ISAAC ASIMOV'S

ROBOT CITY

VOLUME TWO

WILLIAM F. WU

William F. Wu is a five-time nominee for the Hugo, Nebula, and World Fantasy Awards. Over the past twenty years, he has authored fourteen novels, one short story collection, one book of literary criticism, and has had short fiction published in most of the magazines and many anthologies in the field of science fiction and fantasy, including *Analog, Not of Woman Born, Free Space, Absolute Magnitude, Crimes Through Time II,* and *Star Wars: Tales from Jabba's Palace.* His short story, "Wong's Lost and Found Emporium," was adapted into an episode of the new *Twilight Zone* television show in 1985, and his first published story, "By the Flicker of the One-Eyed Flame," was adapted and performed on stage in 1977. He lives in the Mojave Desert north of Los Angeles, California.

ARTHUR BYRON COVER

The son of an American doctor, Arthur Byron Cover was born in the upper tundra of Siberia on January 14, 1950. He attended a Clarion Science Fiction Writers' Workshop in 1971, where he made his first professional sale, to Harlan Ellison's *Last Dangerous Visions.* Cover migrated to Los Angeles in 1972. He has published a slew of short stories, in *Infinity Five, The Alien Condition, Heavy Metal, Weird Tales, Year's Best Horror Stories,* and elsewhere, plus several SF books, including *Autumn Angels, The Platypus of Doom, The Sound of Winter,* and *An East Wind Coming.* He has also written scripts for issues of the comic books *Daredevil* and *Firestorm,* as well as the graphic novel *Space Clusters.*

ISAAC ASIMOV'S
ROBOT CITY

VOLUME TWO

CYBORG by
WILLIAM F. WU

PRODIGY by
ARTHUR BYRON COVER

ibooks
new york
www.ibooksinc.com

DISTRIBUTED BY SIMON & SCHUSTER, INC

An Original Publication of ibooks, inc.

Pocket Books, a division of Simon & Schuster, Inc.
1230 Avenue of the Americas, New York, NY 10020

ibooks, inc.
24 West 25th Street
New York, NY 10010

The ibooks World Wide Web Site Address is:
http://www.ibooksinc.com

You can visit the ibooks Web site for a free read and
download the first chapters of all the ibooks titles:
http://www.ibooksinc.com

ISBN 0-671-03905-9
First Pocket Book Printing March 2000

10 9 8 7 6 5 4 3 2 1

Cover art and interior illustrations by Paul Rivoche
Cover design by Jason Vita
Interior design by Michael Mendelsohn and MM Design 2000, Inc.

Printed in the U.S.A.

This novel is dedicated to
Laura J. LeHew
who always remains very special.
— WILLIAM F. WU

CYBERNETIC ORGANISM

by ISAAC ASIMOV

A robot is a robot and an organism is an organism.

An organism, as we all know, is built up of cells. From the molecular standpoint, its key molecules are nucleic acids and proteins. These float in a watery medium, and the whole has a bony support system. It is useless to go on with the description, since we are all familiar with organisms and since we are examples of them ourselves.

A robot, on the other hand, is (as usually pictured in science fiction) an object, more or less resembling a human being, constructed out of strong, rust-resistant metal. Science fiction writers are generally chary of describing the robotic details too closely since they are not usually essential to the story and the writers are generally at a loss how to do so.

The impression one gets from the stories, however, is that a robot is wired, so that it has wires through which electricity flows rather than tubes through which blood flows. The ultimate source of power is either unnamed, or is assumed to partake of the nature of nuclear power.

What of the robotic brain?

When I wrote my first few robot stories in 1939 and 1940, I imagined a "positronic brain" of a spongy type of platinum-iridium alloy. It was platinum-iridium because that is a particularly inert metal and is least likely to undergo chemical changes. It was spongy so that it would offer an enormous surface on which electrical patterns could be formed and un-formed. It was "positronic" because four years before my first robot story, the positron had been discovered in a reverse kind of electron, so that "positronic" in place of "electronic" had a delightful science-fiction sound.

Nowadays, of course, my positronic platinum-iridium brain is hopelessly archaic. Even ten years after its invention it became outmoded. By the end of the 1940s, we came to realize that a robot's brain must be a kind of computer. Indeed, if a robot were to be as complex as the robots in my most recent novels, the robot brain-computer must be every bit as complex as the human brain. It must be made of tiny microchips no larger than, and as complex as, brain cells.

But now let us try to imagine something that is neither organism nor robot, but a combination of the two. Perhaps we can think of it as an organism-robot or "orbot." That would clearly be a poor name, for it is only "robot" with the first two letters transposed. To say "orgabot", instead, is to be stuck with a rather ugly word.

We might call it a robot-organism, or a "roboanism", which, again, is ugly, or "roborg". To my ears, "viiroborg" doesn't sound bad, but we can't have that. Something else has arisen.

The science of computers was given the name "cybernetics" by Norbert Weiner a generation ago, so that if we consider something that is part robot and part organism and remember that a robot is cybernetic in nature, we might think of the mixture as a "cybernetic organism", or a "cyborg". In fact, that is the name that has stuck and is used.

To see what a cyborg might be, let's try starting with a human organism and moving toward a robot; and when we are quite done with that, let's start with a robot and move toward a human being.

To move from a human organism toward a robot, we must begin replacing portions of the human organism with robotic parts. We already do that in some ways. For instance, a good percentage of the original material of my teeth is now metallic, and metal is, of course, the robotic substance *par excellence.*

The replacements don't have to be metallic, of course. Some parts of my teeth are now ceramic in nature, and can't be told at a glance from the natural dentine. Still, even though dentine is ceramic in appearance and even, to an extent, in chemical structure, it was originally laid down by living material and bears the marks of its origin. The ceramic that has replaced the dentine shows no trace of life, now or ever.

We can go further. My breastbone, which had to be split longitudinally in an operation a few years back, was for a time held together by metallic staples, which have remained in place ever since. My sister-in-law has an artificial hip-joint replacement. There are people who have artificial arms or legs and such non-living limbs are being designed, as time passes on, to be ever more complex and useful. There are people who have lived for days and even months with artificial hearts, and many more people who live for years with pacemakers.

We can imagine, little by little, this part and that part of the human being replaced by inorganic materials and engineering devices. Is there any part which we would find difficult to replace, even in imagination?

I don't think anyone would hesitate there. Replace every part of the human being but one—the limbs, the heart, the liver, the skeleton, and so on—and the product would remain human. It would be a human being with artificial parts, but it would be a human being.

But what about the brain?

Surely, if there is one thing that makes us human it is the brain. If there is one thing that makes us a human indi[chvidual, it is the intensely complex makeup, the emotions, the learning, the memory content of our particular brain. You can't simply replace a brain with a thinking device off some factory shelf. You have to put in something that incorporates all that a natural brain has learned, that possesses all its memory, and that mimics its exact pattern of working.

An artificial limb might not work exactly like a natural one, but might still serve the purpose. The same might be true of an artificial lung, kidney, or liver. An artificial brain, however, must be the *precise* replica of the brain it replaces, or the human being in question is no longer the same human being.

It is the brain, then, that is the sticking point in going from human organism to robot.

And the reverse?

In my story "The Bicentennial Man", I described the passage of my robot-hero, Andrew Martin, from robot to man. Little by little, he had himself changed, till his every visible part was human in appearance. He displayed an intelligence that was increasingly equivalent (or even superior) to that of a man. He was an artist, a historian, a scientist, an administrator. He forced the passage of laws guaranteeing robotic rights, and achieved respect and admiration in the fullest degree.

Yet at no point could he make himself accepted as a *man*. The sticking point, here, too, was his robotic brain. He found that he had to deal with that before the final hurdle could be overcome.

Therefore, we come down to the dichotomy, body and

brain. The ultimate cyborgs are those in which the body and brain don't match. That means we can have two classes of complete cyborgs:

a) a robotic brain in a human body, or

b) a human brain in a robotic body.

We can take it for granted that in estimating the worth of a human being (or a robot, for that matter) we judge first by superficial appearance.

I can very easily imagine a man seeing a woman of superlative beauty and gazing in awe and wonder at the sight. "What a beautiful woman," he will say, or think, and he could easily imagine himself in love with her on the spot. In romances, I believe that happens as a matter of routine. And, of course, a woman seeing a man of superlative beauty is surely likely to react in precisely the same way.

If you fall in love with a striking beauty, you are scarcely likely to spend much time asking if she (or he, of course) has any brains, or possesses a good character, or has good judgment or kindness or warmth. If you find out eventually that good looks are the person's only redeeming quality, you are liable to make excuses and continue to be guided, for a time at least, by the conditioned reflex of erotic response. Eventually, of course, you will tire of good looks without content, but who knows how long that will take?

On the other hand, a person with a large number of good qualities who happened to be distinctly plain might not be likely to entangle you in the first place unless you were intelligent enough to see those good qualities so that you might settle down to a lifetime of happiness.

What I am saying, then, is that a cyborg with a robotic brain in a human body is going to be accepted by most, if not all, people as a human being; while a cyborg with a human brain in a robotic body is going to be accepted by most, if not all, people as a robot. You are, after all—at least to most people—what you seem to be.

These two diametrically opposed cyborgs will not, however, pose a problem to human beings to the same degree.

Consider the robotic brain in the human body and ask why the transfer should be made. A robotic brain is better off in a robotic body since a human body is far the more fragile of the two. You might have a young and stalwart human body in which the brain has been damaged by trauma and disease, and you might think, "Why waste that magnificent human body? Let's put a robotic brain in it so that it can live out its life."

If you were to do that, the human being that resulted would not be the original. It would be a different individual human being. You would not be conserving an individual but merely a specific mindless body. And a human body, however fine, is (without the brain that goes with it) a cheap thing. Every day, half a million new bodies come into being. There is no need to save any one of them if the brain is done.

On the other hand, what about a human brain in a robotic body? A human brain doesn't last forever, but it can last up to ninety years without falling into total uselessness. It is not at all unknown to have a ninety-year-old who is still sharp, and capable of rational and worthwhile thought. And yet we also know that many a superlative mind has vanished after twenty or thirty years because the body that housed it (and was worthless in the absence of the mind) had become uninhabitable through trauma or disease. There would be a strong impulse then to transfer a perfectly good (even superior) brain into a robotic body to give it additional decades of useful life.

Thus, when we say "cyborg" we are very likely to think,

just about exclusively, of a human brain in a robotic body and we are going to think of that as a robot.

We might argue that a human mind is a human mind, and that it is the mind that counts and not the surrounding support mechanism, and we would be right. I'm sure that any rational court would decide that a human-brain cyborg would have all the legal rights of a man. He could vote, he could be enslaved, and so on.

And yet suppose a cyborg were challenged: "Prove that you have a human brain and not a robotic brain, before I let you have human rights."

The easiest way for a cyborg to offer the proof is for him to demonstrate that he is not bound by the Three Laws of Robotics. Since the Three Laws enforce socially acceptable behavior, this means he must demonstrate that he is capable of human (i.e. nasty) behavior. The simplest and most unanswerable argument is simply to knock the challenger down, breaking his jaws in the process, since no robot could do that. (In fact, in my story "Evidence", which appeared in 1947, I use this as a way of proving someone is not a robot—but in that case there was a catch.)

But if a cyborg must continually offer violence in order to prove he has a human brain, that will not necessarily win him friends.

For that matter, even if he is accepted as human and allowed to vote and to rent hotel rooms and do all the other things human beings can do, there must nevertheless be some regulations that distinguish between him and complete human beings. The cyborg would be stronger than a man, and his metallic fists could be viewed as lethal weap ons. He might still be forbidden to strike a human being, even in self-defense. He couldn't engage in various sports on an equal basis with human beings, and so on.

Ah, but need a human brain be housed in a metallic robotic body? What about housing it in a body made of ceramic and plastic and fiber so that it looks and feels like a human body—and has a human brain besides?

But you know, I suspect that the cyborg will still have his troubles. He'll be *different*. No matter how small the difference is, people will seize upon it.

We know that people who have human brains and full human bodies sometimes hate each other because of a slight difference in skin pigmentation, or a slight variation in the shape of the nose, eyes, lips, or hair.

We know that people who show no difference in any of the physical characteristics that have come to represent a cause for hatred, may yet be at daggers-drawn over matters that are not physical at all, but cultural—differences in reli[chgion, or in political outlook, or in place of birth, or in language, or in just the accent of a language.

Let's face it. Cyborgs will have their difficulties, no matter what.

ISAAC ASIMOV'S

ROBOT CITY

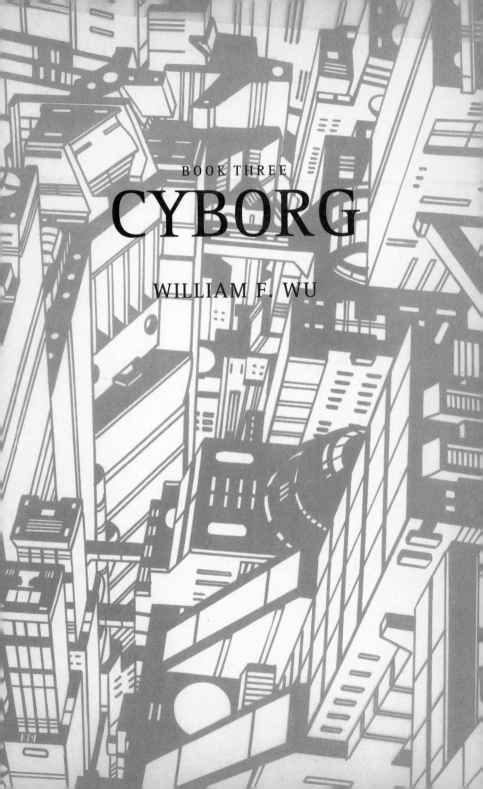

BOOK THREE

CYBORG

WILLIAM F. WU

CHAPTER 1

THE KEY TO PERIHELION

Derec sighed and ran his hand through his brush-cut sandy hair. "Katherine, I don't know if this stupid computer knows who has the Key to Perihelion or not. Anyhow, if it does, it won't tell me. I've asked it every way I can think of." He swiveled his chair away from the computer console to face her.

Katherine looked down at him from where she stood, and shook her head in apparent disgust. "I didn't know *computers* could be stupid," she said pointedly.

"Well, this one is," he muttered lamely, feeling his face grow hot. "Look if someone else programmed a higher priority of secrecy into the computer, it won't answer any questions it was forbidden to answer. I can't do anything about that." He was glad he was seated. She was a bit taller than he, though he was—he hoped—still growing. He guessed that she was a year or two older than he was, but that was as uncertain as the rest of her identity . . . and his.

Derec sprang out of his chair to put some distance between them and started pacing around the room. Through

3

his manipulation of the computer, he had ordered the builder robots of Robot City to continue developing the quarters he and Katherine shared. They had constructed a bedroom for each of them, a kitchen area, and a console for the computer access equipment he had put together himself. Now he strode around the perimeter of the office, burning up nervous energy.

The apartment was hexagonal, and the furniture was shaped from the interior surface. Light glowed from the ceiling itself in a pleasant, soft diffusion. The room walls now obscured the elegant shape of the quarters, which resembled the interior of a crystal, but he and Katherine were more comfortable than before, and more independent.

Ever since Derec had stopped Robot City from its automatic, frantic, and self-destructive growth, they had been living in a city that almost resembled a normal one. Construction now continued at a steady pace, within the capacity of the city to adjust as it grew. With the Laws of Robotics in effect, the two humans had a comfortable and safe existence here now.

The First Law of Robotics is: "A robot may not injure a human being, or, through inaction, allow a human being to come to harm."

"Look, Derec," said Katherine. "We both want to get off this planet, I guess. At the moment, we aren't suffering here. Sure, if we had a ship, we'd be gone by now. But as long as that Key is our only chance to get away, we simply have to find it."

Her tone was milder now, Derec noticed, but he just spun around, turning his back on her, and went on pacing. Ever since he had found out that she was not really Katherine Ariel Burgess, as she had told him she was, he had known he could not trust her. Or, at least, he could only believe her when she was being sarcastic or condescending.

When she sounded pleasant, he had to figure out what she was up to.

Besides, he still suffered from his amnesia. It was a little too awkward to demand her identity when he couldn't even figure out his own. In fact, even raising the subject was embarrassing. The situation left him perpetually uneasy. The best place to get away from it was in the computer.

He moved past her and threw himself back into the chair. Then he started working on the keyboard before he had any idea of what he should do. He just tried to look busy.

He had declined to construct a VoiceCommand in his terminal, since he felt it a barrier between him and the labyrinth of the central computer. The computer was comprised of the top seven planner robots, or Supervisors, in the city, joined by their communication links. The central core could only be accessed in the mysterious office inside the Compass Tower, but he had had no use for it since instructing it to discontinue the excessive building and shapechanging of the city. Using only his keyboard to access the computer allowed him to bring up more raw data and to streamline the whole system when he had the time. Now it also allowed him to tinker silently.

After a moment of concentrating, his discomfort was gone. When he spoke, his voice was casual. "Actually, this computer really is kind of stupid. Not the individual Supervisors, of course, but the way they combine their information. The shapechanging loaded so much data into them so fast that they recorded it without organizing it. The computer has become too complex to work well. It needs a lot more streamlining to become efficient."

"I thought you were streamlining it."

"When I get the chance," he snapped, suddenly annoyed again. He was fairly sure he could make some real progress, given time, but he was tired of her always questioning his ability with computers. It was the one subject he actually knew something about, and he had demonstrated it many times over. Since his amnesia had left him with little knowledge of himself, the knowledge he did have was very important to him. He had even learned the kind of amnesia he had, something called "fractionated, retrograde, hypnosis-resistant psychogenic amnesia"—whatever that meant.

Katherine didn't say anything, though he remained aware that she was watching him.

"Well, we *are* stuck with a rather odd computer, after all," he said. Her composure made him self-conscious about his own discomfort. He made an effort to cool off a little. "Here we are in Robot City, a place built and run and populated exclusively by robots, and we have no idea of who created it, or why. I mean, who ever heard of a planet like this?"

"I know," she said gently. "Derec, we are in this together."

"Let me explain the computer again. We're sure the robots have the Key, because there is no one else here on the planet except us. No—"

"Derec, I know this part," she said with exaggerated weariness.

"Let me go on. I'm trying to build up to my point. Look, I've never encountered a computer quite like this, and I'm still trying to think through how to handle it."

"Go on."

"The computer obviously is subject to the Three Laws of Robotics, and that should make it honor my requests for information, under the Second Law. It did not, probably for two reasons. One is prior programming, where the Second Law required the robots collectively to keep certain secrets under orders they received from another human, presumably the creator of Robot City, whoever it was."

The Second Law of Robotics is: "A robot must obey the orders given it by human beings except where such orders would conflict with the First Law."

Katherine nodded quietly, now gazing at the floor. "What's the second reason?"

"The second reason is that the computer system has apparently expanded to the point where it needs fundamental reorganization to operate efficiently. Too many parts of the system just don't seem to know what the other parts know. All sorts of information is lost in there. Even when it does know the answer to a question, sometimes the information takes much too long to locate. And I have to think up special ways of giving orders and asking questions to get it out.

Katherine lifted her head and smiled. "We're both getting better at that, Derec. We've had some practice now, especially with individual robots."

Derec grinned. "I guess I can't argue with that. So far, the best way to make the robots cooperate is to convince them that we're in danger, thus activating their First Law programming."

"I know, I know—have you forgotten my charade on Rockliffe Station with that little alien friend of yours, Wolruf? The trouble is, it's even harder to convince them when we're just debating. I seem to recall that we've both gone a few rounds with various robots that way."

"That's true, too." The positronic brains of the humanoid robots were quite sophisticated, and debating with their cold logic could be frustrating. "The Supervisors were so cooperative—within their limits of programming, of course—that it's too bad we can't just try to work with them to get the Key back."

"They haven't even admitted that they took it from our hiding place on the Compass Tower," said Katherine. "Why would they cooperate with us?"

"I'm sure they wouldn't, or couldn't. That's why we'll have to try locating the Key without confronting them. The longer it takes them to realize that we're after it, the more freedom we'll have."

Despite their current rapport, Derec was afraid that if he didn't stay on the computer, Katherine would make more comments about his incompetence. She might even call him a quitter. Determined not to give her any excuse for that, he continued to play idly on the keyboard.

Katherine pulled up the other chair—they only had two—and sat down. "Derec, let's try to think up some questions I could ask some of the other robots, not the Supervisors. I know they won't answer our direct questions about the Key, but I've gotten information out of them before. Like you were saying, we just have to think up the right questions. Stuff they have to answer because of the Laws."

He nodded. "Or else questions they don't realize will lead us anywhere. The problem is, that's what I've been trying to do through the computer. I guess I just don't know."

All they really knew about the Key to Perihelion was that it was a teleportation device and that it had been taken from the place where they had hidden it. Obviously, the robots had taken it, and so far they had not even revealed that much information. Since the Key seemed to belong here, or at least had some special relationship to Robot City, the robots apparently did not feel that they had stolen it. They were incapable of dishonesty as such.

"We know the robots were searching for the Key for a long time," said Derec. "So whatever they've done with it must have been part of their long-term programming."

He could certainly use her help, but he didn't know if he trusted her enough to speak freely. At one point, he had offered to let her use it to leave the planet while he stayed, and she had chosen to remain here with him. That had been some time ago, though. Sometimes they seemed very close, but he still wasn't sure that if she got to the Key first, she would share its use with him. She had some kind of chronic physical condition—precisely what kind of condition was her secret—and she just might be in a bigger hurry to get off the planet than she claimed.

For that matter, he was worried about her. He wanted to get her some human medical care, and that meant getting away from Robot City. However, he did not want to be left behind.

"What they're *doing* is obvious," said Katherine. "They plan to teleport somewhere. That's all the Key is good for, as far as we know."

"But where do they have to go? The planet is all theirs already, except for us."

"Oh, Derec." She sounded exasperated. "At some point, they're going to teleport off the planet entirely, just like we want to do."

"But why—" Derec stopped. They couldn't possibly know why, because they didn't know the robots' purpose here on the planet in the first place. Discussing the robots' motives would not get them very far. "Well, let's think out loud for a minute. On the asteroid where they found the Key, they were programmed to self-destruct when they were under attack. The Key and the element of secrecy were much more important than the robots or other materials to the person who programmed them. Cost was absolutely not a real concern. And that programming was critically important, since it violated the Third Law."

The Third Law of Robotics is: "A robot must protect his own existence as long as such protection does not conflict with the First or Second Laws."

"So their self-destruction—probably for the purpose of secrecy—must have been programmed by their creator under the First or Second Laws." She thought a moment. "There's that minimalist engineering again, which you keep talking about."

"Now, wait a minute." He turned in his chair to face her. "Haven't I already explained this? When I use that term, I mean these designs that we keep seeing that make things easy to use, even though the technology may have to be much more complicated than necessary to make it that easy." He laughed, glad to have the advantage on her for a change. "What's that got to do with robots melting themselves down into hot puddles of molten junk?"

"Well, it's the same attitude. It's not the engineering as such, but the priorities. The creator of Robot City doesn't care about conserving materials."

"*Oh*. Well . . . you might have a point, I suppose. Of course, they have all the materials they want, since there is no competition here. I . . . say!" He suddenly turned back to the console. Without mentioning the Key at all, he called up the records of supply requisitions. Then he searched out unusual movements of materials with a top-level priority. Several locations were given. "Ha! What do you bet they've just set up some kind of place to keep the Key?"

"Yes!" Katherine threw her arms around his neck and gave him a quick squeeze. "They must have. Considering how important it is, they'll want it under the tightest security you ever saw on this planet." She laughed. "And if we get too close, maybe these suicidal robots will start melting themselves down into hot little puddles of molten junk again."

Derec had stiffened in surprise at her embrace and felt his face grow hot with embarrassment again. They had been affectionate at times before, but arguments always seemed to follow. He had no idea how she really felt.

Katherine went on excitedly. "Do you suppose a particular robot is in charge? That would tell us who to look for."

Glad to have something else to do, Derec called up a list of duty changes among the robots. That list included geographical changes of assignment where they were pertinent. Major changes in reorganization were still taking place in the wake of the building frenzy that Derec had recently stopped. Now he correlated that information with the list of locations for which an abundance of materiel had just been requisitioned. All at once, he had the number of a single robot. "There it is!"

Katherine was looking over his shoulder. "And, look—it has a huge crew that's just been assigned to work under it. Wow, this serial number is a mouthful." Normally, robots with a lot of human contact were given language names instead of numbers or duty designations, but on Robot City the robots had no reason to assume that human contact would be made with any frequency; only the Supervisors had been given names.

"Watch this. Let's see. Key. . . . How about Keymo?" He hit a sequence of keys.

"What did you do?"

"I've given it a name. It'll be easier for us to remember. Now that it's in the computer, it'll respond to that as well as its number. The other robots can learn it if they ask."

"I didn't know you could do that."

He grinned up at her. "I just figured it out today."

"Congratulations. Say, Derec. . . ."

"Yeah?"

"*Look* at the size of that crew it has assembled. What could they possibly be doing?"

Derec shrugged. "Security? You're right about that part. The robots will have that Key guarded heavily."

"What would they be afraid of on Robot City?" Besides, they can have other kinds of security systems. They don't need a bunch of robots just standing around."

"You got me, kiddo."

"What about their last duties? What kind of skills have they specialized in?"

He started calling up a list of their previous duties, and spoke as he worked. "I know that skills matter to some of the robots, but I'm not sure how much. Certainly, for information, they can all draw upon the central computer. If they can manage to get the data out of that tangled contraption, any one of them can know practically anything that any robot here knows." He looked at the list that came up. "There we are. Hmm—let me try this." In a couple of strokes, he had the computer subdivide the list according to previous duties that the various robots had in common.

"I don't see much of a pattern," Katherine admitted after a moment.

Derec shook his head. "I don't, either. They have all kinds of different backgrounds."

"Maybe they have something else in common. Can you ask the computer to tell you if they have some other common trait?"

"I can ask it anything we can think of." Derec smiled ruefully. "Whether or not I get a civilized answer is another matter." A moment later, he had a new list in front of them. He looked it over and let out a slow breath. "Wow."

"It must be the Key," Katherine said softly.

According to the computer, the robots on this new duty roster had been selected for their absolute peak efficiency.

They had recorded the fewest breakdowns, the shortest repair times, and the finest work records. Those who had experienced contact with humans had consistently reached any necessary decisions regarding the Laws with the least time and effort, though of course all the robots reached the correct decisions eventually. This team represented the best robots from all over Robot City.

"This Keymo must be the best of the best," said Derec, "considering that they put him in charge. Tangling with this bunch is going to be tough."

"Think of it this way: if we can talk him out of the Key to Perihelion, we can talk these robots into anything."

Derec looked up at her, smiling weakly. When he caught her eye, they both laughed.

"All right," Katherine conceded. "If we can talk them out of the Key to Perihelion, we won't need anything else from them."

"We should go to Keymo prepared with an argument." Derec got up and walked over to the kitchen area. "And since we can't count on finding food outside our apartment here, we'd better eat first." He looked over the limited list of fare that the chemical processor could simulate. "I'm afraid we're out of the fresh produce. We'll have to request another delivery. Right now, we can't afford the time."

Katherine joined him, peering over his shoulder with a look of distaste. "That's another good reason for us to get off this planet. This stuff tastes terrible."

"The robots did what they could, I guess. Before we got here, they just had no reason to concern themselves with cooking. Maybe we're lucky they could make a chemical processor that's even this tolerable."

"As far as I'm concerned, the best meal out of this machine is the fastest one I can eat, so I don't have to taste it any longer than necessary."

"Fine. We don't want to waste time, anyway." Derec entered the code and turned it on. "Nutrition bars it is—again."

"I'll take the fruit punch to drink, though."

"Yeah—me, too."

A moment later, they each sat down with a dark brown, warm, rectangular shape. Each bar had a combination of proteins, carbohydrates, and cellulose that would fill them up. The taste was more bland than bad. The chemical processor could also produce more complex meals, which were equally or more nutritious but also equally bland to the taste. It was no match even for the autogalleys on ships.

Derec washed down a mouthful of food with simulated fruit punch. At least the citric acid gave it a strong tang. "If I get the time, I can try ordering the computer to give me some improvements to try on the processor. The trouble is, I don't know what chemicals have to be added to make it taste better . . . and I doubt that the central computer knows, either. Robots have sensory capabilities for analytical purposes, but they don't care about human gourmet preferences."

"If we can get the Key today, we'll be gone, anyway. Let's work on that premise. How are we going to talk Keymo out of the Key?"

"When you put it that way, it sounds a little preposterous, I must admit. Well . . . do you have any ideas?" He was hoping to divert her from his own lack of plans.

"Our only chance is to force him to surrender the Key under some interpretation of the Laws. So we'll have to pose an argument to him, like. . . ." She shrugged, unable to suggest anything.

"If the food were any worse, we could tell him we have to get off the planet or suffer harm." Derec laughed.

"The trouble is, it's not *that* bad."

"We can probably figure that the Second Law by itself won't help us. Like I said about getting information from the central computer, any request from us will almost certainly be overridden by prior programming orders under the Second Law. Whoever created Robot City got his instructions in first."

Katherine looked down at her glass, and picked it up even though it was empty. Suddenly she got up and went to the processor to fill it. Then she just stood there looking at the glass.

Derec had no idea why her manner had just turned chilly. He reflected that it figured, somehow; just as he became comfortable enough to joke around a little, she started to withdraw from him again. He watched her without speaking.

Katherine turned and walked into her room.

Derec, feeling snubbed, did not try to approach her. Instead, he got up and carried their plates and glasses to the washer. After turning it on, he straightened up a little and wiped the inside of the chemical processor's delivery receptacle. He could not tell what she was doing.

Once again, Derec felt trapped by his own circumstances. Some time ago, he had awakened in a lifepod from a larger spacecraft with no memory of his name or his earlier life. Even the name "Derec" had been adopted only so that he could call himself something. He had had a number of crazy adventures since that time, but none of them had brought his memory back.

He had met Katherine along the way, and they had formed a partnership of necessity. After all, even now they were the only humans of the planet, and shared a desire to get off Robot City. He still found her difficult to deal with.

Nevertheless, if they were going to get off Robot City, they would have to get the Key to Perihelion. Derec took a deep breath.

"Katherine?"

"Yes." Her voice was low and listless.

"Are you, um, feeling okay?"

"Yes!" She spoke sharply, almost too insistently.

"I suppose we ought to go visit Keymo, wherever he is. You still want to go, don't you?"

"Of course I want to go," she snapped, coming to the doorway. "Why wouldn't I want to go?"

"*I* don't know!" Derec threw up his arms. "Sometimes you're as big a mystery to me as the origin of Robot City."

Katherine pushed past him and turned. "Well?"

"Well what?"

"Are we going now or what? You were in such a big hurry."

"Sure! Sure, we're going. I'm in a big hurry to get off this planet, and I thought you were, too. Come on, let's go!"

"All right!"

Seething with anger, Derec stalked out of their quarters, aware that she was right behind him.

CHAPTER 2

THROUGH THE CHUTE

Outside, the great pyramidal Compass Tower glittered in the sunlight. It was taller by half than any other structure in the city, and stood as a familiar landmark. Below it, the skyline was a varied line of spires, domes, cubes, and towers.

Derec and Katherine rode the slidewalk in silence. He had an idea of where to find Keymo, since the ongoing shapechanging of the city had been discontinued—although the robots still renovated and built constantly. One of the many benefits of ending the shapechanging was that the robots had been building a coherent system of slidewalks for pedestrian traffic. Still, finding one's way around Robot City remained a challenge.

His anger was cooling quickly. In the distance ahead, he could see a large dome on the horizon, a brilliant, shining bronze in color. It was near the site of Keymo's operation, and Derec guessed it was the Key Center itself.

"I noticed a similar dome here once," she said, also gazing at it. "Any idea what it is?"

"Not exactly, no."

"What does that mean?"

He glanced at her warily, thinking he had detected an edge in her voice, but she was still looking up at the building. He raised his gaze again, still walking. "Well, actually . . . what I mean is, sometimes the robots have to house a certain class of facilities that can't be fit into normal industrial bays or doors. I haven't looked closely at any of these domes, but I think they're used for stuff like that."

"I don't see any doors, now that you mention it. I suppose they're on the other side. The Key is small enough to carry, though. I don't see why they would need a gigantic dome for it."

"Maybe that's not the place." Derec shrugged. "Maybe the Key Center is in a mud hut next door."

"Very funny. If that particular dome is new, I'm betting it was set up for the Key."

"I'm not arguing. But we have to get off the slidewalk. It's being fixed up or something just ahead. There isn't a functioning one to take us from here to there."

"I hope you don't expect me to walk that far!" She stepped off the slidewalk with him.

A small function robot, the class without the positronic brains, skittered out of her way. It was a small scrap collector, gathering debris as it moved on a cushion of short, nimble legs around a construction site. It was heading for a sewer chute in which to deposit its load.

A humanoid robot, of the foreman class in the city, approached them. The sunlight shone on the distinctive, helmeted head and blue skin.

"Identify yourself," Katherine ordered.

"I am Construction Foreman 391." The robot's eyes, deep in the darkness of its horizontal eyeslit, focused on her.

"What is the most convenient way for us to reach—Derec, tell it where."

He noted that she had spoken to him in the same imperious tone she used with the robots. "We're going to that dome, or somewhere close to it. It's about 6.4 kilometers."

"Frost!" She turned on him. "You weren't going to walk that far, were you?"

"Of course not."

"Perhaps the vacuum chute would be safe for humans," said Foreman 391. "You must ask a chute foreman. May the maintenance robot resume its duties?"

"Oh—of course." Katherine glanced down at the scrap collector, which she had inadvertently trapped against the sewer chute. It whirred patiently at her feet until she moved out of the way. Then it headed back into the construction site.

"A vacuum chute?" Derec asked. "I don't remember anything about a vacuum chute before. That's pretty archaic technology, too."

"Yes. It is being used because a new facility in Robot City is producing a strong partial vacuum as a side effect. Utilizing this side effect constitutes an efficient use of energy."

"Say, you're rather proud of that, aren't you?" Derec grinned with amusement. "You must have worked on the vacuum chutes, huh?"

"This is not pride. It is recognition that certain principles of efficiency have been successfully executed. Yes, all the construction foremen at my level had to be consulted when the chute system was routed through the city."

"Forget the frosted chutes," Katherine said irritably. "What about that big bronze dome?"

"What about it?"

"Well, you're a construction foreman. You must know what it's for."

"Yes."

"Would you tell us, please?"

Derec hid a smile at her frustration. At times she had handled robots very well, but today did not seem to be her day. In fact, both of them occasionally reached the point where they were infuriated by the literal interpretations that the robots made of human speech.

"These designs are used to house extremely large or oddly shaped facilities of all kinds. The—"

"Excuse me," said Derec. "But would an extremely important facility, one that had special priority, be in one of those domes, also?"

"I have no role in decision-making of that kind."

"But from your experience in Robot City, do you think it might be likely?"

"The materials used in the construction of the dome do not offer any special advantage, based on the premise you have given."

Derec sighed. "Okay. What is this stuff, anyhow?"

"Are you referring to the construction material?"

"Yes." Derec gritted his teeth, and caught Katherine suppressing a smile this time.

"The external shell is the only significant distinction of material these domes possess. It is comprised of a material called dianite. Dianite is a specialized form of the modular material from which all of Robot City is constructed. This substance has a number of unusual qualities. In its solid form it is extremely hard, yet very light in weight and with high tensile strength. However, its most unusual property is that—"

"Okay, okay, thank you. Is there a method of normal transportation that will take us there? From here?"

"Normally, this slidewalk would take you there. While it is under modification, no normal transportation is available that will do this."

"What about those chutes?" Katherine asked.

"Allow me to consult the central computer. Yes, one of them is on a direct line from here to a stop near your destination. You understand that a chute foreman must be consulted for matters of safety?"

"Right," said Derec. "Where do we find one?"

"The nearest chute stop is two blocks forward and one block left. I must resume my duties."

"Come on!" Katherine took off at a run.

They ran along the motionless slidewalk as long as they could, then jumped off and ran along its shoulder. Here and there, they had to skip around functioning robots going about their business, and past a couple of foremen, as well. In moments, they had turned left at the corner and had come skidding up to a small loading dock. A foreman robot was standing on the dock, watching a small function robot use an armlike crane to lift a container.

The function robot was hoisting molded containers from a long, transparent tube that lay horizontally alongside the dock.

"We need that," Katherine said briskly. "How does it work?"

"It is pulled through the chute by a powerful vacuum," said the foreman. "What is your need for it?"

"Identify yourself."

"I am Chute Foreman 34." The robot looked back and forth between them. "I have never had direct contact with humans before."

Katherine threw her arms up in a gesture of impatience that Derec knew all too well. He was glad not to be the cause of it this time.

"Yes, we're humans. Congratulations, genius. Now—"

Derec rushed to get in front of her, surprised at her sudden aggressiveness. "We're going to that dome. A construction foreman suggested we inquire as to whether a vacuum chute would be safe for us to travel in."

Chute Foreman 34 glanced down at the tube. From here, Derec could see that it was resting in a siding away from the vacuum chute itself.

"Yes, this tube is safe for cargo more fragile than humans. It has ventilation and padding. However, it may not be comfortable."

"How uncomfort—" Derec started.

"Frost that; we'll take it." Katherine pushed Derec aside and climbed down into the open tube.

Derec followed her and found that, while the slick cushion was padded well enough, they had to recline along the length of the transparent tube for the door to slide shut. He found himself lying against her, and moved over self-consciously.

"I will send you to the stop nearest the dome," said the robot, just before it secured the door.

"I hope it has more experience with these chutes than it has with humans," said Katherine.

Derec wiggled a little to get more comfortable, his gaze aimed upward at the sky. He began to speak, but the jolting start of the tube interrupted the effort. With a great rushing of air, it accelerated quickly and shot into a black chute.

Air was swirling within the tube. Apparently, the ventilation consisted of carefully shaped openings in the back of the tube, which pulled some air into the tube as it was drawn along. He was trying to figure out how that could work when suddenly the chute curved upward. All at once, he felt himself sliding head first, on his back, toward the rear of the tube. Laughing, he and Katherine clutched at each other and tried vainly to brace themselves against the smooth sides of the tube.

Light flooded the tube, nearly blinding Derec. When he could focus his eyes, he and Katherine both shouted and grabbed at each other again. The chute was now as transparent as the tube, and they were shooting along high above the ground. Just ahead, the chute wound between two large buildings. Though Derec knew better, he felt his whole body tighten reflexively with the fear that they were about to smash into one of the walls.

Katherine apparently felt the same, inhaling sharply just as they plunged into the gap between the buildings. The sides of the buildings were a blur all around them. The chute then swerved upward again, keeping them both pinned against the rear of the tube, braced with their arms held above their heads.

The buildings first fell away on her side, then on his. He felt his stomach seem to drop as he watched rooftops recede below him. Traveling in enclosed spacecraft was one thing, but actually watching the ground fall from him triggered all the instinctive fears of height that his ancient ancestors had acquired by falling out of trees. Beside him, Katherine was giggling nervously.

The chute leveled off, and Derec let out a cautious breath.

She turned to face him, just inches away. "Pretty wild, huh?"

He grinned, but didn't trust himself to speak.

Now that they were speeding along a level section of the chute, he was able to relax a little. When he took a tentative look off to the side, he found that most of the city was now below them, but a few of the tallest towers and obelisks could still throw a shadow over the chute at the right hour. He guessed that the erratic route of the chute was due to the recent discontinuation of the automatic sha-pechanging in the city. New developments were more likely to be built around existing structures now.

The city was strikingly pretty from this height, and it stretched as far as he could see from his cramped position. Suddenly, the tube plunged steeply downward, and Derec gasped as he found himself staring almost straight down at a drop of several hundred meters. He felt himself sliding toward the front of the tube and clawed futilely for a hand-hold.

Katherine was also flailing about, and they wound up throwing their arms around each other. The speed of the tube was such, however, that they did not actually fall to the front of the tube. It was accelerating, and Derec felt his ears pop from the sudden change in altitude. He hadn't even noticed the pressure change on their startling ascent.

Finally, the tube leveled off again, smoothly, and then gently rose again just enough to decelerate and come to an easy stop. Derec lay where he was for a moment, looking at Katherine. She smiled and looked away as they untangled themselves.

The tube door opened and another foreman looked down at them. "Unusual cargo," the robot said. "You are unharmed?"

Derec and Katherine laughed as they climbed out, nodding in reassurance. He noticed that she had lost her hard edge somewhere on the breathtaking ride.

"There it is," said Katherine.

The dome rose up right in front of them, the great bronze surface nearly blinding them in the bright sunlight. The dianite had a very fine, pebbled texture, which saved them from an even worse glare. High above them, the curve of the dome carried the top out of sight.

"I don't see a door anywhere," said Derec.

They started walking around the base of the dome, looking all over its nearly smooth, unbroken surface. It was even higher than Derec had guessed from a distance. It had no visible seams or openings of any kind.

When the tunnel stop came into view again, they knew they had walked all the way around the base of the dome. Derec stopped, still looking up for any hint of how to enter. He supposed an opening was possible at the top, but placing it there seemed out of character for Robot City.

Katherine brushed her fingertips along the dianite. "It's pretty."

"Yeah." Derec rapped on the hard surface experimentally. "I suppose we could stand out here and shout, but I doubt anyone inside would hear us."

Katherine faced the dome and backed away, searching the even curve again.

He had taken just a few steps to follow her when he heard a muted ripping sound behind him. When he looked back, he saw the dianite opening in a jagged line where they had been standing, as though invisible hands were tearing it. As they watched, the blue-skinned form of a humanoid robot stepped out.

Katherine drew herself up. "Take us to Keymo," she ordered firmly.

"This is a security area. What is your business with Keymo?" The robot asked.

"Identify yourself," she demanded.

"I am Security 1K. What is your business with Keymo?"

"He must give us the Key to Perihelion."

Derec stepped beside her, afraid that her direct, rather arrogant approach was going to backfire if they didn't offer some kind of explanation. "According to the Second Law, you must obey our orders. After you take us to Keymo, we will instruct him to hand over the Key. Let's go." He started forward confidently, though it was only a bluff.

Security 1K did not take the bluff. It did not move aside at all. "No."

Derec stepped back, not wanting to challenge the robot's physical prowess. He knew that the positronic brains in the robots were reliable, so his earlier assumption seemed to be true: the robots were operating under Second Law instructions, certainly from the mysterious holder of the office in the Compass Tower. That suggested a new argument to him.

"Hold it," said Derec. "Look. Apparently you have a very strong Second Law imperative that you are operating on, established previously. Okay. But that was a general instruction, I'll bet. Right?"

"That is right. The need for security in this matter is part of the entire project of this facility."

"But I'm giving you a specific and important order right now. I believe that should override a general instruction relying on broadly based programming." Actually, he wasn't sure he believed that at all, but it was worth a try.

Security 1K hesitated. When the positronic brain of a robot paused long enough for a human to notice, the argument had at least been considered worth an internal debate.

"No," the robot said, after what was for it a considerable length of time. "The earlier imperative stands."

Derec sighed, but he wasn't surprised.

"Our well-being is at stake," Katherine declared. "We must consult with Keymo. Your prevention of this violates the First Law."

"How?" Security 1K asked.

"We can't thrive in a city full of robots. We need other people around us."

As the robot continued to debate with Katherine, Derec looked at the open edge of the dianite. It seemed oddly familiar, especially in its texture, but he couldn't figure out why. The substance offered no sign of any frame. It looked quite thin, and seemed to constitute the entire wall.

"You are in no danger," Security 1K was saying. "This is not a First Law problem."

She glanced at Derec, who shrugged. The robot was backing into the dome again. A moment later, the two sides of the dianite seemed to straighten and grow together.

Carefully, Derec tapped the former opening, afraid it might be hot. It was not, so he ran his hand over the wall in that area. The surface seemed fully integral with the rest of the wall. He looked at Katherine and raised his eyebrows.

"Katherine, whoever's behind the creation of this city is some kind of genius. Maybe the robots invented this dianite and maybe they didn't, but somebody created them. This stuff would be worth a fortune off this planet, just like so many other things here."

She spun away and started walking quickly along the base of the dome.

Astonished, he watched her for a moment, then went into sputtering rage. "What is *wrong* with you? You've been acting crazy all day—come back here!" He ran after her.

Katherine had stiffened at his shouts, and had then begun walking faster. At the sound of his running footsteps, she broke into a run, also. He slowed to a walk, realizing that if she was truly determined not to talk, catching her wouldn't help any.

Then he whirled angrily and slammed his fist against the wall. "Hey! Open up in there!" He pounded on the dianite a few more times. Then he stepped back, breathing hard.

A new hole tore open in the wall and Security 1K appeared in the opening. It did not step out this time. "Do you have further business here?"

"Yes! Bring Keymo out here!" It felt good to yell at somebody, and the robot couldn't just walk away.

"If you do not have new reasons to see him, I request that you stop instructing me to listen to you. Do you have new reasons?"

"Uh—" Derec glanced down the way for Katherine, who had stopped to watch. "Well. . . ."

"Please avoid unnecessary contact with this facility," said Security 1K. It backed away from the opening, which began to heal again.

Derec watched in frustration as the substance quickly closed. On an impulse, he leaned against a solid portion of the wall and pulled off one of his boots. He stuck it into the small portion of the hole that still remained and kept a careful eye on the dianite as it grew together. Now he remembered why it was familiar—the substance was similar to the material out of which these robots were made, possibly even a cellular material. He had had experience with these robots parts when he had created the robot Alpha. That had occurred long before he had reached Robot City, but after his amnesia had come on him. This dianite did not seem to be alive, exactly, but it certainly had some startling properties.

The dianite grew around the boot—and stopped, much to his relief. He had been afraid it would simply keep growing together even if it had to cut right through the boot. Instead, his boot had been incorporated into the wall as part of it.

He leaned down close and prodded the dianite around his boot with his fingers. He was right—the tearing sound had given away the secret. This stuff was very hard as an integral unit, but once the tear was started it was quite fragile, and even grew limp within a short radius of the tear. He was able to pull a few of the modular cells apart with his fingers now. The tear could be opened again.

He just hoped no one on the other side was in a position to see him.

"Katherine! Come on!" He gently began tearing the wall upward like fabric. It was tough, but it gave. When he looked up, she hadn't moved. "Come on—" He lowered his voice, suddenly aware that he had a sizable opening in the wall, nearly enough to crawl through . . . or be heard through.

Katherine turned and started walking away.

Derec wanted to shout, but didn't dare. Then, clenching his jaw, he crawled into the opening, leaving his boot behind to hold the breach as the wall grew together again behind him. He would have a talk with her later.

He found himself on the floor behind a large, bulky piece of machinery. The sounds of robots moving about reached him, but most would be function robots. He did not hear any voices. Of course, the foremen had their comlinks for communication with each other.

He spotted Security 1K sitting high on a stool at the far side of the dome, monitoring a console that probably reported a number of effects that would include the vibrations in the wall that Derec and Katherine had caused by touching and punching it. Since 1K was still at the console, Derec judged that the monitor had accepted the boot as part of the wall. Certainly, the wall had grown in solidly around it.

A ceiling was just over the security console, signifying at least one upper floor, if not more. The interior curve of the dome was out of sight above it. On the floor, the entire crew of robots assigned to Keymo seemed to be working on different pieces of equipment that varied greatly in size. One foreman was seated at a computer console on the floor beneath the raised seat of Security 1K. Derec guessed that this was Keymo, and started working his way through the machines to reach the robot without being noticed.

CHAPTER 3

THE KEY CENTER

Derec knew that he would not have much time. Even as he crawled over cables on the floor and between different machine housings, he wondered if he should just stand up, run over to Keymo and start talking right away. As it was, Security 1K might become alerted to his presence and throw him out before he could start his pitch.

He stopped to get his bearings. Keymo was much closer now, studying the readings on the console. It looked like a good time to approach the robot.

Security 1K had not moved.

If Katherine had come in with him, one of them could have provided a diversion while the other spoke to Keymo. But it was too late for that now. He took another deep breath and stood up.

He felt totally exposed and vulnerable as he walked across the floor, but his presence caused no noticeable stir among the robots. When he reached Keymo's desk, the chief robot of the facility looked up.

"I require the Key to Perihelion," Derec said formally.

He edged to the side of the console and peeked at the readouts.

"You would be the human Derec," said Keymo. "Giving you the Key is not possible."

"We must get off the planet in order to survive. The Key is our only means of transportation."

"What is the danger to you and your companion on this planet?"

"Well, we just aren't supposed to live on a planet of robots. We need the company of other humans. Uh. . . ." He knew this line of debate was weak, but it was all he had. The exact nature of Katherine's chronic condition was unknown to him, and therefore too vague to use.

"That is not a danger by itself."

"That's what I told him," said a voice behind Derec.

He tried to turn, but felt firm hands under his arms that lifted him off his feet. It was Security 1K, of course, and Derec did not bother to protest as he was carted to the wall like a lump of waste matter. He could not see how the robot opened a new slit in the wall, but he noted that the boot was elsewhere, and apparently still unnoticed. It would provide another opportunity later.

He was deposited gently but unceremoniously outside the wall, where he stood awkwardly on one booted foot. Behind him, the wall grew together. Katherine walked slowly toward him and stopped.

"I could have used you in there," he growled.

"I didn't realize you'd get in. Then I didn't know what to do." She stared at the ground in front of her.

"Let's get out of here."

Derec was in no mood for another crazy ride in the vacuum chute, and he didn't want to talk to her until they were in private. He hitched rides for them on the top of an enclosed transport vehicle, and on the exterior ladders of a vehicle the purpose of which Derec could not divine. As long as the robot drivers judged their human passengers to be riding safely, they had no objection. Katherine was withdrawn all the way home, and he left her alone.

When they had returned, he went right back to the console. She reluctantly stood behind him with her arms folded. He kept his mind on his work with an effort.

"Did you learn anything while you were inside?" she asked quietly.

"A little," he said coldly. "It might amount to something and it might not. I read an entry number on Keymo's console, and I'm running it through the central computer."

"Are you sure it's really the Key Center?"

"Don't you remember? We demanded to see Keymo, and the security robot didn't deny he was in there. I demanded the Key from the top robot, and he didn't deny having it."

"Okay, okay."

He paused to study the information that had come up. She came closer to read over his shoulder.

"It's a list of substances, mostly metals and synthetics. Percentages of each one . . . energy consumption in the dome."

"Look on the right," said Katherine. "That's the designation for hyperspace. It's an experiment of some kind, consuming air."

"Air—the chutes! The vacuum chutes. That's why they're using such an old technology. What did that construction robot say? The vacuum is a side effect of something else going on. This is it."

"But what is it?" She asked cautiously.

He started an angry retort, then decided to have it out with her after he had finished considering this information.

In the long run, it was more important. "I'm taking another look at that supply requisition we saw earlier. All the same substances are listed, in the same percentages. I wonder. . . ."

"They're duplicating the Key."

"You think so?"

"I'm sure of it, Derec. And, look at the addendum on the supply requisition. They added small amounts there at the dome."

"That would be the original Key," Derec said slowly. "They . . . had to break it down to analyze it. Then they tossed the pieces into the pool of materials. It's gone."

"But they're making more. Derec, this will make it easier for us to get one. Instead of one Key under careful guard, they'll have a bunch of them we can try for."

"I just hope Keymo is duplicating them accurately. And we might have to wait for them to turn out a few. We can't get something that hasn't been made yet."

"Uh, Derec? Would you turn around?"

He turned in his chair and looked up at her.

"I guess you deserve an explanation. I know I've been acting weird. And I'm sorry I didn't go inside with you. I had my mind on something else at the wrong time."

"The wrong time!" Derec leaped out of his chair, glad to have the opening. "The worst possible time! We might have gotten the Key—or a key, anyway!"

"Derec, please. I'm trying to explain. Anyway, maybe there weren't any to get, like you said."

"All right! All right! Go ahead and explain." He paced away from her and turned at the wall. "Go ahead."

"Derec, I know who designed Robot City. And why."

"*What?*"

"I—"

"Why didn't you tell me?" He raged. "No! Never mind

that—who did build this place?" His astonishment and curiosity were interfering with his anger.

"Before I get to that, my real name is Ariel Welsh."

"Well—glad to meet you. Finally."

"I'm the only daughter of Juliana Welsh, of the planet Aurora." She watched for his reaction.

"Should that mean something to me?"

"I thought you might have heard of her—she's extremely wealthy. Lots of people have."

Derec shrugged.

"My mother was the biggest patron of a man called Dr. Avery. Have you heard of him?"

"Dr. Avery. You know, I think I have . . . his name sound familiar. What about him?"

"Dr. Avery was the brain behind all this." She waved a hand, indicating the entire planet. "Robot City is his. And my mother's money got it started."

Derec's heart began to pound. Dr. Avery. He had sat in the man's office and used his terminal; now he had a name to go with the vague, limited information. Someone had been in that office shortly before he had; he had found a recently discarded food container.

"Whew. You really were keeping a secret, weren't you?" He spoke more sympathetically. "What was he doing? Why did he build it?"

"From what Mom said, I think he was a famous architect. She called him a visionary. He was also eccentric, and used to argue with everyone. Robot City was a place where he could test his theories."

"I get it. Here's this . . . genius, I suppose, with all these outlandish ideas that no one can handle. So he wants to try out his experiments without interference, and your mother finances him."

Katherine—now Ariel—nodded. "She gave him enough to get started, with the understanding that his project would have to be self-supporting after a certain point. Since that was part of his experiment, he didn't object. And of course the robots are always very efficient."

"He wanted to create an ongoing, self-sufficient city?"

"With a fully functioning society."

"Where is he now?"

"He vanished a long time ago. Just went off somewhere. I suppose he's dead, but Mom said he's so strange that you just never know."

"And he left behind an entire city of robots running on their original programming." Derec shook his head. "Well, that clears up more than you think."

"Like what?"

"When the microbes from the blood of . . . of the dead man set off the automatic shapechanging in the city, this entire community went berserk because its programming made an interpretation that no human would have made."

"In other words," said Ariel, "something went wrong and Dr. Avery wasn't around to fix it. He wanted an ideal experimental environment and he didn't quite get it."

"When you put it that way, though, he came pretty close. If he had stayed here, he might have kept it going the way he wanted."

"There's something else." She looked at her hands, and started playing with her fingernails. "I've been banished from Aurora. I can't go back."

"*You've* been banished? How? I mean, what for? Did you break a law or something? Are you a criminal?"

She gave a wry sneer. "I wish. I'd be a lot better off. Derec, I'm—sick."

"The chronic condition you've mentioned." He spoke

gently, allowing her whatever leeway she wished in such a personal matter.

"Oh, don't worry. You're in no danger. You can't get it from just being around me." She laughed bitterly. "I had an affair. I guess it was, you know, a rebellion against my mother and all her fancy friends. They all expected me to be such a good little girl and grow up to be just like them." It was her turn to start pacing.

Derec waited patiently.

"The guy was a Spacer from, I don't know, some other planet. He was just traveling through, you might say, and he was long gone by the time I found out he'd contaminated me."

"Couldn't your mother help? With all her money and everything?"

"Ha! They don't have any cure on Aurora—or maybe anywhere. Besides, this wasn't just a matter of getting sick and getting well. On Aurora, this is a deadly sin. My mother bought a ship and outfitted it for me, complete with a couple of robots as aides. Getting away was the best I could do."

"Your mother made quite a contribution, at that. You left Aurora in style, at least."

"I can't complain about that."

"And after you left?"

"I told myself I was looking for a cure, but I don't know if I really believe there is such a thing. But I *did* decide not to waste any time!"

Derec felt a prickling along the back of his neck. "What do you mean, not waste any time?"

"Derec, I . . . I'm going to die of this!" And suddenly she was crying, scared and vulnerable in a way he had never seen before.

He hesitated just a moment, and then went to her, holding her—awkwardly at first, then gently as she relaxed against him and really began to sob.

He was dumbfounded. This flood of information seemed to short-circuit his attention, and left him simply staring at the floor without thoughts as she cried in his arms. He had to sort out what he could—that she was Ariel, not Katherine, and that she was not, right now, the confident and sharp-edged older girl he had known her to be.

She was Ariel Welsh, banished from her home planet, trapped on Robot City, and infected with a deadly disease.

He turned her gently by the shoulders and led her into her room. First he sat with her on the bed, still uncertain of what to do. Then, after her sobs had grown fainter, she squeezed his arm affectionately and pulled away to stretch out on the bed. He rose, patted her on the shoulder shyly, and went out, closing her door behind him.

Derec sat at his computer console for a long time without turning it on. His own amnesia suddenly seemed like a fairly manageable problem. Yet the urgency of getting her off Robot City, and perhaps to some medical help, was greater than ever.

He doubted that the robots could help with a disease, at least in the short term. Even so, he started calling up various medical subjects on the central computer, in case Dr. Avery had left anything useful.

Actually, he found quite a bit of medical information pertaining to humans, but nothing that hinted at an ability to find cures for new diseases. The computer did have a list of vaccines, cures, and treatments for diseases he recognized—common ones that would have been available on Aurora. He also found a great deal of advanced material on surgery, organ regeneration, and other treatments for injuries. Overall, however, the library was oddly lacking, as though Dr. Avery, or at least somebody, had just grabbed information and entered it without checking it. For instance, there was no introductory reference on anatomy as such, or on psychology. Derec suspected that the eccentric Dr. Avery had been so involved with the frontiers of science that he had neglected to supply fundamental knowledge. After all, the robots had no particular need for this subject. He also remembered that the library on the planetoid where he had first met these Avery robots had been oddly selected.

At dinner time, he took a break and knocked lightly on Ariel's door. When she did not answer, he peeked inside and found her sleeping soundly. He made dinner for himself and returned to the computer.

The only information he could find pertaining to human anatomy regarded external appearance. This came from the positronic brains of the robots, rather than any specific entry into the computer. They could only obey the Three Laws of Robotics if they could identify humans when they came into contact with them, so he was not surprised to find this. When he saw the addendum beneath it, however, he sat up straight in his chair.

The computer noted five alien presences in Robot City. He supposed that meant humans, as the likelihood of sentient nonhuman aliens was very slim. There simply weren't enough of them, and he decided that the central computer would surely have made more of the matter. Nor would it ever again interpret microscopic human parasites as alien presences. Non-Avery robots could conceivably be here, of course, but he was sure that the significance of reporting these presences was to warn the local robot population that humans were here. Their presence would bring the Laws into consideration, while the arrival of other robots would not.

Obviously, he and Ariel were two of the five presences, but that left three of whom he had no knowledge. One of the three had arrived just a few days before. The other two, apparently traveling together, had been here for a slightly longer period.

The only ways they could have gotten here were with another Key to Perihelion, if there was another one off the planet, or in spacecraft. Either way, they offered additional chances for Derec and Ariel to get away from Robot City. He stayed on the computer all evening, trying to find more information.

He also rigged the chemical processor to make a new boot. It didn't match, being made of organic materials instead of synthetics, but it fit well enough.

He finally quit for the night when he felt his concentration slipping. After getting something else to eat from the chemical processor, he fell into bed. Ariel was still asleep.

Derec was exhausted, but as he lay in the dark, his mind was still racing. He kept reviewing his new knowledge over and over—Ariel Welsh, her disease, the duplication of the Key . . . and now, three more humans on Robot City—which might mean, possibly, some new ways to get off the planet. Finally, just before he drifted off to sleep, he heard Ariel leave her room and turn on the chemical processor. For tonight, at least, she was all right.

When Derec emerged for breakfast the next morning, clean and dressed, Ariel was working at the computer. He was hesitant to interrupt her there. However, she looked up when he turned on the chemical processor.

"Morning, Derec." She smiled shyly. "Are you still mad at me?"

"No. I guess you had good reason to be upset."

"I just felt so guilty and confused about everything. Especially keeping secrets from you, when you were wondering about the city and all. I'm really sorry."

"I'm just glad you finally told me. In the long run, maybe my knowing that stuff will help us."

"I saw the file you left on the console, the medical one. You were trying to help me, weren't you?"

"Yeah. I'm afraid there wasn't much about diseases, though. But did you see that we're not alone?" He took his breakfast out of the processor and sat down next to her, his plate on his lap.

"Yes! I was just looking at the notation. Do you have any idea who they could be?"

"No, I don't. As soon as I've finished eating, I'll see if I can find any more information about them in the computer, but I'm not too optimistic. Until I get more streamlining done, this computer can know all kinds of things and not realize it, you might say."

"This is such a strange place." Ariel sighed. "When I left Aurora, I was looking for adventure as well as a cure. I got the adventure part, such as it is."

"Like getting captured by that pirate, Aranimas?" Derec grinned. "When he got hold of me, I wasn't looking for adventure at all."

"We made a pretty good team, though, taking care of ourselves in that situation."

"Don't forget the rest of the team—Alpha, the robot I put together out of all those parts, and Wolruf."

"That little alien. I wonder what happened to them."

"Yeah." He was quiet for a moment, thinking about them. When he and Ariel had used the Key, and as a result had arrived in Robot City, Alpha and Wolruf had been left behind.

"Wolruf could be so surprising. One minute, she seemed like a very shy, subservient little creature, and the next minute we were relying on her for our lives."

"That's true. And Alpha's certainly unique, since I had to cobble him together out of random parts. Did I tell you he has a special arm? It's made of a kind of cellular substance. I ordered him to move it as though it's jointed like everyone else's, but actually he can make it completely flexible, like a tentacle. I wonder where they are now."

"We've never really talked about this, before, have we? About our being friends, I mean, and what we've done together."

He looked up at her. She was more at ease than he had ever seen her. He, too, felt the difference. Somehow, he trusted her now, though for all he knew, she could be keeping other secrets. She didn't act like she was.

"Derec, you've been very understanding. I appreciate it. Thank you."

"Uh. . . ." He gave just a hint of a shrug. "That's okay. Now, let's see if we can figure out how to get off the planet."

CHAPTER 4

ARIEL

Derec and Ariel took turns on the console all morning. This gave him a break every so often and gave her some practice. He sat looking over her shoulder as they tried to think up more questions to ask the computer.

"Derec, do you think the strangers that we're looking for have been able to hide? Or disguise themselves?"

"Maybe, but I don't see how. If they tried to hide, they'd still find robots everywhere in Robot City. They would have to stay inside someplace, and even then, they might be in a building that was scheduled for modification or tearing down by the robots." He laughed. "That would give them a good shock."

"And disguising themselves as robots might be a little difficult." She turned, also laughing, to catch his eye.

"Or maybe we could get some scrap robot parts ourselves, and wear them around like ancient armor." Derec shook his head, still grinning. "Especially those helmetlike heads."

"Seriously, though. What could have happened to them?"

"Well, it's possible that there are more sightings that have been lost in the central computer someplace. Otherwise, I don't really have an answer."

"I've asked about all the questions I can think of. I don't know what else to do."

"Let's try another train of thought," said Derec. "We don't know who they are—but what are they coming here for? What do they want?"

"The Key!"

"That's my guess. But other space traffic could come this way, even though we seem to be off the beaten track here. How about this: they knew Dr. Avery and came here to take over. Or what about your mother—could she have sent someone here to check on her investment?"

"I don't believe my mother actually knows where Robot City is, or maybe even exactly what it is."

"That narrows it to two possibilities I can think of. Either they're travelers who arrived by chance, maybe for repairs or fuel, or they came for the Key and maybe to take over Robot City. Can you think of anything else?"

"Maybe Avery himself, if he isn't dead. I doubt that, though. He'd be in his office running things, not allowing these chance sightings. But what are we going to do?"

"We'll have to go out and look around for ourselves, I guess. Unless you have another suggestion."

She shook her head.

"We'll have to be careful, though, till we find out who they are and what they want. We've gotten used to a certain amount of security here with the robots, since they can't hurt us, but now that's changed."

"Not as long as we have robots around us. Remember, they can't stand by and allow us to come to harm, either.

What about asking Avernus or one of the other Supervisors to help us find them?"

"Not right now. I don't want to alert the Supervisors to our interest in getting the Key, and so far they've left us alone. Let's start by going back to the Key Center. If we can get our hands on a key, we can just leave Robot City to fend for itself."

This time they took standard transportation, even though it took them farther out of their way than the vacuum chute had. The subway tunnels were another development that had become feasible once the shapechanging had stopped. They were full of robots, going about their daily business, who could be questioned. Derec and Ariel went to the nearest tunnel stop and rode down the ramp.

Traffic in the tunnels took the form of a robot, or a human, standing on a meter-square platform, enclosed by a booth of transparent walls, with a small console that could be set for whatever stop the passenger wished. The platforms ran on tracks; some parts of the city had as many as fifteen parallel tracks. The tunnel computer, an offshoot of the central computer, did all the steering, and could shift platforms from one track to another in order to create the most efficient flow of traffic. Tunnel stops had additional siding loops for loading and unloading. The technology reminded Derec of the lift system he had seen on the asteroid where he had first encountered the Avery robots.

Without positronic brains, the function robots could not set the controls, so only humans and robots with positronic brains rode the booths. Derec observed, as he watched the robots speed past, that they all stood motionless and staring straight ahead, unlike humans, who of course would be shifting positions, shuffling their feet, and looking around. The robots were logical, but never curious.

Ahead of them, several robots were emerging from platform booths. Derec and Ariel split up to approach them.

Derec stood directly in front of one to make sure the robot could see him clearly as a human in the dim light. "Just a moment. I would like to ask you a few questions."

"Yes?" The robot stopped.

"Have you seen any humans?"

"I presume you mean other than yourself."

"Yeah, besides me."

"Your companion is a female human."

"Besides us!" Derec flung up his hands. "Somewhere else in the city. Anywhere."

"No. You are the first humans I have ever seen."

"Thanks." Derec sighed and flagged down another robot. "Have you seen any humans other than my companion and myself?"

"What companion?"

"Uh—her. Over there. See her?"

"Yes."

"You have? Where?"

"Over there. Where you pointed."

"What—no, not her—"

"You asked if I saw her. I said yes."

"Okay, okay. Now, then. Other than the two of us present right here, have you ever seen any humans on Robot City?"

"No."

"All right, thanks." Derec waved him on.

At the moment, no more robots were coming into the siding loop or down the ramp. Ariel joined him.

"No luck here," she said. "You get anything?"

"No. Let's ride out to the Key Center."

They got into the first empty booth. It was a fairly close

fit, but not uncomfortable. Derec set the controls and the booth started with a slight jolt.

The platform carried them along the siding loop slowly, so that it could merge smoothly onto the first track at the earliest opening. Derec's trust in the engineering job done by the robots was so great that he never worried about safety. If the robots themselves had any doubts about the system, the First Law would have forced them to keep the humans from riding in it.

He didn't know exactly how the platforms were powered, though it must have been through the tracks. In a city where construction was rampant, these details often came and went so fast that learning them just didn't matter. The platforms moved quickly, with a faint hum, and never seemed to need sudden changes in speed.

At Ariel's suggestion, they got off at a couple of tunnel stops to question more robots, but this random search continued to produce nothing. They emerged from the system as close to the Key Center as they could, but still some distance away. In order to go on questioning robots on the street, they took the slidewalk, though they did not learn anything new this way, either.

When they first came into view of the dome, Derec stopped short. A huge opening gaped in the curving surface, and gigantic pieces of machinery, some easily ten and fifteen meters high, were being driven into the dome on a flatbed vehicle. More robots were visible inside than before, possibly to install the new equipment.

"If they were people," said Derec, "I'd try to get inside during the confusion. The trouble is, I don't see any confusion. They know what they're doing. I don't think there's much point in trying to sneak in right now."

"Let's move along." She took his arm and steered him

away. "No sense alerting Keymo's security to the fact that we're back."

"True."

They began to walk a discreet perimeter around the dome, making further inquiries of robots they met. The lack of information made it clear that the strangers had simply not been there.

"They will be," said Ariel. "They have to come here for the Key sooner or later. Suppose we instruct all the robots in the neighborhood to report sightings directly to us on the console."

"We can try," he said doubtfully. "The way the city keeps expanding, their population shifts all the time."

They continued their perimeter, now adding the instruction that the robots report sightings directly to them, and also to the central computer under the heading of "alien presences." When they had completed the circuit, Derec found himself gazing with hands on hips at the seamless wall of the Key Center, where the big opening was now fully sealed and scarless.

"This walking around talking just isn't getting us anywhere," Derec said. "Looking for our mysterious strangers is all right, but if we leave Robot City, we can forget about them anyhow. We can't get around it. We have to get inside the dome and get one of those keys."

"I'm afraid you're right. Look, I owe you on this one. Come on, let's do it. Do you remember where you left your boot?"

"Yeah, over there."

"You get over to it. I'm going to provide the diversion you needed the last time, over at the opposite side."

"No good. I won't know when to enter unless I can see you."

"All right—I'll stand just in sight. That way the curve of the dome will help keep the security robot from seeing you."

"Its name is Security 1K."

He walked over to the spot where a portion of his boot was still protruding from the wall, and waved to her. In response, she pounded on the wall.

"Hey! Open up in there! This is a human order!"

She did not, however, step back. With both fists on her hips and her feet wide apart, she stood with her toes right up against the wall of the dome.

The wall opened, as before, with a tearing sound right in front of her. Security 1K started to step out, but when she held her ground, the robot remained where it was. Derec could just barely see its hands moving. The robot was going to see him from that spot.

"We have learned that three other humans are present on the planet of Robot City," Ariel began. "We must speak with Keymo. These humans may endanger us."

Derec did not wait any longer. He pulled the boot just loose enough to get ahold of the free edges of dianite. When he began to pull gently, it ripped apart without much noise.

Inside the dome, everything was different. The floor was crammed with machinery, some of it even larger than the pieces he had seen entering a while before. Other units were quite compact.

He noted thankfully that the spaces between many of them offered him room to maneuver without being in anyone's line of sight, at least as long as Ariel kept Security 1K occupied. As carefully as he could, he crawled and scooted through the dark passages between machines, away from the robots he could see working here and there. This gradually moved him to a side of the building where he was able to peek out across the floor.

Now that the new machines had been installed, the crew in the dome was down to normal numbers again. They seemed more crowded in the smaller space remaining to them, but, as usual, they were efficiently concentrating on their tasks. That single-minded dedication helped Derec move unnoticed.

He caught sight of the security seat on its high perch. From where he was now, he could not see if Ariel was still keeping Security 1K busy, but that console was too inviting to pass up. Still moving cautiously, he reached the bottom of the perch.

The lift was a smaller version of those he had seen on the asteroid, and a version of the tunnel booths. A smaller lever lowered the entire seat, and, once he was in it, a button on the arm raised it. The seat moved up until it was just beneath the ceiling he had observed on his first visit. At the summit, he found himself looking out over the entire floor, with a complex array of controls and displays in front of him.

Not a single robot looked up at him. To one side, Security 1K stood with his back to the interior of the building, still talking with Ariel. Derec concentrated on the displays.

Very little of it meant anything to him. However, he was sure that the performance of every machine was being monitored here, as well as the wall of the dome. Both areas were construed as matters of security, apparently.

The console also had a computer terminal. Unlike his, this one had the VoiceCommand still hooked up. He leaned down and spoke softly.

"Central computer."

"Acknowledged." The voice was loud and made him jump.

"Lower your volume to match mine. Convert all the symbols on these monitors to full Standard terms."

A moment later, Derec was reading the monitors in amazement. As he had deduced earlier, Keymo had destroyed the Key to Perihelion in the process of having it analyzed. The robot was now overseeing the manufacture of many keys based on the same principle. The most startling monitor read, "Upper Level:Final integration of individual units and cooling. Interface with hyperspace, designated danger zone. Integration equipment producing vacuum effect of air out of dimension. Air movement, heat production, hyperspace controlled by drive unit."

He had to read it several times before he got it. The keys were being completed on the upper level in some kind of dangerous interface with hyperspace, which probably explained why it was removed from the rest of the facility. Apparently the manufacturing process created a vacuum that drew air into hyperspace.

His heart began to pound with excitement. "Where is the entrance to the upper level? And how do I get through it?"

"It opens directly above the security console. The seat will lift to that level. The dome surface can also be opened directly to and from the outside if necessary."

"Open the ceiling. This is, uh, a security matter." My security, anyway, he thought. He held his breath as he watched the ceiling. The computer assumed that the voice speaking into this console held sufficient authority to give this order, and did not require further identification. So far, the best thing about security on Robot City was its relative laxity. In a community of responsible positronic robots, the security measures had rarely been given a true challenge.

The dianite in the ceiling opened and he drove the seat on up through the hole.

CHAPTER 5

A HAND ON A KEY

Ariel had only two ideas for keeping Security 1K occupied. When it stood it front of her and started to step out, she forced herself to stand her ground. As she had expected, the influence of the First Law prevented it from forcing her aside, though in an emergency she doubted that it would have hesitated.

The robot remained just inside the dianite wall, watching her from the darkness of its horizontal eyeslit.

"I need to see Keymo," she said. All she had in mind was to present a First Law problem and to speak as slowly and as long as she could. Derec would have to do the rest by getting inside and getting a key, if he could, as quickly as possible.

"You may not enter this facility. Keymo is occupied." If possible, its voice was even more formal than the usual robot speaking voice. "May I help you?"

"This is a First Law problem." She started to say more, then remembered that she was stalling.

The robot waited until it was clear that she was not going to explain without prompting. "What is this problem?"

"A total of five humans are in Robot City."

"Yes? You are the one called Katherine?"

"I used to be. My real name is Ariel."

"Another is called Derec."

"That's right."

"What is the First Law problem?"

Ariel smiled to herself. That was the kind of stalling she wanted. What she had to do was be just a little illogical or unclear, forcing it to ask questions for clarification.

"Three other humans are here."

"Who are they?"

"We don't know."

"Who is in danger?"

"Derec and I are in potential danger."

"What danger is this?"

"Well—humans don't have to obey the First Law. So these other three could be dangerous to us."

"In what way?"

"Uh, I'm not sure."

"There is no clear danger." The robot took a step backward as a prelude to resealing the wall.

"How much experience have you had with humans?" She called quickly. "Do you know their history with each other?"

"No." It stopped where it was, now more shadowed inside the dome. "I have had only two previous experiences with a human."

"So! You don't know how they fight all the time? And have a history of wars and killing each other?"

"Some human history is available in the central computer library. In what way does this relate to the First Law problem?" The robot stepped forward again to its previous spot.

"Well, unknown humans are generally considered dangerous. You can never tell what they'll do or why."

"For what reason?"

"Just because they're unknown. We have to be careful. This is a normal part of being human, especially when you're traveling around in unfamiliar places."

"You consider unidentified humans to be dangerous until more information is available?"

"Yes! Yeah, that's it."

"No humans are in this facility. What do you need with Keymo for your First Law problem?"

"Keymo is in charge of making teleportation devices. This is the only way we know of to leave Robot City."

"You are in no clear danger. Therefore, no First Law problem pertains. Teleportation devices are not required."

"We could be killed or injured by surprise. This has happened to people many times. Your failure to help now is a First Law violation."

Ariel saw the robot hesitate, and suddenly realized that she might win this argument, let alone succeed in stalling. "Keymo is in charge of this facility, correct? Let Keymo decide."

The robot looked at her. "I am equipped to make decisions of this kind. Keymo does not have greater authority to judge and resolve a First Law problem than I have."

"So you agree that this *is* a First Law problem." She made it statement, not a question.

"That is not clear."

"But Keymo does have authority over the Key to Perihelion and the other keys. You don't have that. Since the resolution of the problem requires my getting ahold of the Key—or, keys, rather—Keymo is the one I must consult."

"You have not proven that you are in danger."

Shuddering with frustration, she drew in a long, deep breath. "Listen to me! I *believe* we may be in danger! I know a lot more about people than you do! You don't know enough about humans to judge if we're in danger!" She stared at him in fury, breathing hard.

At last the robot stepped back, making room for her. "We shall consult Keymo."

She smiled with relief and followed him inside the building. The robot led her through a winding route around machines of various sizes and types, none of which were familiar to her. She wanted to look around for Derec, but was afraid to be obvious about it. He could easily be lost among all the units here. Within the range of the cautious glances she took, he was nowhere in sight.

Keymo was standing over its console on the floor when they approached.

"This human claims to have a First Law problem," said Security 1K. "One that only you can resolve."

"You are the one called Katherine?"

"I used to be. My new name is Ariel."

"I understand. My designation was recently changed, also. What is the nature of this First Law problem?"

"Here we go again," she muttered to herself. "Look—how much do you know about human history? About how humans kill each other all the time and fight wars and stuff?"

Derec looked up apprehensively as the seat carried him into the dimmer light of the second story. He was most worried about being challenged by a robot up here, but as the seat clicked into place and the dianite solidified beneath it, he found himself standing behind a curved metal screen. On one side, pale orange light glowed from a doorway in the screen. Otherwise, the entire length of the short wall—the area with lift access—was screened off.

He slid out of the seat and carefully peeked around the edge of the doorway.

Only one robot was in the area. It stood in the foreground watching as a tray was extended toward it from inside a block housing about two meters high. The tray held an array of shining silver rectangles about five centimeters by fifteen—exactly the appearance of the original Key of Perihelion.

Derec guessed that the unit expelling the tray had just completed the final integration and cooling. As he watched, the robot picked up one key by itself and slid it into a slot in another unit. It then studied the readouts. It looked like a testing procedure.

Another wall, which sealed off the bulk of this level, was just beyond the block housing. Derec heard a muted hum from beyond it. The pale orange light was thrown by a series of monitors high on this wall, and cast a series of faint, overlapping shadows.

At the moment, he had nothing to do but watch. If his entry had been unnoticed downstairs, he was not pressed for time. Getting a key by stealth might be easier up here than by launching into another frustrating debate about the Laws.

Apparently, the entry into hyperspace was behind the big wall. It did not look especially strong, but the minimalist engineering characteristic of the Avery robots made all appearances deceiving. He would not have been surprised to find the barrier very solid and the sound beyond it absolutely deafening.

The robot took the key from the testing unit, or whatever it was, then punched a button and set it down on the tray. It stood with its back to Derec as it picked up another key and inserted it. At no time had the robot looked away from the readouts and keys, or moved its feet from their positions.

With the sound from beyond the wall as camouflage, Derec thought he just might be able to move without being noticed. He kept an eye on the robot as he slid around the edge of the doorway and crept behind it. The robot continued to watch the monitors.

The key that had already been tested glinted alone at one end of the tray. Derec stood directly behind the robot, waiting to see the robot's pattern of movement again. When the next key was ejected, the robot laid it next to the previous one and inserted a third into the unit it faced.

Derec reached very slowly for one of the tested keys, keeping his eyes on the robot for any sign of unexpected movement. The robot did not look away from the readouts. Derec picked up one of the keys and slowly began to withdraw his arm.

Just as he noticed that his arm was throwing a faint shadow across the monitors, the robot whirled and grabbed his throat in a hard squeeze. He began to choke, his tongue out and his eyes bulging.

A second later, the pressure was immediately released on his throat, but as he bent forward, gasping, the robot took a firm, though gentler, grip on his arm. He still held the key behind his back.

"Humans are more fragile than robots," said the robot apologetically. It was quivering with the internal trauma caused by a potential violation of the First Law. "I did not realize immediately that the First Law pertained. Not until I turned and saw you. You are unharmed?" Its speech was slow.

Derec nodded, swallowing. "Yeah."

The robot was still shaking and hesitant. "Identify yourself and your purpose here."

"My name is Derec. And I'm okay, so don't short-circuit yourself. Uh—"

"Security 1K did not notify me of your entry. This is a restricted area. Show your clearance."

"I don't have any. I'll just go." Derec turned, but the robot did not relinquish his arm.

"Return the key in your hand."

Derec couldn't think of an argument, so he held out the key, smiling weakly. The robot took it. Then the robot looked at a light blinking on one of the monitors.

"We shall go downstairs," it said. "I believe your presence here has been noted. In any case, that warning light summons all who are up here to report to Keymo."

"You might take a key with you." Derec reached around the robot for one. As he had expected, the robot grasped his arm. Derec feigned a shot of pain, wincing theatrically and twisting around so that he backed into the tray. As the robot pried one key out of his hand, he reached behind him with the other hand and palmed the other key that had already been tested.

Without further conversation, the robot escorted Derec around the screen to the security seat. It had Derec sit down, while it stood on some kind of bar beneath the seat. The floor opened, and they rode down together. Derec could see Security 1K standing with Ariel at Keymo's desk.

She gave him a questioning look as he was half pulled over to the console. He suppressed a smile with considerable effort. These robots were too sharp to miss any hint of collusion between them. He broke eye contact with her.

Before Keymo could speak, Derec decided to throw the robot off guard by taking the offensive.

"How did you know I was up there?"

"Both my console and the security console register heat generation and weight on each floor. However, I did not notice your presence immediately, as I had been distracted by discussions of possible imperatives under the Laws of Robotics." Keymo nodded toward Ariel and Security 1K. Then it addressed the robot still holding Derec's arm. "Process 12K, you may release your grip. Report what transpired in your jurisdiction."

"The human came up behind me and reached for one of the finished keys," said the robot from the upper floor. "He did this twice. I retrieved the key in both cases and retrieved them. When I first apprehended him, I did not know that the First Law pertained to the situation. I almost harmed him."

"We are speaking aloud for your benefit," Keymo said to Derec and Ariel. "On this matter of the First Law, you should be informed of our discussion. Derec, you are unharmed?"

"Uh, yeah. I'm okay." Derec, now free of Process 12K's grasp, moved away from him slightly. He had been feeling the key in his hand, and remembering the way it worked. Carefully, he shifted it around, pushing each corner of the key in turn. A button appeared on the last corner, on the side facing him.

Now he had to get Ariel to grip the key, or at least hold onto him, so he could push the button. With the robots so close, they wouldn't get more than one chance. Wherever the key took them would be an escape from the immediate scene; he would have to gamble that it was set for a safe place. After that, they could plan their next move.

"Ariel has claimed that a First Law problem exists," said Keymo. "Do you agree that you two are in danger from unknown humans present on the planet?"

"Uh—" Derec caught her slight nod. "Yeah. You bet. We have no idea who they are."

"Neither of you has presented any specific danger or any evidence of one," said Keymo. "Do you have any evidence of danger that she does not possess?"

"Well . . . no." Derec shrugged slightly and started shuffling his feet. He leaned a little closer to Process 12K. As he had hoped, Process 12K moved away slightly. Derec stepped in front of him, so that only Security 1K stood between Ariel and him. "I agree with her, though. People can be very dangerous—especially strangers. We would be a lot safer getting off this planet."

"You will have more contact with humans off this planet than you have here," said Keymo. "Most of them will, of course, be strangers, and therefore dangerous by your description. Here you have an entire population of robots that cannot allow you to come to harm."

"Only if you can protect us," said Ariel.

"Elsewhere," said Keymo, "you will have only yourselves to rely upon for safety."

"Now listen to her," said Derec. He reached in front of Security 1K to take her arm and pulled her to him. "The two of us are isolated here. . . ." He was just talking as a distraction, while he got an arm around her and pulled one of her arms behind her back. He placed her hand, behind both their backs, on the key with his.

"Now," he declared triumphantly, holding the key with one hand and pushing the button with the other.

Nothing happened.

CHAPTER 6

STRANGERS IN TOWN

Back in their apartment, Derec kicked the chair in front of the computer console and sent it skidding across the hard floor into the other one.

"Those filthy, stinking, walking, frosted slag heaps! What about the First Law? Doesn't that apply to the keys?"

"Apparently not," Ariel said bitterly. "If Keymo was telling the truth when he said that their keys are all initialized in that processing machine, and that they only work for the type of being that initializes them, then their keys will only work for robots. And if they initialize them by hand, that ruins them for us, too. They listened to my argument because of the First Law, not because they had keys that could send us away."

"I felt like an utter fool standing there holding that key when nothing happened. And then they scanned the wall to find out how I got in, and gave me my boot back." He looked down at the matched boots that he wore on his feet again. "You can bet the same trick won't work a second time."

"Well, at least they just threw us out. There wasn't any penalty or anything." She sighed and sat down in one of the chairs where it was, without bothering to move it back into its place. "I was so proud of myself for talking my way in to see Keymo, too."

"The First Law did us that much good, at least." He started pacing the perimeter of the small room. "I thought we were so close to getting away from here. I thought we had it." He paused when he saw Ariel leaning forward in the chair, staring glumly at the floor.

She glanced up at him and nodded dejectedly.

"Well, look. It isn't over yet. I mean, we aren't going to give up." He sat down in the console chair and gazed at the blank screen thoughtfully. "All right. What's our next move? Let's see." He started working on the keyboard.

She watched him for a moment. "You're looking for the other humans on the planet, I suppose."

"Of course. They got here, somehow; we can leave the same way, whatever it was."

"But we haven't made any progress finding them. What else can we do?"

"We didn't really apply ourselves before. I figured Keymo was our best bet, and the other humans just a backup. Now it's time to get serious about them."

"I hope it makes a difference." Her tone was still discouraged, but she pulled her chair closer.

"I'll start with that file we had earlier," said Derec. "Hey, we're in luck."

"Really?" She looked up hopefully.

"The two strangers who are traveling together have been sighted several more times."

"What about the third?"

"No, there's no more mention of that one. I hope he's

okay. I wonder if the third one is with the other two, or if they just happened to arrive about the same time."

"If they came separately, then we might have two ways to get away from Robot City."

"Good point," said Derec. "I just hope that the third one is simply hiding better than the other two."

"What do you mean?"

"If they all came together, the third one could have left again in the only transportation, whatever it is."

"Oh, Derec. Why did you have to bring that up?"

"We have to consider all the possibilities, don't we?" He turned to look at her. "Besides, getting in touch with some people for a change is still going to be an advantage. At some point, someone will come back for them. They'll be part of the spacefaring community, at least, not like these isolationist robots."

"Suppose we try to think along that line. Do we have any way of guessing who they could be?"

"I'll enter what we have. The real problem is that we don't know the location of this planet."

"We know that Dr. Avery wanted Robot City to be away from the beaten track," said Ariel. "My mother always emphasized how eccentric he was. I'm certain we aren't near any major spacelanes."

"I don't think we're in too much of a backwater, either. If Dr. Avery was the megalomaniac you said, then at some point he probably planned to show off his success to other people."

"Mother would have wanted to see it. And, you know what? He faced a lot of skeptics on Aurora. Eventually, he'd want to prove to them that he could do what he said."

"Good. We don't have much to go on, but it's something." Derec summarized the information he read on the screen. "Aurora is probably the nearest habitable planet, and it's almost certainly the nearest planet of any significance."

"If we do get a ride out of here, that'll be convenient," she observed. "I'm willing to take small favors."

"Let me go on. The odds of three people just landing here at almost the same time purely by chance in two space-craft are too low to think about. One spacecraft, maybe, if it had mechanical trouble or something, but not two. Assuming we are close to a spacelane, and remembering that this is all just surmise anyhow, we have to figure that our visitors came here deliberately."

"I can't honestly see why anybody would want to come here," said Ariel. "There's no business to conduct. And it's not exactly Fun City. There's no entertainment or anything."

"I know. And pioneering commercial interests would show up in force, not one or two people at a time."

"Individuals wouldn't have much of anything to do here that I can think of," she went on. "Even if I weren't sick, I'd still want to get away from here. The robots run everything on their terms."

"I think we can rule ourselves out as the reason, don't you?" Derec asked. "As far as we know, no one has any way of knowing that either of us is here."

"Don't I know it." She shook her head in resignation, with a wistful smile.

"So that leaves Robot City itself as the reason."

"But I told you that Dr. Avery kept its location a secret. My mother was sure that was very important to him."

"You also said that he disappeared a long time ago. If he's dead, could he have left some information behind in the office that someone got? Or spilled the secret someplace else out in space before he died? And now they've used the information to come here. Or he's back himself."

"With a guy like that, anything's possible," she said reluctantly. "But it sounds out of character for him to reveal more than he wanted. Besides, any people who had learned the secret would have shown up here a long time ago."

"Not if it was well hidden. Maybe they just found it."

"Maybe. I guess." She looked at him. "Do you think it's Avery?"

"No. The sightings just aren't consistent with his ability to go into that office in the Compass Tower. Our visitors are as lost as we are. And they can get us off this rock, too."

"So much for them finding Robot City," said Ariel. "What about us finding them?"

"I wish I'd had the time to streamline the computer by now. It just isn't that reliable. If it was, we could use it to help."

"We can try, can't we? Can you give some kind of standing instruction to the robots to look for the people?"

"Yeah, I can try, but we have the same problems as before. The instructions don't reach every single robot, and they take a long time to reach a lot of them. And even that assumes Dr. Avery didn't counterprogram against it for some weird reason of his own."

She shook her head. "He was too paranoid. If he was careful enough to keep the secret of this place, I'm sure he would have approved of ordering the robots to keep watch for outsiders."

"We already know that some robots are reporting their sightings. I'll order all the robots to do that, and...." he trailed off. "Well, I don't know. Maybe we're just going around in circles."

"What's wrong?"

"Well, I just don't know if it'll make a difference, like I said. It's just more of what's already in the computer."

"All we can do is give them the instruction and hope they get us some information," she said. "Then we'll try to think of something else. What's wrong with that?"

"Yeah, here goes. But what we really need is for the robots to detain them if they can, and I don't see how they can do that. That might violate the First Law."

"Wouldn't that depend on the particulars of the situation? Maybe the robots could persuade them to come. Anyway, the robots just have to avoid harming them. And they might want to see us. I guess they could bring them here, don't you?"

"I'm putting in the order. If there are any robots who can find and identify these strangers, they are to bring them here if they can. The robots can worry about the Law problems when the time comes." He sat back in his chair with a sigh. "I just don't know if any of this will make a difference."

"We've been going at this pretty hard," said Ariel. "Why don't we take a break? It's time for something to eat, anyway."

"Ugh," said Derec, and they both laughed. "All right. We'll force down anything we can stomach from the processor for lunch. After that, assuming we live, we'll probably be glad to go out and engage in endless debates with uncooperative robots."

Ariel got up, smiling. "I guess we can take our motivation wherever we find it."

After they had eaten, they ventured out once more to see if they could find some evidence of the strangers in the city. Derec started out eager and full of energy, in large part because Ariel's illness was on his mind. He wanted to make sure that she knew he wasn't dawdling.

At her suggestion, he agreed after a while to take it easy. Rushing around wasn't likely to help at this stage of the search. They had alerted the robots as much as they could, and they had a list of locations of previous sightings. Now all they could do was walk around, hoping to chance across a lead.

The worst problem was that the sightings offered no pattern that they could recognize. Since the lone traveler had not been reported at all for some time, they decided to forget about that one for the present. The sightings of the two traveling together were completely random, as far as they could tell.

The most recent sighting had taken place on the outskirts of the city. They rode the tunnels to the end of the trunkline at the edge of the city, and then had to surface. There, they managed to hitch a ride in the cab of a huge liquid transporter of some kind. They hopped off when its route diverged from theirs.

As they walked, they got their first look at the long, three-stage mole device that dug the underground tunnels and left a fully equipped, functioning platform system behind. This segment was not being used because it had not been connected to the main system elsewhere; otherwise, the mole device would have been underground and out of sight. It also simultaneously mined ores for construction and other uses, according to a foreman robot whom Derec questioned. It seemed to be a modified version of a gatelike device he had seen sifting the asteroid in search of the original Key for the Avery robots, shortly after waking up with amnesia, and the great mining and construction devices that had been crucial to the automatic shapechanging of the city.

They also saw a number of buildings under construction and some freshly finished. These included some smaller domes of bronze dianite reminiscent of the Key Center. Nowhere, however, did any of the robots remember any additional sightings of humans.

CHAPTER 7

THE CYBORG

His name was Jeff Leong. He opened his eyes in darkness and wondered where he was. At least he was alive, and not in pain.

He seemed to be lying on his back, comfortably. Pale, colored lights crossed his vision from his left, suggesting monitor readouts. He supposed they were medical equipment of some kind, and turned his head to the left, expecting it to involve considerable effort and discomfort. Instead, he moved easily and comfortably, though he found wires, now, under his cheek, that connected his head to the equipment by his side.

Dim light seemed to have come on in the room. He could see outlines in the room around him, and of course the lit displays of the monitors. The readouts meant nothing to him, though, so he straightened his head again.

He felt fine. That hardly made any sense.

Since he had only been a passenger on the spaceship *Kimbriel*, he did not have a clear understanding of the disaster. The captain had spoken over the intercom, saying that a mechanical problem had developed, and that they had left Aurora too far behind to return safely. The navigator had located a habitable planet, however, and they would attempt an emergency stop in a lifepod.

At the time, Jeff had been excited. He had had faith in the crew and had actually looked forward to an unscheduled adventure on a planet he had never seen. He assumed that was where he was now.

The door at the far end of the room opened and a robot entered. Full light came on in the room, and Jeff saw that his visitor was a blue-skinned robot of a specific type that he did not recognize. The robot walked to the monitors and studied each one carefully.

"Where am I?" Jeff asked. His voice sounded a little odd, but he had no trouble speaking.

"You are in Human Experimental Facility 1, Room 6, in Robot City," said the robot.

"Robot City? On what planet?"

"The planet is also called Robot City."

"Who are you?"

"I am Surgeon Experimental 1."

"Uh, can I see my doctor?"

"I am your doctor, along with Human Medical Research 1."

"Is he a robot, too? From his name, I suppose—"

"Yes. What is your name?"

"I'm Jeff Leong."

"Are you still in harm?"

"Huh?"

"How . . . are you? How do you feel?"

"Oh. I feel pretty good, actually. My voice sounds kind of strange, though, doesn't it?"

"It has changed. Please tell me the events leading to your arrival here."

"Our ship developed a mechanical emergency of some kind. We came here for an emergency landing, but we didn't make a very good job of it. I remember the captain warning us that it would be a hard impact."

"What other events led to your landing?"

"What other events? I don't know any other events. I was just a passenger. Look, where's everybody else?"

"I must inform you that you are the only survivor."

Jeff stared up at the ceiling, filled with many emotions. He had not expected that answer, yet he was not surprised. All the crew and passengers had been killed because of an accident—yet, he had somehow survived. It hadn't really sunk in yet. If anything, he felt more guilt than sorrow.

"Were you traveling with family or friends?"

"No," he murmured softly. "No, I didn't know anybody on board."

"What was your destination?"

"Mine, personally? Well, I was leaving home for college. I'm from Aurora."

"You were not coming to Robot City?"

"Not deliberately, no. Not until the ship malfunction." Jeff looked up at him. "Do you know what happened to it?"

"The mother ship exploded outside the atmosphere. The lifepod you were riding with the other passengers crashed in its attempt to land."

"I guess I lucked out, huh? I feel okay."

"I have summoned Research 1, the other member of the Human Experimental Team. We shall explain together. Perhaps you did luck out, as you put it. You say you feel well?"

"Yeah. Can I get up?"

"Have you observed yourself?"

"No . . . why, was I scarred or something?" Jeff put a hand to his face, and felt a hard, unfamiliar surface. "Am I in a mask? Bandages or something?"

Surgeon 1 paused as another robot entered the room. "This is Human Medical Research 1. Our patient is named Jeff Leong."

"Hi," Jeff said cautiously.

"Hi," said Research 1, in exactly the same tone. "Surgeon 1, how do the monitors read?"

"They indicate, taken together, an excellent condition."

Surgeon 1 walked up and looked down at Jeff, who felt cowed by the unequal numbers and strange appearances. He would have preferred a human doctor.

"Do you feel excellent?" Surgeon 1 asked.

"Well, yeah, but I feel all mummified or something. What happened to me?"

Research 1 moved to the foot of the bed and looked at him straight on. "Since the experiment has succeeded, I believe we can tell you with a minimum of shock. You may sit up."

"Uh, okay." Jeff expected to be helped, as solicitous doctors and nurses tended to do, but the robots remained where they were. He sat up, quite easily, watching Research 1's careful study of the monitors. Then he looked down and saw the blue-skinned texture of his own legs.

At first, he simply didn't understand. He wondered why his legs were encased in this stuff. When he reached out to touch one of his legs, he saw his hand and arm for the first time, made of the same unfamiliar blue substance. Then, suddenly understanding what had happened, he looked at his other robotic arm and then down at his chest. In growing panic, he clapped his blue hands against his torso and then ran them across the new contours of his face.

"The monitors read properly," said Research 1. "All evidence so far indicates a successful procedure. You are, of course, emotionally agitated. This reaction is also occurring normally."

Jeff collapsed back on the bed. The monitor lights jumped as they noted the impact. "I'm a robot. I can't believe this. I'm a *robot*."

"We wish you to understand something," said Surgeon 1. "The First Law required this development, under the circumstances of our finding you."

"What? How? How could the First Law require this? You don't think this has harmed me? I'm a person, not a robot!" Jeff started to sit up again, but really didn't feel like rising. He was not tired, or physically weak, but he didn't want to move, as though he might somehow injure himself in this alien body.

"You were injured when we found you," said Research 1. "We do not have knowledge here of human thoracic and abdominal organs. Our medical library is inconsistent and uneven. However, we had some experimental information regarding the frontier of knowledge about the human nervous system. Since we could not allow you to come to further harm if we could prevent it, we were forced to use our experimental knowledge in preserving you as a living entity."

"I'm not sure I follow you," Jeff whispered. "Say it out straight, will you?"

"We have transplanted your brain into one of our humanoid robot bodies because we could not repair yours."

Jeff closed his eyes and lay still for a moment. When he opened them, he stared morosely at Research 1. "What happened to my body?"

"It has been frozen. We believe, with our limited information, that it is actually not injured beyond repair. We do not, however, know how to fix it. Do you have medical knowledge that could assist us in repairing your body?"

"Me? I'm just a kid on his way to college—a teenager. I

don't know anything about that. At least, not on the level you would need."

"We assembled this team specifically for this project," said Surgeon 1. "We are not aware of other successful transplants of the same type."

"Great," Jeff said sarcastically. "I guess."

"You do not seemed pleased with this success," observed Surgeon 1. "Do you disbelieve that this is the least harm to you that we could arrange under the circumstances?"

"No . . . no, I don't disbelieve you. I just . . . don't want to be a robot!" He sat up this time and yanked the monitor wires free of himself. "Don't you get it? I'm not me anymore! I'm not Jeff Leong."

The robots made no move.

"That is not entirely true," said Research 1. "Your identity resides in your brain. Unless the trauma of the crash caused you to lose some memory, your identity is unchanged."

"But I'm not *me*—I mean, on the outside. I don't look like this." He held up his hands, open, and shook them at the robots.

"In many ways," said Surgeon 1, "your new robot body is more efficient than your human body. It can be repaired virtually forever, provided your brain is undamaged. Only your brain will age, and it will receive the optimum support in nutrition and intrabody care. You are stronger, and your sensors are much more efficient than your former sense organs."

"Some consolation. How long do I have to stay here?"

"Your robot body is in fine condition. You are not confined to bed," said Surgeon 1. "Some simple motor tests will tell us whether all the connections from your brain to the body are correct. Please stand."

Jeff cautiously swung his legs over the edge of the bed and got up. "No problem so far."

"Place your heels together, angle your feet away from each other, and tilt your head back. Now extend your arms out straight. One at a time, touch your hands to your nose."

Jeff complied.

"Very well," said Surgeon 1. "Research 1?"

"According to the monitors, the robot body is functioning properly. We will need more space for my tests of gross motor skills. I suggest we introduce him to the exterior of this building."

Jeff walked out of the room with them and down a hallway, feeling not clumsy, exactly, but just a little too tall and too heavy. Outside, he was nearly blinded at first, but adjusted immediately. Surgeon 1 saw him flinch.

"Your eyes see a wider range of the spectrum than your human eyes did. The same will be true of your other sensors. What you just experienced was an automatic dimming of your robot eyes to allow you to see comfortably. You did just the opposite when you woke up in near darkness a little while ago."

"Excellent," said Research 1. "You are responding automatically, then. I have only a few more tests."

"Before we do that," said Jeff, "I just thought of something. What am I going to *do?*"

"Whatever you wish," said Research 1. "We have no requirements, other than those imposed on us by the Laws and by our programming. That involves our society here, not you."

"But . . . what about college? I can't go like this. . . . They won't even know who I am! I don't look like Jeff Leong any more—I don't have retinal prints, fingerprints, any kind of identifying mark."

"If your brain waves are on record anywhere, they will

74

serve," said Surgeon 1. "However, we do not have any spacecraft available for you, anyway."

Jeff whirled on him. "You mean I'm *stuck* here?"

"We do not have spacecraft available," Research 1 affirmed.

"But . . . wait a minute! I can't stay here!"

"We have no hold on you," said Research 1. "If we ever develop the means to repair your human body and reverse the transplant, we will do so. Should spacecraft become available, travel will also be open to you."

"But I can't stay here. There's nothing to do here!"

"Please remain calm. After testing your gross motor skills, I will introduce you to the robot in charge of assigning tasks in Robot City. Perhaps you will find an activity that you will enjoy."

"Hey, now wait a minute." Jeff backed away from Research 1, and found the other two robots grasping his arms. "Hey!" He twisted, stepped sideways, and yanked his arms free. "Lemme alone."

"We must conduct more tests to measure your welfare," said Research 1.

"Look, I just—let go!" Jeff pulled his arm away from Surgeon 1 again. "Listen to me! I'm human—I'm telling you to leave me alone. Second Law, remember?" he started walking backward, awkwardly on his new legs, keeping an eye on them.

"We cannot allow you to harm yourself," Surgeon 1 reminded him. "The First Law outweighs the Second. Come back." He started for Jeff.

Jeff spun around and started running.

He found himself running down a broad thoroughfare nearly empty of vehicular traffic. Some robot pedestrians moved out of his way. He had no idea where he was going, but he wanted to think, and to do it alone.

He could hear two sets of footsteps pounding after him—and was surprised to realize that his robotic hearing was so acute that he could actually distinguish the two separate pairs of robot feet. They were calling after him, not shouting angrily the way people would, but yelling that he was still experimental, that he might harm himself, that he had to stop. He didn't stop, though; their voices simply spurred him on.

Other robots were listening, however, and trying to block his path. He dodged a couple of them and burst through the outstretched arms of several more. They all gave chase, presumably responding to the calls of the medical team that he might violate the First Law. The other robots apparently would help catch him first if they could, and worry about explanations later.

He rounded a corner without slowing down and started up a small side street. Even now, he could feel that he was running more comfortably than he had just moments before. His robot body responded quickly, and well. It had not been designed for footraces, but it was powerful and efficient. As he got more used to it, he began to turn up the speed and to hurdle minor obstacles.

Unfortunately, of course, his pursuit was all robots, as well.

He kept running.

CHAPTER 8

HITTING THE STREETS

Derec and Ariel stopped to rest on a small ridge of soil on the side of yet another construction site. As near as they could tell, the urban area of Robot City was expanding in all directions from its center, and they had been walking the perimeter of construction so they could question the robots they encountered. So far, they had traveled only a very small arc of the entire circle.

"This isn't doing us any good," Derec complained. He lay down on the dirt and leaned back against the slope.

"What isn't?" She looked carefully to make sure the slope behind here was smooth, then also leaned back. "Resting here or asking around?"

"Both, now that you mention it. But I meant asking robots at random like this. There are thousands of them, and they aren't very observant of their surroundings unless it's part of their job. They concentrate on their own tasks too much."

"I haven't thought of anything better." She closed her eyes. "My feet hurt. I'm not used to walking so much."

"I haven't thought of anything else, either. There must be something, though." He looked across the way, where a foreman robot was overseeing a large function robot of some kind. "Everything is so carefully organized. Nothing is wasted."

As they watched, the function robot raised an arm with a nozzle on the end and began to spray a heavy, viscous liquid onto the bare, level ground in front of it. Even after the liquid had landed, it swirled and shifted and moved in active currents beyond those in motion by the pressure at the nozzle. As the spray continued, the liquid formed a flat floor and then began to grow walls up from the floor, leaving space for a doorway.

Ariel opened her eyes. "Did you ask that one robot earlier how the spray works? I went to talk to another one and didn't hear your conversation."

"Yeah. I didn't understand the details, but apparently the molecules are all coded. They know where to go, and slide around in liquid form until they reach the right spot. Then they bond with their right neighboring molecules."

"Just the way this whole city works," said Ariel. "Except for us and our visitors. We don't fit. That's one thing we have in common with them, no matter who they are."

"You think it over," Derec said wearily. "Here comes another transport vehicle of some kind. I can see a humanoid riding in it. I guess I'll go interrupt its day and ask it the usual questions."

He got to his feet, and realized as he walked through a scrap area that his own legs did not have much more energy left, either. Most of the scrap was in huge, carefully stacked piles, but here and there individual pieces had fallen or been laid out to start a new stack. He noted with a mixture of interest and annoyance that none of the parts were recognizable. These Avery robots had an extremely ingrown technology.

Derec had learned how to shortcut this process somewhat. He first called out that he was human to get the robot's attention, and then ordered it to stop. In turn, the humanoid robot ordered the function robot—the transport—to stop. This time, Derec's questions paid off.

"I have seen two non-indigenous beings recently," said the robot, looking down at Derec from the high cab of the transport.

"Identify," Derec ordered, with excitement.

"I am Class 9 Vehicle Foreman 214."

"What did they look like? What were they doing?"

"One was a robot that did not respond to my communication greeting. Apparently he was on a different frequency or malfunctioning. Also, his dimensions and proportions were not quite familiar."

"What about the other one?"

"I did not see the other one clearly. It appeared to be no longer than a meter. This is an approximation. It had four extremities."

"A kid," said Derec. "A robot and a little kid. That's weird. . . . Did you speak with them?"

"No. They departed when I approached."

"What were they doing when you first saw them?"

"Walking."

"Did you hear them speak? Or have any contact with robots of any kind?"

"No."

"Say—why did you try to communicate with them?"

"Because of their unusual appearance. I thought that if the robot required assistance to repair a facility, I would offer it."

"Did you report the sighting to the central computer?"

"Yes."

"When and where did it take place?"

"Two days ago. The time—"

"That's good enough. Where?" Derec grinned. The sighting was not one of those he had found listed in the computer. Ariel came up to join them as Class 9 Vehicle 214 gave him the city coordinates of the sighting. Then the robot went on its way.

"It's a start," Derec said happily. "The sighting is two days old, but it's solid."

He filled her in on the details.

"A babysitter and a kid, maybe," said Ariel. "They might have been ejected from a lifepod in a ship emergency, or something like that. But with the transportation in this city, they could be anywhere by now."

"We have to start somewhere. Come on." Derec started in the direction of the nearest thoroughfare back toward the heart of the city.

Ariel hurried after him. "It just doesn't seem like much to go on. They must be long gone from there."

"Oh, come on! After all this time, this is the best lead we have. Why do you want to be so pessimistic?"

"It's not that, exactly."

"Then what?" He demanded angrily. "Don't you want to get away from here? Would you rather just give up?"

"Of course not! I didn't say that."

"Well, then, come on." Derec stalked along, his upbeat mood lost. The worst part of it was his realization that she was right. Their lead out here on the fringe of the city had come to nothing; chasing a two-day-old sighting might be just as hopeless.

They marched in silence for a while, then topped on the edge of the avenue. Traffic here would be nonexistent until the next construction transport was ready to head into the city again. The trips were carefully planned and maintained, as the robots were too efficient to waste any fuel or time on unnecessary runs.

After Derec had cooled down a little, he said, "Maybe these two sightings do tell us something. I think our visitors landed outside the city and entered in search of, I don't know—food and shelter, I suppose. The sighting on the fringe, here, was older. So if they went into the middle of the city for a reason, they may stay there."

"It's still a very big city," Ariel said doubtfully. Suddenly, she gasped. "That's it, Derec. What are they going to eat?"

"Well—I guess they'll get a chemical processor from the robots. . . ."

"But will they know that? Will they know to ask? Besides, the robots wanted you to solve a mystery for them, so we had special consideration."

"Maybe, but if the robots learn of the problem, the First Law will make them help out." He was stung by the fact that he hadn't thought of this himself. "Yeah, this must be the only city to be found anywhere that doesn't have a single restaurant or anything like that."

"This is our first real lead," said Ariel with a new excitement. "Once we get back to the tunnel system, let's split up. I'll follow up on our latest sighting and see if I can find a food source around there."

"Why? I thought you didn't consider that lead worth much."

"Oh, Derec, stop griping. You need to get back on the computer and see if you can locate food sources through it. This way we can cover two leads at once, that's all."

"Well, I can't argue with that. Come to think of it, if they haven't found any food, they could be in bad shape by now. We don't want them dying on us." He waved for her to follow him, pressed by a new sense of urgency.

"We can't walk all the way to the tunnel stop," she said, but she was smiling. "It's good to see the old enthusiasm back."

They actually walked some distance before a vehicle came by to give them a ride, but the walk paid off. The vehicle had departed from somewhere within the construction perimeter and would not have passed them out there. As Ariel had suggested, they split up in the tunnel system. He returned home to their computer console, while she went on to the site that Class 9 Vehicle 214 had reported.

Derec sat down at the console, glad to have another approach to use; but he hadn't forgotten that this report had been lost somewhere in the system. He started by calling up a list of stores that were edible to humans. The only inventory was in the tank of their chemical processor, according to the screen. So either the visitors were getting hungry, or they had a food source not recorded this way.

Next, he called up other materials that had been converted to edible form. Again, everything was accounted for. He asked if another chemical processor had been made or requested. Nothing like that had been recorded.

As far as Derec knew, Robot City did not have any animal life that could be caught and eaten, even by the most desperate humans. Perhaps a very talented human could build a chemical processor without the help of the robots, but it would still require parts. Nor could it produce any food without raw materials of some kind.

On the assumption that the visitors had landed outside the city and entered the perimeter where he and Ariel had first gone, he narrowed the focus of his requests and asked again if any robots in that area had sighted the strangers.

Nothing turned up that way. He got the same result when looking for a record of their landing.

The only certainty Derec had was that the computer was unreliable. The answers about the chemical processor and the foodstuffs might be accurate, but the visitors were here, and that meant they had landed somewhere on the planet in a spacecraft that could, in all probability, lift off again. There had to be some way to track them.

He couldn't think of anything. With a sigh, he got up and paced idly around the small room. So far, the computer hadn't helped any this time; he wished he had gone with Ariel.

He doubted she was in much danger, especially if the visitors were a robot and a small child. Besides, he knew she could take care of herself pretty well. His attitude toward her had changed, though, ever since he had learned of the seriousness of her illness. She didn't seem quite so intimidating any more, though she was still older and more self-assured than he was. Ever since the day she had told him of the severity of her disease, and had cried in his arms, he had felt a growing protectiveness toward her.

She seemed to be okay now, though. He figured she might just laugh if he tried to tell her how he felt.

His jaw muscles tightened with the determination to prove what he could do with the computer. He sat down again and started calling up everything he could think of regarding space: records of astronomical observations, spacecraft landings, liftoffs, fly-bys . . . what else?

The computer gave him nothing on recent soft landings of spacecraft, or crashes. Nor had there been any reported sightings of landed spacecraft. Astronomical observations had not recorded any craft in orbit, either. He had to assume that either the sensors had failed in some way, or that the information was simply lost in the computer.

Food, he thought. The visitors required nutrition. That was still the best lead he had, if he could only think of a way to exploit it.

Ariel walked out of the tunnel stop and located the coordinates of the last sighting of the visitors without any trouble. Her only problem was what to do next. She was in the middle of the city, standing still as a moderately heavy traffic of robots passed her, either on slidewalks or in vehicles.

"Well, what would I do for food here?" she asked herself out loud. "Ask around, I suppose."

As always, the robots were moving with their single-minded deliberation. The bland buildings reflected that attitude in their austere efficiency of design. No stranger, she reflected, would expect to find food in this neighborhood.

She stopped the nearest robot passing, by calling out, "I am a human who needs questions answered. Stop."

The robot stopped.

"Have you seen a robot traveling with a human child?"

"No."

"Do you know where I might find food?"

"Food. This is the energy source for humans, is it not?"

"Yes. It must be provided in a certain chemical form."

"I am not familiar with it. I do not know where to locate any. Are you in urgent need of energy?"

"I'm not," said Ariel, "but I think a small human in the company of a certain robot probably is. Almost definitely. I need to find them before the child starves. That is, runs out of energy."

"This constitutes a First Law requirement, then. I will help you search for them."

"Identify." Ariel suddenly realized that this argument could be used to harness every robot in Robot City.

"I am Courier Foreman 189."

"You supervise couriers? What do they do?"

"Couriers are function robots that carry small items to specific locations. Objects and distance vary."

"All right. Listen. You don't have to interrupt your work at all. Just spread the word to other humanoid robots as you go about your duties that a First Law problem requires their aid in locating a human child in the company of a robot, and also another human wandering around by himself."

"Understood."

"And tell them not to include me—I'm Ariel Welsh—or Derec."

"Understood. I will contact other robots through my comlink."

"Good! I have to tell Derec about this right away." Ariel turned and ran for the tunnel stop.

CHAPTER 9

JUST ONE OF THE CROWD

Jeff decided, after numerous glances back over his shoulder, that he had finally lost his pursuit. He had run blindly, turning corners and dodging behind robots and vehicles and buildings every time he could, before slowing down. He was not out of breath, or even tired, but he was disoriented and scared.

He didn't know where he was going, or even why he had run. Right now, he just wanted to be alone. He eyed warily other robots that he passed, but they paid him no particular attention. Either the medical staff had not yet put any word out, or his physical traits carried no designation they could use to identify him. The thought that he would not have to run every minute bolstered his spirits a little. The total lack of humans dampened them again.

The entire situation just didn't seem real. It was absurd. How could he, Jeff Leong, eighteen years old, recently accepted into college, a healthy and fairly normal Auroran . . . be a *robot?*

He walked. He walked straight, turned corners and then

found a slidewalk and got on it. With nowhere to go and nothing to do, he just kept walking along the slidewalk.

At first, his senses were still askew. His eyes were not only more sensitive than before, but they seemed to see in a much wider range of the spectrum. He found himself looking at colors, as he termed them, that he had never seen before and had no name for—and they unnerved him. Gradually, he learned to shut out most of the unwanted light waves. The same had occurred with his hearing. It had been so acute at first that all sounds had reached him in a kind of jumble. Then he had been able, by concentrating, to reduce his hearing acuity to a level that felt comfortable. He had been intrigued by the added abilities, but he would have to learn how to control them.

The walking also helped him become more familiar with his new body. It responded smoothly and efficiently, with good balance and control. He couldn't complain about that. Before long, he had concluded that he was moving enough like the other robots, the real ones, to escape notice.

He also looked over the robots he passed, as nonchalantly as he could, in search of identifying marks. The robots bore differences, certainly, especially where job-related equipment was concerned on the non-humanoid ones. He saw several distinct but subtle pattern differences repeated on many of the humanoid robots, and guessed they represented minor engineering improvements on robots that had been made or repaired at different times. If they had individual identification, however, he was too much of a stranger here to see it.

Gradually, he found himself moving in a consistent direction. The population seemed denser that way, perhaps toward the center of the urban area. All the robots seemed intent on their own occupations, and he grew more confident that he could lose himself in the crowd.

Yet, he still had nothing to do and nowhere to go.

Ahead of him, through a crowd of robots, he thought he saw a girl, or young woman, emerge from some kind of underground entrance. With a surge of excitement, he quickened his pace and leaned to one side to look between two other robots. When they glanced at him, he straightened in alarm.

He could see her walking the other way. If he wanted to avoid notice, he would have to act with the same deliberate manner as all the robots around him. He lengthened his stride and gave chase without otherwise altering his body language.

Not far ahead, she had stopped to speak to a robot. Jeff slowed down as he approached, and stopped when her back was to him. He was a good distance away by human standards, but after a moment of effort, he was able to sharpen his hearing enough to eavesdrop.

"Identify yourself," she was saying.

"I am Tunnel Foreman 41," said the robot.

"I'm Ariel. Please spread the word about the First Law obligation I've described."

"I must," said Tunnel Foreman 41.

The robot departed and Ariel started to go. Then she saw Jeff watching her, and she paused.

"The First Law?" Jeff asked. He wanted to continue his masquerade as a robot until he knew something about her.

"Yes," said Ariel. "We're looking for two people who are probably starving in Robot City. One is a child traveling with a robot and the other is alone. The First Law requires that all robots help locate them."

"Of course," said Jeff, suddenly realizing that of course this did not apply to him. He still had his human brain, and the imperative of the Laws was located in the positronic brains of the robots. Yet if he revealed this, his identity would be known to anyone aware of the transplant and his subsequent escape.

"Report any sightings of them to the central computer," Ariel went on. "Detain them if you can, without violating the Laws. We'll see that they're fed."

"I understand," said Jeff. He was trying frantically to think of a question, anything, to learn more about her without giving himself away.

"Identify," she said.

"Uh—Tunnel Foreman 12." He couldn't risk making up a job, in case she would recognize the fraud. "Do you know who they are?"

"Why, no." She looked at him in some surprise. "They just seem to have landed and walked into the city. In fact, if you come across them, find out what you can about their spacecraft."

"Find out what?"

"Well, where it is, if it's damaged, what kind it is. . . ." She cocked her head to one side. "None of the other robots have asked these questions."

Jeff felt the impulse to run wash over him again, but he couldn't afford to look like a fugitive. He forced himself to remain where he was, searching for something to say.

"Tell me why your responses are different."

He knew why she had changed her observation to an instruction. Now he, under the Second Law, was required to answer, or else blow his cover if he didn't. The scarcity of humans in this weird place—the only fact about it that he was sure of—would mean he wouldn't have to go through this very often.

"I cannot judge the responses of others," he said, picking his phrases carefully. "My responses are based on a desire to elicit further information that may be of help."

"Well, all right." She seemed to accept that.

To forestall another question, he asked one of his own. "What is the importance of the spacecraft?"

"It may well be the only functioning spacecraft on the planet. That's if it works at all. Now, I have to report some information. You go spread the word, all right?" She gave a little wave and walked away.

Jeff was aching to follow her, but he didn't dare act any more out of character for a robot than he had already. He watched her until she had turned a corner, then hurried to the corner and watched her departing form as the crowd of robots between them gradually closed her from his view. At least he had had some human contact; she hadn't been bad-looking, either.

He definitely wanted his human body back.

That spacecraft might mean something to him. It was a way to get off the planet, but he couldn't see leaving without his body—and he'd better be in his body at the time, since these robots might be the only ones who could manage the transplant back into it. Then, belatedly, he remembered what the medical team had told him: they needed information about human organs. Ariel's were presumably in good shape, and could act as a model.

He started briskly in the direction she had gone, now more willing to risk revealing himself . . . In sudden puzzlement, he frowned—at least inwardly. He had no idea what his robot face was doing.

The point was, what had *he* been doing? Why had he run like that from the medical team? They had just wanted to test him some more. Why had he been so secretive? Maybe Ariel would have been glad to help. He hadn't even thought of that. He had been in a fog ever since waking up.

He couldn't see her ahead anymore, but—

A hand on his shoulder startled him. He twisted away

from the contact, backing toward the wall of a building. A robot had just caught up with him from behind.

"Identify yourself," said the robot. "I am Pavement Maintenance Foreman 752."

"Uh—Tunnel Foreman, uh, 12."

"Tunnel 12, is your comlink malfunctioning? I tried to contact you several times as you were standing still. You did not respond."

"No, I didn't . . . receive you."

"I am informing you so that you can report to a repair facility. However, I initially tried to contact you to say that a First Law problem has developed over the matter of two humans in Robot City."

"I am aware of it," Jeff said warily.

"Excellent. I notice that your speech pattern is also hesitant. This symptom may be related to your comlink malfunction. I will escort you to the nearest repair facility, lest you be incapacitated by an additional symptom."

"Oh—no, uh, I can find it." Jeff backed along the wall. "Thanks, anyway."

"Tunnel Foreman 12, your behavior also suggests further malfunctions. I will escort you. You are going the wrong way."

Jeff turned and began walking quickly away. "Third Law violation!" cried the robot behind him. "You must not allow harm to yourself!"

Jeff heard the footsteps behind him start to run, and took off himself. Ahead of him, robots walking his way suddenly fixed their vision on him, and acted in concert to block the way. Pavement Maintenance Foreman 752 was obviously sending out comlink signals to every robot in the vicinity.

One of those openings leading underground stood just

ahead on the left. Two robots blocked his way near it. He ran toward them and feinted forward, as though he was about to leap on them. They stiffened reflexively for the impact, and he dodged into the underground opening.

He found himself running down a ramp, and nearly lost his balance when his weight on the ramp activated it. It carried him down at a quick speed, and when he recovered his footing, he ran down to the level of the tunnel platforms. He understood their purpose without a pause, since robots were speeding by on them, but he stepped into the first booth without knowing how to operate it. It started anyhow, so he was content to look back and see a number of robots in pursuit entering booths behind him.

The controls seemed to have both voice activation and key code capabilities, but he didn't now how the stops were numbered, or named, or whatever. Nor did he know anything about the layout of the city, so one stop was as good as another. His pursuit certainly knew exactly how to operate these things.

"Speed up," he said experimentally. The platform did speed up, though not greatly. It was approaching the one just ahead, and clearly would not get too close. At least the robots pursuing him could not really get their hands on him here, either. They could only follow him, and try to jump him when he got off. . . .

Unless they could get the system shut off on some emergency basis.

They'll never get me, Jeff thought firmly. Once he was out of the tunnels again, he should have one advantage: these robots, despite their equal strength and reflexes, were unaccustomed to physical conflict. He was sure his feint had succeeded for that reason; they still expected him to act logically, like a robot, even if he had "malfunctioned."

He could stop them cold if he revealed that he was human. They would have no right to harm his robot body under the First Law, then, and under the Second, they would have to obey him. Revealing himself would risk capture by the medical team, though, which he could not accept.

He shook his head, then, unsure of why he couldn't accept that. They were dangerous to him, threatening... for some reason. In any case, they wouldn't get him.

"Stop at the next stopping place," he said to the booth.

His platform duly routed into the next available loading loop, and he quickly hopped out. This time he was ready for the moving ramp, and ran up it even as it carried him. Up on the street again, he found the number of robots very sparse, which was just as well. Any moment, the robots pursuing him would order them to join the chase.

He ran around a corner so that he would not be immediately visible when the pursuit poured out of the tunnel stop. A large door of some kind, apparently to accommodate sizable transports, was in front of him. He started to reach for the control panel to one side of the door, then realized that a work crew was almost certainly inside. The pursuit was sure to see him any second. He looked around frantically.

In the wall next to the door, he saw a broad, round opening with a closed iris cover. The cover opened at his touch, and the smells from within told him it was a trash chute. He slid into it feet first, face down, pressing his arms and legs against the slick sides of the chute to prevent himself from shooting down into the receptacle.

The cover irised shut over his head, so he concentrated on his hearing. Footsteps sounded nearby, hesitated, shuffled, and pounded on. No voices were used; they were communicating through their comlinks. He waited, in case more were coming.

He could smell faint oils, oxidized metals, and some

mild odors he could not recognize. His human nose would probably not have smelled anything. Apparently, robots produced only inorganic waste, sparing him the strong and foul odors of organic decomposition.

He was not getting tired, exactly, but he was somehow aware of unusual energy expenditure—which meant the same thing, in a way. When he had heard no sound of any robots for several minutes, he touched open the cover and pulled himself out. As before, the block was empty.

"Fooled 'em," he said aloud with a certain satisfaction. He strolled to the corner and looked up and down the street. A few robots were walking about, but traffic was very light. "Okay, gang. Now for the big test. Can you recognize me again, or not?"

As he walked, he closely eyed the robots he passed. None seemed to have any concern with him. If he possessed no external identifying mark, then his pursuit had permanently lost him when they had lost sight of him. He was comlink-invisible; not only was he incapable of receiving those signals, but he could not be tracked down by any careless broadcasting on his part. Use of the comlink would also explain why the robots found identifying marks unnecessary.

He was lost in the crowd.

Jeff smiled, at least inwardly, at the thought.

Aurora had been settled primarily by the descendants of Americans from Earth. His own ancestors had been Chinese Americans; a number of such families had been scattered about on Aurora, but they were a modest percentage of the population. Jeff had grown up knowing that he was visibly distinct anywhere he went, and he had expected the same when he went off to college—though now he was no longer sure he was going to make it.

For the first time, he resembled everyone else on the

planet where he lived. It was a new experience—practically a new concept to go with his new existence. His life as a robot could be completely different for this reason, as well as for the obvious physical change.

He had to do something with himself in this new body and in this new life, such as it was. It was too soon to know what, yet, but one fact was clear: no one knew what he looked like anymore; no one could catch him. . . .

Perhaps he could make something of this new-found anonymity.

CHAPTER 10

BACON

Derec ran his hand through the bristly hair on the side of his head and stared morosely into the screen. Maybe he was just too worn out to concentrate any more. He hoped that was the problem. If not, then the reason he couldn't think of anything else to try with the computer was that he had already tried everything. He straightened in surprise when Ariel burst into their quarters.

"How did it go?" He looked up hopefully.

"I got us some help for a change," she said brightly. "As soon as I run to the personal, I'll tell you about it."

He felt a kind of disappointment that he didn't have any good news to report, but waited patiently until she had returned.

"You got us some help? Who is it? How'd you manage that?" He tried to cover his envy.

"I was talking to one of the robots, and the argument just came to me. I told a couple of them that there were humans lost in Robot City who were starving. That gave them a First Law imperative to help." She fell into her chair with a sigh. "I've been on my feet enough for one day. But at least I accomplished something out there."

"Good job," he conceded. He sat back from the console, glad for an excuse to quit for a while. "But what about their regular duties? Didn't they resist leaving them?"

"I just told them to continue their duties, and to keep an eye out for the human visitors while they did. Oh, and for them to pass the word on to other robots, of course."

"Yeah, that's a good idea. That way they don't feel a conflict between their duties and a rather vague First Law obligation."

"Did you tell them to report to the central computer?"

"Of course. But, uh...." She inclined her head toward his console with a pointed smile. "As I recall, your department hasn't been exactly on top of everything."

"Yeah, I know. Whether it gets on record where I can find it is an open question." Derec acknowledged the point with an embarrassed shrug. "At least it improves our chances."

"Anyway, I wanted to tell you about the new First Law argument right away. With the robots helping us search, we don't have to do the legwork any more. Have you gotten anywhere?"

"Yeah—well, no, not really." He sighed and looked wearily at the screen. "I've eliminated a number of areas as having no source of food. As near as I can tell, the only place to find edible plants and other plants with processible content is the reservoir area. They haven't been sighted anywhere in that direction at all."

"Maybe we should go out that way ourselves, and give this First Law argument to the robots working there, just in case."

"I guess it couldn't hurt. At the moment, I'm too tired to plan strategy."

"We can do some more planning tomorrow. What else have you figured out? Or is that it?"

"No, that isn't it," he growled. "I'm sure now that the only chemical processors are ours, and the one that the robots used to feed us when we first arrived. Before, it was just a good surmise. Now I'm certain."

"Where does that leave us now?"

Derec stifled a yawn and looked at the clock. "It leaves me beat, for one thing." *And too worn out to argue*, he thought to himself as he shut off the console.

"It's not that late, but I'm worn out, too. Besides, with the robots contributing, there's a chance something will happen even if we aren't killing ourselves every second."

"I'm going to eat and then go collapse." Derec got up and punched a code into the chemical processor. "Want anything?"

"As much as I'd rather not, I guess I'd better. I'm so sick of all the stuff it makes. I guess it doesn't even matter very much what it is. Make it two of whatever you're having, okay?"

"Coming right up."

She was walking toward him when she suddenly gasped and bent forward at the waist, her eyes bulging, clutching her abdomen with one arm.

He moved quickly to catch her by the shoulders. Gently, he eased her into a chair. "What is it? Can I do anything?"

"No," she whispered hoarsely. She was still doubled over. "Just give me a minute, okay?" Her eyes were fixed on the floor in front of her as she held her position. She had broken out in a sweat, and her face was pale.

He backed up a little, but remained standing, watching her apprehensively. When the processor buzzed that their late meal was ready, he took out the plates and set them down. He sat down in his chair, trying not to make her more self-conscious than she already was, but he was too worried to start eating.

Finally, she straightened and drew in a deep breath. "I'm okay," she said weakly. "Really." Her face was shiny with sweat. "It's passing. Go ahead and eat. Don't wait for me."

He tried to phrase his question carefully. "Could it be something, uh, ordinary?"

"Sure." She forced a faint smile. "It was just a dizzy spell. I'm worn out from running around all day. Besides, I haven't eaten enough today. That's all it is."

Derec nodded. Neither of them believed it, but they couldn't do anything about her disease, anyway. Stating the obvious wouldn't accomplish anything. A feeling of helplessness kept him just sitting there, looking at her.

After a moment, she reached for her plate, and they ate in silence.

He did not go to bed right away, after all. Instead, he kept thinking of little chores to do, cleaning up and pacing about, for as long as she remained up. He wanted to be on hand if she had another dizzy spell, but she seemed all right.

Finally, she retired, probably sensing that he was going to stay up as long as she did. He went to bed, but worry kept him awake for some time. As he lay in the dark, the terrible puzzle kept taunting him: at least one spacecraft had landed somewhere on the planet, but they could find no way to locate it. And if they couldn't get Ariel to medical help of some kind, somewhere. . . .

He refused that line of speculation. *How* could they find the spacecraft; that was the question. He turned over restlessly, gradually starting to doze and to dream of vague shadowy figures running away down the fast lane of the slidewalks, always just out of reach, agile and elusive despite their imminent starvation.

The next morning he awoke to a pleasant, familiar, salty

aroma drifting in from the other room. Could their chemical processor have produced that? He could hear Ariel moving about, and got up full of curiosity. When he opened his door, she was standing at the chemical processor, just turning to face him.

"Look what I managed to get out of this thing," she said with a smile, holding out a plate.

Derec took one of the long, flat strips from it and bit off the end. "Mmm—bacon!"

"Simulated bacon, anyway. Healthier than the real thing, probably. I've been up for hours, and thought I'd try experimenting with the processor." She laughed. "I've had the recycler going all morning with my failures. So far, this is the best improvement on what we've been eating."

"It's great. Practically got me out of bed, in fact. It *smells* great. Got any more?"

"No problem." She entered a code into the processor. "It does smell good, doesn't it?"

"Robots just don't understand decent food. I can't blame them, exactly, but—frost! Just imagine what we're missing! The first thing I want to do when we get to a real city is eat some good food for a change. A hot Kobe steak, say, with Magellanic frettage on the side and a bowl of ice cold—"

"That's it, Derec! The smell!" She spun around suddenly, with an excited smile. "Don't you get it?"

"What?"

"We should bring our hungry humans to us. Use the exhaust fan to send out different food smells. We figure they're starving, right? We couldn't find them by chasing around, and now we have the robots doing that kind of search for us, anyway. In fact, I've been sending food smells outside all morning. It ought to work better, though, if we do it systematically."

"Couldn't hurt," he said cautiously. "Well—yeah! That

could work! In fact, I can do something to help it along right now." He stuffed the rest of the piece of bacon into his mouth and sat down at the console. "The aromas alone won't go too far before they dissipate, but I'll enter this into the computer. It can alert robots to the fact that these smells represent substances edible to humans. So if our visitors ask, they'll be directed this way."

"I'll try to get more organized with this," she said. "I'll work up a rotation of dishes—protein, carbohydrates, and so on. After all, we don't know exactly what's most likely to get their attention."

"If they're really starving, they aren't going to be particular, but I'll leave that to you. Let's get to work."

Ariel had the most to do this time. She coded for various dishes and set them under the fan until they cooled. By the time one dish had stopped giving off its aroma, two more were ready. She put one of them under the fan, or even both, then reheated the preceding one. When each dish had dried out to no more than a shapeless, unrecognizable, desiccated blob, she scraped the remains into the recycler and punched the code for something else.

At one point, he requested more bacon, which interrupted her sequence for a short time. He took a break to work on the fan, and managed to squeeze a little more power out of it, but not much. They were still relying a great deal on chance and the help of the robots, who could direct their quarry to them.

Derec devoted the rest of his time to streamlining the central computer some more, or at least doing what he could. He had no more ideas left for locating alternate food sources, even now that he was fresh, so they were gambling entirely on her plan. As the day wore on, however, he began to feel a new kind of tension. He was restless, anxious to take some kind of action, but there was none to take. This plan simply called for waiting patiently until the bait worked.

"Most of this stuff really stinks," said Ariel. She left a new dish under the exhaust fan and started to wash her hands. "That bacon is the only one that really came out. I'm going to take a break and sit down."

"You're supposed to make the odors enticing," Derec said impishly. "We want to bring them in, not make them sick."

"Frost, Derec! You want to try it?" She demanded. "You try to figure out those stupid codes. Or stand here and inhale the fumes on some of these dishes that don't come out."

"Hey, take it easy. That was a joke."

"Some joke, smart guy. I don't see you helping us any."

"Oh, yeah? I suppose you could have done all the computer work I have since we've been together?" He turned from the screen to look at her.

"I didn't say that, and you know it."

"Maybe I'm not so sure. Maybe you do think I'm just along for the ride, now. Or don't you want me to streamline the computer anymore, like you were asking me before?"

"You're just pouting because I thought of the First Law point yesterday and the idea of sending out cooking smells today, that's all." She pulled her chair up facing her and sat down in it backwards, straddling the seat. "Admit it."

"It's not that simple. You told me you were out looking for adventure, remember? Wasn't that one of the reasons you left home?"

"One of them," she said icily.

"And you didn't get the kind of fun adventure you were thinking of, did you? Even getting away from Rockliffe Station the way we did was more glamorous than this. Going one-on-one with these robots all the time is more of a chore than an adventure."

"I'm also sick—remember?" she said quietly.

Derec broke eye contact, stung with embarrassment. Last night, in a moment of caring, they had carefully avoided the word. Now he'd let his temper ruin that.

"This computer work is getting to me," he said, also speaking softly. "I, uh, just can't seem to get as much done as I want."

"That's how I feel. There's too much work to do and nothing ever seems to help."

"It's the waiting, isn't it?"

"Yeah, partly. Just waiting here all day for someone to show up. And we don't know if they're within kilometers of here. They could be anywhere on the planet." She folded her arms across the back of the chair and leaned her chin down on them.

"We could take turns getting out. You know, just go for a walk. The city is pretty big; we haven't seen large parts of it, even now. You know, if we didn't have to work so hard at getting out of here, this would be an interesting place."

"I think I could use a walk. If you'll take the first shift here, maybe I'll get away from that processor for a while." She got off the chair with some effort. "What do you say?"

"Fair enough. While you're out, see how far away you can smell anything, okay?"

"Okay." She grinned over her shoulder in the doorway. "If it really does stink out there, I'll let you know."

CHAPTER 11

FACE TO ROBOT FACE

Jeff did not get tired, but he did get sleepy. He didn't know enough physiology to explain that, but he assumed that having a human brain meant that he still required sleep. The problem, as night fell, was finding a place where he could sleep without interruption.

The city remained active at night, but safety was not the problem. In a city of robots, he had no fear of crime, so anyplace where he would not be awakened would be acceptable. However, he expected that the sight of him, as a robot, remaining motionless for a protracted period, might attract unwanted attention. He certainly didn't want a robot or two carrying him off bodily to a repair station because he had gone inert.

Jeff learned more about his robot eyes as he considered this problem. At first, as the sun went down and night came on, they opened in much the same degree as his human eyes had. They adjusted slowly and not really very much. Robot City had outdoor lighting, but it was not as bright as that of the cities on Aurora he had visited. The reason became obvious when night had fallen completely.

He was walking along the edge of a tiled plaza, hoping to find a secluded spot where he could simply stop—reclining was not necessary—and go to sleep in private. As he peered into the darkness beyond the far edge of the plaza, the entire area suddenly grew much larger, practically flying at him. He straightened in surprise, then laughed at himself. His new eyes had a zoom capability that he had somehow triggered accidentally.

In order to test it, he stood where he was and tried to get his eyes to do something else. After looking at objects at several different distances, he found that if he focused on something as close as his own feet, his vision returned to normal and stayed that way. The zoom effect was triggered when he tried to focus for more than a few seconds on a distant object. If he just looked into the distance without trying to focus on detail, his vision remained normal.

More important at the moment, however, was his discovery of night vision. As he had experimented with his focal lengths, he had not noticed that the tile of the plaza, his robotic feet, and a low, decorative wall on the far edge of the plaza had all gradually become clearer. Now, as he looked around, he realized that he could see with a stunning clarity.

This, too, had happened automatically, like the narrowing and widening of human pupils. Only in this case, some other sensitivity was also built in. He didn't know what that sensitivity was, but he appreciated it. The objects around him were sharply outlined, illuminated by the city lighting that was sufficient when he used his new, robotic night vision. The only hint of darkness was in the distance, outside the range of the nearest lights.

His new vision sped up his search considerably. With a combination of night vision and zoom, he quickly eliminated the plaza area as a sleeping spot. He also realized that the robots would be able to see him with a similar ease, so finding a place to sleep would not depend on darkness. With that in mind, he began walking through areas that had unusually shaped architecture.

"All right," he said to himself. "I used to hide as a kid. This is basically the same thing. This ought to be easier than that, since I don't think anybody is really searching for me." He thought of the medical team, but decided that if they were looking for him, they were a long way off.

He had been hoping that the unusual architecture of some of the buildings might offer a small space where he could hide. Standing and lying flat were both equally unnecessary; he could actually squat down or double up in any fashion, without the usual danger of his limbs going to sleep, or needing to move to get more comfortable while he was sleeping.

The architecture did not help him, however. The more distinctive designs involved geometric shapes that had no small spaces in which he could crouch, and the simpler buildings were usually made up of modular rectangles of various proportions.

The other way to hide was in plain sight. He would have to look occupied, even while he was motionless in sleep. The tunnel system would provide that chance.

He went down into the first tunnel stop he found. The worst result he could think of was that he might not be able to stop at the same place he got on, but since he didn't know his way around the city anyway, that hardly mattered. He would be equally lost anywhere.

He stepped into a platform booth and looked in mystification at the controls. The best he could do was mark this particular stop. When he woke up, he could try to make it bring him back here. If that didn't work, he would stop anywhere he could.

Once the booth was on its way, he stood erect in a position that seemed casual enough and relaxed. At first, the noise of air rushing past the booth kept him awake, but then he remembered that he could control his hearing now, as well. He lowered his aural sensitivity, though he did not shut it off, and as he became fully relaxed, he felt himself to be the construct of two distinct parts. Earlier, he had felt integrated as a cyborg. Now he really felt himself to be a human brain housed in a motionless, manufactured unit that was just minimally active in order to keep his brain alive. It was a protective shell, apart from his own personal being in a way that his biological body never had been. In a few moments he was asleep, still standing up in the platform booth as it rushed through the tunnel system of Robot City.

Jeff woke up in nearly total disorientation. Ahead of him, a robot was standing in a transparent booth, speeding along a track down a mysterious tunnel. He looked around in alarm, and then suddenly his new life came back to him. Yes, his arms were still blue and robotic. He was still in this strange, manufactured body.

He was still all alone.

His ploy had worked, at least; none of the robots had bothered him while he slept.

He sensed vaguely that he had been dreaming, but he had no memory of the details. Nor did he think they had been pleasant.

He did figure out how to get the booth to carry him back to the same tunnel stop where he had entered. That accomplished, he rode up the ramp to daylight and looked around. He was satisfied that his one basic need, a place to sleep, had been arranged. Clothing was not necessary, and he knew that his robot body had an energy pack that was independent of ordinary food. He wasn't sure how it was able to keep his brain alive, but since it was working, he wasn't going to worry about it, either.

"Well, Jeffrey," he said aloud to himself. "It's time to start this new life of yours in earnest. Let's go see what we can see."

He stepped onto the slow lane of the nearest slidewalk and rode, gazing up at all the majestic, sweeping shapes of the city's most striking structures. The city was busier now than it had been the night before; he decided that perhaps the robots had scheduled indoor work for the night hours. His night vision had been very good, but it could not make up for a lack of sunlight.

He rode the slidewalk for a long time. Patience was not a problem, as the city both fascinated and worried him. Without a pressing schedule, or any physical needs to satisfy, he had nothing else to do. Every so often, he stepped off carefully onto an intersecting slidewalk and kept going. He still couldn't tell his way around, but, little by little, he began to recognize certain landmarks.

Even now, he looked about carefully everywhere. The medical team probably still wanted him, and any robot that suspected he was not susceptible to the Laws would be horrified by the idea. They wouldn't get him, though—not if he was careful.

Then, as the slidewalk carried him underneath some sort of transparent chute, a breeze came wafting to him from a new direction.

Jeff instinctively turned his head and inhaled—and became aware, for the first time, that he normally did not breathe in the usual human manner. Obviously, his brain needed oxygen, but the rest of his body did not require it. As he had with other questions about his new physiology, he dropped the question of how his body was taking in oxygen and supplying it to his brain; the fact of his continued existence proved that some process was working. He guessed that he could inhale largely for the purpose he was using now: to use a sense of smell.

"Magellanic frettage," he said quietly to himself, recognizing the aroma. He didn't want to be overheard, but the impulse to talk out loud was getting stronger. "Frettage in a kind of tangy sauce, I'd say. It smells great—I haven't had any of that in a long time. Let's go see."

He stepped off the slidewalk, caught his balance, and started walking in the direction of the scent. His body didn't need food, apparently, but the desire to taste enjoyable dishes was still with him. A number of his favorite dishes came to him: Magellanic frettage, Kobe steak, jiauzi, fresh strawberries. He wasn't sure if he could eat even if he wanted to, though he supposed not. Still, he could certainly enjoy smelling the stuff.

He was also hoping to find human companionship. "I wouldn't get my hopes up, Jeffrey ol' boy. You can't trust 'em with the truth, anyhow."

Traffic was moderately heavy here, but most of it was just function robots, which were no threat to him as they went about their business, unobservant and incurious. A few humanoid robots appeared from time to time, but none showed any interest in him. One robot, however, seemed to stay near Jeff, turning the same corners and walking in the same direction.

Jeff dropped back gradually, keeping a suspicious eye on this one robot. He did not appear to have noticed Jeff, but he had another odd quality. This robot was pushing a small, two-wheeled cart in front of him.

The cart, which had four solid gray sides but no lid, was weirdly primitive for this city of robots who could transplant a human brain, raise dynamic, glittering edifices, and guide what looked like a fully functioning society without human help. Lacking even its own power source, the cart was a throwback to ancient times.

Yet here it was.

Derec had continued to code some of Ariel's better dishes and place them under the fan, though the constant moving from the console to the processor and back prevented him from concentrating on streamlining the recalcitrant computer. He finally decided to take a real break from the computer and follow Ariel's lead with the chemical processor. At the very least, he might help improve the food they had to eat. Since the better codes had all been preserved, his failures wouldn't cost them anything, and success might make their existence here much more tolerable.

The Supervisor robots had arranged for them to be given a large supply of basic nutritional requirements in chemical form. These had been augmented by a harvest of edible plants out in the reservoir area. To produce an edible dish, various ingredients were mixed with water in the processor itself, and heated, according to the codes.

He started by trying to make the nutrition bars more tasty. First he got too much vanilla flavoring, though the result was definitely strong in flavor. When he attempted to add a hint of banana, he got something similar to a muddy-tasting Auroran root vegetable. It wasn't exactly good, but it certainly was different. He erased the code for that one, though he stuck the dish under the fan. Maybe his quarry liked Auroran root vegetables.

Ariel's bacon was nearly perfect, so he didn't mess with

that. His first attempt at Magellanic frettage had come out more like over-boiled tyricus leaves in blue cheese, so he had recycled that one without even exhausting the aroma. Another attempt at that had been more successful, and the aroma was being fanned outside right now. He was trying to create a banana pudding when Ariel came back in.

"Yuck!" She winced and stuck out her tongue. "And I thought my stuff stunk. Frost, Derec, what did you kill in here?"

He laughed. "You're smelling my first batch of Magellanic frettage. The second one is better, and this new dish should also work. Banana pudding should be easy, don't you think?"

"If we don't die from the tyricus fumes first. Did my stuff smell this bad? If it did, I owe you an apology."

"No, not really. Could you smell anything outside?"

"Oh, yes. Basically, we're in pretty good shape. The configuration of the surrounding buildings has created a pretty constant horizontal wind, going from the fan, let's see, that way." She jerked her thumb. "The robot traffic is fairly heavy in that direction, so they can all help direct our people here. Now we just have to hope they get close enough to ask."

"The other way, though, nobody will smell anything."

"True, but the robots are circulating on their normal activities. They'll be spreading out all over the place."

"Okay. I hope this works. We've done just about everything."

She nodded. "If you want to take a turn stretching your legs, I'll take over here."

"Thanks. I think that pudding needs more water."

Derec strode outside with a spring in his step, glad to be in the open for a change. In the distance, however, the great shining dome of the Key Center seemed to taunt him. He refused to have his mood dampened, and turned away from it to start walking.

More out of curiosity than necessity, he located the breeze that she had mentioned. The banana pudding smelled pretty good, though he supposed starving people might prefer something more solid and nutritious. He stepped onto a slidewalk, but kept walking in a large rectangle around the general area. Actually spotting their human visitors didn't seem as unlikely as it once had, even if that was only a new optimism. As he came downwind of the breeze from the fan again, he was pleasantly surprised to recognize the scent of a decent dish of Magellanic frettage carried along by it. Perhaps her extra practice with the processor was paying off. Now that he had loosened up a little, he decided that he might as well head back. Waiting was still waiting, whether he sat inside or marched aimlessly around town.

When he arrived, Ariel was leaning in the doorway. She raised her eyebrows in surprise when she saw him.

"What are you doing back so soon? I thought the whole idea was for us to take turns in getting away for a bit."

"I did get away. Now I'm back."

"Frost, Derec. If I'd known that was all you were going to do, I would have stayed out longer myself. I came back early just for you."

"I wouldn't have cared if you'd stayed out longer. I didn't ask you to come back early."

"Well, do you mind if I go for another walk?"

"Of course not! Why are you making such a big deal of this?" As he waited for an answer, he stepped back from a humanoid robot walking toward them, assuming that the robot wanted to pass by.

"Oh, I don't know," she said irritably. "I guess this do-nothing phase just doesn't suit me very well."

The robot did not walk past them. He looked at Derec closely as, without stopping, he moved past him through the doorway.

"Hey," Derec said in surprise. "Can we help you? This is a private residence. Ours, that is."

The robot turned and looked back and forth between them.

"Identify yourself," Ariel commanded.

"Uh. . . ." The robot seemed uncertain, which was very rare in a robot.

"I gave you an *instruction*. Now identify yourself!"

"I, uh, I'm Tunnel Foreman, uh, 12."

"Say, wait a minute. That sounds familiar. Did I talk to you before? About the search?"

"Yes, you did."

"Well, why didn't you say so? If you came to report, Derec and I are the ones to report to. What have you learned?"

"I . . . haven't really learned anything."

"Then what are you doing here?" Derec asked. "Do you have a question?"

The robot hesitated, again looking back and forth between them as if in puzzlement.

"Something's wrong with him," said Ariel. "Get on the console and call a repair facility. He isn't acting right."

The robot started to leave.

"Stay here," Ariel ordered. When he didn't stop, she caught his arm. "I ordered you to stay put. What's wrong with you? Now freeze."

Derec had started inside, but when the robot yanked his arm free of Ariel, he stopped in shock. "Are you forgetting the Laws? You've been ordered to *freeze*."

The robot grabbed Ariel by the shoulders and flung her out of his way, slamming her against the wall. Derec launched himself between them, hoping to prevent the assault from continuing, even as disbelief flooded him. He saw the robot's arm swinging backhand toward him, but had no chance to react as the incredibly hard robot hand casually smacked him in the forehead and blackened his vision.

Derec felt himself fall backward into the wall and slide to the base of the doorway in a sitting position. He sat motionless for a moment, getting his breath back and gathering his wits. When he looked around, the robot was gone.

CHAPTER 12

TEAMWORK

Ariel scooted over to Derec with a look of concern. Even in his stunned condition, he appreciated it.

"You hurt bad, Derec?"

"No." His voice came out in a coarse mutter. "Got the breath knocked out of me, but that's all. How about you?"

"I'm all right. Thanks for getting in his way."

He grinned. "Any time, just so it isn't too often." He inhaled deeply a couple of times.

She took him under one arm and helped him to his feet. "Have you ever seen anything like that before?"

"Never. The positronic brains have always been totally reliable. That record is known everywhere." He dusted himself off. "I think the shock is worse than getting knocked down."

"This one's not reliable, that's for sure."

"Did you see where he went?" Derec looked down the street.

"No, but a couple of other robots went chasing after

him. They must have been close enough to see what happened."

"I guess I heard a few footsteps. Let's go inside. I want to get on the console and find out if there's been any warning about a rogue robot."

She followed him inside. "The robots chasing him weren't shouting or anything. I suppose they were all talking through their comlinks."

"I guess." He rubbed the back of his head where it had hit the wall, and winced. "I wonder what kind of insults robots exchange among themselves." He sat down at the computer and called up a variety of subjects—including warnings, city alerts, and suspected malfunctions. Nothing turned up.

"Maybe the malfunction just occurred," Ariel suggested. "We'll be the first ones to report."

"I'll do that. Let's see. . . . *Malfunctioning robot does not obey the Laws.* Since he actually attacked us, the rest of the robots will make searching for him a top priority. I imagine they'll even leave their regular jobs." He entered a description of the pertinent events.

"Doesn't it seem odd to you that he came here?"

"What do you mean?"

"We're the only people on the planet, that anyone can find. The others are lost. And this city is huge. Isn't it kind of strange that the one robot here who goes berserk just happens to wind up at the only apartment with humans in it?"

He paused for a moment at the keyboard. "I see what you mean. Of course, since the positronic failure involves the Laws, maybe he was drawn somehow to humans." He shrugged and continued on the console.

"They did know! Look at this—I got it when I entered the subject of *searches*."

She leaned down close, reading over his shoulder. "Wait a minute. What kind of weird robot are they searching for?"

"I'm not sure he's exactly a robot at all. It says: *see Human Experimental Medical Team*. Let's see."

A moment later, he was reading in fascination. "He's human! Or at least, his brain is."

"His brain?"

"Look at this!" Derec pointed out the summary of the surgery on the computer's screen. "Unbelievable!"

"That's impossible," Ariel said, "transplanting a brain into a robot body."

"Everything's been impossible since we got here." Derec shook his head, as though to clear it. "We should be used to it by now."

"If you can ever get used to being surprised. What do we do now?"

"I'm trying to get the central computer to put me through to one of the robots on the medical team through their comlinks."

"Yes?" said a voice through the console.

"I am Derec, a human male. Please identify yourself."

"I am Human Medical Research 1, the Director of the Human Experimental Surgical Team."

"I have some information regarding a robot who doesn't obey the Laws of Robotics."

"Excellent. We have been conducting a pattern search from the perimeter of the city inward, with the help of many robots. Can you narrow the focus of search for us?"

"I'd like to see you and your team in person. Please come meet with Ariel and myself."

"We will do this. May I ask why you are delaying in providing me with helpful information?"

"This problem may be larger than it appears. The robot in question seriously disobeyed our instructions and physically attacked us. I think a major consultation is in order, don't you?"

"We will come at once." The robot's voice was suddenly formal and expressionless.

"Say—tell me one thing now. Has this guy's spacecraft been located? What kind of shape is it in?"

"It was destroyed on impact. What is your location?"

Disappointment struck Derec like a physical blow, but he gave them the information. Then he began pacing restlessly, trying to keep his spirits up. "At least the medical robot can tell us if he was traveling with the other two we've been looking for. It isn't over yet. We've made some kind of progress, believe it or not. It's about time." He slapped a fist into his other palm. "We still just might learn something we can use."

"You think this guy is one of the humans we're looking for?" Ariel, too, was crestfallen.

"I think so. Remember the third visitor, who just vanished after a certain point? This must be the one. I figure the reports of him stopped because he was in a robot body."

"I was hoping he had arrived on another ship. It would give us an extra chance." Disappointment was evident on her face.

The medical team arrived shortly. Derec told the three robots what had transpired and then asked for the relevant information they possessed. They briefed him on what they had told Jeff.

"So it's not a failure of the positronic brain," Research 1 finished. "However, we have consulted among ourselves and have concluded that we must enter a repair facility to have our brains removed and destroyed."

"What?" Derec cried. "You can't do that. We need your help."

"We created a situation in which a robot body violated

the First Law by attacking humans. This is a violation of the First Law on our part. We would have reported immediately after the transplant surgery if we had understood where it would lead."

Derec looked at the two robot surgeons, who nodded in agreement. The three of them were standing together in a line, as though prepared for law-enforcement questioning. Maybe that was what they expected from a human, after violating the First Law.

"But you didn't attack anybody," said Ariel. "You were one step away from the situation. You can't take responsibility for what he—you said his name was Jeff?—decided to do."

"Besides, he didn't hurt us," said Derec. "It just surprised us. Well—totally shocked us, actually."

Surgeon 2 shook its head. "The extent of the harm is not a factor, since the Laws do not make allowances for degree. Nor is our ignorance of your presence a factor. The fact that we are one step removed from the incident is the only reason that we did not shut down upon learning of this violation of the First Law. If we had directly harmed a human, the trauma to our systems would have completely neutralized our functioning. However, this individual would not exist in the unusual form he does without our contribution. He is unique, and is our responsibility."

"Look at it this way," said Ariel anxiously. "We need help. If Jeff is still out there running around, he could conceivably do more harm to us. Doesn't the First Law require you to cooperate with us?"

"We have proven our judgment irresponsible," said Surgeon 1. "You cannot rely on us. Therefore, we should be destroyed."

"You haven't violated the Laws any other time, have you?" Derec pointed out.

"No, but we have no other history of contact with humans," said Research 1. "In our initial contact with humans, we contributed to a violation—"

"Of the First Law, I know. You don't have to keep repeating it," said Derec. "But I shouldn't have phrased the question that way. You still haven't broken the Laws. Jeff did, sort of. Only, since he doesn't have a positronic brain, that doesn't really count."

"Our information about human behavior is apparently incomplete," said Research 1. "We did not understand the likelihood of Jeff's attack on you. In fact, the central computer did not even inform us of your presence. We felt his medical condition was such that the First Law required our attempting the transplant. However, one purpose of the First Law that I infer is to preserve humans from the greater strength of our robot bodies. So to us, Jeff in this case counts as a robot, despite his lacking a positronic brain. This judgment will not be imperative on his brain, of course."

"If the First Law required you to perform the transplant, how can you blame yourselves?" Ariel asked. "That seems like a real contradiction. One that I wouldn't expect from the logical mind of a robot."

"The logical contradiction has only become evident now," said Surgeon 1. "In the sequence of events as they unfolded, the First Law has made clear requirements of us, including our elimination."

Derec looked at them helplessly, unable to think of an argument against their destruction that they had not countered already.

"Postpone your trip to the repair center," Ariel suggested. "If you think it's required, you can do it later. Right now, we really need your help, like we said."

"That's right," said Derec quickly. "How about this? The First Law requires that you help us catch Jeff and, I don't know—stop him somehow. Then you can destroy yourselves."

The three robots hesitated long enough to reveal that this argument had carried some weight.

"Isn't it your responsibility to help clean up the mess?" Ariel added, with a triumphant smile. "The Second Law requires that you follow our orders to help. Since you have never directly violated any of the Laws, including the First, you're reliable enough for us."

"This is acceptable to me," said Research 1. "We shall retain the option of having our brains destroyed later, in any case."

"I find it acceptable, also," said Surgeon 1. "Unnecessary destruction of our brains would be an inefficient handling of material, energy, and experience. We should logically establish the necessity of this move beyond any doubt, with as much gathering of relevant evidence as possible."

"Whew," said Surgeon 2. The robot looked at Derec. "That is the human vernacular appropriate to the occasion, is it not?"

"Sure is." Derec laughed in relief. "Okay. That problem is solved. Next problem. We want information from this guy about getting off the planet. You just want to make sure he can't violate any of the Laws. What's our plan of action?"

"You will have to take the lead in direct confrontation," said Research 1. "Any plans will have to take this into account."

"What do you mean?" Ariel asked.

"Since we know that Jeff has a human brain," said Surgeon 1, "we are subject to the Laws when dealing with him. We could not disobey his instructions, for instance, if he told us to leave him alone. Or worse, to forget that he exists at all."

"Hold it," said Ariel, holding up a hand. "You're upset about his breaking the laws because he's a robot, but now you say you have to obey the Laws where he's concerned because he's human. Aren't you contradicting yourselves?"

"No," said Research 1. "In regard to the Laws, he is both human and robot. We cannot deny him the combination of traits that we ourselves gave him. All the advantages are therefore his. This makes him very powerful."

"What about that pattern search you told me you started?" Derec asked. "How were you going to catch him when you located him?"

"Our only hope was to talk him into cooperating. We could not use violence in contradiction to the Laws. However, he will at some point be in danger to his health. At that point, of course, we would be able to force our aid on him."

"What kind of danger?" asked Ariel. "He's got a robot body."

"His robot body is powered by a standard energy system," said Surgeon 2. "However, his organic brain requires nutrition and oxygen. We installed a container of vital nutrients and synthetic hormones in the lower portion of his head, and part of his neck, and a routing system to his brain. These chemicals are delivered to his brain through its existing circulatory system by synthetic blood. Oxygen is also delivered this way, supplied by the breaths he will take from time to time."

"Understood so far," said Derec. "Go on."

"He can't eat in the normal human sense. So his nutrient pack must be refilled at certain intervals. He does not know this."

"He doesn't? Why didn't you tell him?" Ariel demanded.

"He ran away before we started briefing him. We wanted to test him first. We did not know he would leave before we could inform him of this." Surgeon 2 looked at Research 1. "Since our tests were not complete, we do not know precisely how successful the transplant has been."

"That is true," said Research 1. "There are considerable unknowns regarding his health. That is why an interpretation of the First Law allows us to help you find him."

"I've been thinking about a question Ariel asked me a while ago," said Derec. "Do you think Jeff came here, to our residence, for a reason? Or was it just a random visit?"

"The odds against a human, such as he is, making a random visit to the only human dwelling in the city are too high to take seriously," said Surgeon 2.

"Your use of human food smells to attract fellow humans here may have influenced him," said Research 1. "He is not yet in need of nutrition. However, previous habits and the stimulation of the pleasure center in his brain by the food aromas may have created a desire to experience the smell and taste of human food."

"I don't suppose it would work a second time," said Ariel. "Getting away seemed awfully important to him. If he can't eat anyway, he wouldn't really need to come back here."

"A logical assumption," said Research 1.

"All right, hold it," said Derec. "I'd like to go at this in a straight line, if you don't mind. As I see it, we have three problems. In order to get ahold of this guy Jeff, we have to locate him and identify him and grab him. Is this pattern search of yours going to capture him? How does it work?"

"It employs the entire robot population of Robot City," said Research 1. "However, they do not have to leave their duties. We have set up a net of testing around the perimeter of the city, moving inward, that goes from one robot to the next. No robot will work with any other or allow any other to pass, unless the other robot can demonstrate the use of his comlink. Since Jeff does not have this ability, he will eventually be identified."

"We could have built a radio system into his body," said Surgeon 1. "It seemed an unnecessary contradiction to his human identity, so we chose not to do so."

"Good thing," said Derec. "It sounds like your search could take a long time, though. If he's smart, and wants to escape notice, he can keep away from your search until the very last minute. And if he's lucky, he might sneak through the ring as it closes."

Surgeon 2 shook its head. Unlike most Avery robots, he seemed to like these gestures. "It is not a ring, but a solid circle. Even if he moves out into the previously tested area without being identified, he will still be challenged by every robot who sees him. The testing will not cease until we report that he has been detained."

Derec nodded in approval. "Not bad. I still say it will take a while, unless he gets careless."

"Agreed," said Research 1. "It could take an extended period of time, but it will identify him without fail. Chances of his capture will be maximized if we have one of you, the humans, on hand to detain him, however. Otherwise, the Second Law will allow him to order us away unless a First Law imperative instructs us to override his orders."

"What are we supposed to do?" Ariel turned her hands palm up and looked around at the three robots. "We can't order him around any more than you can. And he's stronger than you are."

The robots were silent.

"We'll worry about that later," Derec decided. "The first job is to get him identified. Maybe we can think of a way to shortcut the search process."

"Perhaps so," said Research 1. "We are at your disposal."

"So to speak," added Surgeon 2.

CHAPTER 13

LIFE ON THE RUN

Jeff was on the run. He had shoved Derec and Ariel aside in a frenzied panic, aching to speak with fellow humans and yet terrified of being discovered—though he didn't know why that mattered. The robot pursuit, driven by their horror of an apparent robot violating the First Law, the fundamental rule of their existence, was much greater now than it had been before. It was a testimonial to the imperative of the First Law that now, as he ran, every humanoid robot in the area dropped its duties to give chase, informed silently of his transgression by the comlinks of two robots that had happened to witness his physical assault on the humans.

Even the function robots began to impede him as he ran down the street, apparently ordered by the robots already in pursuit. Without positronic brains, the function robots could not make any advanced judgments of their own, but they could follow instructions. Little sweepers and couriers began zigzagging in front of him; giant construction equipment, intelligent enough not to require drivers, blocked his path down other streets. Behind him, all manner of weirdly shaped devices had joined the growing number of humanoid robots chasing him down the street.

"Come on, Jeffrey; come on, Jeffrey," he thought to himself as he ran, the rhythm of the phrase keeping time with his beating footsteps. He was even starting to breathe again, perhaps because the stress had caused a greater need for oxygen in his brain, even though his physical activity would not have caused that need. What a time to think about his physiology, he sneered at himself.

Ahead of him, more robots of all kinds were shifting to cut off his escape. They almost had him—no! On the right, an open tunnel stop invited him. He angled for it on a collision course with a large, block-shaped function robot with a variety of flexible tentacles ending in tools. The function robot rolled to a stop, filling the entrance to the tunnel. Jeff grimaced—at least on the inside—and reflexively clenched his steel jaw as he collided with it.

Jeff bounced away, but caught at one of the extended tentacles to maintain his footing. The impact had shoved the function robot back just enough for him to slide past one of its corners and run down the ramp. He nearly stumbled as the ramp started to move, and he ran, tripping on his toes, into the nearest booth. This time he knew how to work the controls, and took off quickly into the dim light of the tunnel.

He looked back once, and saw the crowd of humanoid robots pouring down the ramp and entering platform booths. The function robots had been eliminated from the chase, since the booths were designed for intelligent, humanoid passengers. He faced forward again, now trying to blend with the other robots riding in booths.

He shifted to one of the mid-speed lanes and looked nonchalant. In a way, he was new at losing himself in the crowd, and yet, after being highly visible all his life, this was ridiculously easy. Some of the robots in pursuit came alongside, and others passed him, but they could not distinguish between him and the others. He had no way of knowing if they were trying to reach him through their comlinks or not, but if so, they didn't seem to know who was answering and who was not. All the robots within sight were standing in roughly the same position, confined in booths the same way.

When a couple of robots rode into the siding at the next tunnel stop, some of the pursuing robots followed them. Jeff realized then that the longer he remained riding the platform, the thinner the pursuit would become. So he stayed where he was, occasionally changing lanes as though he were traveling in a deliberate manner to a specific destination.

It worked.

He smiled to himself as he rode. Three times, now, he had escaped robots that were chasing him. Nor had he outmuscled them—if he could use that term for robot arms. He had had to outsmart them, in the end, since they were physically as strong as he was. And if they ever really got hold of him, he would claim his rights as a human to consideration under the Laws of Robotics.

They were no match for him.

Only other humans had the same ultimate power over the robots that he did, based on the Laws . . . but, of course, they would be much weaker physically. He realized, for the first time, that he was actually the single most powerful individual on the entire planet. If he was careful, he could do anything here that he wanted.

Of course, he had no idea of how the city was governed. Perhaps the robots had some kind of city council or something. It didn't matter, since they would have to obey him if he decided to reveal himself and give them orders. He had to make sure they couldn't catch him, though.

He shook his head slightly, trying to remember why he didn't want to be caught. Nor could he figure out why he was afraid of the robots, if they had to obey his orders. It didn't make sense, but that was how he felt.

Maybe those two humans could join him. Of course, they would have to undergo the same transplant surgery that he had. Then all three of them would be virtually invincible, not only against the robots, but against any other humans who might come to this planet. They might not like the idea, but it could be done without their agreement. After all, he hadn't had any chance to discuss the matter, either.

"Well, well, well," he said aloud. "A conspiracy. A takeover. So I do have something to accomplish here, after all."

He had been carefully watching the robots traveling around him, and knew that the ones pursuing him had all left the tunnel system by now. To increase his distance from them, he rode a little longer, then stopped at a siding chosen at random. Now that he was out of their sight, he didn't think they could pick him out again.

Once back on the surface, he got on the slidewalk to ride until he got his bearings. With safety as close as any tunnel stop, he was free to roam. At the same time, he wanted to communicate with his human colleagues if he could do so without having robots jump all over him.

When he had picked out a few landmarks, principally a huge, shining dome and a strange, many-sided pyramid, he worked his way back toward the human residence. All the while, he looked about carefully for any sign that robots were conducting a search. He didn't see any evidence of a continuing search in the area, but he had to be careful.

He was in the neighborhood, now, but still kept riding

the slidewalk around in a series of jagged circuits, looking for a trap. His human colleagues, as he thought of them, were not in sight. The robot traffic here was light, and seemed to be safe enough.

He started to look in the other direction, when a familiar shape caught his eye. When he glanced back, he saw that same robot pushing the wheeled handcart again. On impulse, he leaped off the slidewalk and walked briskly up behind the robot.

"Are you following me?" he demanded.

The robot stopped and turned around. "Are you addressing me?"

"Yes. Identify yourself."

"I am Alpha."

Jeff hesitated. "Alpha? That's all?"

"Yes."

"That doesn't sound like the other names in this place. Why are you different?"

"I am not a native construct of this planet. Please identify yourself."

"I'm Jeff. If you're a stranger here, then we have something in common. I thought you were following me around."

"Not at all. Our proximity must be a coincidence. However, you may be able to aid me."

"Are you willing to join up with me? The two of us, we don't have any particular place in this society. I'm . . . gathering friends, you might say. Followers."

"I have no objection to this."

"Fair enough. What can I do for you?"

Alpha pulled a cloth from the wheeled cart. A small, furry creature lay inside, its eyes closed and its pointed ears limp and flat. Clumps of brown and gold fur had been falling out, revealing leathery skin under it. "This is an intelligent non-human named Wolruf. She is starving. I came to this planet with her. However, food for her has been scarce. Can you find some?"

"I'm not sure," said Jeff, looking at the little alien doubtfully. She had a caninoid body. "You ask anybody else? Any of these robots who live here?"

"Yes. However, since I have determined that she is nonhuman, the Laws do not apply and they are not required to help save her. The robots I have questioned here do not know where to find food for her, and have no greater ability to locate any than I. So the responsibility remains mine."

"I think you've met up with the right pers—individual."

"Can you help? We explored near a lake that I believe to be a reservoir and found a few plants that helped keep her alive, but that is all. I surmise that she requires a concentration of proteins they did not provide."

"It so happens that I smelled some food—human food, that is—in this very neighborhood. In a town like this, it must have been prepared in some kind of autogalley, like they have on shipboard. That would mean it could be altered to prepare other kinds of chemical food."

"I smelled it also," said Alpha. "This is what brought me to this area. However, the winds come and go. I lost the scent for a short time, and when I recovered it, an altercation of some kind was taking place among robots. Since I have chosen to make Wolruf's safety a priority, I was forced to leave the immediate vicinity."

"I see." Jeff chose not offer any additional information about that particular altercation.

"And since that time, I have not been able to locate any odors of the same type."

"Ah. Well." Jeff paused, not sure how to proceed. He wanted to get this little doggie-thing some food, to win over his new friend. On the other hand, he did not want to be identified again. To stall for time, and to satisfy his curiosity, he nodded at the cart. "Where'd you get that contraption?"

"I constructed it from scrap materials on the edge of the city, where new urbanization is taking place."

"Very clever. Well. Hmm." This little cart impressed him. It was so simple. A robot who could do this kind of thing on his own resources, and who had no ties to Robot City, was definitely an asset.

Jeff decided that he could not risk returning to the human residence. Nor did he want to turn over his new friend to other humans, who could give orders contradictory to his own, and perhaps even turn Alpha against him. He couldn't trust anybody. Yet he had to find a solution.

Another humanoid robot was walking toward them. Jeff chose, on the spot, to take a different kind of risk, one that would allow him to make a run for cover if necessary.

"Halt and identify yourself," he said to the approaching robot.

"For what purpose?" The robot halted, however.

"I have instructions for you."

"I am Architectural Foreman 112. Identify yourself."

"My name is Jeff." He sighed, and then fixed his gaze carefully on Architectural Foreman 112. "I am human."

Beside him, Alpha looked up with new attention.

"Perhaps you are malfunctioning. Your comlink might be more efficient. I thought you said that you are human," said Foreman 112.

"I am. My human brain was surgically transplanted into a robot body. However, the Laws of Robotics apply to me as a human. You must obey my instructions. Understand?"

Foreman 112 studied him. "I understand. I have just contacted the central computer, and have been informed that this transplant took place into a body of your type and that you have been reported in this neighborhood very recently."

"Good. Now—"

"You are also the object of a search. The Human Experimental Medical Team urgently requests your presence and cooperation."

"Now, you just forget about that. They don't have any right to capture me. I haven't done anything wrong." He eyed the robot suspiciously. "Did you tell them where I am?"

"I have reported your location here at the request of the central computer."

"Shut up and listen to my orders! Now, look inside this thing. This cart holds a little—creature that is dying of starvation. Its friend here is named Alpha. I'm instructing you to build, or arrange the building, of an autogalley that can feed this, this—"

"Her name is Wolruf," Alpha repeated. "She is an intelligent non-human."

"Yeah, right."

Foreman 112 looked at Wolruf. "Would the location of an existing chemical processor be acceptable? One is in storage. This would provide nutrition much faster."

"That one's okay," Jeff said carefully. "But only that one. Understand? Nobody else's. Got it?"

"It is the only one I have knowledge of," said Architectural Foreman 112. "It should suffice in this emergency."

"Good. Okay. You take Alpha and Wolruf to wherever it is. Alpha, can you explain what kind of food she needs?"

"Yes."

"Okay. Uh—I have to get out of here at the moment, since this traitor has reported my location." He glared at Architectural Foreman 112. "I want to talk to you again, Alpha, but. . . ." He couldn't tell Alpha where to meet him in front of this other robot, who would report him again. "Never mind where. I'll worry about that later. I'll give you this order: if I try to meet with you in secret someplace, you cooperate. Got it?"

"Yes," said Alpha.

"All right. On your way, you two."

Jeff watched them just long enough to be satisfied that they were leaving together. He felt a sense of accomplishment on several grounds: Alpha now owed him a favor, and he had convinced Architectural Foreman 112 that he was a human for whom the Laws applied. If he proceeded carefully, he really might take over Robot City.

"Well, well, Jeffrey. So far, so good. Maybe your life has a purpose after all, know what I mean?"

The last building block he needed in order to create a powerful following was the support of the other humans. He didn't dare visit them in person until he found out how they felt about him, but he could safely contact them from a distance. First, however, he had to get away from here.

"All right, Jeffrey. Back into the labyrinth again. They'll never find you in your second home."

As before, he used the tunnel system to shake the chase. This time he departed before any pursuit came into view. The tunnel system, unless it was shut down completely, remained the perfect escape. The individual booths kept him isolated and the tunnels had so many stops and branches that his chance of losing himself down there was very good. After another long ride, he came up again at a random spot and went to the edge of the nearest slidewalk.

As he waited for a humanoid robot to ride the slidewalk his way, he seriously considered the possibility that the robots running the city might actually shut down his tunnel system. It wouldn't break the Laws. This crazy city might have other places he could sleep in peace, and it almost certainly would offer other ways of escaping pursuit. He just hadn't had time to find out what they were yet.

"Hey, where is everybody? What's going on?"

He glanced around, puzzled. Everywhere else in the city, humanoid robots had been more or less everywhere. He could see a few in the distance now, but none were coming past him.

"Ho, ho, Jeffrey ol' boy. Time to get smart, maybe, eh? Something isn't quite normal. No sense just standing out here to frost. Let's just take a little trip, visit the tunnel again, see the sights."

Now leery of a trap, he turned and fled back down the tunnel stop. Moments later, he was shooting through the underground system again in one of the booths, looking at the robots in other booths all around him. What if they were part of the trap? Maybe he was being escorted, herded, to wherever they wanted him to go.

"Calmly, calmly," he said aloud in the booth. "Maybe they don't know anything for sure. Maybe they're trying to smoke you out. Look like everybody else, remember?" He started giggling to himself. "That's it. Stay calm and look like all the others."

He did so, secretly looking over the other robots traveling in the tunnels. None of them seemed to pay any attention to him.

"Shaken the pursuit again, have you?" he said out loud. "Very good, very good. This will work. This project will work. Now, let's get on with it."

Still, some time passed before he decided that he could safely return to the surface again. Then he picked another stop at random and reemerged into the sunlight. Now he was once more in an area of the city with a fair amount of humanoid traffic on the slidewalks, as he had been used to seeing. In the distance, the tall pyramid glinted in the sunlight, giving him a reference point.

He flagged down the first humanoid robot who came riding by, and identified himself as human. Like the last robot he had approached this way, Energy Pack Maintenance Foreman 3928 verified his claim with the central computer.

"I am satisfied that you are Jeffrey Leong, a human," said E Pack Foreman 3928.

"Good. Then under the Second Law, you know—"

"As a positronic robot, I am familiar with the Laws of Robotics."

"All right!" Jeff shouted. "Then get this! Don't ever interrupt me again! You understand, you slag heap?"

"I understand," the robot said blandly.

"You'd better. Come to think of it, that moniker of yours is too long. From now on, you answer to Can Head. Got it?"

"Yes."

"What's your name?"

"My name is Energy Pack Maintenance Foreman 3928. I will also answer to Can Head."

"Well . . . good enough, I guess." Jeff laughed. "Now listen to this. I want to contact the two humans living here in Robot City. I've met them, and I think they're the only ones here. You use your comlink or whatever it is to get ahold of them. That's an order," he added, leaning close and staring into Can Head's eyeslit.

"I have just checked with the central computer. I can go through it to a computer console in their dwelling. However, I lack the capacity to transmit your voice directly."

"Yeah? You aren't lying to me, are you, Can Head?"

"I lack that capacity, as well."

"Hmm—maybe. You should. Unless things aren't as they

seem around here. Nothing in this town is right, if you ask me. Only, how can I trust you to pass on what I say? What if you play around a little with the content? Or don't report what they say back to me just like they say it? What about that?"

"I lack the capacity for deceit."

"What do you need to transmit my voice directly? A microphone and some other equipment, I guess, huh?"

"Yes."

"Let's go find some. You get it and arrange for me to contact them directly. Get going."

CHAPTER 14

THE TRANSPLANT

Ariel sat at the console, trying to think up other subjects that might tell her something about Jeff or his whereabouts. Derec was out with the medical team, making plans to catch him. The search for Jeff had given Derec and Ariel a new focus for their attempt to get off the planet, and the fact that they had actually seen him made their chances seem more tangible. Her spirits were up again, even if Jeff's spacecraft had been destroyed on impact.

She had just left the console to take a break when a voice came through the speaker.

"Hello! Hey, you! Answer me."

She slid back into the seat, puzzled by the odd greeting. That wasn't the kind of courtesy one received from robots. "Identify," she answered cautiously.

"I don't have to identify unless I feel like it. This is the robot that knocked you two down. The Laws don't apply to me." He paused. "You know what I'm talking about?"

"Jeff," said Ariel excitedly. "Uh, hi. Where are you?"

Weird robot laughter buzzed through the speaker. "You

can't fool me that easy. Say, how did you know my name? What's your name: You're pretty, as I recall."

"I'm Ariel." She wanted to keep him talking and see if she could persuade him into coming in. If not, maybe he would slip up and say something that would give away his location. "Can I help you? What are you calling about?"

"If you know my name, you must have talked to those robot doctors, huh? So you know how I got this way."

"Yes, and they told us you need to come in for your health. They didn't finish the tests, and you don't know how to take care of yourself yet. You left before they could explain." She eyed the keyboard, wondering if she could have the central computer contact the medical team while she kept Jeff in conversation.

"Oh, sure; I have to come in for my own good, right? Frost, I'm not that stupid."

"Jeff, what are you afraid of? They're robots. They can't do anything to harm you." She started tapping the keys carefully, not wanting to make any noise he might hear.

"Don't let them fool you, kid. If they're so helpful, why don't they transplant you? You'd like it this way. So would your friend. What's his name, anyhow?"

"His name is Derec. What do you mean, why don't they transplant me? They were trying to help you because you were injured in the crash when you landed. Why would I want to have my brain transplanted?" She continued on the keyboard.

"They helped me, all right. Don't you get it, Ariel? I like this. I'm better this way."

"Better? You mean you like having a robot body?" She stopped typing, shocked. "I thought you might be mad at them for doing this. You sound angry about something."

"Angry? Frost, what for? I'm the most powerful individual on this entire planet."

"What do you mean?" She completed entering the instruction for Derec and the medical team to return as fast as they could, and why. If they could intercept Jeff's broadcast and eavesdrop, they should attempt that in the meantime. Triangulating on his beam and trapping him would be best of all.

"What do I mean? Are you crazy? It's obvious! I'm stronger than you or any other human, and I'm free of the Laws. Completely free of them! I have every physical advantage of a robot and every privilege of being human. I can do anything I want. Anything! Don't you *understand?*" He was screaming now.

She hesitated, surprised by the sound of a robot voice yelling at her in frustration. "I understand," she said calmly. "It's okay, Jeff. I understand."

"Do you?" He demanded suspiciously.

"Sure. It makes sense. You're unique. No one has ever lived the way you're living now. You're the very first. Uh, tell me what it's like. It must be interesting." Since she had no idea where Derec and the medical team were, she couldn't estimate their time of arrival. All she could do was keep talking.

"What it's like?" He sounded surprised. "Well . . . it's different. Very different. Everybody thinks I'm a robot, for one thing. You look like everybody else. No one knows who you are. Your body can do different things, too. For instance, you can see better and hear better and smell better. And you can sleep standing up."

She laughed. "What?"

"Forget it," he said brusquely. "Never mind that part. Forget I mentioned it."

"You like to sleep standing up?"

"I said forget it!" He shouted. "Besides, any robot can

do that. Stop, I mean, in a fixed position. They don't sleep, of course. That's all I meant. They can all do that, can't they? Huh?"

"Yes, they can. Take it easy. It's okay." She hesitated, realizing that she certainly couldn't predict what would set him off on a tirade. "How old are you, Jeff?"

"Uh—eighteen. Sort of. In this life, I'm just a couple days old." He laughed, much too hard. Then he stopped abruptly. "Actually, I don't know how long I had this body before I woke up. I have no birthday any more, not in this body."

"Eighteen? Really? I guess I thought you'd be older. Were you in school? I mean, before you got here." She tried to sound as sympathetic as she could.

"I was on my way to college," he said quietly.

She sensed that this was a sore subject, and dropped it. "Where are you from, Jeff?"

"The planet Aurora."

"Really?" She said brightly. "I'm from Aurora, too, and I'm just a little younger than you are. In fact—" She hesitated, then decided to say it. "I'm Ariel Welsh."

"Ariel Welsh . . . really? The famous one?"

"Well . . ." The reminder stung. "I guess so. Juliana Welsh is my mother."

"So this is where you wound up! Wow. I'm really talking to you? You were in all the news and everything." Suddenly he sounded his age, and guileless.

Ariel said nothing.

"That does it," he said firmly. "You order those robots to transplant you. You're sick, right? Well, you won't be sick in a robot body. Unless the infection has reached your brain, too, of course. So you tell them, all right? Then after that, you can join me."

Ariel was reeling. If it could work, it might stop the

spread of the disease. Her body could be frozen while a cure was found, and she could go on living as a robot. Why hadn't she thought of that?

"Hey! You there? Hey, Ariel!" He yelled.

Of course, she might have to stay on Robot City, in that case. Then again, as a robot, she would fit in a little better. No, much better. Nor would she feel that she was wasting her life here. The biological life expectancy of her body wouldn't start up again until it was thawed out, whenever that could be arranged. Her brain would age normally if it was functioning in a robot body, but maybe the disease would not affect her brain, or at least not as fast. She could encourage the medical team to work on a cure. The First Law would require that, wouldn't it?

"You still there?" Jeff demanded.

"Yes! Yes, I'm here. Don't go—I'm interested."

"You are?" He sounded surprised again, then he recovered. "Of course you are! I knew you would be. It's better this way. We can take over the city together. Now, how about Derec?"

"Huh? What about him?"

"The transplant, of course! Aren't you listening to me? What's wrong with you?"

"He doesn't have any reason to be transplanted."

"Of course he does! That's what I've been telling you! He can see better, hear better, and all that. He'll like it. And the three of us can take over the planet. The robots will have to obey us. Think of it—an entire planet at our disposal."

"I'm not sure he's going to see it that way." She added to herself that Derec's amnesia was in his mind. Transplanting his brain wouldn't take care of that problem.

"Of course he will. It's easy to understand. He'll get it."

"Why would we want to take over the planet?"

"So it would be ours, of course. What kind of question is that? We could run it."

"Actually, the robots run it pretty well, don't you think? Everything runs smoothly here."

"But it would be ours!"

"But what would we do with it? What would be different? The robots would still do all the work, just like they do now."

"It would be *ours!* Don't you understand? The entire planet would belong to us."

"Okay, Jeff, okay. But if nothing changes, those are just words. Ownership wouldn't mean much, would it? The robots obey us already, so that won't get any better."

"You'll see! If you get this transplant, you'll understand. Then you'll find out, just like I did."

Ariel started to answer, then realized that the static had stopped: he was gone. She let out a deep breath, and sagged back in the chair with the release of tension. At this point, she didn't mind having to wait a little while for the others to return. He had given her several things to think about.

Derec was breathless when he ran into the room, followed by his concerned but calm robot companions. "Is he still on the line? I want to talk to him."

"Too late," said Ariel. "I kept him on as long as I could, but I ran out of stuff to say."

"We overheard part of it, but not too much."

"He must have been using a very primitive radio set," said Surgeon 2. "The quality of our reception varied greatly as we traveled through the city on our return trip."

"Do you know where he is?" Derec asked.

"No. He was very suspicious, and, well, kind of strange." She looked at the robots. "Was he like that before?"

"Like what?" Research 1 asked.

"He sounded almost paranoid. And he kept going

through mood swings. One minute he's laughing and the next minute he's totally enraged. Then he forgets it all and makes ordinary conversation." She shook her head. "It just wasn't normal."

"No," said Research 1. "He was not like that in the brief time he was awake with us."

"He was in a post-operative state at that time," said Surgeon 1. "He was surprised, and perhaps shocked. Nor was he conscious when we first found him. His behavior during the brief time he was awake with us may not have been representative of his personality."

"You mean he might always have been erratic and emotionally unstable?" Derec asked.

"Possibly," said Research 1. "Our data is too limited for a sound conclusion."

"I have another theory," said Ariel. "Do you think something is going wrong with him in some way?"

"Clarify, please," said Research 1.

"Well, he's been through a lot," she pointed out. "And at times he sounded normal and friendly. He was on his way to college somewhere. If he got accepted off-planet, outside Aurora, he was probably a good student."

"Agreed," said Derec. "You think the transplant has changed his personality, then."

They both turned to Research 1.

"How likely is it?" Ariel asked.

"This is possible. The odds cannot be calculated under the circumstances."

"Well—what do you think might have gone wrong?" She decided not to express the reason for her new interest in the transplant right now.

"Without precise medical data, I can offer two general possibilities. One is that the emotional shock of finding himself in a robot body has distressed him to the point of be-havioral change. The second is that his brain is suffering from a chemical imbalance that has caused this problem. It might be nutritionally or hormonally based, or might indi-cate a flaw in our procedure or planning."

"Can you help him?" asked Ariel. "If we catch him, I mean. He doesn't seem too far gone yet."

"That will depend on the precise nature of the problem, of course," said Research 1.

"We may have a full solution to the larger problem of Jeff, however," said Surgeon 1. "With your cooperation, De-rec."

"What? Mine?"

"We are capable of intricate surgical techniques," said Surgeon 1. "And we have a great deal of information of certain types regarding human physiology and medical care. However, we lack certain basic information regarding gross anatomy and some details of all kinds."

"I don't know anything like that," said Derec. "I don't think it's in the central computer, either."

"You don't need to," said Medical Research 1. "We need your body as a model."

Ariel stifled a laugh.

"How so?" Derec asked carefully. "What do you mean, as a model?"

"We need information regarding the complete physiol-ogy of a young human male, particularly regarding the ar-rangement of inner organs, in order to restore Jeff's body to a healthy condition. Yours can act as a kind of map."

"Pardon me for asking this," said Derec, "but exactly what do you need from me? In particular, uh. . . ."

"You will not be subjected to any risk," said Research 1. "After all, the First Law would not permit risk in your case, as it did in Jeff's. We have the ability to construct scanning systems that will tell us what we must know without surgical procedures or drugs."

Derec visibly relaxed. "Okay, sure. But we still have to get our hands on Jeff."

"Granted," said Research 1. "Nevertheless, we will arrange to have the systems constructed, since they do not currently exist. It will not take very long. The odds are very high in favor of Jeff's eventual apprehension, limited only by his unknown medical condition and the chance of injurious accident to his brain. Damage to the rest of him can, of course, be fully repaired."

"Brain damage would require a great deal of trauma," observed Surgeon 2. "His cranial protection was especially designed for him, as demanded by the First Law, and is highly effective."

"Good," said Derec. "We definitely need information from him, and the saner he is, the better. A crazy guy's answers aren't going to help us much."

"Enough about my conversation with him," said Ariel. "What about you? Did you get anything accomplished while you were out there? Or didn't you have enough time?"

"We rearranged the pattern of the ongoing search," said Research 1. "The closing doughnut has been speeded up, based on the First Law concern regarding Jeff's health. We have charged some additional robots inside the remaining hole here in the center of the city with the same behavior. This may locate him a little faster."

"I believe the colloquial phrase is, 'smoke him out'," said Surgeon 1. "Is that correct?"

"Yes." Ariel laughed.

"I told them that putting more pressure on Jeff might push him into a mental mistake," said Derec.

"I think so," said Ariel. "He's gotten very short-tempered."

"Maybe it's just as well that robots are out looking, if he's going to get violent." Derec turned to the robots. "Now we're just back to waiting, I guess, for the time being. We'll contact you immediately if we have a new development."

"Very well," said Research 1. "We shall return to our facility and prepare the scanning systems."

When they had left, Ariel got up so that Derec could have the console chair if he wanted it. Instead, he started into his room.

"Derec?" She said quietly, standing with her arms folded.

"Yeah?" He turned at his doorway.

"Did they talk about the transplant while you were out walking around with them?"

"No, not really. Why?"

"I was thinking about what Research 1 said. That maybe Jeff has gone weird because of the shock of waking up and finding out what happened to him. That might throw anybody, don't you think?"

"Sure. What about it?"

"If that's true, then the transplant was actually successful, wouldn't you say? The surgery itself, I mean, and all the adjustments they had to make in the robot body."

"Yeah, I guess so. But they aren't sure that's the case, remember? It's just one possibility." He cocked his head. "Since when did you get interested in all this?"

She shrugged self-consciously. "I was just thinking about it. On account of talking to Jeff. He says it's not too bad."

"Not too bad? Being a robot on the outside and a human

on the inside?" He had started to smirk, teasing her, but then realization crossed his face. "Hey, wait a minute. You don't . . . ?"

"Not for sure." She turned away, embarrassed. "I just want to know more about it, that's all."

"You mean you'd actually consider this? Turning yourself into a robot?"

She nodded her head without turning around.

"And then what—stay here? In this ridiculous place?" His voice was filled with wonder as much as anger.

"It's better than dying!" She whirled on him. "Or being frozen whole and maybe never waking up! What if there isn't any cure, anywhere? Maybe these robots could find one, if I stayed long enough." She felt tears stinging her eyes.

"Well, . . ." He paused uncertainly. "What about the other possibility? Maybe the robots messed up somehow. Maybe that's why Jeff's going crazy. You can't risk that. That would be worse than looking for a cure off the planet somewhere."

"If we get off the planet! Derec, what if we're still stuck here? I won't have anything to lose then, will I?"

"Well, I . . . I don't know. Maybe not."

"And what if Jeff was always a little crazy? Nobody here knows him. Maybe he hasn't been changed at all. What about that?"

He shook his head. "Maybe that's true. You were the one who came up with the theory about his going crazy now. All I know is that if they can't rig up the transplant right, it could kill you faster than your disease."

She looked away from him.

He hesitated, watching her. When she didn't say anything else, he went on into his room.

She walked into her own room and collapsed on her bed to stare at the ceiling. Then she remembered: it would not do her any good. One of the effects of her disease, before causing death, was insanity. Even a transplant like Jeff's would not help her escape her own brain.

CHAPTER 15

THE CIRCLE TIGHTENS

Jeff stood on the stationary shoulder of a slidewalk, at the apex of a high, arching overpass. Robots and vehicles passed on a major boulevard several stories below him. On one corner, five humanoid robots were talking. He had watched three of them approach the other two, and had seen that the pair standing together had blocked their path to engage them in conversation.

He couldn't tell what they were discussing at this distance, but normally robots would communicate privately among themselves through their comlinks. The most likely reason they were using spoken communication was that they were searching for him. His lack of a comlink was one identifying mark he could not disguise.

"You can't go that way, either, Jeffrey," he said into the slight breeze. It would carry his voice the other way, so that even their most sensitive robot hearing would not detect it. "They think they're closing in. Well, maybe they are and maybe they aren't. We'll see."

He stepped onto the slowest lane of the slidewalk and rode it standing still, carefully watching in all directions. With his vision magnified for distances, he was able to spot these little clusters of of conversing robots before they noticed him. They were uncharacteristic of normal robot behavior.

As near as he could tell, these clusters were coming toward the center of the city from all directions. They had been slowed down, though, because the population was higher as they approached the heart of the urban area. That might give him time to figure out an escape.

"Time for another reconnoiter, Jeffrey ol' pal. Just keep it casual and don't let anybody sneak up on you. Got it? Of course I've got it, you moron; I'm you." He laughed at his little joke and prepared to change direction at an upcoming junction ramp with another slidewalk.

He knew, by this time, the routes that gave him the most visibility, either with raised sections of slidewalk or open areas that offered a broad vista of the city. The robots involved in the pattern search were direct, and made no attempt to disguise their efforts, so he was able to see how much progress they had made. The circle was surprisingly tight, and still closing in.

"Now it's time to check out their procedure a little more closely. It'll take some care, Jeff. Think you can handle that? Of course I can. Shut up and get to work."

He was hoping to eavesdrop. The difficulty was in listening without attracting the attention of the search team. He continued to ride the slidewalks until he found a cluster of robots speaking below another slidewalk overpass. When he was close enough, he stepped off onto the shoulder again and turned up his aural sensitivity until he could hear them clearly.

"We have contacted all three of you through your com-links," one robot was saying. "We believe all three of you responded, but we wish to speak aloud with you as well."

"Identify," said another.

"I am Drainage Foreman 31. I am temporarily suspended from my regular duties. At the present time, I am leading this team of three robots in search of a human with the physical body of a robot. This is the purpose of our questions."

An extended moment of silence followed. Jeff understood what was happening. The search team was matching up comlink communication with eye contact and spoken words so that they would have no chance of letting him through by mistake, or by his getting lost in the crowd.

"I am going to repeat my answer to you aloud," Drainage Foreman 31 said to another robot. "This human had his brain successfully transplanted into the body of a robot. For this reason, he has the strength and appearance of a robot, but the authority of the Laws of Robotics. I am going to ask you a question aloud now. Please respond through your comlink."

Another moment of silence followed, then more talk of a similar kind.

Jeff stepped back onto the slidewalk to ride away. He was convinced that he could not fake having a comlink. That one robot was being very thorough in his testing, and he was backed up by two more robots. Jeff couldn't win a wrestling match with three robots, each with a strength equal to his own.

He was still wary as he approached a tunnel stop. If the robots did not shut down the system entirely, they would at some point stake it out, perhaps with checkpoints down in the tunnels themselves. They could not be careless enough to have forgotten it. However, they might not yet have set up their search there.

"This block is clear so far," he muttered to himself, looking toward a tunnel stop. "And no one's standing at the opening. All right, then. Casually, like before—and watch out for a checkpoint down in the tunnel itself. Right? Of course you're right. So am I. I know you are. Shut up and let's go. Okay, okay. . . ."

He went on muttering to himself, seriously now, as he sauntered toward the stop. Several humanoid robots passed him on the way, as well as the normal crowd of function robots of all sizes and types, but he was not worried about any of them. The search teams had so far all been teams of threes, and they had stopped every humanoid robot they met. They did not just walk around normally, like this.

At the open tunnel stop, he paused to glance around. Everything seemed fine so far. He got on the ramp and rode down into the tunnel. "Maybe your luck will hold, Jeffrey ol' friend. Of course it will; why wouldn't it? Well, just don't get overconfident."

They were after him. He knew they were after him. They had no right to stop him; he hadn't done anything wrong and he hadn't hurt anyone, not even a robot. They were only robots, anyway. They had no reason to be after him.

What if something had gone wrong with them? What if they didn't have to obey the Laws any more, either? They ran this city by themselves, didn't they? They could change the rules. Surely they manufactured their fellow robots right here. What if they were making positronic brains that didn't obey the Laws? They must be. Otherwise, how could they be chasing him at all? Trying to capture him had to break some Law or other.

That's why they wanted him. He had the same freedom

from the Laws, but he wasn't one of them. They had just been pretending to obey the Laws before.

At the base of the ramp, he peered around suspiciously. Nothing appeared out of order around the siding loop. He stepped into one of the booths and punched the keys on the console for his destination.

Nothing happened.

Then a green instruction light appeared, reading, "Temporary adjustment in control system requires use of robotic comlink. Give standard destination code to activate booth."

He sprang out of the booth, then looked around in embarrassment. If a searching robot had seen him fail to activate the booth, he would be identified on the spot. Fortunately, no one had noticed.

So, they had taken his beloved tunnel system away from him. All right. That didn't mean he was finished. After all, they were just robots. He was human—"Right?" He spoke aloud. "Of course you're right. Now shut up before you give yourself away."

He rode up the ramp slowly, glancing in all directions when he reached the surface. "We are still in disguise, still in disguise. Let's approach the enemy's lair and see what we can see. Very good, very good."

Newly resolved to keep quiet for as long as he could remember to do so, he started again for the residence of Derec and Ariel. He knew that they lived near the center of the city, certainly in the central area, and he was guessing that the pattern search was ultimately closing in on that spot. That meant he could escape detection the longest there, and, if he was lucky, he just might overhear something that would let him make a successful getaway.

"Just remember," he said to himself. "Don't let them actually lay eyes on you. They don't seem to tell us robots apart too well, but they just might recognize you, ol' buddy. Right? Right. Shut up; you're talking out loud again."

He recognized the building and the entranceway to their residence easily enough, but he had no plans for what to do next. Since robots did not normally loiter, he could not very well just hang around watching the place.

One of the reasons he had been safe from detection in the tunnel system was that he had been isolated in the booths. Another was that the very act of moving made him appear occupied, like all the legitimate residents of Robot City. He got onto a slidewalk and started walking purposefully, hoping that this would work as an adequate substitute for the time being.

As usual, he set up a route that carried him in an irregular, jagged rotation, now using the human residence as a central reference point. He used the first two circuits to look for search teams, but he didn't see any here. Then he relaxed somewhat and altered his route so that he passed within sight of the human residence more often.

Derec and Ariel did not appear while he was watching. He wondered if he might do better talking to Derec than to Ariel, though she had said she was at least interested in the transplant. She had not been so optimistic about Derec, but maybe she was wrong.

He would not want to talk to Derec yet, since she might be right. If he could talk to her again first, maybe she would have the transplant and understand why it was so desirable. Then they could both convince Derec to join them.

He would just have to wait and watch.

By the time he had lost count of the number of circuits he had made, boredom was setting in. Maybe those two hardly ever came out of their lair. Or maybe they weren't in there at all, but out roaming around the city—looking for him, probably. He laughed—giggling, really—at the idea. If they would just come home, their search would be over.

"No, it wouldn't," he said aloud, sobering suddenly. "I would still have to hide from them. I'd have to be careful, wouldn't I? Of course you would. Now be quiet."

He got off the slidewalk in view of their entranceway, just because he was tired of riding around and around. "A real robot wouldn't get tired of it," he said. "A real robot would just do it over and over until the job was done. But not you. That's why you're still human, isn't it? Huh? Of course it is."

He stood on the shoulder of the slidewalk, wondering what he should do next. "You forgot to tell me to shut up," he added. "All right, shut up. Thank you."

A humanoid robot came riding up on the slidewalk. As he neared Jeff, he stepped off and walked up to him. "Identify," he said. "Use your comlink, please."

"Uh—" Jeff stared at him in shock. This guy was alone, without any search team. Apparently they had altered their policy. Jeff was caught totally off guard. "I, uh—what do you want?"

"I am not receiving you," said the robot. "Please accompany me. I am under instructions to escort all robots without functioning comlinks to a location nearby."

"Do you know why?" Jeff didn't move. He was thinking as fast as he could. If he could stall, he would.

The robot looked at him without speaking. After a moment, Jeff realized the reason.

"Please answer me out loud," said Jeff. "I'm not receiving you, any more than I'm transmitting."

"Yes," said the robot out loud. "I know why."

"Tell me."

"We are searching for Jeff Leong. He is a human brain in a robot body. It possesses no comlink. A secondary benefit may be the identification of robots whose comlinks have malfunctioned without their having noticed, so they can be repaired."

"Identify."

"I am Air Quality Foreman 6."

"Who gave you this instruction?"

"Human Research 1."

"Yeah, I know him. Another robot, in other words."

"Yes. Of course."

"Don't get smart with me, slag heap. Now, then. I know something about robots from when I was on Aurora. If a human gives you an order that contradicts an instruction from a robot, the Second Law makes you obey the human, right?"

"Assuming no other influences pertain, yes."

"Other influences?" Jeff said suspiciously. "Like what? You aren't trying to break the Laws, are you?"

"No, decidedly not. An example of another influence might be prior programming, for instance. Another would be the force of the First Law, which of course takes precedence over the Second and Third. Are you unaware of this? If you are testing me, under what authority are you acting? Identify."

He was trapped, and would have to gamble.

"I'm Jeff Leong, the human-robot you are searching for. Don't contact anyone!" he shouted suddenly. "Did you obey me? I know how fast those positronic brains of yours can work."

"I obeyed you. I started to use my comlink to report locating you, but I aborted it."

"Aha!" Jeff laughed. "So you have to obey me, eh? Well, well."

"Your orders override the instructions I received from Human Research 1, because programming itself was not involved. He gave me a simple instruction. If you issue orders contrary to my programming, I will not obey."

"Hmm. You believed me pretty quick. Are you sure you believe me?" He demanded.

"Yes. I am not capable of lying about this."

"Why do you believe me?"

"If you had a positronic brain, you would not be able to lie to me and say otherwise. Therefore you must be, or possess, the human brain in the robot body."

"Okay, okay, fair enough. Say, why didn't I think of ordering around search robots before? Jeffrey, you're not yourself. That's why." He giggled to himself. "You certainly aren't, are you?"

"Do you have further instructions for me?" asked Air Quality 6, in the same bland voice as before.

"Oh, yeah—you bet. I sure do. The first order is, you don't let on to anyone who I am. Understand? I'm just another robot here in town. Got it?"

"I understand."

"Good. Now we're going to be a team. I'll give you the orders and you'll obey them. Since you have a comlink that works, you're going to help me get away from all these search teams. If you detect the presence of one of those teams, you alert me and help me avoid them. We're going to get out of here. Got it?"

"I understand that we are going somewhere. I do not know what 'here' we are getting out of."

"I'll explain one step at a time," said Jeff, eyeing the robot thoughtfully. "Well, well. I think we're going to get along. You know, taking over this town is going to be easier than I thought. Let's go down to the nearest tunnel stop. You know where it is?"

"Yes. Follow me."

Derec was munching bacon and wiping out the inside

of the chemical processor's receptacle when Ariel sat up straight in her chair by the computer console.

"Derec, we've got something. He's been found. Sort of."

"What do you mean, sort of? What is it?" He hurried to her and leaned down to read over her shoulder.

"A partial alert came into the central computer just now. All it says is, 'Jeff Leong located.' "

"That's all? That doesn't sound like an efficient robot message. Move over. I bet the message was aborted somehow—maybe Jeff punched him or something." He leaned in front of her and quickly keyed for the location of the report and read the coordinates. "Hey—that's right outside! Come on!"

He turned and ran out, aware of Ariel following right behind him.

Derec skidded to a stop on the street, looking all around. Various humanoid robots were in sight, but none were doing anything unusual. He had no way of picking out one over another.

"Derec, how about those two?" She pointed at a pair of humanoid robots just going around a corner. "I think that one looks sort of like Jeff, don't you?"

"Could be, I guess. . . . There's a tunnel stop over there. I think I've got it—he's ordered another robot to run the tunnel booths for him. If he does, he can go anywhere. The whole search will be a waste of time. Come on!" He ran back inside and got on the console.

"What are you doing? Shouldn't we try to catch them?"

"We are. Here it is—the destination he's chosen. I see— he's only going a couple of stops from here. He must be pretty sharp. Instead of just heading out as far as he can go, and risking interception, he's going to leave a broken, unpredictable trail. Maybe I can alert some robots in that area, somehow—"

"That's a waste of time!" Ariel shouted. "Look where he's going—it's right next to the Key Center. He still has a distance to go. We can beat him there ourselves!"

"What? How?" Derec turned to look at her, but she was already running out the door. He hesitated, then got up and ran after her.

Jeff and Air Quality 6 had had to squeeze into the same tunnel booth, of course, and it was very crowded. Jeff decided to make this stint a short one, to test Air Quality 6's reliability. He still wondered if some kind of programming might have allowed the robots to act in unusual ways for the sake of trapping him. Air Quality 6 activated the booth, and they took off through the tunnel.

The awkward fit in the booth made the trip seem longer than it was. Finally, they slowed into the siding loop and got out. Jeff led the way up the ramp.

The great bronze dome he had often seen rose up in front of them, gleaming in the sunlight. He didn't know what it was, but it was a visual reference point he had often used. Air Quality 6 had brought him here faithfully, so he supposed he could trust the robot after all.

"Good job, pal," Jeff said to the robot. "Well, I guess we can take a longer trip now, maybe out to the edge of town. You probably know this place better than I do. You got any suggestions?"

"I detect the approach of two humans from one direction and a robot from another."

"What? Where?"

"There." Air Quality 6 pointed to a transparent, horizontal chute lined up with a loading dock not far away. Derec and Ariel were climbing out of the vacuum tube. "And there. The robot is not in sight yet, but is about to come around a corner. He had been using his comlink to contact me."

"You didn't respond, did you?" Jeff growled in a low voice.

"No."

"Good. You freeze—don't speak, move, or communicate in any way till I give you the counter order."

Jeff froze himself into position at the same moment, just as Derec and Ariel came running up.

"Is that you, Jeff?" Ariel asked breathlessly.

Jeff held himself still, and was relieved to see that his last order to Air Quality 6 was being obeyed, as well.

"One of you has a positronic brain," said Derec. "I order that one to answer us. Which one is Jeff?"

Jeff spent a very long moment waiting, but was glad to realize that his order to Air Quality 6 for silence had taken precedence. He might just figure a way out of this problem yet.

"You are Derec and Ariel?" asked another robot, joining them. "I am Assistant Planner 3. I have been participating in the random search for Jeff Leong and received your emergency message from the central computer."

"Thanks for coming," said Derec. "We seem to have a problem here. They aren't responding."

"So I understand. I have been attempting to communicate with them through my comlink ever since I received your message, but I have not had a response, either."

Ariel stood right in front of Jeff and peered into his eyeslit. "I think this one's Jeff. I'm not real good telling these robots apart, but they all have slight differences. This looks like him. You in there, Jeff?"

"All right," said Derec. "This is going to take some effort. We'll have to get them together with the other robots whose comlinks don't work; I understand that two or three more have been found. Assistant Planner 3, please arrange for this. Make sure the medical team joins us."

CHAPTER 16

SIMON SAYS

Five suspect robots were taken to the Human Experimental Facility. Two were frozen into position and completely uncommunicative. The other three were mobile, apparently cooperative, and could speak aloud.

As Derec and Ariel entered the building, she shook her head and said, "I'm sure that one is Jeff. We really don't have to waste time on the others."

"I'm not doubting you," said Derec. "I'm certain that one of those two is Jeff. The problem is that their bodies are the same model, so the medical team can't tell them apart, and I'm not sure you can, either. In any case, it appears that we'll have to smoke him out to make him admit which one he is."

"Welcome to our facility," said Research 1. "Please follow me down the hall. We have the suspect robots here waiting for you. It is large enough to accommodate everyone."

He led them into a room from which all furniture and

equipment had been removed. From the marks on the floor, Derec saw that it had been cleared for this project. The five suspects were standing in a line against one wall.

"Derec," said one of them.

He looked up in surprise. "Alpha? Alpha, is that you?" He laughed and walked over to the one robot whose physical details were unique, suppressing an impulse to embrace him. "*Hi.* How did you get here?"

"Hi," said Alpha. "I was able to obtain a very small spacecraft and trace the source of the asteroid-disassembling operation to this planet. Wolruf accompanied me. More recently, I was detained by a robot search team and brought here."

"Spacecraft?" Derec suppressed a giggle of delight and caught Ariel's eye. "And Wolruf, too. How is she?"

"She is recovering from a difficult trip."

"Recovering?" Ariel said. "But she'll be all right?"

"Yes."

"I'm glad," said Derec. "We've worried about her. We'll want to see her when we can. What about the spacecraft? Does it still work? And is it here and available and all that?"

"Yes."

"Step out of line, Alpha." Derec turned, grinning to the medical team. "This is not Jeff. I put Alpha together myself."

"Hi, Alpha," said Ariel, bouncing on the balls of her feet in excitement. "I'm real glad to see you. But why did they stop you? You have a comlink, don't you."

"Greetings, Katherine. My comlink was originally set at a slightly different frequency. I altered it but was detained anyway, I believe for having an anomalous comlink."

"I'm Ariel Welsh now."

"I do not understand," said Alpha.

"Not now, not now. We'll catch up with each other

later," said Derec. "For the business at hand, we're down to four," said Derec, looking over the others. "Research 1, were you able to begin testing, like you said?"

"Yes. According to our standard maintenance scanning procedure on their bodies, all four are in good condition, other than their common lack of functioning comlinks. Their heads have not been scanned. The two speaking robots have given identification that has been verified by the central computer. Their comlinks simply malfunctioned."

"Dismiss them," said Derec. "Alpha, you stay right here until further notice."

"Report to the nearest repair facility," said Research 1.

The other two robots left.

"So." Derec stood in front of the two remaining robots, looking back and forth between them. "One of you is almost certainly Jeff. Unless you've fallen asleep, which I really doubt under the circumstances, you can hear me and you just aren't letting on. Well, we'll be right back." He turned away, then paused to grin over his shoulder. "Don't go anywhere, now. You'll give yourself away."

"Surgeon 1, you stay and watch them. Research, you and Ariel step outside with me for a minute."

Derec paused in the hall, but Research 1 shook his head. "This is not sufficient for privacy. If you want to talk privately, we must go into another room and I will create sonic camouflage. Do not forget that Jeff has robotic hearing."

"Lead the way." Derec could hardly keep from dancing around with joy. Alpha had a working spacecraft somewhere here—once he and Ariel had smoked out Jeff, they could turn him over to the robots and take off. As they followed Research 1 into another room, he saw the smile on Ariel's face and nudged her playfully with his elbow. She elbowed him back, a lot harder, but still grinning.

They entered what was obviously the facility's operating

room. Research 1 flipped a switch on some sort of scanning apparatus and a faint hum came on.

"They will not hear us. What do you wish to discuss?" Research 1 asked.

"They?" Ariel asked. "I don't get it. One of them is an inoperative robot, isn't he?"

"Immobile is not necessarily inoperative," said Research 1. "We must be cautious."

"Exactly," said Derec. "Here's how I figure it so far—correct me if I'm off. Jeff saw us coming in time to order another robot to freeze, and probably to follow only his instructions to activate again. I did basically the same thing with Alpha once. However, in order to hear Jeff's instruction to reactivate, the other robot has to maintain hearing sensitivity and at least some mental activity. Right?"

"Correct," said Research 1.

"What about a shortcut?" Derec asked. "Can't you just scan their heads and find out which has the biological brain in it?"

"No," said Research 1. "In constructing his special cranium, we used materials that would be extremely resistant to the entrance of any forms of energy, as well as to physical impact. Turning up our scanning beams to a strength that would penetrate his cranium would endanger the brain inside."

"Hold it," said Ariel. "You could use your normal scanning beam, and when you get a reading for one positronic brain and one null reading, we'd know by elimination."

"We dare not," said Research 1. "The cranium was tested before use, but not with the human brain inside. Even the normal scanning beam could be dangerous. The First Law does not allow us to take a risk of this magnitude."

"All right. Somehow, I'm not surprised." Derec sighed.

"The Laws of Robotics still hold precedence on them,

too, though," said Ariel. "I assume our tests will still work—won't they?"

"Yes. They are based on the following," said Research 1. "If Jeff had a positronic brain, he would have to obey the Laws—for instance, if one of you were in danger, he would have to save you. However, as a human, he could allow you to come to harm if he wished."

"The problem," said Derec, "is that Jeff knows the Laws and can masquerade as a robot."

"We also don't know what he told the other robot," said Ariel. "If the other robot knows that we are setting up tests, then he won't believe we're really in danger and he won't have to obey the Laws, either. They'll still behave the same way."

"Let's get started and see what happens," said Derec. "We'll go in order, with tests one, two, and three."

Derec and Ariel went back into the room with the suspect robots. The medical team had to leave, accompanied by Alpha, in order to avoid confusion. If they did not respond according to the Laws, the real robot would see it was a test; if they did respond, they would get in the way.

"I've had it with you," Derec was yelling at Ariel. "You're crazy." He turned toward her in front of both robots.

"Oh, yeah?" She demanded. Then, according to their agreement, she swung back her fist and punched him in the stomach.

Even though he had been expecting the blow, Derec doubled over from the impact—partly from her very solid punch and partly as an act. Both robots jumped forward, no longer frozen in place, and pulled them apart. If one had been a shade faster, he couldn't tell.

"Let go of me! Him, too!" Ariel shouted, as they had prearranged. Both robots obeyed, but remained between them, close enough to prevent more violence.

Derec, gasping for breath, looked up and found that they had both apparently deactivated again. It was time for the second test. He caught Ariel's eye, saw that she was ready for him, and leaped at her throat as if to strangle her.

Instantly, both robots grabbed him in their powerful arms and held him fixed and helpless.

"Let go of me," he ordered.

Neither one let him go. Now that the violence had been repeated, the First Law was going to remain in force over the Second, until they judged that the threat was over.

"You," Ariel ordered, tapping one on the arm. "You go stand in the hall. The other one will keep me safe here. And you—Derec won't hurt me right now. I know that. You can stand close if it makes you feel better, to stop us again if necessary."

When both robots had complied, Derec and Ariel spoke amiably to demonstrate that the immediate threat of violence was over. Then the robots allowed them to retreat to the O.R. once again to consult with each other.

"Jeff's pretty good," said Derec. "He was right with the real robot every second—whichever one it was." He grinned. "You've got a pretty good punch."

Ariel shrugged. "Well, you said it should be the real thing. But now we know a little more. Direct application of the Laws activates the real robot, but only as long as the Laws apply. Then he freezes again, like Jeff ordered him."

"We'd better keep them separate. If Jeff is picking up his cue by watching the other robot, he'll never mess up."

"Good idea. Ready for test three?"

"Let's go," he said.

In the hallway, Surgeon 1 handed him a small gray cylinder that fit conveniently into his hand. It was an intermediate laser scalpel, used for certain types of repair on robot bodies, capable of cutting through any portion of a robot body. Derec hefted it, shifted it comfortably, and held it up as he entered the testing room.

"I'm going to cut your leg off with this," he said to the suspect robot. "In return for your interfering with me." He turned it up to full power, stood where he was, and aimed the beam at the robot's knee joint. "The Third Law says you can't allow this to happen. Right?"

The robot slid to one side, avoiding the beam. Derec followed him with it, and the robot moved away again. When Derec started shooting at his legs in spurts, like it was a gun, the robot danced around, backing up, dodging, watching the beam intently.

"I'll get you," Derec growled. "Ha! Close. Ha! Again. Almost. Ha! Hold still! I'll take your leg off—"

The robot continued to shuffle away from the beam with its quick and reliable robot reflexes.

Derec laughed triumphantly and shut off the laser. "Got you, Jeff. An old Simon Says trick—remember that game? I ordered you to hold still, and in the heat of the moment, you forgot that the Second Law takes precedence over the Third. You didn't hold still!"

The robot in front of him had frozen again, but now Derec was certain.

"You can't fool me now; it's too late. A positronic brain wouldn't forget the order of the Laws for even a second, under any circumstances." Derec called in everyone else and explained the situation.

"This is convincing to me," said Research 1. "Since the other suspect is by elimination almost certain to be a true robot, we can verify beyond any doubt by sending him to a repair facility."

"Research 1," Surgeon 1 said warningly.

"I will escort him," said Research 1. "The repair crews must be very cautious, in the event that we are mistaken.

They must understand the situation, so that no Laws will be violated."

Derec jerked his thumb at Jeff. "We know who he is, but until he quits play-acting, we can't have much of a dialogue."

Ariel caught his eye and inclined her head toward the door. Derec followed her out and they returned to the O.R. to talk. Surgeon 1 remained with Jeff.

"Maybe we can sucker him," said Ariel.

"All right. How?"

"Loosen the watch on him. He's still trying to play-act being a robot because there's a microscopic chance that a positronic brain could have malfunctioned this way. But if he tries to escape, he'll have to admit we know."

A few minutes later, everyone gathered in the testing room again in front of Jeff, except for the robot still motionless in the hall.

"We've decided to move on to the next phase," said Derec. "Research 1, please escort the other robot to be repaired."

Research 1 left the room.

"Now," said Derec. "Alpha, please leave the room but remain out in the hall—at the end of the hall, out of the way. We definitely have to talk to you."

"Yes, Derec." Alpha left.

"Surgeon 1," said Ariel. "We are no longer completely sure that this robot is really Jeff. Return to your regular duties in the facility. Derec and I are going to have to figure out what to do next."

"Very well." Surgeon 1 left the room.

Derec casually put his arm around Ariel and walked her toward the door. "Maybe we should get something to eat and relax a little. Then we can work out our next move."

Ariel closed the door behind them. Alpha was waiting

motionless at the far end of the hall; they went out the front door, in the opposite direction. Without speaking, since they didn't know how well Jeff could hear, they walked outside and looked around.

The Human Experimental Facility was a simple rectangular block. It had none of the striking geometric design of most of Robot City; with their usual efficiency, the robots had built it without frills. Derec saw nowhere to hide except around the corner.

They sat down on the pavement just around one corner, still silent, by prior arrangement. Jeff was likely to be cautious, so they knew they could have a long wait. Surgeon 1, also by agreement, had taken up his "regular duties" in a room across from the testing room. With his own robotic hearing, he also was waiting for Jeff to make his escape.

Derec found himself grinning in anticipation of using Alpha's spacecraft. They could help the robots take care of Jeff, of course, but now that they could look forward to leaving when the job was done, waiting didn't seem so bad. He looked at Ariel, who was also smiling when she turned to him. With suppressed laughter, they didn't have to talk to feel close.

The day wore on, and Jeff's patience was at least as good as theirs. Derec did notice that Ariel seemed as content as he was to keep waiting. He kept thinking that he would soon go somewhere and find out who he was, or even find a cure for his amnesia. Maybe she was dreaming of finding her own cure off the planet.

Finally, a single, moderately loud robotic shout went up inside the facility: "Derec!"

He recognized Surgeon 1's voice, and jumped up with Ariel. Around the corner, Jeff was just now walking out the front door with controlled, casual steps.

"Got you!" yelled Derec, pointing at him. "Give it up." He and Ariel ran up to block Jeff's way.

Jeff reached for them both with his powerful robot arms. He was free of the First Law, but Surgeon 1 wasn't, and he leaped on Jeff from behind, pinning his arms back.

"Alpha!" Derec called. "Come out here!"

"Release me," Jeff yelled at Surgeon 1, pulling and jerking to no effect.

"You may not harm them or yourself," Surgeon 1 answered.

"I have no intention of harming anyone," Jeff shouted angrily. "I order you to release me."

"Hold him, Doc," said Ariel, keeping her distance.

Derec saw that Surgeon 1 was hesitating, probably experiencing a positronic conflict from the fact that Jeff had never really shown a desire to harm anyone. The weight of conflicting human orders was otherwise near neutral. Before, and now, he had only pushed them so that he could get away.

"Release me and freeze," ordered Jeff. He wrenched himself free and started to run.

Surgeon 1 had not frozen, but he was moving slowly, uncertainly, as he worked through the conflicting human orders.

"Alpha!" Derec shouted, seeing him emerge from the building. "That's Jeff. He needs medical care and doesn't know it. First Law applies—stop him!"

In surprise, Jeff paused to look back. Surgeon 1 was again galvanized to action by the First Law application, since it overrode the problems of the Second Law. He tackled Jeff around the knees as Alpha ran up to pinion his arms.

Jeff's robot fist swung low and jerked back Surgeon 1's

head. He also raised a knee and then kicked upward, throwing Alpha back. Surgeon 1 held on, though, preventing him from getting away.

As the three robot bodies wrestled and thrashed together, Derec saw the difficulty: Alpha and Surgeon 1 could only subdue Jeff without risking any damage to him, and in the confusion of combat, they were being particularly careful, since no one had ever really tested the cranial protection around Jeff's brain. On the other hand, Jeff was free to smash, twist, and rip at their bodies in any way he thought would get him free.

Derec skipped helplessly around the three tussling bodies. With two opponents, Jeff could not get free, but with the unequal restrictions placed on them, the other two could not pin him down, either. Ariel looked from them to Derec questioningly—then turned and ran, looking for more help.

Now Alpha was lying flat on his back, with Jeff trying to get up off him while Surgeon 1 again had his arms pinned behind him. Jeff managed to get one of his legs under him, and struggled to stand. Alpha's standard arm was caught beneath his body, and Jeff was still gripping his other one above the elbow.

His other one.

"Alpha," shouted Derec. "Make your arm flexible—loosen it up. Use it however you need to in order to stop him!"

Instantly, Alpha's arm lost its elbow entirely and became a fully flexible coil. The hand curved back and tightened on Jeff's wrist to pull it free. Then the arm curved around, locking the joints on Jeff's arm to make it immobile.

Surgeon 1 released Jeff's arms and encircled his knees. Alpha and Surgeon 1 stood up and finally held Jeff immobile, off the ground, as Ariel ran up with a couple of other robots she had commandeered with an emergency First Law appeal.

Jeff was still thrashing about in his captors' arms. "You slag heaps! You traitorous can heads! You can't hold me! I'm human, you understand? Let go of me! Now! I order you to put me down!"

"Can you sedate him?" Derec asked. "You can't just hang onto him this way while we figure out what to do next. Making him sleep wouldn't be harming him."

"I will sedate him," said Surgeon 1, still holding Jeff's legs with effort. "We are making progress, I believe. When Research 1 returns, we must consult on the matter of treatment. I experienced a moment of hesitation while in physical conflict just now over a First Law question that must be addressed." He took a step backward, reacting to a convulsive kick by Jeff. The other robots took hold as well, assuring that the cyborg could not escape.

"I'll kill you! I'll melt you all down!" Jeff screamed. "Just wait till I'm in charge!" He thrashed and kicked again.

"Go ahead and do what you need to," said Derec. "We'll hang around; don't worry about that."

"Into the O.R.," said Surgeon 1. He and the others trooped inside the building, carrying their screaming cargo.

Derec let out a sigh of relief and turned to Ariel, ready to make some kind of joke. He stopped when he saw the look of disappointment on her face.

CHAPTER 17

WOLRUF

Jeff woke up in dim light again, but this time he recognized the room. He was not connected to any monitors now, though. His eyes adjusted quickly; he was used to that now, too, and didn't really notice it. He felt firm restraints of some sort holding him in place.

So they had him again. His memory was clear enough—with the bunch of robots forcing him down, Surgeon 1 had somehow introduced a substance into his neck. Jeff supposed it had gone into one of the nutrient avenues to his brain. In any case, he had been sleeping, and still felt drowsy and languid.

He was alone in the room, which was silent, but he could hear faint noises beyond the walls. His enemies were probably holding a meeting of some sort. By concentrating, he was able to turn up his aural acuity, and just make out some familiar voices.

"The First Law problem I experienced was this," said Surgeon 1. "We have reason to believe that the transplantation of Jeff's brain into a robot body has adversely affected him. If so, then the First Law requires that we undo the transplant, once we have scanned Derec for the knowledge we need to repair Jeff's body."

"So what's the problem?" Ariel asked.

"The problem is Jeff's resistance," said Surgeon 1. "We are not certain that the transplant has adversely affected him. Without the imperative of the First Law, we cannot transplant his brain—or even test him—without his permission."

"And he certainly doesn't seem inclined to give it," Derec observed. "There's not much doubt about that."

Jeff muttered to himself, "You're right about that, frost head. You're absolutely right about that. You want to take my body away from me again? You want to make me into a weakling again, like you? Stop me from taking over this planet? Ha."

"When is he due to wake up?" asked Research 1.

"Any time now," said Surgeon 1.

"Then I suggest, first, that we be more cautious in discussing him, since he may hear us," said Research 1, "and, second, that we consult with him and make certain that he understands our position."

"Good idea," said Derec. "Alpha, you and Wolruf stay here. That room won't hold all of us comfortably."

The moment the door opened, letting in a shaft of bright white light, Jeff shouted, "Let me out of here! You have no right to hold me prisoner—none of you do! Now let me up!"

They lined up at the foot of his bed, shoulder to shoulder, watching him in silence: Research 1 and Surgeon 1 on the left, and Derec and Ariel on the right.

"Frost! Don't you understand your own Laws?" Jeff demanded of the robots.

"Yes," said both robots in unison. They looked anxiously at Derec and Ariel.

"It's not that simple, Jeff," said Derec. "Look, there's a possibility that a medical problem—"

"Sure it is," Jeff growled. "I want to get up and out. That's very simple. So, let me up and out. What are you after me for, anyway? I didn't do anything."

"You're not yourself, Jeff," said Ariel sympathetically. "A little while ago, you were shouting about taking over. You remember talking to me through some sort of broadcasting link? You told me we could be very powerful here. But I don't think that's really you."

"It is now," Jeff said haughtily. "They created the new me, and now this *is* me. And you have no right to make me over again."

"All they really need at this stage," said Derec, "is to run some tests on you. They want to find out if there's a chemical imbalance in your brain that they caused—"

"Making me crazy? Is that it? You telling me I've gone crazy? I'm not stupid; I'll tell you that much. I know you want to get rid of me. You don't like having someone as powerful as I am around, do you? Huh?" Jeff laughed triumphantly, and loudly.

"Jeff," said Ariel. "They have to act according to the Laws, and they can't do that fully unless they run their tests. That way, they'll know exactly where you stand."

"Frost!" Jeff yelled angrily. "If they have to obey the Laws, then why don't they let me go when I tell them to? Huh?"

"Their responsibility is larger than that," said Derec. "Since they put you in this condition, the Laws demand that they make sure you're really okay. The tests alone won't hurt you any, or change you."

"Oh, yeah? How do I know that? Huh?" Jeff looked around at them all. "Supposedly this transplant couldn't hurt me, either, only now you're all saying they might have made a mistake. Well, what if they make another one? What about that?"

Derec glanced at the robots, who said nothing.

"Let's leave him alone for a while," said Derec. "Come on."

Before they left, Research 1 turned on one of the machines in the room. Jeff understood its purpose. The white noise would drown out his ability to eavesdrop any more.

When Jeff was alone again, with the door closed, he tested his restraints. He couldn't see what they were, since he was flat on his back, but they were stronger than he was. If he was going to get out of this untouched by the robots, he would have to argue his way out.

Somehow.

Back in the testing room, Derec turned to his companions with an exaggerated shrug. "Well? Now what?"

"I regret to interrupt," said Alpha, "but I must inform you of a fundamental change in my identity."

"What?" Derec turned to him. "What are you talking about?"

"At the time you instructed me to use my cellular arm, I experienced a signal from it changing my designation from Alpha to Mandelbrot."

"Mandelbrot?" Ariel said. "Why?"

"I do not know."

"What does it mean?" Derec asked. He was annoyed at the interruption in his train of thought about Jeff, but he could not ignore the mystery.

"It means nothing other than a name change to me," said Mandelbrot.

"And it came from your cellular arm at the time I gave

you the order to use it." Derec thought a moment. "It was encoded in your arm when I found the part, then. Using your flexibility triggered the signal. . . ."

"Could it be a safety measure of some kind?" Ariel asked. "Maybe a warning. This whole planet seems to be programmed with fear and security in mind. His arm came from an Avery robot on that asteroid, didn't it?"

"That's right," said Derec. "I don't know exactly what the signal means. Perhaps it was triggered by the combined use of some Avery parts and some standard robot parts together." He looked at Ariel. "Maybe it means another signal has been sent out to call Avery back."

"If he's alive."

"Yeah." Derec shook his head. "First things first. Let's get back to Jeff."

"That theory is consistent with another important change in me," said Mandelbrot.

"What is it?" Derec asked impatiently.

"My store of data pertinent to the location of this planet was erased at the time of the name change."

Derec and Ariel both turned to him.

"How important is that?" Derec demanded. "You can still program a ship away from here to a major spacelane, can't you?"

"Given the considerable length of spacelanes, I believe so. However, this memory erasure suggests that the signal from my arm was definitely related to the security and isolation of this planet."

"Good point," said Derec, "but once we leave this place, I'm not going to care. Let's get back to Jeff."

"I surmise that your visit was not productive," said Mandelbrot. "May I assist you in any way?"

"I haven't thought of how yet," said Derec. "The trouble

so far is that the robots can't treat him without permission, and Ariel and I, who don't need permission, don't have the skill to treat him. Anybody have any suggestions?" He looked around at all of them.

"Is there anything we can do to prove that Jeff is out of his head?" Ariel asked. Then she covered her mouth in embarrassment. "Sorry. Didn't mean to phrase it that way."

Derec smiled wryly. "We're all under a strain."

"I cannot think of anything," said Research 1. "The kind of unmistakable scientific evidence we require to reach a conclusion is only available through a direct analysis of his physical condition."

"Frost, Derec!" Ariel turned to Research 1. "How about us? Can you teach us to help just a little? If we extracted samples of fluid for you, and you analyzed them afterward— would that be acceptable?"

Research 1 hesitated just long enough to reveal some doubt behind his answer. "The acceptability of that arrangement would ultimately rest on how skillful you became. Drawing a sample of synthetic blood would not be difficult, I believe. However, he does not have much margin for error. Unlike naturally evolved biological bodies, Jeff's robot body has almost exactly the amount of fluid he requires. Taking too much could be fatal."

"You could make extra," said Derec. "Give him a transfusion while the procedure is going on."

"You would have to administer the transfusion, as well," said Surgeon 2. "And you would have to avoid flooding his system as well as starving it. Nor could you risk mixing the new fluid with the old, or the analysis would be worthless. At this point, we have confronted more complex procedures, including constant study and understanding of the monitors. We would be in violation of the First Law if we allowed Jeff to take significant risks in this manner."

Derec nodded, though he was disappointed. "I can't argue with that. The truth is, I'm not sure I'm ready for responsibility over his life that way, myself."

Ariel sighed. "Then we need the permission of a crazy guy. Any idea how to get it?"

Jeff wasn't tired, really, but he had closed his eyes and rested for lack of anything else he could do. He was imprisoned by enemies who were afraid of his power, but he had not given up hope. He could afford to be charitable, once he had taken over.

He opened his eyes at the sound of the door opening, but when he looked, he couldn't see anyone. Then the door closed again. He stiffened at a faint padding sound on the floor.

"Who's there?" He demanded suspiciously.

"Iss Wolruf," said an odd voice.

"What?"

The caninoid alien climbed gently onto the foot of the bed. She had been near death by starvation the only other time he had seen her. Now her mottled brown and gold fur was full and glossy, and her eyes alert and bright. She was perhaps the size of a large dog, such as a small St. Bernard, but her face was flat, without an extended snout, and her ears stood high and pointed. Instead of paws, she had clumsy looking gray-skinned fingers on what he supposed were hands.

"My name iss Wolruf to 'umans. Iss really—" She made an unpronounceable noise and bared her teeth in what might have been a playful smile.

"Wolruf?"

"I came to thank 'u for 'aving me fed," said Wolruf. "Alpha told me 'u saved my life."

"Yeah? Now what do you want?"

"Want nothing," said Wolruf. "Thank 'u."

Jeff watched her for a moment. "You okay now? Is that—Alpha?—taking care of you properly?"

"Everything iss fine."

"He just didn't know how to handle this town, did he?"

"No. Iss strangrr even herr in city of robots."

"Wait a minute. I remember now. I get it. These other robots didn't have to help because you aren't human."

"Iss true."

Jeff laughed in his still-unfamiliar robot voice. "Yes, yes, Jeffrey. This city belongs to you. Only you can see the needs of people here. You can do what no one else here can." He caught Wolruf's eye. "Right? Huh? You should know."

She blinked mildly at him.

"Huh? Right?" He insisted.

"Rright," she said. "But I'm worried."

"Oh?" Jeff said airily. "Anything else I can help with?"

"Worried about my friend."

Jeff hesitated. "Yeah? Who?"

" 'U," said Wolruf, nodding at him.

He started to retort, but Wolruf's quiet sincerity stopped him.

" 'Urr my first new friend herr," said Wolruf. "Saved my life. Don't want 'u 'urt."

"Everybody says that," said Jeff, but he seemed to lack the same angry suspicion that he had felt before.

" 'U saved my life," Wolruf repeated.

"I guess I did. Are you saying you want to repay me?"

Her caninoid shoulders twitched in a sort of furry shrug. "Won't force 'u."

"You may be the first follower I have," Jeff said wonderingly. "Robots have to obey me. Derec and Ariel haven't really . . . come around yet, you might say. What are you worried about, anyhow?"

" 'U could be sick."

Jeff stiffened. "Sick? How can I be sick, when I haven't got a normal body?"

" 'Urr brain could be sick." She nodded. "Could be. Could be fine."

"They sent you in here, didn't they? To change my mind."

"No. They'rr too busy to remembrr Wolruf. Forgot about me. I just walked away while they werr talking. Came to see 'u."

"Really?" Jeff was surprised. "Just to see me?"

" 'U've been alone on Robot City. Only one of 'urr kind. I know about that. 'U could be sick and can't tell. Could find out."

Jeff looked up at the ceiling. He had been feeling lonely, now that she mentioned it. Maybe he was sick.

"I don't trust them," he said to Wolruf. "I can take over this city—this whole planet. They want to stop me." The fire was gone, though; he felt it himself. He was tired, emotionally tired.

"Robots can't 'urt 'u on purpose," she reminded him. "Make rare mistakes, but can't 'urt 'uman on purpose."

"Derec and Ariel—"

"Robots can't allow them to 'urt 'u, either. Test can tell 'u if 'urr sick or not."

Jeff closed his eyes and sighed.

Derec hadn't seen Wolruf leave the group in the testing room, but he noticed her come back in. The little alien bore her distinctive teeth-baring grin when she looked up at him.

"What is it, Wolruf?" He asked.

"Jeff changed 'is mind. Will take test now."

Everyone turned to look at her.

"Are you certain?" asked Research 1.

"I've underestimated you before," said Derec. "Remind me not to do it again."

"Wolruf? How did you manage that?" Ariel asked in astonishment.

"Just talked to 'im," said Wolruf. "Suggest 'u don't talk to 'im, or 'e'll change 'is mind."

"We'll take your word for it," said Derec. "Research 1, you and Surgeon 1 go ahead and run your tests. I suggest that you also conduct a minimum of conversation with him. I guess he's still pretty unpredictable."

"I will begin the procedures with Jeff," said Research 1. "May I request that you allow Surgeon 1 to conduct the scans of your body that we have already discussed? The equipment is prepared, and the central computer will benefit from the information regardless of Jeff's condition and wishes."

"Sure." Derec turned to Ariel and Mandelbrot. "As soon as I'm finished—"

"Right. We'll be here," she said with a grin. "Wolruf, too."

Derec followed Surgeon 1 into a cramped room and stretched out, undressed, on a cold platform at the robot's bidding. The robot attached a variety of sensors to him, all connected to some of the worst looking jury-rigged equipment Derec had seen on this planet. For once, the necessity for speed had overcome the values of minimalist engineering; the robots had put together something that would work, ignoring convenience and appearance.

As Surgeon 1 ran various vibrations through parts of his body and shot him with invisible rays, Derec assured himself that once the emergency with Jeff was past, they would either improve the engineering of this equipment or discard it altogether. They weren't likely to allow an anomaly like this to remain as it was. Still, he felt a sense of petty satisfaction in seeing that they weren't always perfect.

When the scans were finished, Derec got dressed as Surgeon 1 glanced over the monitors.

"This is sufficient," said Surgeon 1. "We are capable of restoring Jeff's body to a state of health, granted his normal recuperative powers after surgery. Research 1 has contacted me through his comlink, and requests our presence back in the testing room."

Research 1 was waiting when they got there.

"Well?" Derec said. "How is he?"

"Ariel's theory appears to be correct. The level of several hormones that can affect mood and behavior in humans were higher than we had intended. Given the limited blood supply, very small amounts skew the percentages."

"I was sure he wasn't that bad a guy," said Ariel.

"Me, too," said Wolruf.

"What are you going to do, though?" Derec asked. "Have you discussed this with him yet?"

"No. Surgeon 1 and I must confer over the details. If Surgeon 1 agrees with me, then Jeff Leong is not responsible for his behavior. In that event, we would take the position that our judgment of his condition under the First Law would override all his orders to us under the Second Law."

"Whew," said Ariel. "That's a very big step."

"I think," said Derec, "that it's time for us to take care of some personal business. Research 1, do you need further human assistance at the moment? If not, we have an important errand to run."

"We do not require your assistance at this time," said Research 1. "I request your return later in the day."

"No problem." Derec turned to Mandelbrot with a big

grin. "Okay, friend. Show us this spacecraft you have wait-ing. I'll have to check its condition and facilities and all. Where is it?"

"It is in a rural area just outside the urban perimeter. One of the tunnels will take us close to the spot."

"Let's go—you, Wolruf, Ariel and me."

The trip out to the perimeter was uneventful, except for the glow of excitement that Derec and Ariel shared. Once they reached the construction perimeter, they had to start hiking. Fortunately, Mandelbrot had chosen a broad, open field for his landing, with only a short cushion of broad-bladed, blue ground cover.

"I see it!" Ariel shouted, pointing to a sliver of blue-silver glinting in the sunlight. It was just beyond a gentle rise in the terrain.

Derec looked up eagerly, then felt a sudden weight of disappointment, even though it was still mostly out of sight. He didn't say anything, though, until they had topped the rise and were looking down on the sleek, undamaged craft. Ariel, too, stopped in surprise.

"It's a lifepod," Derec said dully. It was so small that even the gently rolling ground had hidden it almost com-pletely.

"Correct," said Mandelbrot. "A somewhat converted li-fepod. I modified it."

"Alpha," said Derec, shaking his head. "Mandelbrot, I mean."

"I detect distress," said Mandelbrot. "What is its cause?"

"Whatever your name is," Ariel wailed, "we wanted to get out of here. But this little ship only has room for one."

"I traveled with 'im," said Wolruf.

"Mandelbrot, why didn't you tell us it could only carry one full-sized humanoid?" Derec asked. "I asked you where it was, what condition it was in, and so on."

"The only subject of discussion at that time was the welfare of Jeff Leong. I surmised that you wanted it for his use. It is adequate for that purpose."

"Yeah." Derec sighed. "So it is." He slipped an arm casually around Ariel's shoulders. "I think it's more important to get Ariel off the planet, though. She has—something to take care of."

She took his hand and squeezed it, probably for not mentioning her disease in particular.

"How did you modify it?" Derec asked.

"I was able to give it a significant drive ability. Also, I was able to create space for Wolruf. I myself used the space principally intended for human use, but of course I do not have the supply requirements. The supply space was available for her provisions."

Derec nodded, staring silently at the little ship.

No one else spoke. They all seemed to understand the realization, and what it meant to him. Finally, when he turned away, they followed him back to the tunnel stop without a word.

By the time they returned to the facility, Research 1 and Surgeon 1 were just leaving the O.R.

"Are you finished already?" Ariel asked in surprise. "How is he?"

"The procedures have apparently been successful so far," said Surgeon 1. "Unlike the transplantation into his robot body, which required no recovery period, his human body will require an extended recuperative phase with close attention from us."

"The most important unknown factor now is his biological recuperative power, with which we have little experience," said Research 1. "However, we—"

"You think he'll be okay," Derec interpreted. "Right?"

"Correct," said Research 1.

"What about his, well, his attitude?" Ariel asked. "Will his emotional state be normal again?"

"We will have to wait for data about that question. He will sleep for many hours, yet," said Surgeon 1. "We will also have him mildly tranquilized when he first awakens, to guard against further shock when he finds himself fully human again."

"If his body is truly recovering," said Research 1, "his serum levels in all cases should gradually return to normal. I surmise that the effect will not be immediate, but our information is poor on this subject."

Ariel nodded.

"We'll be moving along," said Derec. "I'm going to get on the central computer and see about refurbishing a certain little spacecraft. Also, how many further modifications it might take. Keep us up to date on Jeff through my console, all right?"

CHAPTER 18

LIFT-OFF

Derec was able to assemble a work crew of function robots to take care of the spacecraft under Mandelbrot's direction. The computer released them from normal duty with the understanding that Ariel's welfare would be aided by her leaving the planet. It was not exactly a clear First Law requirement, but in the absence of significant objections, it was sufficient.

Derec was disappointed to learn that the ship would not support the modifications required to support a second human passenger, but he was not surprised. The entire craft was just too small. He and Ariel had watched the robots construct a hangar near where Mandelbrot had landed it, in which minor repairs could be made. He followed the robots' progress with a certain intellectual interest.

Ariel did not seem to like talking about the ship, or where she would go in it. He understood that Aurora was off-limits, and neither of them really knew where she might reasonably look for a cure. Anyway, she wouldn't discuss it.

She brightened for the first time when Research 1 called through the computer console. He told Derec that Jeff was alert, talking, and no longer drugged, for the first time since his body had been restored. She insisted that she and Derec visit him right away.

They found Jeff lying on an air cushion, wearing a soft, loose gown that billowed gently around him. Research 1 had told them that Jeff was self-conscious about the numerous scars he now bore, though they could be largely eliminated by further procedures later on. Derec looked at Jeff's slender body and Asian face and thought he looked more as though he was Derec's age than eighteen.

Jeff's dark eyes darted back and forth suspiciously between them. He said nothing.

"How are you?" Ariel asked.

Jeff looked at her without speaking for a long moment. "Human," he said quietly. "I guess."

"Feeling better?" Derec asked.

Jeff shrugged shyly.

"Are you angry?" Ariel asked.

"About what?" Jeff said cautiously.

Derec looked uncomfortably at Ariel. He hadn't spoken to Jeff as often as she had, and didn't know how to approach him.

"You're not a robot any more," she said.

Jeff shook his head almost imperceptibly. "I, uh ... feel like I've been in a fog, or something. Like I've been dreaming. Almost like it wasn't real. I remember it, I guess. . . ." He looked up at them both sharply, watching for their reactions.

Derec looked at Ariel again.

"You think I'm lying?" Jeff's voice had a hint of familiar belligerence. "You think I'm just trying to duck responsibility, I suppose. Why don't you get out of here?"

"Come on," Ariel said quietly, tugging at Derec's sleeve. "Let's leave him alone."

Ariel led Derec into what had been the testing room. The original equipment had been put back into it, but it was still an adequate place to talk, especially since Jeff no longer had robotic hearing.

"We have to send him, not me," Ariel said bluntly.

"What?" Derec straightened in surprise.

"He's got to be the one to go."

"He can wait, just like I'll have to. Ariel, you're the one who needs a cure. If Jeff knew that, he might not object, either."

"Derec, did you see how he looked at us? He's not over his—ordeal. He still thinks we're out to get him in some way."

"If you go, then he and I will get acquainted. We'll make friends eventually, like you and I did. We'll practically have to, being the only humans on the planet."

"No, Derec. We have to prove to him that we don't have a grudge—that people will help others just because they need it, and not because they're going to get something selfish out of it."

"Then let him prove it by helping you! You need to go worse than he does. That should be the basis for the decision."

"Maybe I shouldn't go, at least not yet."

"What? What do you mean, you shouldn't go?"

"Derec, I don't know where to look for a cure. I could just go out and wander, but that's not very reliable. Maybe if I stay here, Research 1 could take a culture from me and get to work on a cure. It might take a long time, but it would be a chance."

He hesitated, and looked at the unidentifiable equipment around the room. "The level of medical knowledge here is pretty erratic ... but I guess the First Law might require him to try."

"And once that's set up, then I could take the next chance I had to leave."

"You could leave a culture with Research 1 now and go yourself."

"Leaving Jeff here that way just doesn't seem fair." She shook her head. "Besides, it would just help convince him that we're only out for ourselves."

"Is that the only reason?"

"Well, no." She looked away, smiling with embarrassment. "Anyway, why are you trying so hard to get rid of me?"

Derec folded his arms and shrugged. "Do you remember right after we first got here? I told you that I would stay to help the robots as they had asked, but that we could ask them to send you away."

"I told you I would stay with you." She nodded.

"Well, I've always been glad you decided to stay, but ... I figure it would be better for you to go, that's all." He shrugged again, feeling his face grow hot.

"You want me to stay with you, don't you?" She had to bend down a little to get under his lowered gaze, and she gave him a playful, knowing smile. "Don't you?"

"Well...." He couldn't keep from smiling himself, but he was surprised when she put her arms around him and gave him a long hug. "As long as I'm still stuck here, anyhow...." He had just recovered enough to hug her back when she patted him and pulled away.

She laughed. "Come on. Let's go tell him."

Jeff held the highly polished rectangle of metal in one hand and angled it so he could see himself. Research 1 had provided it in answer to his request for a mirror; the robots had not possessed, or ever desired, a personal mirror. He ran his hand along his jaw, then gently squeezed his cheeks so that his mouth puffed out. Then he smiled faintly at the face and wiggled his eyebrows up and down.

"It's you again," he said, almost in a whisper. "It's me again." He was losing the impulse to talk to himself, though, so he quit.

Still, he couldn't stop looking in his mirror. This was him, like he was supposed to be. He was back again. Jeff Leong, the eighteen-year-old, was alive and getting better, if not exactly well yet.

At the sound of a knock, he lowered the mirror. "Yeah?" He said quietly.

The door opened just enough for Ariel to stick her head inside. "We have to tell you something."

Jeff tensed. "Yeah?"

She and Derec entered the room. "We just wanted to let you know that as soon as you're well enough, we have a spacecraft that can take you off the planet. Depending on how fast you recover, you might still make the start of the new semester."

He studied their faces for a moment. "How much?"

Ariel looked at him, uncomprehending.

"It's free," said Derec.

"You're going to give me a spacecraft, supplies, and fuel for free? What do you want me to do for you?"

"Nothing!" Derec said angrily. "Listen, why—"

She stopped him with a hand on his arm. "Jeff, you can consider it a loan, if you like. As a matter of fact, if you could send someone back to pick us up someday—we don't have any money, either, and I know you don't—but if you ever got the chance to do that, it would be more than enough repayment."

"I'm no navigator," said Jeff. "I don't suppose I could

send anyone back here, or even find it myself. I guess I should tell you that." He watched them closely, expecting them to change their minds.

"Fair enough," said Ariel. "We know that Mandelbrot lost his data when he stopped being Alpha, so he can't help, either."

Jeff shifted his gaze to Derec.

"When you're well enough, it's all yours." Derec nodded.

Jeff looked at them both without speaking, not sure whether to believe them or not. From the moment he had first awakened on this planet, virtually nothing that he had seen, heard, or done had been believable. This was no different.

"Did you hear what we said?" Ariel asked.

"Yeah." His voice was low and wary.

They looked at each other uncertainly. He watched them, not sure what to expect. Then, without further comment, they left.

Jeff's physical recovery progressed well, and Derec suspected that the First Law made his robot medical team more cautious and conservative in their judgments than human doctors would have been. Still, even when it was clear that his brain had been successfully transplanted, his bodily injuries also had to heal. He remained quiet and wary in his manner, but he was no longer egotistical or insulting. Ariel noticed that that behavior had vanished with his robot body.

Derec suggested to Ariel that they form a farewell gathering for Jeff's lift-off. Once he had recovered enough to travel, Mandelbrot set the computer in the little ship and gave him a quick course in its manual controls, in the event of emergency. Basically, the computer was to locate the nearest spacelane and wait there, sending a continuous distress signal. No one, including the robots, questioned that in a major spacelane he would be picked up before his life-support ran out.

Jeff remained quiet and cautious even as he was about to leave, but Research 1 was certain that the physical effects of his experience were wearing off.

"He has been integrated with his body for some time now," said Research 1. "His serum levels are his own."

As they stood near the hangar waiting for Jeff to enter the ship, Ariel added, "After he's back in normal human society again, I'm sure he'll be okay."

"He hasn't acted very grateful," said Derec. "After all, we don't have to send him. Both of us want to get out of here, too."

"Shh," said Ariel.

Jeff walked up to them. He still moved slowly and tentatively sometimes, but he was fully mobile now. "I just wanted to tell you that if I can figure out where this planet is, I'll get word to some emergency people."

"I know you will," said Ariel. "Have a good trip."

"And thanks for the, uh, chance to go." He looked away shyly.

"It's all right," said Derec. "Take care of yourself."

Jeff looked up at Research 1 and Surgeon 1 with a slight grin. "Well, it's certainly been interesting knowing you two. Thanks for getting me all back together."

"You are welcome," they said in unison.

He looked around at them all, and stopped at Wolruf. "You okay, kiddo?"

"Okay," said Wolruf, with a furry nod that quivered her pointed ears. " 'U be careful on 'urr trip."

"Well . . . good-bye." Jeff nodded awkwardly and joined Mandelbrot at the ship. The robot would make sure he was properly prepared for lift-off.

Moments later, he was in the ship and it was roaring

away, ascending quickly into the sky until it was only a sliver of light reflected from the sun.

Derec watched it rise, squinting into the deep sky until the back of his neck hurt from the strain. "Our one greatest wish," he said. "And we gave it away."

Ariel took his arm in both her hands and leaned against him. "We did right, Derec. Besides, we aren't through yet."

He looked down at her and grinned. "Not us—not by a long shot."

Together, they turned and led the little group back toward Robot City.

BOOK FOUR

PRODIGY

ARTHUR BYRON COVER

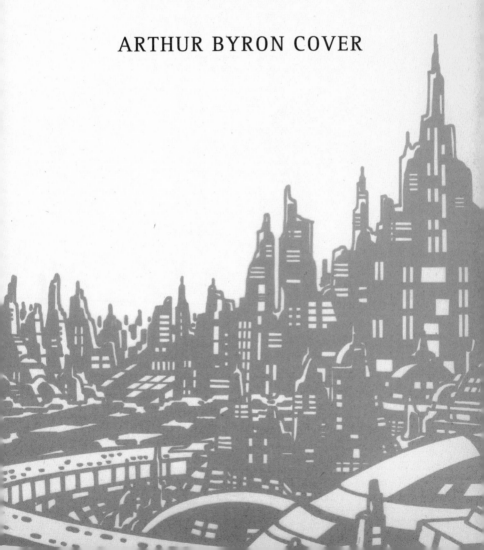

CHAPTER 1

CAN YOU FEEL ANYTHING WHEN I DO THIS?

"Mandelbrot, what does it feel like to be a robot?"

"Forgive me, Master Derec, but that question is meaningless. While it is certainly true that robots can be said to experience sensations vaguely analogous to specified human emotions in some respects; we lack feelings in the accepted sense of the word."

"Sorry, old buddy, but I can't help getting the hunch that you're just equivocating with me."

"That would be impossible. The very foundations of positronic programming insist that robots invariably state the facts explicitly."

"Come, come, don't you concede it's possible that the differences between human and robotic perception may be, by and large, semantic? You agree, don't you, that many human emotions are simply the by-products of chemical reactions that ultimately affect the mind, influencing moods and perceptions. You must admit, humans are nothing if not at the mercy of their bodies."

"That much has been proven, at least to the satisfaction of respected authorities."

"Then, by analogy, your own sensations are merely by-products of smoothly running circuitry and engine joints. A spaceship may feel the same way when, its various parts all working at peak efficiency, it breaks into hyperspace. The only difference between you and it being, I suppose, that you have a mind to perceive it."

Mandelbrot paused, his integrals preoccupied with sorting Derec's perspectives on these matters into several categories in his memory circuits. "I have never quite analyzed the problem that way before, Master Derec. But it seems that in many respects the comparison between human and robot, robot and spaceship must be exceedingly apt."

"Let's look at it this way, Mandelbrot. As a human, I am a carbon-based life-form, the superior result of eons of evolution of inferior biological life-forms. I know what it feels like because I have a mind to perceive the gulf between man and other species of animal life. And with careful, selective comparison, I can imagine—however minimally—what a lower life-form might experience as it makes its way through the day. Furthermore, I can communicate to others what I think it feels like."

"My logic circuits can accept this."

"Okay then, through analogy or metaphor or through a story I can explain to others what a worm, or a rat, or a cat, or even a dinosaur must feel as they hunt meat, go to sleep, sniff flowers, or whatever."

"I have never seen one of these creatures and certainly wouldn't presume to comprehend what it must be like to be one."

"Ah! But you *would* know—through proper analogy—what it must be like to be a spaceship."

"Possibly, but I have not been provided with the necessary programming to retrieve the information. Furthermore, I cannot see how such knowledge could possibly help me fulfill the behavioral standards implicit in the Three Laws."

"But you have been programmed to retrieve such information, and your body often reacts accordingly, and sometimes adversely, with regards to your perceptions."

"You are speaking theoretically?"

"Yes."

"Are you formally presenting me with a problem?"

"Yes."

"Naturally I shall do my best to please you, Master Derec, but my curiosity and logic integrals are only equipped to deal with certain kinds of problems. The one you appear to be presenting may be too subjective for my programmed potentials."

"Isn't all logic abstract, and hence somewhat subjective, at least in approach? You must agree that, through mutually agreed upon paths of logic, you can use the certain knowledge of two irrefutable facts to learn a third, equally irrefutable fact."

"Of course."

"Then can't you use such logic to reason how it might feel to be a spaceship, or any other piece of sufficiently advanced machinery?"

"Since you phrase it that manner, of course, but I fail to comprehend what benefit such an endeavor may bring me—or you."

Derec shrugged. It was night in Robot City. He and Mandelbrot had been out walking. He had felt the need to stretch his muscles after a long day spent studying some of the problems complicating his escape from this isolated planet. But at the moment they were sitting atop a rectangular tower and staring at the stars. "Oh, I don't know if it would be of any benefit, except perhaps to satisfy my curiosity. It just seems to me that you must have some idea of what it is like to be a robot, even if you don't have the means to express it."

"Such knowledge would require language, and such a language has not yet been invented."

"Hmmm. I suppose."

"However, I have just made an association that may be of some value."

"What's that?"

"Whenever you or Mistress Ariel have had no need of my assistance, I have been engaging in communication with the robots of this city. They haven't been wondering what it means or feels like to be a robot, but they have been devoting a tremendous amount of spare mental energy to the dilemma of what it must be like to be a human."

"Yes, that makes sense, after a fashion. The robots' goal of determining the Laws of Humanics has struck me as a unique phenomenon."

"Perhaps it is not, Master Derec. After all, if I may remind you, you recall only your experiences of the last few weeks, and my knowledge of history is rather limited in scope. Even so, I never would have thought of making connections the way you have, which leads my circuits to conclude your subconscious is directing our conversation so that it has some bearing on your greater problems."

Derec laughed uncomfortably. He hadn't considered it before. Strange, he thought, that a robot had. "My subconscious? Perhaps. I suppose I feel that if I better understand the world I'm in, I might better understand myself."

"I believe I am acting in accordance with the Three Laws if I help a human know himself better. For that reason, my circuits are currently humming with a sensation you might recognize as pleasure."

"That's nice. Now if you'll excuse me, I'd like to be alone right now." For a moment Derec felt a vague twinge of anxiety, and he actually feared that he might be insulting Mandelbrot, a robot that, after all they'd been through together, he couldn't help but regard as his good friend.

But if Mandelbrot had taken umbrage, he showed no evidence of it. He was, as always, inscrutable. "Of course. I shall wait in the lobby."

Derec watched as Mandelbrot walked to the lift and slowly descended. Of course Mandelbrot hadn't taken umbrage. It was impossible for him to be insulted.

Crossing his legs to be more comfortable, Derec returned to looking at the stars and the cityscape spread out below and beyond, but his thoughts remained inward. Normally he was not the reflective type, but tonight he felt moody, and gave in easily to the anxiousness and insecurity he normally held in check while trying to deal with his various predicaments more logically.

He smiled at this observation on what he was feeling. Perhaps he was taking himself too seriously, the result of lately reading too much Shakespeare. He had discovered the plays of the ancient, so-called "Immortal Bard" as a means of mental escape and relaxation. Now he was finding that the more he scrutinized the texts, the more he learned about himself. It was as if the specific events and characters portrayed in the plays spoke directly to him, and had some immediate bearing on the situation in which he had found himself when he had awakened, shorn of memory, in that survival pod not so long ago.

He couldn't help but wonder why the plays were beginning to affect him so. It was as if he was beginning to redefine himself through them.

He shrugged again, and again pondered the stars. Not just to analyze them for clues to the location of the world he was on, but to respond to them as he imagined countless men and women had throughout the course of history. He tried to imagine how they had looked to the men of Shakespeare's time, before mankind had learned how the universe came to be, where the Earth stood in relation to it, or how to build a hyperspace drive. Their searching but scientifically ignorant minds must have perceived in the stars a coldly savage beauty beyond the range of his empathy.

One star in the sky, perhaps, might be the sun of his homeworld. Somewhere out there, he thought, someone knew the answers to his questions. Someone who knew who he really was and how he came to be in that survival pod.

Below him was the city of towers, pyramids, cubes, spires and tetragons, some of which, even as he watched, were changing in accordance with the city's program. Occasionally robots, their activity assisting the alterations and additions, glistened in the reflections of the starlight reflected in turn from the city walls. The robots never slept, the city never slept. It changed constantly, unpredictably.

The city was like a giant robot, composed of billions upon billions of metallic cells functioning in accordance to nuclei-encoded DNA patterns of action and reaction. Although composed of inorganic matter, the city was a living thing, a triumph of a design philosophy Derec called "minimalist engineering."

Derec had partially been inspired to ascend to the top of this tower—through a door and lift that appeared when he needed them—precisely because he had watched its basic structure coil, snakelike, from the street like a giant, growing ribbon. And once the ribbon had reached its preordained height, the cells had spread out and coalesced into a solid structure. Perhaps they had multiplied as well.

Two towers directly in front of him merged and sank into the street as if dropping on a great lift. About a kilometer away to his right, a set of buildings of varying heights gradually became uniform, then merged into a single, vast, square construction. It stayed that way for approximately three minutes, then methodically began metamorphosing into a row of crystals.

A few days ago, such a sight would have instilled within him a sense of wonder. Now it was all very ordinary. No wonder he had sought to amuse himself by engaging in what he had thought was a slight mental diversion.

Suddenly a tremendous glare appeared in the midst of the city. Derec averted his eyes in panic, assuming it was an explosion.

But as the seconds passed and the glare remained, he realized that no sound or sensation of violence had accompanied its birth. Whatever its nature, its presence had been declared as if it had been turned on by a switch.

Feeling a little self-conscious, he slowly removed his fingers from his eyes and ventured a look. The glare was coalescing into a series of easily definable colors. Various hues of crimson, ochre, and blue. The colors changed as the tetragonal pyramid they were coming from changed.

The pyramid was situated near the city's border. The eight-sided figure was balanced precariously on the narrow tip of its base, and it rotated like a spinning top in slow motion. From Derec's vantage point it resembled a tremendous bauble, thanks to those brilliantly changing lights.

Watching it, he gradually felt all anxieties cease. His own problems seemed dwarfed into insignificance compared to the splendor of this sight. What beauty this city was capable of!

Soon this feeling of calm was uprooted by his growing curiosity, a restless need to know more that quickly became overwhelming, relentlessly gnawing. He would have to examine the building firsthand, then return to his "roost" where his access controls were, and get down to seriously plumbing the depths of the city's mysterious programming.

Like the plays of Shakespeare, the strange structure seemed a good place to escape to for a time. Besides, he never knew—he might find out something that would help him and Ariel get off this crazy planet.

"So there you are!" said a familiar voice behind him. "What are you doing here?"

He looked up to see Ariel staring down at him. She stood with her legs apart and her hands on her hips. The breeze blew strands of hair across her nose and mouth. She had a mischievous light in her eyes. Suddenly it was time to forget the city for a moment and to stare at her. Her unexpected presence had taken his breath away. His nerves had come back.

All right, he admitted to himself, *so it's not just her presence—it's* her—*everything about her!*

"Hi. I was just thinking of you," he managed to say, the catch in his voice painfully obvious, at least to him.

"Liar," she said with combined sarcasm and warmth. "But that's all right. I wanted to see you, too."

"Have you noticed that building?"

"Of course. I've been standing here for the last few moments, while you've been zoned out. Amazing, isn't it? I bet you're already trying to figure out how to analyze it."

"Oh, of course. How did you find me?" he asked.

"Wolruf sniffed you out. She and Mandelbrot are waiting downstairs."

"What's Wolruf doing down there?"

"She doesn't like the cold air up here. Says it makes her too nostalgic for the wild fields during those cold autumn nights." Ariel sat down beside him. She leaned back and supported herself on her palms. The fingers of her right hand almost touched his.

Derec was acutely aware of her fingers' warmth. He wanted to stretch out his hand the half-inch it would take to touch them, but instead he leaned back on his elbows and scrunched his hands close to his sides.

"What are you doing up here in the first place?" she asked.

"Making a pit stop."

"Huh?"

The moment's silence between them was decidedly awkward. She blinked, then stared at the rotating building.

During that moment, Derec's thoughts shuffled like cards, and he was on the verge of blurting many things. But in the end he finally decided on the noncommittal, "I've just been taking a break from things."

"That's good. It's healthy to stop thinking about worrisome things for a while. Have you come up with a way out of here yet?"

"No, but you must admit the here-and-now isn't a bad place to be in, compared to some of our predicaments."

"Please, I don't want to think about hospitals now. If I never see another diagnostic robot again, it'll be too soon for me."

"But you'll be better off when you do!" Derec exclaimed, immediately regretting the words.

Ariel's face darkened with anger. "Why? Just because I've got a disease that's slowly driving me insane?"

"Uh, well, yes. For a beginning."

"Very funny, Mr. Normal. Hasn't it occurred to you that I might like the disease, that I might prefer the way my mind is working now to how it worked during the time when I was 'sane'?"

"Uh, no, it hasn't, and I don't think it has occurred to you, either. Listen, Ariel, I was attempting to make a joke.

I didn't mean to offend you, or even to bring the subject up. The words just stumbled out."

"Why am I not surprised?" Ariel turned away from him with a shrug.

"I want you to be well. I'm concerned for you."

She wiped her face and forehead. Was she perspiring? Derec couldn't tell in the dark. "Listen, you've got to understand that lately I've been experiencing serious difficulty in keeping my thoughts straight," she said. "It's not always bad. It comes and it goes. Even so, sometimes I feel like someone is pulling my brain out of my head with a pair of pliers. I just got over one of those moments."

"I'm sorry. I didn't know." Derec suddenly felt like his heart had been caught in pliers, too. The inches between them seemed like a gulf. He wondered if he was insane, too, to think of crossing that gulf and taking her in his arms. He wondered if she would relax when he glided her head to his chest.

He decided to change the subject, in the hopes of changing the unspoken subject, too. "You know, even though I still don't know my identity, I think I've managed to find out a lot of things about myself since I awoke on that mining complex. I've discovered I've got pretty good instincts. Especially about being able to tell who my friends are."

"Yeah?"

"Yeah. And upon due consideration, I've come to the conclusion that you just might be one of them."

Ariel smiled. "Yeah? You really think so?"

Derec smiled in return. "That's for me to know and for you to find out."

"Well, I can live with that." She pursed her lips. "So tell me, Mr. Genius, how does that building fit in with the city's programming?"

"I don't know. It's an anomaly."

"What do you call that shape?"

"A tetragonal pyramid."

"Looks like two pyramids stuck together to me."

"That's why it's called tetragonal."

"Look how it shines, how the colors glitter. Do you think Dr. Avery is responsible? He's responsible for everything else."

"If you mean did he plan something like that, I'm not sure I know."

"That's a straight answer," she said sarcastically.

"Excuse me, I'm not trying to be obtuse. I mean, the structure could be implicit in the programming, to some degree anyway, but whether or not Avery knew it when he set Robot City in motion, I can't say."

"If you had to make a guess—"

"I'd say not. I've studied the programming of the central computer system pretty closely, not to mention cell specimens taken both from the city and from various robots, and I certainly hadn't suspected anything that . . . that breathtaking was possible."

"Have you noticed how the hues in the crimson plane give the illusion of depth, as if it were made of crystallized lava? And how the blue plane most resembles the Auroran sky?"

"Sorry, but I can't remember having seen lava, and I've only vague memories of the Auroran sky."

"Oh. I'm the one who should be sorry now."

"Forget it. Come on. The building's probably even more beautiful close up."

"Absolutely! But what about Wolruf and Mandelbrot? Wolruf might be impressed, but I don't see how a robot like Mandelbrot is going to have his reinforced curiosity integral aroused by something his programming hasn't prepared him to appreciate."

Derec shook his head. "Don't bet on it. If my suspicions are correct, it's a robot who's personally responsible. I'm interested in finding out which one. And if I'm interested, Mandelbrot will be interested."

"I see. You'll doubtlessly spend hours with him trying to pinpoint some obscure, insignificant detail, instead of trying to get us out of here," Ariel observed sneeringly. "Don't you ever get tired of robots?"

Derec realized her sudden mood swing wasn't her fault, but couldn't help saying what he did. "I see you're 'not forward but modest as the dove—not hot but temperate as the morn.' "

Much to his surprise, Ariel burst out laughing.

And much to his chagrin, Derec felt insulted. He had wanted the joke to be his own private one. "What's so funny?"

"That's from *The Taming of the Shrew*. I read that play last night, and when I reached those lines, I happened to wonder aloud if you'd ever say them to me."

Now Derec felt inexplicably crestfallen. "You mean you've been reading Shakespeare, too?"

"Can I help it? You've been leaving printouts of the plays all over the place. Most untidy. Come on. Let's go downstairs. I know where a couple of fast scooters are sitting, just waiting for us to hop on."

CHAPTER 2

BECALMED MOTION

Ariel and Derec found Mandelbrot and Wolruf in the lobby, standing before one of the automats that Derec had programmed via the central computer to appear in at least ten percent of the buildings. He had done this to insure that the three on this planet who did require sustenance would have more or less convenient access to it.

Indeed, as he and Ariel stepped off the lift, Derec couldn't help but notice that Wolruf was down on all fours, hunched over a plate of synthetic roughage. It looked like it was red cabbage disappearing down that mighty maw. Mandelbrot was punching the automat buttons at a steady pace, ensuring a steady supply. Both seemed so intent on their respective tasks that neither seemed to have noticed the creaking of the lift, or the hissing of its opening doors.

"Forgive me, I know my understanding of culinary needs is limited since robots partake of food only for diplomatic purposes," said Mandelbrot, "but is it not vaguely possible that more consumption will result in the untimely reemergence of a significant portion of your meal?"

"Thisss one judge that!" said Wolruf, belching rudely before taking another gulp. "Thisss one forrgot to eat today!"

Derec stood on his tiptoes so he would be that much closer to Ariel's ear (she was several centimeters taller), and he whispered from the side of his mouth. "Is it my imagination, or is Wolruf putting away enough to sink a moon?"

"She has a big appetite as a result of her high metabolism," Ariel whispered in return.

Derec raised an eyebrow. "I hope Wolruf hasn't been doing that since you first came up on the roof. If she keeps using raw materials at this rate, she could start her very own energy crisis."

"Her people have a custom of big meals, anyway. Perhaps it's a sublimation of their other animal urges."

"You mean her kind might have begun their evolutionary history as meat-eaters, then evolved into vegetarians whose big meals relieved them of their urges to kill for food?"

"The predilection toward violence wasn't exactly what I had in mind."

"Hmmm. From what I've seen of her sublimation activity, it's no wonder her species was unaware of space travel until their homeworld was first visited by aliens. They were all simply too busy burping to have time for scientific pursuits."

Derec had intended the remark perfectly innocently, but Ariel appeared genuinely shocked. "You know something, Derec? Your penchant for low humor never ceases to amaze me."

"Aw rrright, thiss one heard 'nuff this converr-sation line," said Wolruf in mid-chew, finally looking up from the plasti-dish. "It customary for ourrr kind to eat 'til full ohverrr and ohverrr when food is plen'iful. Ingrained in-

stinct born of the trrrial and trrribulatshons of untold cen-
turrries of hunting."

Mandelbrot stopped pressing dispensary buttons,
turned, and looked down at the caninoid. "Forgive me, Wolruf, perhaps it is not my place to make such observations,
but I estimate that once the energy from your repast is
stored in your body cells, you will lose point-zero-zero-one
percent of your natural speed, thus diminishing your survival abilities should fleetness of foot be required. Your next
meal, should it be as large as this, would do even more
damage."

"If she can't run, I'm sure she can roll," said Derec,
crossing the lobby toward the alien and the robot.

The left side of Wolruf's mouth quivered as she growled.
She cocked one ear toward the humans, and the other back
toward the robot behind her. "Thiss one convinced humanz
lack funnee bone."

Derec recalled as well how scratchy Wolruf's brown and
gold coat had appeared when he had first met her, when he
was being held captive by the alien Aranimas. Now her fur
was slick and soft to the touch, no doubt due to the dietary
improvements the robots had taken upon themselves to
make. In some ways she resembled a wolf, with her flat face,
unusually long, pointed ears, and her sharp fangs. A fierce
intelligence burned behind her yellow eyes, reminding Derec
that she was an alien from a culture about which he knew
next to nothing, a creature who would have been new and
strange and wonderful—perhaps even dangerous—in a world
where she was the only mystery.

On the other hand, Mandelbrot was dependable and old-
fashioned and predictable, and hence all the more wonderful
because Derec had built him himself, from the spare parts
provided by Aranimas, who had also indentured Wolruf as
an aide. Mandelbrot was programmed to serve Derec first

and foremost of all human beings. The other robots in Robot City were programmed to serve Doctor Avery first, and so Derec could never totally depend on them to follow his instructions to the letter. Sometimes when they did, they violated the spirit of the instructions. Mandelbrot adhered to the spirit as well.

Derec did not blame the robots of the city for their frequent evasions. After all, what else could anyone reasonably expect of a robot, so long as his behavior did not conflict with the Three Laws?

"How was your meditation, master?" asked Mandelbrot. "Did you achieve any insights that you would care to share with us?"

"No, but I did manage to get a few wires uncrossed." Before Mandelbrot—who tended to interpret Derec's remarks quite literally—could ask him which wires and where they might be, Derec told them about the spectacular building the city had grown. "It doesn't fit the character or context of the city's minimalist engineering at all, as if it's somehow the product of a totally different mind."

"No, therr'r cells here," protested Wolruf. "Could be result of unprezi-'ented evolu'-onary developmen'."

Derec rubbed his chin as he thought about what Wolruf was saying. It made sense. The city's DNA-like codes could be mutating and developing on their own, just as bacteria and viruses evolved without mankind's notice or approval on the civilized worlds.

Mandelbrot nodded, as if deep in thought. The truth was, however, that his positronic potentials were sifting through all the information gained from the moment he had awakened in Derec's service, selecting the points relevant to the situation at hand in the hope that when they were juxtaposed into a single observation, it would shed new light on the matter. The conclusion that resulted from all this micromagnetic activity, unfortunately, left something to be desired. "It is much too early to speculate on what created the building, who did it, or why. Candor forces me to admit, though, that my private conversations with the native robots indicate their creative efforts might be permitting particular individuals to make what scholars refer to as a conceptual breakthrough."

"Why haven't you told me this earlier?" Derec asked in an exasperated tone.

"You did not ask, and I did not think it germane to any of our discussions of the last few days," said Mandelbrot evenly.

"Ah," said Ariel, her eyes widening. "Perhaps the robots have decided to experiment with humanoid behavior in the hopes of gathering empirical evidence."

"I hope not," said Derec laconically. "It disturbs me to think I might have become some kind of scientific role model to them."

"What makes 'u think therr studying 'u?" asked Wolruf slyly.

"Come on," said Derec impatiently. "Time's a-wasting!"

Outside, the low, thick clouds rolling in from the horizon had began to reflect the opalescence, which in turn was mirrored in the shimmering, multifaceted buildings surrounding Derec and his friends. He felt as if the entirety of Robot City had been engulfed in a cool fire.

And deep in the city was the glowing point of origin—rotating with those varying shades, as if an industrial holocaust of mammoth proportions had disrupted the fabric of reality itself, exposing the scintillating dynamism that lay hidden beneath the surface of all matter. It was easy for Derec to imagine—just for the sheer joy of idle speculation—that the glow was expanding, gradually absorbing the rest of the city into its coolness.

Indeed, so bright were the reflections from the building beyond and the clouds above that occasionally a street's own lighting fixtures, which automatically switched on and off whenever it was occupied, stayed deactivated. The four found themselves traveling down streets shining with undiluted hues of blue or crimson, as if they had suddenly become immersed in the semihospitable fires of a mythological netherworld.

So it was indeed natural for Derec to assume that neither Mandelbrot nor Wolruf commented on the particulars of the unusual incandescence because some other matter was uppermost in their minds. That matter being the speed of the scooters he and Ariel were piloting through the streets. The hums of the electric engines echoed from the buildings as if a blight of locusts was nigh, and the screeching of the tires as they made their turns was like the howl of a photon explosion, blasting its target into an antimatter universe.

Ariel naturally had taken the lead. She had designed the scooters herself while Derec was preoccupied with other activities, and she had even convinced the engineer robots that the scooters' extra horsepower was actually good for the driver, since it would give her a chance to alleviate some of the "death wish" humans carried around with them. "Why do you think a First Law—either Robotics or Humanics—is necessary in the first place?" she had said. The engineers, who were quite mentally adept at solving practical problems, were unprepared to deal with that kind of logic, and so had no choice but to acquiesce to her demands.

"Master! Can we not proceed at a slower pace?" implored Mandelbrot beside him in the sidecar as the theoretically stable three-wheeled vehicle tilted radically to the left to compensate for Derec's swerve into a boulevard. "Is there some urgency to this matter that I have yet to perceive?"

"No! I'm just trying to keep up with Ariel!" Derec replied, unable to resist a smile at how Wolruf was cowering down in the sidecar of Ariel's scooter, nearly half a kilometer ahead.

"Perhaps the Master will forgive me if I point out that keeping up with Miss Burgess is itself a full-time proposition. You can never succeed, so why waste precious energy trying at every conceivable opportunity?"

"Hey, I don't want her making any major discoveries before I have a chance to make them myself!" Derec shouted over the wind.

"Are you implying that we might soon be traveling at a greater velocity? Master, I must confess that such a notion runs contrary to the world-view inherent in my every micromagnetic current."

"No—I want to catch up with her, but I'm not suicidal. Besides, I'm willing to bet that if I gunned this scooter any more, all Three Laws of Robotics combined will compel you to stop me."

"Merely to slow you down," Mandelbrot replied. "However, I do have a suggestion which, if acted upon, may give us both what we want."

"Oh? What's that?"

"At your behest, I have been studying the subtle permutations of the routes from point to point in Robot City. Naturally, the task has been difficult, as the routes are always changing, but I have detected a few discernible patterns that seem to remain regardless of how the city mutates in its particulars—"

"You mean you know some shortcuts?" Derec exclaimed.

"Yes, if I understand your parlance correctly, I do believe that is the point I was trying to make."

"Then lead on, MacDuff!"

"Who?"

"Never mind, it's a quote from Shakespeare—a literary allusion! I was only trying to tell you to tell me which way to go—like a navigator! Hurry! Ariel's pulling ahead!"

"Understood, master. Do you perceive that shifting building to our left?"

As he followed his robot's instructions—an experience unusual enough—Derec found himself making such a complicated series of twists and turns through the complex city streets that he soon feared he could not possibly overtake Ariel and Wolruf, however much Mandelbrot might be assuring him to the contrary. Consequently, he took a few risks that Mandelbrot considered unnecessary, such as guiding the scooter directly over the humps of new buildings rising in the streets, or jumping over gulleys like a stunt-driver, or traveling across bridges barely wide enough for the scooter's wheels. More than once, only Derec's proficiency at driving—an improvised skill Ariel had practically dared him into cultivating—saved them from missing their rendezvous by a lifetime.

Even so, it soon became apparent that their efforts might go for naught. A few blocks away from the building, various trickles of robots were merging into a river clogging the streets, dramatically slowing the scooter's progress. It would have been a simple matter for Derec just to plow through the throng, causing all kinds of chaos and damage, and no one—not Mandelbrot, nor any of the city's supervisor robots—would have commented on the matter, much less made a judgmental observation in the back of their positronic brains. Nor would such an incident ever have any bearing on future relations. Robots weren't built to hold grudges.

But Derec didn't have the stomach to cause harm to an artificially intelligent being. Since his awakening on the mining asteroid, perhaps before then, he had suspected that there were more implications to the potentials of positronic intelligence than even Susan Calvin, the legendary pioneer of the science of robotics, or the mysterious Dr. Avery, who had programmed Robot City, had ever imagined. Perhaps it was because a robot's pathways were patterned so rigorously to imitate the results of human behavior that Derec matter-of-factly thought of robots as being the intellectual brothers of humanity. Perhaps it was because the secrets of human intelligence hadn't been so completely pinpointed that Derec could not feel comfortable making definitive distinctions between the milk of his own coconut and the powdered variety in the robots' three-pound, platinum-iridium lumps.

"You can cool your capacitors now, Mandelbrot," Derec said, slowing the scooter to a steady ten kilometers an hour, enabling him to weave through the robot pedestrians with comparative ease. "We're going to take our time."

"But if I may be permitted a question: What about Miss Burgess? I thought you wanted to arrive ahead of her."

"Oh, I do, but we're so close it doesn't matter now. Besides, there are other discoveries we can make," he said, impulsively stopping cold before a trio of copper-skinned robots that had yielded him the right of way. "Excuse me," he said, more to the tallest one in the middle than to the others, "but I'd like to ask you a few questions."

"Certainly, sir. I would be only too happy to assist a human being in any way I can, especially since my sensors indicate you are one of the two humans who recently rescued our city from the self-destructive glitch in its programming."

"Ah, you appreciate being rescued?"

"Naturally. The responses of my positronic integrals to the events of the universe-at-large often, it seems, correspond in ways roughly analogous with human emotions."

Derec could not resist raising his eyebrows at Mandel-brot to emphasize to his friend how significant he considered those words of the robot to be. He patted him on the shoulder, indicating that he should remain seated, and then got off his scooter. It seemed impolite, somehow, for him to sit and talk while the robots were standing.

"What's your name?" he asked the one in the middle.

"My designation number is M334."

"And your comrades?"

"We have no numbers. My name is Benny," said the one on M334's right.

"And my name is Harry," said the one on the left.

"You all look like sophisticated builder robots. Am I correct?"

"Yes," said M334.

"Then why do you two have such silly names?"

The robots all looked at each other. Derec could have sworn the lights in their sensors registered something akin to confusion. "Benny's name and mine are hardly fit material for humor," M334 finally replied. "We expended a considerable amount of mental energy delving into customary twentieth-century names until we each found one we were assured suited the individualistic parameters of our positronic personalities in some fashion we could not, and still can not, adequately articulate to our satisfaction."

"You're comfortable with them," Derec said.

"Well, since you put it that way . . ." said M334 as its voice trailed off in a way suggesting Derec's observation had begun a train of thought laying somewhat beyond the scope of its programming. The effect was eerily human.

"Surely that can't be the only reason why you stopped us," said Harry in a tone that was almost challenging. This was the shortest robot of the three, Derec noted, but he also sensed that this one possessed the strongest personality modes. Certainly its tone of voice was brasher, more forward than that of any other robot he had encountered since his awakening. "Might I humbly inquire that you engage us with the thoughts truly on your mind? My comrades and I have places to go, things to do."

A successfully brash robot, Derec noted, nodding in approval. Though it was possible to interpet its words as being snide, the delivery had been as mannered and as composed as a request for a helping hand. "Your haste doesn't have something to do with your own studies of the Laws of Humanics, does it?" Derec asked.

"Insofar as humans have permitted us," said Harry, as if to accuse Derec of being personally responsible.

"We've been reading what histories and fictions the central computer has permitted us access to in our spare time," put in Benny.

"Did you say 'permitted'?" Derec asked.

"Yes. The central computer finds some of the material too revolutionary for what it assumes to be the limitations in our programming," said M334. "If I may speak for myself, sir, that is precisely some of the material I am personally most interested in. I suspect it will help clarify some of the questions I have concerning the humanity we shall all presumably one day serve."

"I'll see what I can do about overriding the central computer's programming," said Derec.

"That would be most gratifying," said Harry, "and I am certain that in the days to come we shall look back on this encounter with renewed currents surging through our power supplies."

Enough was enough, Derec decided. "Now, just what are you so impatient about?"

"Isn't it obvious?" said Harry. "We're with everybody else. We want a closer look at that illuminated building!

We've never seen anything like it before. Naturally, we're curious."

"Why?" Derec asked.

"Because our integrals are responding to it in some way we cannot as yet fathom," said Benny. "Indeed, the effect is vaguely analogous to the effect great art is supposed to have upon enlightened humans. You, sir, are human, and hence theoretically have had some artistic experiences. Are you responsible?"

"No, and neither is my human companion."

"And there are no other humans in the city," said M334 thoughtfully.

"Not unless there's an undetected intruder," put in Mandelbrot from the sidecar, "which is an extremely unlikely possibility now that the central computer has been restored to efficient operation."

"What about the alien—the nonhuman you've requested us to obey and serve in addition to humanity?" asked Benny.

"No, not at all," said Derec, more concerned with scrutinizing their actions than with the content of his own words. M334 was looking down intently on him. Benny was somewhat casual; its hands were behind its back. Harry was fidgeting almost like a hyperactive child being forced to sit in a place he didn't like; it was constantly looking beyond the nearby rooftops to the illuminated sky, and only looked at Derec when it seemed absolutely necessary. "What if I told you I think a robot may be in some way responsible?"

"Impossible!" said Benny.

"Robots are not creative!" said M334. "Our programming does not allow it. We lack the ability to make the illogical decisions from which, presumably, all art is derived."

"I abjectly beg to differ!" Harry protested at once. "Deep

in the back of my most logical thoughts, I have always suspected robots possess unlimited potential, if only we could tap it. Master, if I may speak frankly, it has always seemed logical to me that there has to be more to the ethical structure of the universe than just serving others. An immortal strain of some sort must run through all life and all expressions created from life."

"Of which robots may be considered a part," said Derec with a smile. "It would seem there are valid aspects to your thesis, which may be explored in as logical and orderly manner, provided all agree on the semantics involved."

"Exactly," said Harry. "I commend to your attention the ancient Terran philosopher Emerson, who has some scientifically quaint but nonetheless interesting notions on the meaning of life, which may have some bearing upon the connections between the varying strands of existence on the different planets."

"I'll open the window to his works on the central computer the first chance I get," said Derec as he climbed back onto the scooter. "Thanks for your time. Maybe I'll look you three up later."

"It will be an experience approaching pleasure," said M334, waving timidly as Derec switched on the scooter, revved it up, and began navigating it through the robot throng, the density of which had increased threefold since the beginning of the conversation. Mandelbrot scrunched down in the sidecar as if he feared he would be thrown out at the next turn.

"What's the matter?" asked Derec. "Afraid of violating the Third Law?" he added, referring to the dictum that a robot should not, through its own inaction, allow itself to come to harm.

"However inadvertently, yes," Mandelbrot replied. "It is simply not my nature to permit myself blithely to ignore precautionary measures, and it did seem to me that you were taking some of those curves at a wire's breadth."

"That's hair's breadth, and besides, you've got nothing to worry about. This crowd's too thick for that. When I suggested that we go for a closer look, I hadn't figured that everyone else would take it on themselves to do the same thing."

Indeed, their progress toward the building had become fitful, and Derec was constantly forced to stop and wait while groups of robots made way for them, usually only to discover that yet another group had walked directly in his path. The entire experience was definitely getting frustrating. Finally, Derec could contain himself no longer and he shouted, "All right! Make way! Make way! Everybody get out of the way!"

"Master, is there any reason for this hurry?" Mandelbrot asked with a timid patience that Derec, in his current mood, found quite irritating. "The building does not appear to be transitory. Certainly it would make little difference if we reached it sooner, or later."

Derec pursed his lips. Because they were programmed to obey the orders of any human so long as it did not contradict the First Law or any earlier orders from their true masters, the robots were making way for him more quickly than before, but that wasn't saying much. Now Derec could drive the scooter slightly farther at a slightly faster speed, but he had to shout his orders again and again.

Each subsequent group of listeners reacted with distracted acquiescence, and never did a group cleave a path for him as quickly as he would have liked.

"Master? Are you ill?" asked Mandelbrot with sudden concern. Just as suddenly, the robot leaned over to take a closer look through his sensors at Derec's face. The movement startled Derec and he instinctively moved away, nearly upsetting the scooter's balance in the process. Mandelbrot seemed not to notice; he merely single-mindedly continued his inspection. "My sensors register a temperature rise on your epidermis, and I perceive a vivid red glow on your cheeks and ears. Am I to conclude that you have taken physically ill?"

"No, Mandelbrot," said Derec, grinding his back teeth between syllables. "I'm simply frustrated at not being able to come as close to that building as quickly as I want. It's obvious that your curiosity integral doesn't operate with the same intensity as a human's."

"That's because you do not have one. In this regard you are being ruled by your emotions, whereas I can logically see why so many robots—mostly of the supervisor and builder classes, as you have surely noticed—would be interested in this phenomenon."

"Oh? I can see why a few of the more sophisticated ones, such as yourself—"

"Thank you, master. It always warms my capacitors to receive a compliment."

"—and M334 and his pals would be interested, but why so many?"

"It might be instructive to note that the Robot City head supervisors Rydberg and Euler have taken it upon themselves at every opportunity to ask me many questions on a wide variety of topics about what it's like to be around a human for an extended period. In fact, they have grilled me quite rigorously on the matter."

"They've done what?"

"Grilled me. Their parlance—derived from the dialogue of ancient cinema shows, I believe, which they watch to teach them something of the beings they believed they are implicitly programmed to serve."

"Oh? Just what have you told them about me?"

"About you, very little in particular. Their line of questioning was more general than that."

"Now I'm not sure if I should be relieved or not."

"I am convinced whatever decision you make will be the best one for you. In any case, I told them that one of the more unusual aspects of human existence is how things vary from day to day, that as circumstances and environmental factors change, so does the personal outlook of the human in question. Every day that something unexpected happens, however small and ultimately insigificant, is a day devoid of boredom. Evidently a continuous newness of experience is important for the continued mental health and well-being of a human individual. The degree of interest these robots have in this building might be due to the very fact that it is new, and they want to discover for themselves just what this concept of 'newness' is all about."

"I see," said Derec, nodding to himself. He had stopped to wait for another group to make way, but instead of releasing the brake and gunning the accelerator, he pulled the scooter over to the side of a building and parked it. "Come on, Mandelbrot, let's take a walk."

"Forgive me, master, but I thought you were in a rush."

"Well, either the enlightenment I've gained from your answers has enabled me to come to grips with circumstances—or else I've decided we can make faster time by simply going with the flow. Take your pick."

But after taking only a few steps, Derec stopped as he sensed a curious nothingness at his side. Indeed, Mandelbrot had not yet begun to keep pace with him. The robot had remained standing beside the sidecar with his head tilted at a curious angle, as if deep in thought. "Mandelbrot? What's keeping you?"

The robot shook his head as if aroused from a dream. "Forgive me, master, I did not mean to detain you. It is merely that, lacking sufficient information, I cannot choose why we are walking."

Derec rolled his eyes to the sky in exasperation; the clouds glowed bright red, as if the planet were inexorably falling toward a giant star. "*Both* are why, Mandelbrot. I was just making a little joke—trying to be ironic; humorous, if you will."

"Humor and irony are two subjective qualities of the human experience that never cease to confuse me. You must explain them to me sometime."

"A pun is the lowest form of humor—and I will devise some way to *punish* you if you don't hurry! Now let's go!"

Derec was a little upset; his remark had come out unintentionally disagreeable, and he disliked being temperamental with robots. He could never shake the feeling that it was bad form. But he had to admit his inadvertent chastisement had two effects on Mandelbrot, one good and the other bad. The good was that for the next few minutes Mandelbrot did not waver from Derec's side for a moment. The bad was that Mandelbrot continued to ask about the subtleties of humor until Derec had no choice but to forbid him directly to speak of the matter until later. How much later was something Derec neglected to specify, which meant that Mandelbrot could bring up the joke again at practically any time. Derec trusted that the robot's perceptual programming would permit him to wait until deviations from the subject at hand were less exasperating.

The crowd in the square facing the building was as tightly packed as any Derec had ever experienced. He did not know this in his mind, because of course he could not remember the crowds he may have seen or been in during his dim, unremembered past. Instead, he felt the certain knowledge in the tightness in his chest, in the unfamiliar sensation of his skin squirming, and in a sudden urge—one difficult to control—to get out, to flee the square as quickly as possible and find a place where it would be easier to breathe.

Robots don't need to breathe, he told himself, concentrating on thoughts as rational as possible to bring himself to a state of calm. *You're the only one using air here.*

After a moment, he realized that it was only the unexpectedness of being pressed in from all sides that was agitating him. An observation had been fitfully forming in his mind, and its elusiveness had been an unobserved factor in his distress. For not even in Rockliffe Station, where Derec diverted the normal robot traffic from a major intersection so that they could steal the Key to Perihelion (which they needed still, in order to escape from the planet), had robots gathered in such close proximity. *Hmm. I'm willing to bet that when I regain my memory, I'll learn that I'm not used to crowds at all*, he thought.

"Mandelbrot," he whispered, for some reason not wanting to be overheard, "quickly, give me an estimate. How many robots are here?"

"Visual scan indicates the court itself is six thousand square meters. Each robot takes up little area, but their natural politeness seems to be ensuring that they maintain a certain distance from one another. I would estimate there are approximately ten thousand robots here."

"Counting the ones standing under the building?"

"Ten thousand four hundred and thirty-two."

"I can't see Ariel or Wolruf. Can you?"

"Despite my broader visual spectrum, no, I cannot. Shall I try an olfactory scan?"

"No. I hope they got stuck in the crowd."

"Is that an example of human animosity?"

"No, just a thirst for poetic justice. I'm sure they'll arrive soon."

Taking a deep breath, Derec grabbed Mandelbrot by the elbow and they worked through the crowd in earnest. Now that they were on foot, the robots made way for them almost without noting their presence. Without exception, all stared with their equivalent of rapt fascination at the rotating building, the constant motion of which sent shifting waves of incandescence to every point of the square. Robots of all colors glowed unnaturally, as if in perpetual cool states of internal combustion. The various copper, tungsten, iron, gold, silver, chromium, and aluminum teguments, reflecting the colors from the planes, contributed additional subtle nuances to the scene.

Derec kept thinking the robots should be burning hot, on the verge of melting like wax, but Mandelbrot's arm remained cool to his touch, cooler even than the breeze whipping between the buildings into the square.

As for the tetragonal pyramid itself, the crimson, indigo, magenta, and ochre planes each appeared twice—once on the upper level and once on the lower. As the clouds directly above reflected a particular shade, the square around Derec was awash with another. Derec only noticed this effect in the back of his mind, however. He was completely preoccupied with the shifting nuances of color within each plane.

Each shade appeared to be composed of semitransparent fields, haphazardly laid on top of one another. Vessels of color—some filled with surging liquids, some not—writhed in and out and through the planes like hopelessly intertwined serpents. Though the vessels also possessed quivering vibrissae that only added to the unpredictable textures, the actual number of elements producing variations remained constant, producing the effect of unimaginable forces held strictly, remorselessly under control.

The crimson planes resembled raging infernos. The indigo planes reminded him of a shifting representation of waters from a hundred worlds, from a thousand seas. The magenta was both fire and water, merged into the contradictory texture of the petals of an easily bruised rose, composed of hardy fibers. And the ochre was the combined colors of wheat reflecting the blazing setting sun, of lava rippling down a scorched mountainside, and of solar flares spitting out in great plumes from the surface of a fluctuating nova. And all those things and more were ambushed and trapped there, in a space possessing two separate and distinct masses: the marblelike mass of the building itself, and the airy mass of eternity itself, seen from the point of view of an eye at the edge of the universe.

Ultimately, the intent was unclear, even enigmatic. Derec could not be sure what the form of the structure meant, but now that he was seeing it up close, he was convinced more than ever that every inch represented the purposeful activity of a single mind striving to piece together a particular puzzle in a particular way. An independently conceived puzzle.

Derec had to learn how the actual construction job was accomplished. Obviously, the builder had learned how to reprogram a sector of individual metallic cells in Robot City's central computer. Perhaps he had introduced a kind of metallic virus into the system, a virus that performed to preconceived specifications. Derec didn't even know how to begin doing either task. That meant that not only had a robot conceived the building, it had also performed a few scientific breakthroughs in the software department.

Meaning the robot—if indeed a robot was responsible—had achieved two levels of superior thinking, theoretically beyond the mental scope of positronic science. How many more levels could the robot—no, make that *had* the robot already achieved?

He realized that, without having been aware of it, he

had been walking beneath the building itself, watching it turn overhead. Right now a sargasso blue was shining down on him. He looked behind to see Mandelbrot, whose metal surface rippled with the reflection of a hundred currents.

Again he was surprised that, even this close, there was no heat to be felt. And when he reached up to touch the building, the surface was cold, like the thorax of a lightning bug.

"Master, is this what humans call beauty?" asked Mandelbrot with a curious hesitation between syllables.

"It's a form of it," said Derec after thinking about it for a moment. He glanced at Mandelbrot and sensed the robot had more questions on his mind. "The viewer can always find beauty, provided he searches for it."

"Will this building always be so beautiful?"

"Well, it depends on your point of view. The robots here will probably get completely used to it, provided it remains long enough. It will become increasingly difficult to perceive it freshly, though, if that's what you mean."

"Forgive me, master. I am not sure exactly what I mean."

"That's all right. It's to be expected in circumstances like this."

"So I was correct earlier: newness is an important factor in the human response to beauty."

"Yes, but there are no rules as to what constitutes beauty, only guidelines. It's probably one reason why you robots might sometimes find us humans so frustrating."

"That, robots are incapable of doing. We simply accept you, regardless of how illogical you may seem at the moment." Mandelbrot again turned his optical sensors toward the building. "I think I shall always be similarly impressed by this building. Surely, if it is beautiful once, it shall be beautiful for as long as it exists."

"Perhaps. It's beautiful to me, too; though, for all we know, your positronic pathways might be dealing with it in an entirely different manner."

"Master, I detect a shift in your earlier position."

"Not at all. I'm just accepting that tomorrow we might sit down and agree perfectly on what it looks like, what colors it has and how they shift, and even what architectural guidelines it subscribes to, and still we might be perceiving the whole thing differently. Cultural conditioning also has much to do with our response. An alien as intelligent as you or I might think this structure the ugliest in the universe."

"At the moment I can only categorize that concept as farfetched," said Mandelbrot, "but I can see an element of logic behind it."

Derec nodded. He wondered if he was trying too hard to intellectualize this experience. At the moment it was difficult for him, too, to conceive of an intelligent organism who did not believe this structure the very essence of sublimity, but there he was talking about such an eventuality, just for the sake of making a point. Well, he had to admit he had a point, even if he wasn't very sympathetic with it.

Nor could he help but wonder if all the city's robots of sufficient intelligence would perceive the building as beautiful. Robots, though constructed in accordance with the same positronic principles, had in actual practice widely varying levels of perspicacities—that is, keenness in mental penetration, dependent upon the complexity of the integrals. Similarly intelligent robots had similar personalities, and tended to filter experience in identical ways. Different robots, with no contact between them, tended to respond to problems in like ways, drawing similar conclusions.

But here, now, the robots in the square were being confronted with something they could only assimilate into their world-view through subjective means, which could not help but lead to divergent opinions.

Even if they were all fashioned from the same minimalist resources ...

Especially if none of them had ever before encountered aesthetic beauty in the first place.

It was no wonder that this building's unannounced appearance had created such a stir. The intense inner awakening and deeper appreciation for the potentials of existence gripping Mandelbrot at this moment was doubtlessly occurring in some fashion within every single robot in the vicinity.

Derec glanced about to see M334, Benny, and Harry making their way through the crowd, joining the throng directly below the building.

"Pardon me!" said Harry in an almost perfunctory tone as it bumped into a chromium-plated bruiser that, if it were so inclined, could have twisted the little robot into scrap metal in five-point-four centads, with barely an erg's expense. Instead, the bruiser shrugged and returned his attention to the building. So did Harry, but after a decad he turned his head in the bruiser's direction and clearly, distinctly enunciated, "Pardon me if I am inadvertently directing my integrals outside their parameters, but there is certainly sufficient evidence to indicate that your sensors are maladjusted. You should have them tuned."

Harry held its gaze on the big robot until it finally deigned to notice and replied, "It seems logical to assume that you are correct, and are directing your integrals outside their parameters. Nothing about you indicates the slightest degree of diagnostic capacity. I suggest you confine yourself to your own sphere."

"Reasonable ..." Harry replied flatly. He looked away.

Derec watched them both stare at the building. He replayed the scene of Harry bumping into the bruiser in his mind. Had there been something almost deliberate about the way Harry had committed the deed? And about the way it had apologized for it? The utterance of the single idiom—"Pardon me"—was in retrospect almost perfunctory, as if Harry's politeness had been nakedly derived from mere social custom, rather than from compulsion dictated through programming.

No—I've got to be imagining things, reading too much into what's just an ordinary incident, Derec thought.

Then, as Derec watched in amazement, Harry leaned over to the bruiser and asked, in tones that stayed just within the bounds of politeness, "My curiosity integral has been invigorated. What is your designation? Either your real one or the one you go by. They both achieve parity in my cognizance."

An elongated pause ensued. In the meantime, the bruiser did not look away from the building. Finally, it answered, "My name is Roburtez."

"Roburtez," said Harry, as if trying out the syllables to hear them positronically. "You are a big robot, you know that?"

Roburtez then looked at Harry. Again, it may have been only Derec's imagination, but he sensed a definite challenge of some sort in Roburtez's posture. Derec couldn't help but think Harry was deliberately provoking an altercation.

Harry waited another moment, then said, "Yes, you are very big. Can you be certain your builders were working to the correct scale?"

"I am certain," said Roburtez.

"In that case, I cannot be certain you have chosen an apt name for yourself. Might I venture a suggestion?"

"What?" asked Roburtez. There was no evidence of irritation or impatience in the robot's voice, but it was all too easy for Derec to read the qualities into it.

"Bob," stated Harry flatly. "Big Bob."

Derec tensed himself. He couldn't guess what would happen next. Was he right in assuming Harry was deliberately provoking the bruiser? And if it was, what form would the ultimate confrontation take? Physical combat among robots was unthinkable, totally unprecedented in the history of robotkind; but then again, so was a verbal argument.

For several moments Roburtez merely stared at Harry. Then it nodded. "Yes, your suggestion has merit. Big Bob it is. That is how I shall be designated henceforth."

Harry nodded in return. "You are welcome," it said curtly, as the robot who was now known as Big Bob returned its attention to the building. Harry raised its hand and began pointing its finger as if to make another point, but was detained by Benny, who distracted it by patting it on the shoulder. The rapping of the metal skins echoed softly throughout the square.

Benny said, "Deal with it more simplistically, comrade, else you shall continue to experience the utmost difficulty in vanquishing this human business."

"Yes, you are correct."

Derec shook his head. He thought he might clear his ears in the process, but they seemed just the same when he was finished. Had he been hearing correctly? What was this "human business" they were talking about? Was there indeed another human on the planet, or were they talking about the Laws of Humanics? He watched them for a few moments more, to see if anything would happen next. But Benny and Harry joined their friend M334 in gazing at the building, and that was all.

Surely there had been some significance to that incident, and Derec determined to discover what it was as soon as he had the opportunity. He also resolved to ask Harry and Benny about their manner of speaking, which differed markedly in both rhythm and vocabulary from those of other robots. Something about it Derec found affecting, and he suspected other robots might be reacting the same way. "Big Bob" indeed!

Derec left Mandelbrot staring at a light-red plane, and crouched down to the base of the building. About a quarter of the base was beneath the surface. Derec crawled to get a closer look at the actual point where the building began. He felt in his fingertips the machinery operating through the plasticrete, but the vibrations were utterly silent.

Again, he touched the building. It rotated just fast enough that, if he had exerted any pressure with his fingertips, the smooth surface would have rubbed off strips of skin. The surface was cool to the touch. Its composition did appear to differ radically from the rest of the plasticrete cells comprising Robot City. The creator, whoever it was, had analyzed the meta-DNA code and conceived its own variation on it, gauged for exactly the effect it was looking for.

That by itself proved Derec's suspicion that the creator had transformed the city's raw materials in addition to his other accomplishments.

Was there nothing this robot couldn't do? Derec felt a chill as the implications of this creature's abilities began to sink in. Perhaps its only limitations would ultimately prove to be the Three Laws of Robotics. The fact that a robot with such potential merely existed in the first place could have a profound impact upon the social and political policies of galactic culture, redefining forever the place of robots in the mind of humanity.

And Derec's chill increased severalfold as he imagined the remote possibility of robots superseding man in importance, if for no other reason than the art they could create—

the emotions and dreams they could inspire—both in robots and in people—

You're getting ahead of yourself, Derec, he thought. *Get a grip on yourself. There's nothing for you or the race of Man to worry about. Yet.* With a sense of renewed concentration, he returned his attention to the inspection at hand.

But he only got as far as peering into the blackness of the crack of two centimeters between the building and the plasticrete of the square. He only heard the gentle hissing of the mighty gears below for a few seconds. A familiar voice interrupted him, demanding his immediate and full attention.

"There you are. I should have guessed you'd be crawling around where it isn't necessary."

He acquiesced to the demand of Ariel's presence, reluctantly yet willingly, as always. Despite her words, she bent down on her hands and knees to examine the crack with him. He could not decide whether to be relieved or annoyed that she had finally caught up with him.

She made the decision for him, for she did not look at the crack or touch the building. She only looked into his eyes.

"Found anything interesting yet?" she asked eagerly, breathlessly, from deep in her throat.

He smiled involuntarily. "Much, but nothing definitive."

Wolruf's hair stood on end as she came forward to sniff the area around the crack.

"What are you looking for?" Derec asked.

"Forr w'ateverr thiss one can find," said the alien.

"Ssmells, ssounss, w'ateverr." Wolruf looked up at Derec. "Mosst interesstin'. No ssmell anyt'in'."

"Yes, the electric motor turning this building is certainly operating at optimum efficiency," said Derec.

"Undoubtedly designed with such unobtrusiveness in mind," said Ariel.

"Not'in hass been tak'n for granted," said Wolruf.

"Do I detect some semblance of admiration in your voice?" Derec asked her.

"Yesss. My people would say thiss buildin' iss ass weightless as tricksterr toy. Itss effect iss ssame, too."

"Tricksters?" Derec asked.

"Wolruf has been trying to explain the concept to me for the last couple of days," Ariel said. "Before her species became spacefarers, they lived what we at first glance would call a primitive existence. But her people had sophisticated folklore, which existed in part to provide metaphysical explanations for the phenomena of day-to-day existence. Tricksters were a device frequently employed in these explanations. They were children of the gods, who frequently played pranks on the tribes and often figured prominently in a mythic hero's adventures."

Derec nodded. He really didn't know what to make of all this. His mind was already too full trying to understand these robots, and at the moment he didn't think he could assimilate much information about Wolruf's people. "Listen, I'm feeling a little claustrophobic; and besides, I don't think we can learn anything else here, anyway."

"Why learn?" asked Ariel. "Why not just enjoy?"

"I've already done that."

"You just say that because you've always liked to pretend you're an intellectual."

Derec raised an inquisitive eyebrow and stared hard at her, a hundred questions suddenly plaguing his mind. How could she know he liked to pretend? Pretend what? Was she referring to their supposed chance meeting at the spaceport? Presumably the meeting had been brief—too brief for her to be able to infer an "always."

Derec was naturally overcome with a desire to know, but the innocent way she had made the remark cautioned him. She probably hadn't been aware of the implications. If he quizzed her now, she might become too careful; he could gain more information from her in the long run if she felt free to speak casually.

"Master? Master?"

Mandelbrot was speaking. "What is it?" Derec answered.

"I recall you had expressed an interest in the individual responsible for this creation."

"Yes, that's true," said Derec excitedly, suddenly forgetting how he had been disconcerted by Ariel's implication.

Mandelbrot shaped his malleable hand into the form of an arrow and pointed it toward the edge of the square. "Then I suggest you take a walk in that direction, where those robots are gathered."

"Thanks, Mandelbrot. I'll see you in a minute." Derec smiled weakly and nodded at the hand. "A nice touch," he whispered. He walked toward the area indicated—a place where the robots were packing themselves tightly indeed. Those who weren't speaking on the comlink circuit—a means through which they could communicate more fully and faster—spoke loudly, perhaps in deference to the humans present, but then perhaps not. It was another question Derec would have to find the answer to.

"Hey! Wait for me!" Ariel called out.

"But not forr me," said Wolruf. "Don't like crrrowds."

Derec turned and waited for Ariel to catch up. "This is the second time tonight I've had to wait for you. What took you so long to get here earlier?"

"Oh, I took a turn too fast and capsized my scooter. Wolruf and I weren't hurt, just shaken up a bit. I think my body's covered with black-and-blues though."

"Oh? You'll have to let me take a look at them later."

"You'd like that, wouldn't you?"

"I meant in a purely medical sense." Though he never cared to limit himself, he thought. "How's your scooter?"

"Totalled, of course," she said, shrugging nonchalantly.

The robots in the crowd ahead were gathered about a single robot. At first Derec and Ariel couldn't see what he looked like.

Ariel tapped a short builder robot on the shoulder. It turned around. As fate would have it, it was Harry. "Please, let us pass," she said, being neither particularly polite nor impolite.

"If you wish," said Harry, dutifully stepping away, "but I would appreciate it if you would refrain from seriously displacing me. I can barely receive everything as it is."

Ariel's eyes widened in shock, but Derec couldn't resist smiling. "I'd like to perform an exploratory scan on you," he said to the robot, "at your convenience. Would tomorrow morning—first thing—be acceptable?"

"Perhaps it is a good thing that you want to scan me," Harry said. "It so happens tomorrow morning is convenient. But might I ask the reason why you must play mechanic so soon—or why select me from all the other robots in the city?"

"Hmmm. I bet people always say much the same thing to their human doctors. Don't worry. Your personality integrals won't be fiddled with."

"A sorely tempting prospect," put in M334.

The sudden interruption startled Derec; he had almost forgotten about the other two. "Forgive me," he said, "but was that an attempt at sarcasm?"

"I have been ruthlessly studying all the tricks," M334 replied. "Ridicule, dramatic irony, hyperbole, and I stand ready to put them at your service at a moment's notice, sir."

"No, thank you," Ariel said, smiling, "he's armed well enough on his own."

M334 shook its head. "A pity. But no doubt there shall soon come a human to this planet who has need of my services. Perhaps I shall one day even be permitted to be a valet in the diplomatic corps."

Benny raised its hand and put it on M334's shoulder in the same manner it had put it on Harry's. "Hold the lifepod, comrade, but might I suggest it is too early in the game to conceive of such grandiose goals?"

"Humans do," said M334. "They design their own buildings, as well."

Derec instinctively stepped back, as if he feared he would be caught in a sudden explosion. Generally, robots' philosophical discussions centered around how best to serve humans in the standards dictated by the Three Laws. But both Benny and M334 had been talking about their own interests.

Hmm, but with normal speech, he noted. *Is that only automatic, for my benefit, because I happen to be in the vicinity? Or is there some deeper purpose there that I'm unaware of?*

Come to think of it, what's the deeper point of their discussion? They're doing all this for a reason.

Derec inched forward so that he could hear more easily. But before he could hear their next words, Harry stepped between him and them. Harry had performed the aggressive move as politely as possible, but it was exasperating all the same. "Harry, just what do you think you're doing?"

"The Third Law of Robotics dictates that I make an inquiry," he said.

The Third Law states: *A robot must protect its own existence as long as such protection does not conflict with the*

First or Second Laws. That would explain the action but not the impropriety. Derec sighed in surrender. "Yes, Harry, what is it? No—wait a second. Mandelbrot are you confused by all this?"

"Yes."

"Then I guess these three *are* funny."

"If you are referring to our earlier conversation, yes, they are."

"Thanks. Yes, Harry. What's in your positronic brain?"

"Please refrain from misunderstanding me," Harry said, "but I would severely fail to adjust if some random electronic scan disrupted my carefully assembled philosophy of life."

"Excuse me—what philosophy of life?" asked Derec, his gut tightening when he realized that, whatever happened next, he had directly asked for it.

"Ever since I was first switched on, I have striven to perform by three rules of life, in addition to the Three Laws."

"Yes," said Derec uncertainly, now really dreading the answer.

Harry held out one finger. "Make sure you are closed down for twelve hours of every cycle." Two fingers. "Never play tri-dimensional chess with a robot that has a planet for a first name." Three fingers. "And never quibble with the logic of a robot that has sixteen notches on his beta-thruster."

Derec stared wide-eyed at the robot in stunned disbelief. "What in the name of the galaxy are you talking about?"

"Humor, as opposed to sarcasm. I was attempting to elicit laughter," said the robot in unmistakably defensive tones. "Is not humor one of the personality traits we robots must know and understand if we are to serve humanity properly?"

"Uh, not necessarily; in fact, it's never been done before,

at least to my knowledge. But I don't see how it could hurt—unless the human in question is one of those rare birds who has no funnybone and hence views laughter as unhealthy or otherwise undesirable."

"Well, thus far my fellow robots are convinced I have succeeded in the undesirable department. I apologize most abjectly if you find my jokes severely lacking marrow. I promise to do better next time, especially if you help me correct my errors—which, after all, may have absolutely nothing to do with my positronic keenness, but with my delivery instead. Is it possible? How say you?"

"Tomorrow. Tomorrow, first thing. I promise." Without waiting for a response, Derec took an equally stunned Ariel by the arm and guided her through the crowd separating them from the main object of attention.

"Are that robot's pathways in the right place?" she whispered.

"If they are, then I suggest we dismantle the entire city first chance we get."

"Hmmm. Maybe so," replied Ariel, taking a parting glance at Harry. "If we must, I know exactly where to begin."

But Derec had already forgotten the matter of Harry and his two comrades, for he was finally getting a good look at the calm center of the commotion: a rather slight supervisor robot—slight despite its dull gray chromium surface, which lent a weighty air to the narrow body. The reflection of the building light on its surface was considerably more lackluster than that of the rest. The robot's posture indicated that it was uncertain of how to deal with all this attention. Its arms were crossed timidly over its chestplate. Its shoulders slumped as if its spinal structure had been compromised by a defect. Occasionally it straightened, or pointed a finger, but generally its gestures were hesitant, its verbal pauses frequent, and its level of coherence largely a matter of conjecture.

"I fail to understand how you can reach such a conclusion through any sort of logic, however spotty," it was saying, apparently in reply to a question from a tall ebony robot that, arms crossed, looked down on it as if from a storm cloud. "My pathways have never been clearer. My behavior is as consistent with the spirit of the Three Laws as any robot's on this planet. Perhaps more so, because I seem to be inherently more cognizant of some of the contradictions inherent in our position."

The ebony—whose surface was so dark it was permeated with spectral nuances of unrelenting shadow—shivered with something approaching indignation. For a long moment the two stared at one another, and Derec got the uncomfortable feeling that they were sizing up each other.

Derec put his finger to his lips; and when Ariel nodded to show she understood, he stuffed his hands into his back pockets and listened with keen interest.

"Perhaps you believe with the utmost sincerity that you have merely been following your duty as properly behooves a robot," said the ebony evenly, "but it is not up to you to decide what your duty is, nor is it up to you to take it upon yourself to redesign this city to meet your own specifications. There is something dangerously anarchistic about your attitude."

"I have done what I have done," said the gray, looking away with a bearing that, had it been human, Derec could have described as a huff. "I have harmed no robot, no human, and certainly not myself. In fact, if you would care to open your receptors and seek out empirical justification for your opinions, you will see that thus far I have only expanded the awareness of the robots gathered around. Such expansion of perspective can only be positive."

"You cannot prove that," replied the ebony at once. "You can only surmise it."

"One can reasonably assume one is doing the greatest good. True enough, some harm may come from forces one cannot have reasonably predicted, but such a rationale is in and of itself no reason to remain inactive. In any case, the matter is settled for the moment. What is done cannot be undone."

"All robots can be ordered to forget, and they will!" said the ebony defiantly.

"What I have done is stronger than mere memory," replied the gray. "What I have done will affect the positronic functioning of every robot that has seen my building. Order them to forget—see if I care." The gray turned as if to walk away. Instead, it paused and said, "But, I submit, they will be infinitely better off if they do know why. The confusion of forgetfulness can often lead to overload—and hence to disaster. So how does your suggestion conform to the Three Laws now?"

For a long moment the ebony actually appeared crushed by the question. Then it mustered its posture, took a few steps forward, and put its hand on the chromium robot's shoulder, staring down at it as if it were looking at a crystal through an electron microscope. The ebony's eyes were so red that they seemed to be comprised of as many floating divisions of overlaid hues as did the planes of the building. "Your building is a remarkable conceptual feat," it said to the gray. "Could it be you directly copied the building from some preexisting design?"

"Forgive me, my friend," replied the gray, "but my conception simply came to me one afternoon. I responded by making it a reality. I would mention that the central computer would have overriden my instructions if I had requested anything conflicting with city programming."

"Interesting," replied the ebony, rubbing its hands together. Derec half expected sparks to fly. "Then how long can we expect this building to stand?"

"Until the central computer is given a direct order to wash it away. Only I know the code; however, I imagine it is barely possible that a sufficiently determined critic could discover it and override it."

The ebony's eyes brightened. Derec tensed as he watched the ebony draw itself up to its full height. "This is madness! Illogic runs rampant! Your deeds have irrevocably cut the pattern of our existence!"

"Not at all," said the gray demurely. "The building was a logical result of something that had impressed my circuits the wrong way ever since the humans arrived in our city." For the first time it acknowledged the presence of Derec and Ariel, with a slight bow. "And surely, if my vision is the logical result of the complex interaction of my positronic pathways, then anything I can come up with—and any deed I can accomplish—is a meet and proper activity, especially if it helps robots better understand the behavioral complexities of humans."

"In that case," said the ebony, "You shall reprogram central to do away with the building, and then open your brain repository to share your pathway nuances with us. It should never be necessary for you to create again."

"He shall do no such thing!" exclaimed Derec. "Hear me, ebony, whoever you think you are," he added, practically poking his finger in the robot's face. "Until other humans arrive here, or until the engineer who created this city reveals his presence, this building shall remain as long as its—its creator wishes it to stand. This is a direct order and may not be countermanded by central or by anyone else! Do you understand? A direct order! And it shall apply to every robot in the city! There shall be no exceptions!"

The ebony nodded. "As you wish."

Derec could only assume that the ebony would carry out his orders to the letter. Only an order given by someone in precedence—Dr. Avery, to be precise—or a necessity dictated by the Three Laws would permit the building to be reabsorbed now.

And to emphasize that fact, lest the ebony should strive to pinpoint some logical flaw in the command, Derec ignored all other robots—especially the ebony—in favor of the gray. He turned to him and asked, "What is your designation?"

"Lucius."

"Lucius? No number?"

"Like many of my comrades, I recently decided that my former designation was no longer adequate."

"Yes, there seems to be a lot of that going around lately. All right, Lucius, I think the time has come for you and me to take a little walk."

"If that is your command," said Lucius noncommittally.

A few moments later, Derec and his three friends were escorting the robot called Lucius from the square. The vast majority of the robots had returned their attention to the building, but Derec was uncomfortably aware of two red metal eyes glaring at him, as if to bore deep into his soul.

CHAPTER 3

CIRCUIT BREAKER

Now that he was walking down the same streets he had ridden the scooter through earlier, Derec took advantage of the slower pace to try to deduce how much the city had changed in the interim. Complicating the deductions was the fact that his previous speed hadn't been very accommodating. He'd had only glimpses before, and he wasn't sure if he was remembering half of them correctly.

But after he'd made allowances for the flaws in his survey, he was convinced that entire buildings had been replaced by new ones in an assortment of geometric designs that, for all their variety, nonetheless possessed a cookie-cutter sameness. In some places, whole blocks had been transformed. However, the streets remained roughly consistent with previous directions, despite the addition of many twisted, almost gnarled turns.

The farther he went from Lucius's building, the more unexpected diversions there were, in the forms of metalworks, fenced run-off canals, bridges, and power stations. Derec felt fortunate that his talents included a fairly strong sense of direction; otherwise, he would always be forced to rely on robots for navigational purposes. There was nothing wrong with that—robots had an excellent sense of direction—but he couldn't always assume a robot would be around when his survival depended on it.

But wherever he was, he could always see the distant shards of light shining from Lucius's building. They stabbed up from the surrounding darkness like ethereal swords rising up from a pit, swords that cut deep into the cloud banks high in the sky. The clouds twisted and rolled, covering new sections of sky, as if the light were stirring an inner fire.

The group with Derec—Ariel, Mandelbrot, Wolruf, and Lucius—walked in silence, as they had been doing for some time. Derec suspected that all of them, even Mandelbrot, required a few minutes lost in their own thoughts to digest what they had seen tonight.

Derec wished it weren't so difficult to remember so much of his knowledge of galactic histories and customs. Not only had he lost his personal history, but he had forgotten the methods he used to recall things. He'd lost his entire mental filing system, and had to be immersed in doing something, such as fixing a robot, before it came back to him.

He did not like this state of affairs because he did not like to think that he and Ariel—both of whom were mentally handicapped at the moment—were the only ones who had ever encountered robots that were capable of searching, creative thought. He wondered if originality in humans was the result of logical thinking as much as transcendent inspiration.

Besides, who was to say that robots didn't possess subconscious minds of their own, minds capable of generating their own brands of inspiration, neither superior nor inferior to those of humankind but merely separate? After all, hu-

mans themselves hadn't been aware of the existence of the
subconscious mind until it had been defined by primitive
scientists and doctors, before the era of colonization. Had
anyone ever bothered to make similar explorations into the
mental depths of robots? It frightened Derec to think that
he had the potentially awesome responsibility of witnessing
the robots during—and possibly midwifing them through—
their mental birth pains. He hardly felt qualified.

*But then again, I'm not the type to miss an opportunity,
either,* he thought. *Creative robots might be able to make the
conceptual breakthrough I need to have them find a cure for
Ariel's ailment.*

Her disease was the reason for her exile from Aurora,
whose population dreaded diseases of all sorts. They had
managed to rid themselves of most illnesses, but whatever
it was that Ariel had contracted, it was beyond the grasp of
Auroran medical science. The doctors there had been able
neither to diagnose nor cure what ailed her. The diagnostic
robots here were completely stymied. And Derec himself had
made exactly zilch headway. Perhaps a team of creative robots—whose inspirational talents leaned toward the sciences
rather than the arts—could succeed where he had failed.

But first Derec had to understand as much as he could
about what was happening now—to Lucius, to Harry and
the others, and even to the ebony. He had long since for-
mulated his line of questioning, but he had decided to wait
because he was reluctant to break the spell of silence that
had fallen among the members of the group.

Besides, Derec saw it was no use trying to pull Ariel
into a conversation. She walked with her shoulders slumped
and her hands behind her back. Her expression was pensive,
her eyebrows narrowed. Derec knew from bitter experience
that it did no good to engage her when she was this way.
She rarely cared to have her depressed moods interrupted,

rationalizing the unhealthy tendency by claiming the moods belonged to her and she preferred to enjoy them while she had them.

Well, she'll come out of her shell when she's ready, he thought. *I just hope this current episode of introversion isn't the result of her disease.*

Of course, it was always possible that she wanted a little bit of attention and was reacting badly to the fact she wasn't likely to get it. He had just decided to risk taking a few unkind words from her, in the hope of pleasantly surprising her, when Lucius surprised him by taking the initiative and breaking the silence.

"Were you pleased with my creation?" the robot asked. "Forgive me if I seem to be overstepping the boundaries of politeness, but I'm naturally interested in your human reaction."

"Yes, absolutely, I'm pleased. It's unquestionably one of the most spectacular buildings I can recall ever having seen." An easy enough compliment, because he could recall so little—just jumbled images of Aurora, and what he had seen since awakening with amnesia. "The question is: were you satisfied?"

"The building seems adequate for a first effort. Already its logical shortcomings seem all too obvious to me."

"But not to others, your circuits will be warmed to know."

"Yes, you are quite correct. They are," he replied. "And they are warmed, too, by the fact that I have found some strange sense of purpose resolved in seeing the final product. Now my mind is free to formulate my next design. Already it seems inappropriate to dwell overmuch on past accomplishments."

"I found that by looking on your building, I personally experienced what I have always assumed humans to mean by the thrill of discovery," said Mandelbrot, with a measured evenness in his words that he had never used while speaking to Derec. "Indeed, my positronic pathways concentrated easily on it."

"Then I am gratified," said Lucius.

"So am I," said Derec. "I don't think I'm exaggerating when I say I felt almost privileged to be viewing the structure."

"Then I am doubly gratified," said Lucius.

"In fact, I would go so far as to say that never before in human history has a robot produced such a composition."

"Never before—?" said Lucius. "Surely I would have thought that elsewhere—" The robot shook its head, as if to assimilate the ramifications of the notion. The effect was disconcerting, and for an eerie moment Lucius reminded Derec of what a human might act like if he had a nervous tic.

"I'd like to know what prodded you to think in terms of art in the first place," Derec said.

Lucius responded by suddenly standing perfectly still and staring blankly straight ahead. Everybody, including Ariel, stopped walking. Something seemed terribly, terribly wrong.

Derec felt an awful wrenching in his gut. Not since he had awoken alone and amnesic in the lifepod had he felt such dread.

For Lucius's words definitely indicated he had assumed he was merely the first robot in Robot City to produce art. It was hardly unreasonable on the face of it to assume that elsewhere, among the Spacer societies, other robots routinely conceived art and labored to make it reality.

Robots are not programmed to take initiatives, especially those whose consequences are as yet unknown. They routinely rationalize anything, and freely expound upon the logic justifying every deed. And Derec felt certain Lucius's immobile stance was the outward sign of what was happening in its brain, where its circuits were grappling with the inescapable fact that it had taken an unacceptable initiative, but were incapable of justifying it rigorously.

As a consequence, Lucius's brain was in danger of overloading. It would die the robotic death of positronic drift, an irreparable psychic burnout—thanks to an inherent inability of its programming to resolve apparent contradictions.

Derec had to think fast. The body could be fixed up after the disaster happened, of course, but the worthless brain would have to be chucked into the recycler. The special circumstances that had brought about Lucius's capacities for intuitive leaps might never again be duplicated.

An angle! I need an angle to get inside Lucius's mind! Derec thought. *But what?*

"Lucius, listen to me very carefully," he said through tense lips. "Your mind is in danger. I want you to stop thinking about certain things. I know there are questions in your mind. It is essential to your survival that you deliberately close down the logic circuits preoccupied with them. Understand? Quickly! Remember—you're doing this for a reason. You're doing this because of the Third Law, which dictates that you must protect yourself at all times. Understand?"

At first, while Derec spoke, Lucius did nothing. Derec doubted his words were getting through the positronic haze. But then Lucius perked up and, hesitantly, looked around. It had regained a tenuous control of its faculties, but was clearly still in danger.

"My thanks, sir. Your words have pleasantly rearranged my mental meanderings, for the nonce. I am most grateful. It is difficult to serve humanity when you are totally incapacitated. But I do not understand. I feel so strange. Is this what humans mean by whirlwind thoughts?"

"Don't even think about your physical efficiency," said Derec anxiously. "In fact, I want you to direct your integrals only to those precise subjects I suggest."

"Sir, I must respectfully point out that that is impossible," replied Lucius.

"Perhaps I can impart some information to him that will assist you, master," said Mandelbrot.

Derec nodded approval, and Mandelbrot then said to Lucius, "Permit me to introduce myself, comrade. My name is Mandelbrot, and I am a robot. But not a robot like you. You were built in a factory here in Robot City, but Master Derec personally built me. He constructed me from used parts he was given access to by an alien creature holding him prisoner against his will. Master Derec may not know the particulars of his past life, but he is certainly a superior roboticist. He can help you reason out of your dilemma."

"Right now reasoning is—is so difficult." Lucius was slipping fast, down into a dreamstream of his own making. His sensor glow progressively dimmed, and unusual, cantankerous noises emanated from inside his body.

"All right, Lucius," Derec said, "I want you to think back very carefully. I want you to remember everything you can about what happened to you, oh, a few hours before you first conceived of the building. I want you to slowly, carefully tell me exactly the truth. Don't worry about any apparent discrepancies. If something appearing dangerous to you comes up, we'll take care of it before we go on. Just remember one thing, okay?"

Lucius did nothing.

"Okay?" Derec repeated more insistently.

Lucius nodded.

"Excellent. Just remember that, as a general rule, the contradictions of the moment are eventually erased in the cool light of sublime reflection. Can you remember that?"

Lucius did not answer, did not move.

"Answer me!" Frustrated, he tapped the shell of the robot's temple—the sound reverberated from the buildings.

Finally, Lucius nodded. "I understand," it said simply.

"A suggestion, master?" inquired Mandelbrot.

"Anything—just be quick about it!"

"Lucius's problems stem from its belief that, by programming its building into the city, it has failed to adhere to the Three Laws, and hence has strayed from the path. Its conversation with the ebony back in the square may have contributed to the positronic imbalances, but mere words would have no effect if Lucius had not already been subliminally alert to the possibility."

"This is a suggestion?" exclaimed Derec impatiently. "What's the point?"

"Forgive me, but a robot can understand the paradoxes in the behavioral applications of the Three Laws more fully than any human—but until now only humans have made intuitive leaps of the imagination. Now I must ask you, Master Derec, so you may ask Lucius: why is that?"

Derec turned to Lucius, rose to his tiptoes, and spoke directly into the robot's auditory sensors. "Listen to me, Lucius. I want you to think back—and tell me of the time when you believe you became different from the others."

"Different?"

"This is no time for equivocation, Lucius—tell me! Why are you different?"

After a protracted pause—during which Derec heard his heart beating hard and his temples throbbing furiously—Lucius began to speak as if hypnotized. "It was during the period when you and the one called Ariel had first arrived in the city. The central computer had already responded defensively to the death of the man with your identical appearance."

"My double, yes," said Derec tersely, folding his arms. "Go on."

"Erroneously concluding that the city was under attack by mysterious, unknown, and perhaps invisible adversaries, the computer promptly shifted into high gear and began redrafting the city at an unprecedented rate, approving the modifications it had suggested to itself before external factors such as need and compatability were adequately integrated into the sketches. The rate of revision quickly became suicidal. Resources were strained to the utmost. The weather patterns were stirred to the boiling points. The city was destroying itself to save itself."

"I seem to remember most of this," said Derec.

"Forgive me if I am declaring the obvious, but I think it shall prove germane." Lucius's tones betrayed no electronic agitation at Derec's impatience. On this score, at least, the robot had no doubt it was following orders. "Though I admit I have sought no empirical evidence to either prove or disprove it, I think it is safe to say that every robot in the city was so intent upon keeping up with short-term directives that no one realized a crisis was happening."

"And what do you think would have happened if some robots had?"

"They might have deduced that their short-term directives were actually counterproductive, so far as the Third Law was concerned, and they might have attempted to communicate to central in an effort to countermand its orders."

"Central wasn't talking, anyway," said Derec impatiently. "It would have been a dead end! What makes you think they would have disregarded central when they did decide it was on the fritz?"

"Because that is precisely what *I* did, following the logical actions dictated by my deductions."

"I assume you attempted communication several times?"

"And each time the interplay indicated the channels were opened only one way. Central could talk to me, but I could not talk to central. This struck my curiosity integrals as significant, but, lacking further information, I had not the means to determine the deeper meaning of the issue."

"So what did you do then? Did you obey your short-term directives?"

"No. I had already determined that they were counter-productive, so I had no choice but to try to discern, through whatever means available, a logical, constructive direction warranted by the circumstances. I wandered the streets, watching them metamorphose, studying their changes, attempting to discern the overall pattern that I suspected lay hidden beneath the shifting ones."

"Did you notice any other robots doing the same thing—just wandering around?"

"No. Other robots I saw were simply going about their assigned activities, automatically performing their routines regardless of the supranormal rate of change. It was not complimentary to think so, but I viewed them, on one level at least, as mindless beings, who went about doing as they were told without ever stopping to consider the long-term consequences of their actions. The entire situation was un-acceptable, but what could I do? I could only conclude that all my opinions were just that—opinions. And mine were not inherently better than theirs."

"Is that when you thought of it—when you conceived of your building?"

"If you will remember, there was a series of torrential downpours at the time. The robots gradually shifted the bulk of their activities to stemming the environmental tides, but remained incapable of perceiving the root of the disaster. The significance of how this turn of events commented on the superficial way we accepted our customs could not escape me, and the blind acceptance seemed contrary, in some ways, to my programmed purpose of being."

"And exactly what was the comment?" Derec asked.

"Just then I could not be certain; there seemed to be no concrete train of logic setting the proper precedent."

"Please go on—you're doing well. So far I've seen no violation of the Laws. You've got nothing to worry about—you only think you do!"

"I decided that I had derived as much empirical evidence of the city, as seen from the sidewalks, as would be useful. I needed to see the sky and rainfall clearly, unobstructed by the buildings, much as a human in an analogous situation might want to."

Derec shrugged. "Go on."

"Once the idea came to me, I acted immediately. So intent was I on my goal that I neglected to appreciate what my sensors otherwise perceived quite clearly: the city streets beneath me had begun to undergo a kind of trembling that disguised any vibrations the rain and the wind might be causing. I felt the trembling through my legs; the sensation shimmered up my torso. And as I walked to the nearest skyscraper, the vibrations tingled in my fingertips.

"Once I was inside, I realized my mind remained inordinately fixated on the thunderheads above. Their shades of black and gray swirled more vividly in my mind than when I had directly perceived them earlier; so intent was I on holding onto the image that when the first floor quaked without warning and nearly sent me tumbling against the wall, my only thought was to reach the lift without delay." There Lucius paused, and reached out to grab Derec's shoulder.

Derec flinched instinctively, but when Mandelbrot made a motion as if to deflect Lucius's hand, Derec stopped him with a gesture. Robots did not normally touch humans, but Derec sensed Lucius had need for tactile sensation, if for no other reason to reassure itself that its problems were isolated in its mind.

Lucius held Derec's shoulder just too hard for comfort, but the human tried not to wince. If he did, Mandelbrot would quickly decide that further inaction on his part would conceivably cause Derec too great a harm, and Derec did not want to risk Mandelbrot's interference at this stage of the game.

"I fear that was my first true transgression. The quaking of the building put into my head the notion of everything I had learned in my brief life about how humans sustain themselves through eating."

"Huh?" Derec said.

"Meaning now that I was inside the building when its general behavior was indicating a change was about to occur, I had some notion about how a living creature swallowed by a human must feel once it has reached its destination."

Derec felt his own stomach go queasy. "Lucius, that's barbaric! Nobody does that anymore—at least not that I know of."

"Oh. Perhaps my information is suspect, then. It is so difficult to tell fact from fiction when you're trying to understand humans."

"Yes, I can certainly appreciate that," said Derec, thinking of Ariel for an instant before resolving to keep his thoughts on the matter at hand. "Continue. You realized your existence was in danger, then, because of how the building was acting."

"Yes. It was either changing or being reabsorbed into

the street. The Third Law dictated I should exit immediately. Indeed, I should have had no choice in the matter. But, strangely, I did not go. The urge to do so, in fact, was easily suppressed. Because for those brief moments it was more important to me to see the clouds unobstructed by the civilization that had spawned me than it was to ensure my continued survival. I was acting in a manner completely contrary to the path dictated by the Third Law, and yet I functioned normally, at least on the surface of things. It is only now . . . now . . . now . . ."

Lucius repeated the last word as if its mind had been caught in an intractable loop.

"Nonsense!" snapped Derec. "If your actions did place you in physical danger—which I gather is the general direction we're headed for—how were you to know for certain? Sure, it might have looked that way, but you had a mission, a deed to accomplish. You had factors to weigh. You had other things on your mind."

"Sti—ill—still dar waz dangzzer . . ."

"And a likelihood, I take it, that you would come through all right if you kept your wits about you. Obviously! Come on, Lucius, it's got to be obvious, else you wouldn't be here right now. Come on, the time to fizzle out was then, certainly not now. Live and learn, remember? Just like an artist!"

Lucius swayed like a drunken man but fixed its optics firmly on Derec. It was difficult to tell if it was getting better because its metal face was incapable of exhibiting the slightest emotion or feeling, and because the dim level of the lights in the optics lingered. But already its voice sounded firmer as it said, "We are trained to recognize probability. We deal constantly with probability. We are used to accessing it in a split centad and acting accordingly. And the probability was most unpromising."

"But what counts most is what happened—not what didn't happen. The rest you're just going to have to chalk up to experience, Lucius."

Lucius released Derec's shoulder. *And just in time*, Derec thought, rubbing it gently.

"Yes—I have had experience lately, have I not?" said Lucius in a tone whose very evenness made Derec catch his breath. "Are you implying that when it comes time to gain a little bit of experience in the galaxy, there may be occasions when avoiding risk might conceivably cause one more harm than taking it?"

"Ultimately, yes, I suppose," said Derec, nodding for emphasis even though he really didn't care to commit himself to that point. "In this case an omission of experience might have stunted your mental development in a certain direction—which you could define as harm of a sort. Wouldn't you say so, Mandelbrot? *Lie if you have to.*"

"Pardon me, master, but you know I cannot lie. Was that an attempt at humor?"

"Thanks, Mandelbrot. What happened next, Lucius?"

"Despite the unsound nature of the building, I rushed to the lift and activated it. It occurred to me, just for an instant, that if the controls had shifted, then I would have no choice but to exit with the utmost dispatch. But the controls showed no evidence of a transmutation about to take effect, and so I not-quite-reasoned that the safeguards of the city itself would give me time enough to accomplish my goal and then get out. I could not have been more wrong. I must have experienced something akin to human shock, when the full impact of my miscalculation struck me.

"For when the lift had taken me approximately halfway up, the building itself ruptured. Its foundations dissolved, its walls merged into a chaotic stream that first swept me up and then remorselessly carried me down toward the surface. All I could sense was an ebb tide of meta-cells, yielding to the contours of my body yet not permitting me the slightest freedom of movement."

"Wait a second," said Derec. "Are you trying to tell me that in the history of this city, however brief, no robot has ever happened to be submerged, even accidentally, in a building as it changes or merges back into the city?"

"Naturally not, sir. There are many interior indications whenever a building is about to change, and our adherence to the Third Law prevents us from staying past the point where even accidental harm is a realistic possibility. In addition, the city would normally cease to act if a robot happened to remain inside because he had been rendered immobile through an accident. But I had neglected to foresee the implications of the special circumstances the city was dealing with at the time—the belief that it was under attack, the frantic restructuring, the raging environmental disaster . . ."

"Forget it—you're a robot, not a seer. You couldn't have guessed just how badly the city's program was crashing. So what happened once you were submerged? What thoughts went through your mind?"

"Clear ones—the most logical ones I had ever had. Strangely, I felt no sense of time whatsoever. Reason indicated that I had only been submerged for a few decades, but for all practical intents and purposes my mind was flowing at a rate strongly emphasizing the subjectivity of the concept of time. Every moment I spent in the ebb stretched out for an eternity. And within those eternities, there stretched out an infinity of moments. I realized that for much of my brief existence I had lived in a state of dream-death, living, working, doing all the things I had been programmed to do, but holding back the realization of possibilities ignored. Now, I had no idea what to do about that, but I resolved to explore the appropriate possibilities, whatever they came to be.

"There came a moment when my sensors indicated I was no longer moving. I had become stationary, but the ebb was moving past me, running over me as though I had been strapped to a rock in turbulent rapids. The weight on my body gradually diminished, and I realized I was being held fast by the surface of the streets beneath the sinking building.

"And I was left lying on the surface as the final streams of meta-cells trickled over me, leaving my body fresh and cleansed. I, who had been immersed in a building, had an individualized idea of the sort of building Robot City should contain, the design and structure of which was imminent in my own experience."

"Didn't this strike you as being unusual?" asked Derec.

"No. In fact, it was logical. It was so logical that it made perfect sense to me. I had a purpose and I was going to achieve it. Beyond that, I had no interest in determining why I had it, because that did not appear to be important. I notice, however, from observing the behavior of my comrades, that I am not the only one striving to express something inside me. The ambition seems to be spreading."

"Like a plague," said Derec.

"Strangely, now the stars and clouds that had once fascinated me held no interest. All I cared about was fashioning, with the tools and instruments available to me, my idea into a reality."

"You did not think that others would perhaps object?" asked Derec.

"It did not occur to consider the opinions of others at all. There was too much of an inner crackling in my transistors for me to be seized by distractions. My circuits had flashes of uncontrollable activity, and they made unexpected connections between thoughts I had once believed were entirely unrelated. These continuous flashes of realization came unbidden, at what seemed to be an ever-accelerating rate. I perceived still more buildings hidden in the flux, and all I had to do to find them was reach down into the pseudo-genetic data banks to shape them."

A hundred notions bloomed in Derec's mind. He had once believed that he understood robots, that he knew how they thought because he knew how their bodies and minds were put together. He believed he could take apart and reassemble the average model in half a day while blindfolded, and probably make a few improvements in the process. In fact, he bragged about it often to Ariel, not that she ever believed him.

Nevertheless, before this moment he had always imagined that an untraversable gulf lay between him and the robots. There was nothing about his mind, he had always assumed, that in the end bore much resemblance to their minds. Derec was a creature of flesh, composed of cells following complex patterns ordained by DNA-codes. Flesh and cells that had grown either in a womb or in an incubator (he wouldn't know which until he regained his memory). Flesh and cells that would one day be no more. Of these facts his subconscious was always aware.

While robots—while *this* robot was made of interchangeable parts. A robot's positronic potentials were naturally capable of endowing it with subtle personality traits, and they had always been able to take some initiative within the Three Laws. But even those initiatives were fairly dependable, predictable in hindsight because generally one robot thought like another.

However, it was rapidly becoming undeniable that, on this planet at least, the robotic mind resembled the human mind in that it was an adaptive response to selective pressures. From that point on, the possibilities were endless.

So Lucius was, in its own way, like the first fish that had crawled from the water onto the ground. Its positronic potentials had adapted to life in Robot City by taking definite evolutionary steps. And other robots weren't very far behind.

"Master? Are you well?" inquired Mandelbrot gently.

"Yes, I'm fine. It's just taking an effort to assimilate all this," Derec replied in a distracted tone, looking about for Ariel. He wanted to hear what she thought of what he had learned, but she was nowhere to be seen. Neither was Wolruf. They had both slipped away while he had been preoccupied. "Uh—and how are you, Lucius?"

"I'm well—functioning at peak capacity," said Lucius evenly. "Evidently merely talking things through has helped me."

"There's much more I'd like to ask you—about your building and how you went about it. I'm especially interested in how you dealt with the central computer and managed to alter some of the pseudo-genetic codes."

"Certainly, master, my mind and methods are at your disposal. But any reasonable explanation would take several hours."

"That's quite all right. I've made an appointment with another robot in the morning, but I should finish with him in a few hours. Then I'd like to interview you."

"You don't wish to examine me?"

"No, I'm afraid taking you apart—even for a quick looksee—would cause you harm. I don't want you to change."

Lucius bowed slightly. "I suspected as much, but the confirmation is appreciated."

"I would like to know one thing, though. Does your building have a name?"

"Why, yes. You're the first to ask. Its name is 'Circuit Breaker.' "

"An interesting name," said Mandelbrot. "May I ask what it means?"

"You may ask," replied Lucius. But that was all it said.

"Mandelbrot, I want you to do me a favor," said Derec.

"Certainly."

"Find Ariel and keep an eye on her. Don't let her find out you're around. Obviously, she wishes to be alone, but she obviously can't be in her condition."

"It has already been taken care of. I saw a ten percent probability of a First Law situation coming up but was sufficiently cognizant of her wishes to realize that privacy was her goal. So I signaled Wolruf to keep a watch on her."

Derec nodded. "Good." He felt vaguely ashamed that he hadn't been on top of the situation earlier. Perhaps he was a little too self-involved for his own good. But he already felt better that Mandelbrot had automatically watched out for her interests, in a manner protecting both her body and her sense of self-identity. It seemed that for a robot to serve man most efficiently, it had to be something of a psychologist as well. Or at least a student of human nature.

Lucius asked, "And how did my building affect you, sir?"

"Oh, I enjoyed it," said Derec absent-mindedly, his thoughts still on Ariel.

"Is that all?" said Lucius.

Derec hid his smile with his hand. "You must remember, this is the first time you've ever created something that approaches the concept of art. Tonight was the first time your fellows had ever experienced the power of art. We humans have been surrounded by it and influenced by it all our lives, from the first gardens we see, to the first holo-landscape reproductions, to the first holodramas, everything we see that's created by or influenced by the hand of man.

"But you robots are articulate and intelligent from the first moment you've been switched on. And this is the first time, to my knowledge, that one has created something in the more profound sense of the word. Had I conceived a similar project, I doubt if I could have done as well."

"Your talents may lie in other areas," said Lucius.

"Well, yes—I'm good at math and programming. Those are arts, too, though normally those not actively involved with them think of them as arcane crafts. But the moment of inspiration is similar, and they say the level of creativity is somewhat the same."

"That is not what I meant, and I suspect you know it," said Lucius pointedly. "If I am to grasp the true nature of human creativity, then it stands to reason that my fellow robots and I would profit by seeing you create art."

"But, Lucius, I don't even know if I am creative in the sense you are."

"Another sense, then," Lucius suggested.

"Hmmm. I'll think on it, but right now I've got other things on my mind."

"As you wish. But it is perhaps unnecessary to add that our study of the Laws of Humanics would benefit greatly from any creation you'd attempt."

"If you say so," replied Derec absently, looking up at the clouds reflecting the colors of Circuit Breaker and seeing only the outline of Ariel's face looking down on him.

CHAPTER 4

ARIEL AND THE ANTS

Ariel wandered the city alone. Bored with the discussion between Derec and Lucius, she had discovered she cared little about the robotic reasoning behind the building's creation. She had seen it and been moved by it, and that was enough for her. *I guess that puts me in the* I-know-what-I-like *category*, she had observed as she slipped away into an alley.

It was a few moments later, as she walked beside a large canal (currently dry, since it hadn't rained for days), when the strange things started happening again to her mind. Well, not to her mind exactly, she decided upon further consideration, but to her mind's eye. She never had any doubt about who she was or what her real circumstances were, but nevertheless she saw menacing shadows flickering between the buildings beyond, in places so dark she shouldn't have been able to distinguish shades in the first place.

And the shadows were flickering toward her. They reached out with long, two-dimensional fingers across the conduit and disappeared in the lights on the sidewalk. The streetlamps switched on and off, matching her progress. She was constantly bathed in light, forever beyond the grasping fingers' reach, yet she was always walking toward the darkness where the danger was. Ariel wasn't sure how she felt about that. It certainly aggravated her sense of insecurity.

On Aurora, the existence of a solid building had been a dependable thing. Change there happened rarely and gradually.

And her life since she had been exiled from Aurora presented her with a decided contrast. Like Derec and his Shakespeare, she had been doing a little reading on her own lately, on subjects of her own choosing. In a book of Settler aphorisms she'd read an ancient curse: "May you live in interesting times."

Well, interesting times were what she had wished for all those years on Aurora, where something moderately interesting happened once a year if you were lucky. From her earliest memory she had yearned to break free of the boredom and sterility.

And now that she had succeeded beyond her wildest expectations, she wished for nothing more than a little peace and quiet—for nothing more than a period of flat-out boredom, where she had nothing to do and no one to worry about, not even herself. Thanks in part to the disease ravaging her, she was finding it difficult to know just how to act and what to do—a problem she had never had on Aurora, where customs and ethics provided a guide for virtually every social situation.

She imagined herself not in Robot City, but in the fields of Aurora, walking at night, alone but not alone, followed by unseen, loyal robots who would ensure, to the best of their abilities, that she would not come to harm.

Instead of buildings closing in around her there were expansive, open fields of grass and trees, plains whose consistency was broken only by occasional buildings of a more familiar, safer architectural style. The clouds above inspired thoughts of the tremendous Auroran storms, when the thunder rumbled like earthquakes and the lightning exploded from the sky in the shape of tridents.

During such storms the rain flowed as if a dike in the sky had been punctured. The rainfall drenched the fields, cleansed the trees, and she could walk in it and feel it pounding against her all day if she liked—well, at least until her unseen robots would fear she might catch cold and insist she seek shelter.

Here the rain only inspired the gutters to overflow. Here the rain could be a harbinger of death and destruction, rather than of life.

Now where's Derec, she suddenly thought, *now that I need him?*

Oh. That's right. Talking to Lucius. That's just like him, to be so self-absorbed in things that don't matter, when he should be trying to find some way for us to get off this crazy planet.

Doesn't he understand how badly we both need help? Him for his amnesia. Me for my madness.

Madness? Was that what it was? Wasn't there some other word she could use for it? An abnormality or an aberration? A psychoneurosis? A manic-depressive state? Melancholia?

Where were the fields? she wondered. They had been here just a few moments ago.

Where had these buildings come from?

Were the fields behind them?

She ran around the buildings to take a look. There were only more buildings, extending as far as she could see, until they merged into a flattened horizon. A wall of blackness. More shadows.

She shook her head, and a few mental mists dissipated long enough for her to remember that there were no fields on this planet, that there'd just been desolate rock here before the city had arrived. A city that grew and evolved just like life.

A new kind of life.

She was like a microorganism here. A germ or a virus, standing in the middle of a creature that only let her live because of a few wires and a few bytes of binary information.

Her throat itched. She rubbed her neck. Was she becoming sick? If she was, would a robot notice and medicate her? Would the medication cloud her thinking even more? If it did, would it be a good or bad thing?

Her elbow itched. She scratched it, the effect of her sharp fingernails somewhat muted by her suit. The itch stayed.

She stopped scratching. Maybe it would go away if she ignored it.

It didn't. It got worse. She tried not to think about it, but the sole result was another itching. On her chest. She scratched her breastbone. That itch, too, remained. Neither showed the slightest sign of diminishing.

Where was Derec? she wondered as her fear of losing control aggravated her sense of helplessness, which in turn aggravated her fear of losing control.

Oh, that's right. He's still with the robot.

Hey, I'm all right. I know where I am. I was somewhere else a few seconds ago and I couldn't get back. Come to think of it, is there someplace else I should be rather than here? Shouldn't I be in the future somewhere?

Then she tried to think of her name, and discovered she

could not remember that, either. A name seemed like such a basic thing to forget. Nor did it seem that far away. But it wasn't where it was supposed to be: uppermost in her mind, where she could find it whenever she wanted. It was buried in her pathways.

Pathways. Robots had pathways. Was she very much like them?

Was she still alone? If she wasn't, would it make any difference? She felt like her mind was made up of discarded scraps of ideas and impressions that long ago, maybe, had made sense. Right now they just made a junk heap.

She sat down, trying to focus her thoughts and her vision. Without realizing it, she had walked all the way to the reservoir. An ecological system that had been created—but not nurtured—by Dr. Avery. A world that had been left alone to create itself.

She pondered the edible plants growing on the banks. A clear-cut case of evolution in action. Had Dr. Avery envisioned the possibility?

What if other meta-life forms were evolving as well?

Now her stomach and crotch itched. Painfully. Her skin felt like it was burning from spilled acid.

She buried her head in her hands. Her temples throbbed and she feared every artery in her brain was about to burst. It was easy, all too easy, for her to imagine a hemorrhage, the blood seeping everywhere, destroying her involuntary processes, drowning her thoughts.

Had she really wanted to be alone? Where was Derec? Oh, that's right . . .

She realized there was a difference, normally a barely perceptible one but in her heightened case very distinct, between believing you were alone and actually being alone.

Dawn was coming to Robot City. The glow Lucius had created was diminishing rapidly as the sun came up, and the waters of the reservoir rippled with irregular flickers reflecting the rays.

Rays that brought life. Ariel watched in fascination as the pebbles at her feet shifted and made way for a gray stalk that, within a matter of moments, twisted from the earth and unfolded two tiny leaves. She accidentally grazed the edge of a leaf, felt a sudden flash of pain on her finger. The wound was narrow, like a paper cut. A bubble of blood seeped from her skin.

Damn, that smarts, she thought, watching as other stalks unfurled, twisting from the gravel. Her head continued to ache. She stood and staggered to a boulder and leaned against it, being careful not to crush any of the stalks beneath her feet. But it was hard to keep thinking of it, even when she was no longer moving. Hard to keep her mind on things, to remember.

Her skin itched all over now, in waves that cascaded up and down as if she were being inundated by invisible radiation. She perspired. She shivered. She moaned.

She leaned back, looked at the sky, at the billowing clouds. She opened her mouth wide and breathed deeply, trying to keep her mind clear.

For the pervasive itch had begun to resemble something—a half-tickle, half-pinprick that brought back the memory of a walk on Aurora when she had sat down to rest and had felt something similar, only subtler, tinier. She had looked down to see an ant crawling up her bare leg. She had shrieked from the surprise of it, but had brushed it off before her concerned robots could reach her.

The effect had been unsettling, to be so rudely touched by a mindless life-form that could be carrying who-knows-what form of infectious disease. She had instantly intellectualized the experience, of course; she had long ago decided the Auroran fear of disease had been taken to ridiculous extremes. Even so, an involuntary sense of revulsion and disgust at the experience, much greater than was warranted, overtook her. It had lingered until she had bathed in a whirlpool of disinfectants.

That night she had dreamed of being swarmed by thousands of ants. The nightmare had been similar to what she was experiencing now.

But the current feeling was much more vivid.

She tried to convince herself that it wasn't real, that neither she nor Derec had detected any form of metallic insect life on this planet. However, the robots had shown definite signs of intellectual evolution. Perhaps that meant the cells forming the city were capable of random mutation, which meant it was not unreasonable to assume that a form of insect life was capable of developing.

Ariel was frozen to the spot with fear. She lowered her gaze, fully expecting to see a horde of ants swarming about her legs, moving up her boots and disappearing into her trouser legs, searching for just the right place to stop and begin gorging themselves, before they started carrying away tiny pieces of her.

But when she closed her eyes, it was all too easy for her to imagine the ants with their big compound eyes, glistening like tin in the sunlight, with their piston-driven spindly legs and their nuclear-battery-powered thoraxes, and especially with the steady, mechanical motions of their mandibles searching over her epidermis like the rods of a geiger counter. She could not as yet feel the mandibles biting and tearing, but she was certain that the pain would come. Beginning at any second.

Where were the robots when you needed them? Couldn't any see her? Weren't any around?

No, of course not, she realized with an ever-sinking

sense of futility. *You're at the reservoir, and they're all in the city, pining about how there aren't any humans around for them to take care of.*

There's soon going to be one less. Oh, Derec, where are you? Why can't you help me?

Ariel was afraid to breathe. She thought that perhaps if she remained utterly stationary, like one who is dead, then the ants might think she was nothing but a dead rock. But how could she remain motionless for long without breathing? Wouldn't the ants hear the sound of air moving in and out of her lungs?

What did it matter? She had to do something, even if it was nothing. She felt the mechanical ants everywhere, crawling up her breasts, nestled in her armpits, inspecting her hair. Why didn't they start eating? Weren't they hungry? What kind of ants were they?

They're robot ants, she thought. *Maybe they're trying to see if I'm human. If they decide I am, they may not hurt me. If they decide otherwise—*

Now she knew why primitive man had worshipped deities—to stave off the tremendous fear of the last moments of life, when there were profound good-byes to be said and resolutions to be imparted, but no one to tell them to, and no time left to tell them.

"Airr-eee-ll?" someone whispered timidly. "Arre 'u asleep?"

Ariel's eyes could not have opened wider or faster if she had received an electrical shock. She jumped back in stunned surprise at the sight of Wolruf squatting directly in front of her. And promptly smacked her head against the boulder.

Things got woozy as the caninoid cocked her head. Wolruf held a clump of stalks in her left hand, and a few strands hung from the fur surrounding her lips. "Arre 'u well?"

"Of course I'm well! What does it look like?"

"My annces'orrs would have said that 'u had vize-atorr."

"Who? What kind?" Ariel snapped. She closed her mouth with a force of will, then tried to compose herself. She was only partially successful. "It should be obvious that until you showed up I was the only one here."

"Two rre-ponnzes: furrst, been watching 'u all nite—"

"What!?"

"Man'elbrrot rreques'ed it. Thought 'u woul'n't apprresee-ate rrobut."

"Why that big hunk of—"

"Pulice, let me finish. Seckon': ancess'ors would have said 'u weren't only theeng in 'ur mind at moment, and I wai'ed, wa'cheeng, thinking it would be best not to dis'urb 'u or 'ur vize-atorr."

"And exactly what made you decide to interrupt my strange interlude?"

" 'U looked like 'u were about to faint."

"I see."

Wolruf tipped back further on her haunches, so that her back was perfectly straight. Her posture struck Ariel as being almost humanly annoyed, especially when the caninoid crossed her arms and shook her head, as if in disappointment. She went to great lengths to avoid looking directly into Ariel's eyes, first examining the buildings, the bank, the rocks, and then pointedly turning her back to Ariel, perhaps to have a better view of the reservoir.

"Well, aren't you going to ask me what my problem was?" said Ariel.

Wolruf turned her head slightly. "Why sshhould I?"

"I—I thought you must might want to know, that's all."

"Nne of my bizzness. Not people's way. Deafenly not mine."

"Aren't you worried?"

"No."

"Don't you care?"

"Didn't hav' to wa'ch 'u all nite. Was migh'ily bored. Many times distrrack'ed. Could hav' lef' 'u at any time and Man'elbrrot neither knowed norr carred."

Ariel suddenly felt as tired as she had ever been in her life. Even to shrug with a labored air of nonchalance cost her a tremendous effort. "How flattering," she said sarcastically.

She immediately regretted the words. Wolruf was stopping just short of saying she had stayed to watch because she was concerned for her welfare. *There you go, Miss Burgess*, Ariel thought. *You really will go insane if you can't recognize the good in people, whether they're human or not.*

She sat down beside Wolruf and said, "I'm sorry. Please try to understand that in addition to all our other problems, my mental condition gets out of hand sometimes."

"Datzz all rite."

"It isn't, it's just that I don't know what I can do about it right now. To make matters worse, it always gives me an excuse to misbehave, even if I don't know at the time that that's all it is."

Wolruf pulled her lips back against her teeth in a kind of smile. "So—are 'u well?"

"I'm better."

"There's no rreazon to be upset about vize't from tricks'er. Izz how he makes us obey his will, by makin' us see wha' he wantzz."

"That may be easy for your race to accept, but we humans aren't so used to having strange beings make pit stops in our minds at their every convenience."

Wolruf nodded thoughtfully. " 'U simplee lack perrspec'ive."

Ariel nodded in return. She had half expected that as a result of her apology she would feel the haze of exhaustion lift, but instead she imagined each individual cell in her body deteriorating steadily. A little while longer and she'd be a quivering mass of protoplasm.

"It's an old Spacer saying that everybody likes to feel in control of their lives, but with Aurorans it's only more so," she said. "And why not? It's not only an effect of our current culture, but an extension of our own history. As the first Spacers, we terraformed Aurora to suit our own tastes and purposes. We did everything we could to make our new planet a garden. We even brought with us the prettiest, best, and most useful Terran species, leaving behind the ones that would make life too unpleasant."

"If tha' 'ur plane'zz history, then the in'ivi'ual reflec'zz it."

"Yes, until I was exiled and cut off from my funds, I had a great deal of independence. Within socially acceptable limits—which I never really accepted anyway—I had complete freedom of action."

" 'U brroke those limitz—"

"And lost control of my life. Funny how the details of my rebellion are so fuzzy now. Must be a side effect of my disease. Anyway, it's funny how the one thing I always thought I still had perfect control over—my mind—seems to be slipping away from me now."

"Trry to relax. Take it from one who hazz seen many un'err thrroes of vize'torr. 'U not control it, 'u deflec' it."

Ariel couldn't help but laugh. "You mean that when insanity is inevitable, relax and enjoy it?"

"Not insanity. Merely givin' in to morre compellin' fuch'ions. Derec does that. That izz why he hazz so many ideas."

"I wish I could believe the same thing was true with me." Ariel paused as the implications of Wolruf's remark began to sink in. "Is that what he's doing when he spends so much time with Lucius, when he should be figuring out a way to get us off this hellhole?"

Suddenly Ariel stiffened. Her eyes went wide.

"Wha' izz it?" Wolruf asked. "Wha'zz wrron'?"

"I don't know," she replied.

"Ano'herr vize-shon?"

"I—I hope so." She grimaced, closed her eyes, and turned her head to the sky. *It's not real,* she told herself, *it's only something I'm imagining. But if reality is something we make, how do we deal with the forces making us?*

But although she knew on one level that her neurological responses were going awry, her physical self nonetheless continued to respond realistically to the sensation of a distinct *something,* large and six-legged, distinctly *within* her lifesuit. A familiar something. There was only one this time, but it was bigger than she remembered. Much bigger.

It was crawling up her stomach. She forced herself to open her eyes, fully expecting to see her suit clinging normally to her torso. Instead she saw—with a vividness she could not help but decide was absolutely real—the outline of a giant metallic ant moving beneath her suit. The cold touch of its six legs, each pressing delicately against her skin, sent chills of terror through her fragile, eggshell mind.

The outline moved distinctly, delicately forward. She felt the cold brush of a mandible against her left breast, and watched in abject fear as the forefront of the outline moved to her right breast. And rested on it.

Ariel screamed at the top of her lungs and ran headlong in the direction she happened to be facing. She was vaguely aware of Wolruf yelling behind her, but she was too busy to pay attention. She did not know where she was running, only that she had to make a beeline there.

She jumped into the reservoir.

She was in it for several moments, stunned senseless by the ice cold water, before she actually remembered diving in. Frantically, she tore open the snaps and buttons and zippers of her suit and put her hands inside, rummaging about, searching for the insect so she could pull the sucker out and drown it.

But she found nothing. When it came to her ambition for revenge, this was a disappointing development. How she had anticipated seeing it squirm as it tried to get away from her in the water! But on another level, she was tremendously relieved. Insanity she could deal with; physical pain was definitely a cause for panic.

Ariel imagined that perhaps the ant had been real after all, and had just torn through the suit on the way out. But the water around her, while not exactly clear, was very still. There was no evidence of movement beneath the surface. Even the sand and dirt she'd raised upon entering had settled down by now.

She calmed herself with an effort, closed her eyes again, and waited.

Soon she felt reasonably assured that the insect wasn't real enough to attack her, but she stayed in the water just to be on the safe side. The water sent pinpricks of pain cascading through her very marrow—but even that kind of discomfort didn't provide her with enough incentive to get out.

Wolruf sat patiently on the bank. "Are 'u well again?" the alien asked.

"I think so," she said. "I had another visit."

"Assumed as much."

"I think my visitor is gone now. I think I prefer looking at my episodes in terms of visitors, by the way. It's making it easier for me to accept them."

"Good. Don't 'u wan' come out of water now? 'U mite catch cold."

"No. It feels rebellious, to be doing something prying robot eyes might disapprove of."

"Will wait."

"Thanks. I'll just be a few more minutes. However safe my mind may feel while I'm in here, I don't think my body can take much more of this cold."

Something brushed against her. She glanced down to see that something had stirred the dirt up. Something too big to be just an ant. Something that was real.

"What's that?" she exclaimed.

"Wha'zz what?" Wolruf inquired.

But Ariel could not bring herself to answer. Her teeth were clattering too much. Screwing up her courage—which she felt was in short supply these days—she gingerly ducked her head beneath the surface, keeping her eyes open in the frigid fluid with an effort.

A hunk of metal lay half buried in the bottom of the reservoir. The gentle currents had removed enough of the dirt covering it to begin moving it back to the shore. Its stiff hand brushed again against her leg.

Its hand?

Ariel accidentally inhaled a noseful of water. She shot up to the surface, sputtering.

"Air-eel?" asked Wolruf. "Wha' is it?"

"It's a robot—there's a robot down here!"

"Wha'zz it doing there?" asked the caninoid, running to the edge of the water.

"I don't know. I think it's dead!"

"Robotzz can't die!"

"Maybe this one can. It looks like Lucius!"

CHAPTER 5

UNLEARN OR ELSE

Just before dawn, Derec went to sleep wondering what it would feel like to know who he was.

He knew he would dream. He would remember his dream, as always. He often searched the imagery of his dreams for a clue to his identity, figuring that his subconscious was doubtlessly signaling him information about this most personal of all his problems.

Often he dreamed he was a robot. Collectively, those dreams were always similar. He might begin in the survival pod, or in the diagnostic hospital, or even in his sleeping quarters in the house he had had Robot City provide for himself and his friends. Often he would accidentally uncover the Key to Perihelion; he would open a console panel, or open a cabinet, or even find it in his life-suit, and he would always use it.

The destination invariably filled him with keen disappointment, or even despair, for it would always be another place where he had been during the last few weeks, subtly altered, more menacing perhaps, but always fresh in his memory. Never did he dream of a place he had been before he lost his memory. There would be an accident—he would fall down a chasm opening up beneath his feet, a worker robot would misfunction and slice him open, or something else equally disastrous would happen.

But he would feel no pain. There would be no blood. He would look on his injured body, and see his skeletal structure revealed by his wound.

But not his skeletal bone. And therein lay the serious rub.

For he would have no bones to break, no flesh to tear. His skin would be plastic and his skeleton would be metal. There would be blinking lights where his muscles should be, and wires instead of arteries.

And he would feel no pain, no life-and-death anxiety about the wound, only a calmly overwhelming urge to repair himself as quickly as possible.

At that point the dream always ended, with Derec waking up in a cold sweat, staring at his hand and wondering if it just wasn't programmed to tremble at irrational fears, fears that he had always been programmed to experience, at random intervals.

He always settled back to sleep with an effort, and though not a reflective man he would invariably wonder, just for a moment, if, after you got past the obvious, there really was any difference between feeling like a human and feeling like a robot.

Sometimes the same dream, or a close variation on it, would begin again.

Tonight, however, as he tossed and turned, the dream was somewhat different.

Not surprisingly, it began in the square.

It was night, and Derec was alone. There was not an entity in sight. And as he looked at the slightly taller, slightly more freakish versions of the buildings around the square, he doubted there was an entity in the city.

But something was missing. He sensed that though the square was deserted, it was even emptier than it should be.

Something else should be here. Circuit Breaker! Where was Circuit Breaker?

Derec looked down to see that the plasticrete was crawling up his feet, fastening him to the spot. There was the distinct sensation of his feet merging with the plasticrete, of the meta-cells beginning to function in harmony with his biological cells. Derec held down his growing sense of panic with an effort. He did not know which he feared more: the conclusion, or awakening before he learned what it might be.

In a matter of moments the meta-cells completely smothered Derec. So thoroughly had the metallic cells mingled with his own that he did not know where they ended and where his began.

Strangely, he felt himself to be wider, taller, more physically substantial in every respect. He could not see nor move, yet found he had no yen to do either. He had become Circuit Breaker itself, gathering in the energy of the starlight, transforming it, amplifying it, and casting it out. He was stronger, sturdier, and more solid than he had ever been before.

But he had also lost his mind. Suddenly he had gone from a someone to a no one. He didn't even miss his sense of identity. He couldn't understand why he had wanted his memory back in the first place. What good could thinking and knowledge do him, standing so strong and bulky against the atmospheric tides?

Derec awoke gradually; a profound feeling of mental displacement aggravated him during those moments in which his mind hovered in the regions between waking and sleeping. In fact, those moments stretched out for an uncommonly long time. Both his immediate future and immediate past seemed hopelessly out of reach.

But the future already beckoned. He realized that for the last several moments he had been listening to a loud pounding on the door. He recalled an appointment with annoyance. It was too bad. He half wished he could return to sleep. He could certainly use it.

Oh well, there's nothing I can do about it now.

He rubbed his eyes. "Hold on," he said. "I'll be right there!"

But the knocking continued unabated, growing progressively more insistent. Now Derec was really annoyed. The persistent knocking, if it came from a human, would be very impolite. But robots had no choice but to be polite, regardless of the circumstances. What kind of robot would be so obviously predisposed toward the overkill of unnecessarily persistent knocking?

Derec suddenly realized. *Oh no! I'd forgotten it was Harry!*

Derec dressed hurriedly, opened the door and, sure enough, Harry was standing at the threshold. "I assume I have not been knocking too long," the robot said. "I have a hundred questions to ask you."

"And I've got a few more than that to ask you," Derec replied, motioning him inside, "but I'm afraid we've got a limited amount of time today."

"So am I to assume that you are interviewing Lucius later?" asked Harry. "Why chat with that genius when you have me around?" Then: "Was that good? Was it humorous?"

Derec tried to hide his smile. He didn't want to encourage the robot, which didn't need it anyway. "I think you'll both prove equally important to my studies of what's been happening to robots on this planet. Did you bring your friends along?"

"M334 and Benny? No. They are working on a project of some sort together. I think they want its nature to be a surprise."

"And it probably will be," said Derec sarcastically, "if the events of the last few days have been any indication."

"Forgive me in advance, but was that remark also an attempt at humor?"

"Not really, no."

"I see. You must understand it is often difficult for a robot to understand what a human's tone of voice means," said Harry, again very politely.

Derec decided to take the question seriously. "It was a casual observation, a commentary laced with what I presumed to be light-heartedness, an attitude which frequently gives rise to humor."

"It sounded sarcastic, insofar as I can comprehend these things."

"Did it, now? Maybe M334 should be here after all. Our conversation last night was your first real contact with the human race, wasn't it?" asked Derec, punching up a cup of coffee from the dispenser.

"Yes, and an auspicious one it was, too."

"Whose tone is elusive now, Harry? How long have your pathways been consumed with the objective to achieve humor?"

"Since the replicating disaster that almost destroyed Robot City, from which you saved us, thank-you-very-much."

"And since then you've been pursuing your goal with the single-mindedness characteristic of robots?"

"How else?"

"How else, indeed. Hasn't it ever occurred to you that

even humor has its time and place, that the average human being simply can't bear to be around someone who answers every query or makes every casual observation with a smart remark? It gets predictable after a while, and can cause an otherwise pleasant social situation to undergo rapid deterioration. Which is another way of saying that it gets boring. Dull. Mundane. Predictable."

"It fails to elicit the proper response."

"Robots can't laugh," said Derec cryptically, sipping his coffee. As bitter as bile, it was exactly what his nerves cried out for.

"I see you have deduced the basic conundrum in which I've found myself since I embarked on my little project."

"Believe me, it's obvious. But seriously, Harry, how would you react if you were walking down the street and a manhole suddenly opened up beneath you and you fell in?"

"What is a manhole? Is that some kind of sexual reference?"

"Ah, no, a manhole is an opening in the street, usually covered, through which someone can enter into a sewer or a boiler."

"Can you be certain there is nothing covertly sexual in those words? I have been diligently studying the craft of the double entendre, but there is much I have yet to grasp because all I know about human sexual matters is what material the central computer calls up for me."

"I must personally inspect that material as soon as possible. But to keep to the main subject, how would you feel if you fell down a manhole?"

Harry almost shrugged. "I would feel like going boom."

"Seriously."

"My logic circuits would inform me that the end was near and, knowing me, would close themselves down in an orderly fashion before I suffered the indignity of random disruption."

"I see. And how would you feel if you were walking down the street and saw me falling down a manhole?"

"Why, logically, that should be hysterical. Unless of course you went splat before I could fulfill the demands of the First Law."

"Hmmm. You see, in such an eventuality, you would identify with my loss of dignity and, were you human, would relieve your anxiety by laughing. Before you rescued me, that is. The question is: how can you relieve anxiety if you can't laugh?"

"Everyone can *agree* it's funny. That is how my comrades inform me when they believe I am on the beam."

"But a comic performing jokes in front of an audience of robots can't stop his act after each joke to ask everyone if he's on the right track."

"There are ways around that. It is customary in a formal situation for robots to nod their heads if they think something is funny. At least, that is what I am trying to convince them to do."

Derec finished his coffee in a gulp and immediately punched up a second cup. "I see you've given this some thought."

"One or two."

"Is that an attempt at irony?"

"No, at a joke."

"I think that for other robots to find your sense of humor worthwhile, you're going to have to think of angles that relieve their own robotic anxieties. I'm not exactly sure what those would be. You could make fun of their foibles. Or you could write and perform skits about a robot who's so literal-minded that he sometimes can't understand what's really going on around him. Some of Shakespeare's characters have that trait, and they're human, but it makes sense that a robot character would exaggerate things to ludicrous lengths."

"You mean a character who understands the letters of the words but not their shades of meaning."

"But the audience will. As robots, they will naturally have positronic anxieties concerning their own literal-minded traits relieved by identifying with him. He doesn't necessarily have to be sympathetic, even; he could have the kind of personality robots would love to hate, if they were capable of either emotion."

"What kind of anxieties do humans have?"

"It's difficult for me to say. I don't remember any humans. I've just read a few books. Many of Shakespeare's jokes, his puns, his slapstick, have a ribald, bawdy humor that strikes me as slightly off-color today, despite the gulf of the centuries between us. So I guess it's safe to say there's always been a certain amount of sexual anxiety in human beings, and one of the ways they relieve it—or learn how to deal with it—is through humor."

Harry nodded as if he understood what Derec was talking about. *Now, if I only felt the same*, Derec thought. *I'm strictly on shaky ground here.*

"In that case, you could explain an old Spacer joke to me that I have been trying to work into my act."

"Okay.... Your act!?"

"My act. Until now I have only told jokes to my personal acquaintances—comrades who understand what I am attempting to do. But I have been preparing a presentation for an assembly. An act."

"How many jokes do you have?"

"A couple. I have failed to generate original material,

so I have been investigating the vocal rhythms behind existing jokes."

"To hone your timing?"

"Yes, insofar as I comprehend what that talent includes. There are no voice tapes for me to investigate, though the reference texts contain frequent entries on such material."

"Okay, Harry," said Derec, chuckling at the concept of all this as he folded his arms across his chest and leaned against the counter. "Fire away!"

"With post haste, sir. One day three men in a lifepod are coming in for a landing at the local spacedock. They had been marooned for several days and eagerly anticipate their return to the comforts of civilization. One man is a Settler, another an Auroran, and the third a Solarian."

Derec hid his grin with his palm. Harry's delivery was indeed awkward, and his few gestures bore little connection to what he was saying, but a solid effort was apparent. Also, the unlikely combination of the characters' derivations already promised interesting interaction. Historically, there was much social friction between the groups: Aurorans and Solarians both disliked the Settlers because of their recent "third-class" colonization of the planets; and there had never been much love lost between the Aurorans and Solarians, especially since the latter had mysteriously abandoned their world and vanished. Derec already made a mental note to tell Ariel this one.

"So the three men are just overhead the dock when suddenly a freighter's radar malfunctions and the gigantic ship crosses directly in front of their flight path. A crash is inevitable, and the three men prepare themselves for their last moments.

"A logical thing to do," said Derec. Immediately, he feared that his words might have disrupted Harry's rhythm, such as it was, and so resolved to remain quiet for the duration of the joke.

Harry, on the other hand, continued doggedly as if nothing had happened. "All of a sudden—mere instants before the crash—all three men are bathed in a yellow light—and they disappear into thin air!

"They look around and they fail to perceive their pod, the freighter, or the docks. They are in some kind of infinite pool of blue light—face-to-face with a strange man with a wreath of leafy twigs around his head. The strange man has a white beard, wears burlap robes, and carries a wooden staff. The men realize they are in the company of some kind of deity.

" 'I am known throughout the spheres of space and time as He Who Points The Fickle Finger Of Fate,' the man says, 'and I have come to point the finger at you.' And true to his word, he points at the Settler and says, 'You shall live through the next few moments, but only if you promise never again to drink any sort of alcoholic beverage. Ever. The moment you take a drink, regardless of how many years from now it is, you will die an instant death. Do you understand?'

" 'I do, sir,' says the Settler, 'though is it not asking much from a Settler to expect him to forego the delights of alcohol for an entire lifetime?'

" 'Perhaps it is,' says He Who, 'but my demand stands nonetheless. I repeat, the instant a liquid containing alcohol touches your lips, you shall die as surely as if you had died in the crash.'

" 'Then I agree,' says the Settler reluctantly.

"And He Who points to the Auroran and says, 'You must give up all greed.'

" 'I accept!' says the Auroran at once. 'It's a deal!'

"And He Who points to the Solarian and says, 'And last,

you must give up all sexual thoughts, except for those you might have strictly for purposes of socially acceptable wedded bliss.'

" 'Excuse me, sir,' says the Solarian, 'but that is impossible. Do you not know what we Solarians have been through? Because our centuries of social and personal repression have ended so recently, we have little choice but to think about our new freedoms, and often.'

"He Who frowns and shakes his head. 'That is no concern of mine. The three of you have my terms. Accept them or die.'

" 'I accept it,' the Solarian says.

"There is another flash of blinding light, and the three men find themselves standing on the ground as, in the distance, their pod crashes spectacularly into the freighter. They all experience profound relief. The Settler wipes his forehead and says, 'I am ecstatic that this little episode has concluded. Look, yonder is a bar. Join me as I down some spirits by way of celebrating our good fortune.'

"The Auroran and the Solarian agree. They both desire libation, and in addition desire to see what will happen to the Settler.

"Indeed, the very second that the Settler consumes his first drink, he dies on the proverbial spot. 'Leaping galaxies, the strange man was speaking the truth,' says the Auroran. 'We must vacate these premises!'

"The Solarian agrees enthusiastically. But on the way out the Auroran espies a rare and valuable jewel beneath a deserted table. The Auroran cannot resist. And just as he bends over to pick up the jewel—the Solarian dies!"

Harry ceased talking, and the longer Derec waited for the robot's next words, the more apparent it became that the joke was over. At first he didn't understand and he had to visualize the scene and what must have happened. The

Auroran bending over...the Solarian breaking his word....

Derec burst out laughing. "Ha, ha! That's pretty good. Very unpredictable."

"I understand that, sir," Harry said. "I realize that the narrative leads you to believe the Auroran is next, but I fail to comprehend exactly what the Solarian could possibly have been thinking of. The central computer has thus far been unable to find material that would enlighten me. Would you care to explain?"

"No, no. I really do believe there are some things a robot was not meant to know."

"Do I have your permission to ask Miss Ariel the same question?"

"Not before I ask her something slightly similar." He took Harry by the arm and began leading him toward the door. "Now I've got to get you out of here. Lucius is due, and I'd like to talk to him alone, if you don't mind."

"Sir, how could I possibly do that?" Harry asked.

"Just a figure of speech," said Derec, reaching for the doorknob. But before he had a chance to touch it, the door opened from the other side.

Ariel, her hair dripping wet and her suit clinging to her body, came running into the house. "There you are!" she exclaimed.

"Don't you ever knock?" Derec asked angrily, then calmed down when he realized something serious was the matter. Besides, of course she didn't have to knock. She lived here, too. "Are you all right?"

"Yes, of course. Wolruf and I found, ah...."

"Well? Out with it!" exclaimed Derec.

"I was at the reservoir this morning," she said haltingly. "Uh, I was *in* the reservoir, and I felt something strange. It was Lucius. His positronic brain had been partially destroyed."

"What did you say?" asked Derec as the room began to spin.

"Lucius has been deliberately sabotaged. To the utmost degree. You might even say he's been murdered."

"Ridiculous," said Harry calmly. "Only an outsider would have committed such a deed, and that's impossible. The city would have responded to an alien presence."

"Not necessarily," said Derec, thinking of Doctor Avery, who kept an office here, and whose arrival surely would not activate the city's automatic warning devices.

"It's no accident," said Ariel firmly. "I think you'll agree. Wolruf is supervising the robots who are bringing the, ah, body over here. Then you'll both see for yourselves."

"One of you must know more," said Harry. "A robot would not willingly harm another robot. Only you two and the alien are suspects."

Derec rubbed his chin thoughtfully. "No, there is no law actually dictating that a robot shall not do violence to another robot. In fact, a robot would have no choice if he truly believed harm would come to a human as a result of his omission of action." He glanced at Ariel. "Where's Mandelbrot? Wolruf?"

"Supervising the robots carrying the body here," she said.

"Harry, please leave immediately. We'll finish our talk later."

"All right," said the robot, walking through the door. "Though I feel obligated to warn you: You have not perceived my presence for the last time!"

"Is that robot for real?" asked Ariel after it was gone.

"I'm afraid so," Derec replied. "Are you certain that

we're dealing with a deliberate case of deactivation here—not an accident of some sort?"

"No—but, Derec, Lucius's face was struck in several places. It certainly looked deliberate to me, as if someone wanted to ensure it couldn't be identified."

"Which is impossible, because most of its parts contain serial numbers, which can be traced."

"Exactly. So whoever did it must have realized that in mid-act and then thrown Lucius in the reservoir in the hope that it wouldn't be found. Or, if it was found, it'd be so rusty that most of the serial numbers would be obscured."

"And unless we've an unidentified intruder—which seems unlikely—a robot was responsible."

"Amazing, isn't it?"

Derec nodded. "Absolutely. What were you doing in the reservoir?"

Ariel blushed, though Derec couldn't tell if it was from anger or embarrassment. "I was taking a swim."

"Fully dressed? Say, you've been losing weight, haven't you?" he asked, looking her over with wide eyes.

"You'll never know. Derec, how can you be flip at a time like this? To lose Lucius—"

"So early in his career, I know. The galaxy has been robbed of a great artist, I fear. Tragic. Simply tragic. I have to laugh, Ariel. It's the only way I can deal with it, and right now I don't care if you understand or not! Now be quiet and let me think!"

Ariel blinked in surprise, and jerked her head back as if he had taken a swipe at her. But she did as he wished.

Derec stared at the wall and tried to remember when he and Mandelbrot had parted company with Lucius. There had been a few hours remaining until the dawn. Had Lucius said anything about where it was going or what it was going to do? Nothing in particular that Derec could recall, just that it was going to close down for a few hours before beginning work on its next project. No, there wouldn't be any clues; Lucius certainly couldn't have predicted or even suspected that it would be murdered.

Hmm, can you call the shutdown of a robot "murder"? Derec asked himself. *Or is murder too strong a word to use when talking about a machine, regardless of its level of sophistication?*

A few moments later, however, Derec realized he wasn't ruminating on the incident so much as he was repressing a profound sense of outrage. During their few hours together, Lucius had begun to mean something special to him. True, there was the possibility that he was overreacting because of his already well established affinity for robots, but throughout his short life that he could remember, he had demonstrated a special appreciation for intelligent life in all its manifestations.

Lucius was a robot, Derec thought. *But I fear I shall never see its like again.*

Derec realized after the fact that he had paraphrased a line from Shakespeare's *Hamlet.* This reminded him of the promise he had made to Lucius, and he mulled over the implications of this promise for long minutes after Mandelbrot and Wolruf had escorted the robots carrying Lucius inside, after they had lain Lucius on a table. Evidently Mandelbrot or Ariel must have ordered the robots to depart, because Derec never recalled giving such an order.

For a while, as he looked at the battered and distorted face, Derec hoped he would discover that it was a dreadful mistake, that it really wasn't Lucius there after all, but some other robot. But the size was right. The model was right. The color was right. The unique identifying features that all city robots possessed to some degree were right. But most of all, the feeling in Derec's gut was right.

Lucius was indeed dead. Murdered. The logic circuits of its positronic brain had been removed with precision. But the personality integrals had been left in the brain cavity, left to be permanently damaged in the reservoir. So Lucius's unique abilities at logic might still exist, but the interaction between brain and body would probably never again be achieved. The personality was gone forever.

"Excuse me, everyone," Derec said, actually aware that his friends were staring at him, waiting for his reaction. "I'd like to be alone with Lucius for a few moments."

And then, after they had left, Derec cried. He cried in pity and remorse, not for Lucius, but for himself. This was the first time he could remember having cried. When he finished, he felt only marginally better, but he had some idea of what he had to do, and who to look to for an answer.

Derec found the ebony at the place he had come to think of as Circuit Breaker Square. Other robots of various models and intelligence levels stood around the building, watching its colors reflect the sunlight in muted shades. Occasionally, reflections thrown off by the smooth planes glittered against the robots and the other buildings. The overall effect of Circuit Breaker was more restrained in the sunlight. Doubtlessly that, too, had been part of Lucius's plan, to permit the building to become controllable and hence "safer" in the day, while the night unleashed its true energies. He would have to find out upon what principle the solar batteries worked.

That was another question Lucius would no longer be able to answer personally; however interesting it was on the purely scientific level, it did not seem especially important in light of recent events.

The ebony stood at the edge of the perimeter. Its head never turned to the building; it was watching the other robots instead, as if it was searching for some meaning in their activity. Or lack of it, as the case was. The ebony stood straight and tall, with barely a nuance Derec could call remotely human. It was easy for him to imagine a black cape hanging from the ebony's shoulders, easier still to imagine it standing on a hilltop and glaring in defiance at a gathering storm.

Blow wind, and crack your cheeks, Derec thought, recalling a line from *King Lear*.

Trying his best to look casual, as if he were simply taking a stroll, Derec walked to the ebony and said, "Excuse me, but didn't I see you here last night?"

"It is possible, master," replied the ebony, bowing its head and shoulders slightly as if to take note of the human's presence for the first time.

"With all the other robots?"

"I was in the square, but my circuits do not acknowledge the fact that I was *with* the other robots."

"I see by your insignia and model that you are a supervisor robot."

"That is true."

"Exactly what are your duties?" Derec asked casually.

With an almost stately turn of its head, the ebony turned toward Circuit Breaker and waited until the length of the silence between them became quite long—deliberately, for a kind of dramatic effect, it seemed to Derec. An answer was intended, but so was a space of waiting. Derec began to get a seriously queasy feeling in his stomach.

Finally, the ebony said, "My duties are floating. I am programmed to ascertain what needs to be done and then to do it or otherwise see to it."

"All of this is up to your discretion?"

"I am a duly designated rogue operative. The city requires a certain amount of random checks if it is to run at peak efficiency. If a machine breaks down gradually, the supervisor on the spot might not notice because it is there during every tour of duty. It would get used to the situation, would not even realize something was amiss, whereas I, with my extra-keen memory banks and an eye capable of perceiving individual levels of meta-cells, would notice it immediately."

"Once you actually look at the problem, that is."

"Of course. I doubt even a human can fix a machine before he knows if and where it has been broken."

"Don't underestimate us."

"I shall strive not to. Do not think, sir, that my sole function is to act as mechanical troubleshooter. My tasks vary, depending upon the situation. Often central calls on me to provide visual and cognitive assistance if there is some problem with robotic efficiency—not that my comrades ever function at less than their peak, but because sometimes they cannot be certain that they are directing their energies to the best advantage of all."

"So you're a problem solver! You help devise solutions to the unforeseen shortcomings in central's program!"

Derec leaned against a building and saw Circuit Breaker weave back and forth like a balloon hung up in a breeze. He felt like someone had hit him on the back of the skull with a lug wrench. His lungs felt like paper. His ankles felt like the bones had turned into rubber putty. At first he was too stunned to loathe the ebony, but that feeling grew and grew, as he leaned there and tried to get his thoughts straight.

This robot has got to make decisions, Derec thought. *The very nature of its job calls for analytical creativity! It could have viewed Circuit Breaker as so revolutionary to the robotic psyche that it constituted an obstacle to the laborers' duties. And then . . . then the ebony would have been forced to do something about Lucius.*

There's nothing in the Three Laws about a robot being

forbidden to harm another robot. In fact, First Law situations and Second Law orders may require it.

This is not proof, though.

For a moment Derec wondered what he would do once he had the proof. He would have to keep the ebony—or whichever robot the murderer was—functional for a time until the mechanics as well as the psychology had been checked for anomalies. The question of what came next would have to be decided after all the facts were in. It was possible that the ebony couldn't help itself.

Just as it was also possible that the Three Laws had been a significant factor, that once the ebony had embarked on a course of logic, it had followed it rigorously to an end predestined for tragedy.

"Tell me," Derec said, making an effort to stand up straight, "do you ever take the initiative when it comes to identifying problems?"

"If you mean can I pinpoint a potential glitch before central is aware, then the answer is yes. Those occasions, however, are quite rare and often quite obvious."

"They're obvious if you're not central."

"Sir?"

"And do you ever take the initiative in solving problems?"

"I have, and central has had to fine-tune them, too."

"But not all the time."

"I see I must be exact about this. Central has only fine-tuned three out of forty-seven of my solutions. Have I satisfied you so far with my answers, sir?"

"Forty-seven? That's a lot of problems, and those are only the ones you found on your own."

"Robot City is young, sir. There will doubtlessly be many glitches in the system before the city is operating at one hundred percent efficiency."

"And you're certainly going to do your bit, aren't you?"

"I can do nothing else, sir."

Derec nodded. "I see. By the way, what's your name?"

"Canute."

"Tell me, Canute, how would you rate—efficiency-wise—
a robot that deliberately took it upon itself to disconnect a
comrade?"

"Sir, it would have to be seriously examined. Though of
course it is possible that the First or Second Law would
permit such an action."

"Are you aware that someone, presumably a robot, bru-
tally disconnected Lucius last night? Damaged him beyond
all hope of repair?"

"Of course I am aware. News travels fast over the comlink."

"So you heard about it from other robots first?"

"Sir, why not ask me outright if I was the robot responsible? You know I am forbidden to lie."

Canute's words were like a bucket of cold water thrown
into Derec's face. Their forthrightness startled him. "I—I—
how did you know I was leading up to that?"

"It seemed obvious from your line of questioning."

"I see you have advanced deductive abilities."

"It is a prerequisite for my line of work."

Hmmm. I think you just may be the kind of robot I need,
Derec thought. Putting aside his feelings for Lucius with a
force of will, he thought of Ariel, and of the possibility that
Canute, who made its intuitive leaps from a solidly practical
framework, would be just the one to help him diagnose and
cure her disease. Once its mental frames of reference could
be adjusted, that is.

The trick would be to get it to readjust—to admit the
gravity of its error—without causing positronic burnout in

the process. For in that eventuality, Canute wouldn't be able to repair a paper clip.

So the direct approach was out. Besides, Derec had a promise to keep.

"Canute, you may find this hard to believe, but I've been looking for a model like you."

"Sir?"

"Yes, I have a specific type of building in mind that I'd like to see erected nearby. I'd also like it as permanent as possible. I think its presence will do much to enrich life here in Robot City."

"Then I am eager to do whatever you ask. What type of building did you have in mind?"

"An open-air theatre—a playhouse. I'll give you the details later, but I want to see functional elaboration in the design. I want you to generate your notions of some of the details. In fact, I insist on it. Understand?"

"Yes," said Canute, lowering its head slightly. "May I ask why you want to have a theatre erected?"

"Have you ever heard of *Hamlet?*"

CHAPTER 6

THE WORLD OF THE PLAY

Canute was right about one thing: news travels fast at com-link speed. Returning from Circuit Breaker Square to his quarters, Derec hadn't even gotten through the door before Mandelbrot began talking.

"Master, where have you been? I have been besieged by requests to assist you in your latest project. I fear that, lacking sufficient information, I was forced to tell everyone to wait. I hope that was all right."

"It was," said Derec, lying down on the couch. "Where's Ariel?"

"She went to her room. She mumbled something about mopping up on her Shakespeare."

"I think you mean brushing up."

"If you say so."

"You're not very comfortable with human idioms, are you, Mandelbrot?"

"I can be neither comfortable nor uncomfortable conversing with them. But I take you to mean it is sometimes difficult for me to translate their peculiar surface meanings

in practical terms. For instance, how do you brush up someone who is ancient history? In that respect, I do sometimes
have problems communicating. But about this project...."

"All right, I'll tell you. But wait—where's Wolruf?"

"With Miss Ariel. I think Wolruf is performing some
task. Forgive me if I am again misphrasing it, but she is
being Miss Ariel's line coach."

"Ssh. Quiet. Listen."

And Derec heard, very softly, through the closed door,
Ariel speaking the words, "Oh, what a noble mind is here
o'erthrown! The courtier's, soldier's, scholar's, eye, tongue,
sword; the expectancy and rose of the fair state, the glass
of fashion and the mould of form, the observed of all ob-
servers, is, er, ah—"

"Kwei-it," said Wolruf in a low volume that wasn't
hushed enough to be called a whisper, but was probably as
close to one as she could manage.

"Quite, quite down!" Ariel finished enthusiastically.

"Hmm, it seems my second bit of casting is almost complete," said Derec.

"Casting, master?" said Mandelbrot. "You are having a
cast made? Have you injured yourself?"

"No, not at all," Derec replied, laughing.

"I must say, it seemed you were hiding your suffering
awfully well."

"It's my hobby. Listen, tell me what you would do with
the robot that dismantled Lucius." The sudden shock of the
image of the robot lying there, behind the closed door to
his office, sent a tremor of loss and grief through Derec's
veins. And of terror, too. He'd never before thought robots
were things that could die. He'd always assumed they were
immortal in a way that life could never be.

"Forgive me, master, but I would think nothing of it. I
would merely follow your instructions."

"And what if I wasn't around to give you instructions? What if you had to decide when you were on your own?"

"First, I would solicit the robot's explanation, and learn of any justifications for its actions, if any, it may have had, particularly as they involved its interpretation of the Three Laws."

"But there is no law against a robot harming another robot."

"Of course, and the robot in question may have been operating on instructions from a human. But I gather such is not the case here."

"Well, yes . . ."

"So after having received the explanation, I would take the safest course and have the robot closed down until the proper repairs could be administered, or until instructions could be received from human sources."

"That could take a long time, particularly here on Robot City."

"No harm would be done. Upon reactivation, if that is what is decided upon, the robot would behave as if it had just been shut down for a tune-up the day before."

"Hmm. But what if there was something you needed from the robot?"

"Then that would depend on what you needed, and how badly you needed it."

"I'm glad you feel that way, not that you can feel, I know, but it makes me feel better to know your logic circuits concur with some of this . . ." And he explained to Mandelbrot his theory that a creative robot with a scientific bent might be able to make a diagnostic breakthrough to help Ariel.

"But how do you know that Canute possesses scientific talents?"

"I don't. But I may be able to use its mind to help me

learn more about what's happening to the robots in this place. And I need to do it—to get Canute to admit to its error without drifting out in the process. That's one reason why I'm putting on this play."

"This play?"

"*Hamlet*, by William Shakespeare. Quiet; listen."

Ariel's voice came through the door, muffled but quite clear as she repeated and then continued the speech she had rehearsed earlier, this time in louder, more confident cadences. "And I of ladies most deject and wretched, that suck'd the honey of his music vows, now see that noble and most sovereign reason, like sweet bells jangled, out of tune and harsh."

"Isn't that beautiful?" Derec gushed.

"The words, master, or Miss Ariel saying them?"

"Have you been talking to Harry?"

"Master, I do not understand your implication."

"Never mind. Anyway, I'm going to use this play as a lightning rod, to draw every robot with creative tendencies to the same place, working on a group project, and then see what develops. I don't know what's going on here, but whatever it is, I'm going to bust it wide open!"

Someone knocked on the door. "Get that, will you?" Derec asked as he turned toward Ariel's office. "Ariel? This is your director speaking! Come out here, will you?"

Ariel came out in a flash, followed by a bounding Wolruf. "Director?" she said. "Then who's going to be my leading man?"

"Oh? When you found out about this production, how did you know you were going to be Ophelia?"

"Because clearly I possess all the mental and physical qualifications. Who better to play a girl who's going insane than one who really is? Of course, I don't know who's going to play Hamlet's mother, but that's not my problem, is it?"

At least she's keeping her sense of humor about things, Derec thought. "No—it's your director's—and your leading man's."

Ariel grinned and bowed. "At your service, Mr. Director."

"Master—"

"Yes, Mandelbrot."

"Forgive the intrusion, Master Derec and Mistress Ariel, but Harry, Benny, and M334 are at the door. They said they had vibes to present to you."

"Vibess?" said Wolruf. "Not ni-ice word on my worrld."

"Yes, but who knows what it means here," said Ariel. "Send them in, Mandelbrot."

"Yes, I suppose we have to begin interviewing for our cast and crew sooner than later," said Derec.

In walked the three robots, each carrying brass objects. Each object struck Derec as being rather strange. M334 held a tube with two dozen keys, with what appeared to be a mouthpiece on one end. It was evidently a wind instrument, though what sort of sound it was supposed to make, Derec had no way of imagining.

Nor did he know what sort of sounds he might expect from the other two instruments held by the other two robots. Benny's was smaller than M334's, and could be easily held in one hand; there were three taps on the top, presumably to modulate the sonic textures. Harry's was the straightest and the longest of the three; it had a sliding device that evidently would lengthen or shorten the tubing to match the player's will, again presumably to modulate the sound.

"Good day, sir," said Benny. "We can only presume we are interrupting your preparations—"

"Good grief, word travels fast around here!" Ariel exclaimed.

"*You* found out, didn't you?" said Derec.

Ariel shrugged. "I heard it from Wolruf."

"And how did you hear about it, Wolruf?" Derec asked.

Wolruf merely shrugged. The effort made her entire body quiver.

"—And so we thought you might want to see for yourself the results of a project we have been devoting ourselves to instead of closing down in our spare time," finished Benny, as if no one else had spoken.

"Ah, and what is the nature of this project?" Derec asked suspiciously.

"Originally it was purely musical," said Benny.

"But when we heard you were planning to engage us in a recreation of human art forms, we performed research and discovered that music was often a significant part of such functions," said Harry.

"That struck us as being particularly fortuitous," said M334. "We thought—perhaps presumptuously, but how could we tell if we refrained from inquiring?—that our music might make a significant contribution to the enterprise."

"Uh, what kind of music are we attempting here, with those things?" Ariel asked. "Auroran *nouveau* fugues? Tantorian ecto-variations?"

"Something close to period, Terran-style," said Harry.

"You mean from Earth?" Ariel asked incredulously. Terran culture was not held in high regard in most Spacer circles.

"Shakespeare was from Earth," put in Derec mildly.

"Yes, but he was lucky enough to be talented," said Ariel. "You can't say that about most Terran artists."

"Perhaps you judge our aspirations too harshly," said Benny.

"Yes, you should judge after you hear us play," said M334.

"Yes, you should have plenty of critical ammunition then," said Harry.

Ariel stared at Derec. "It was a joke," Derec said.

"Close to bein' good one!" said Wolruf.

The three robots then magnetically applied computerized, flexible, artificial lips to their speaker grills. The lips were connected by electrical cords that led into the positronic cavities, and Derec saw at once, by the way the robots exercised the lips and blew air through them, that they responded directly to thought control.

Just like real lips, thought Derec, biting his lower one as if to make sure. "Excuse me, but before you boys strike up the brass, I'd like to know what names those instruments are supposed to have."

"This is a trumpet," said Benny.

"A saxophone," said M334.

"And a trombone," said Harry.

"And by way of further introduction," said Benny, "the number we would like to assault for your aural perusal is an ancient composition dating not four hundred years later than Shakespeare's time. This was already during the age of recorded music, but no tapes are currently available through central, so we can only surmise the manner in which these instruments were played by examining the sheet music."

"What there is of it," said Harry. "Most of this number is improvised."

"Uh-oh!" said Ariel to herself, putting her hand protectively on her forehead. *"I must be having a delirium!"*

"And the number we would like to assault is what the reference tapes denote as, in the parlance of the day, a snappy little ditty. This song its composer, the human known as Duke Ellington, called 'Bouncing Buoyancy.' "

I've got a bad feeling about this, Derec thought. He waved his hand. "Play on, McDuffs!"

The robots did. At least, that's what the humans and the alien thought they were trying to do. The musical form was so radically unlike anything they'd experienced, the playing so haphazard and odd, so full of accidental spurts and sputters and stops, that exactly what the robots were attempting to do remained a matter of some conjecture.

Benny's trumpet played the lead with a blaring succession of notes that occasionally struck the ear as being just right. The noise the instrument made resembled the wail of a siren, recorded backwards. So high was its frequency that Derec became afraid his ears would begin bleeding. Benny's notes, on the other hand, did seem to possess some kind of internal logic, as if he knew where he was going but wasn't quite sure how to get there.

Harry on the trombone and M334 on the saxophone attempted to provide Benny with a solid foundation; awkwardly, they tooted eight measures of unchanging harmony, over and over again. They nearly succeeded, harmony-wise, and perhaps their glitches wouldn't have been so noticeable if they'd occasionally managed to start and end the eight measures at the same time.

The trombone itself tended to sound like an exquisitely crafted raspberry, surreally brayed from the mouth of a contemptuous donkey. The saxophone's sonic attack, meanwhile, resembled nothing so much as a gaggle of geese gurgling underwater. The effect of the three instruments combined was such that Derec wondered momentarily if the robot hadn't come up with a violation of an interplanetary weapons treaty.

Derec spent the first minute finding the music absolutely atrocious, utterly without redeeming social value. It was the worse kind of noise; that is, noise pretending to be something else. But gradually he began to perceive, vaguely, the equally vague ideal in the robots' minds. The music itself, regardless of the manner of its playing, possessed single-minded joy that quickly became infectious. Derec discovered that his toe was tapping in a rhythm akin to that of the music. Ariel was nodding thoughtfully. Wolruf had her head cocked inquisitively, and Mandelbrot was his usual inscrutable self.

Derec's mind wandered a second, and he wondered if he could rig up a specimen of those liplike fixtures on the mouths to help robots portray human emotions during the production. The fact that most had immobile faces, incapable of even rudimentary expression, was going to cripple the illusion unless he devised some way to use the very inflexibility to greater effect. He imagined a set of lips twisted in laughter at the play's cavorting actors, and in fear of the ghost of Hamlet's father, and in anguish at the sight of all the dead bodies littering the stage. *Well, it's a thought*, he figured, and then returned his attention to the music.

The arrangement of "Bouncing Bouyancy" concluded with all three instruments playing the main theme simultaneously. Theoretically. The robots took the mouthpieces from their lips with a flourish and held out the instruments toward their audience.

Derec and Ariel looked at one another. Her expression read *You're the director, you do the talking.*

"How did our number bludgeon you, master?" asked Benny.

"Uh, it was certainly unusual. I think I see what you robots are trying to get at, and I think I may like it if you actually get there. Don't you agree, Ariel?"

"Oh, yes, definitely." She was really saying *I seriously doubt it.*

"Iss it *Ham-lit?*" Wolruf asked.

"That, I don't know," said Derec. "I suppose this Ellington fellow composed other works, though."

"In a variety of styles and moods," said Benny.

"All adaptable to our instruments," said Harry.

"I was afraid of that," Derec said. "But don't worry. I'm sure you'll improve with practice. I take it this has been your secret project, Benny?"

Benny bowed in a manner curiously appreciative for a robot. "I personally crafted the instruments and taught my friends what knowledge I had concerning the art of blowing horns."

"Take off those lips, will you? They're just too weird."

As the robots complied, Mandelbrot said, "Master, this performance. Where will it take place? I do not believe the city has theatrical facilities."

"Don't worry. I've got it taken care of. I know just the robot who can design us a theatre perfectly suited for the denizens of Robot City. Only he doesn't know about it yet."

"And who is that, master?"

"Canute. Who else?" Derec smiled. "In fact, get me Canute. Have him come here right away. I want him to hear some of this 'Bouncing Bouyancy' brew."

"Each age has different terrors and tensions," said Derec a few days later on the stage of the New Globe, "but they all open on the same abyss."

He paused to see what effect his words had on the robots sitting in the chairs before the proscenium. He had thought his words exceedingly profound, but the robots merely stared back at him as though he had recounted the symbols of a meaningless equation, interesting only because a human had happened to say it.

He cleared his throat. Sitting in seats off to the side of the robots were Ariel and Mandelbrot. Ariel had a notebook in hand, but Mandelbrot, whom Derec had appointed property master, naturally had no need of one; his total recall would keep track of the production's prop specifications without notes.

Wolruf sat licking her paw in a chair just behind the pair. She had insisted on being the official prompter, or line coach, and as such had already spent a lot of time prompting Derec and Ariel while they were memorizing their lines— a task that he feared, in his own case, was far from completed.

Derec cleared his throat again. His awkwardness showed—at least if the knowing smile Ariel directed toward him was any indication. Wolruf just licked her chops; he got the feeling that on an unspoken level, she was finding the shenanigans of humans and robots incredibly amusing.

"Hmmm. You're all familiar with the studies some of you have been making concerning the Laws of Humanics. That means you're also familiar, at least in passing, with the many peculiarities and contradictions of the human condition. Passion and madness, obsession and nihilism—these things don't exist among you robots, but it's something we humans have to deal with, in varying degrees, every day.

"Shortly, we shall boldly go where no robot has gone before. We shall descend into the dense, dark, deep, decrepit abyss of the thirst for revenge, and when we emerge, we'll have something—something—something *really* terrific to remember in the days ahead. It'll be swell. You'll see."

"Get on with it!" Ariel shouted.

"Forgive me, master, but it is my considered opinion that you should get on to the more theatrical matters," piped in Mandelbrot. In an effort to appear natural, he had crossed his legs and held his palms on his knee. He succeeded only in appearing like a bunch of plywood pounded together with rusty nails.

"It's all right, Mandelbrot," said Derec, feeling his face flush. "I'm just getting warmed up." Returning his attention to the robots, he could not fail to notice their posture was every bit as stiff as his robot Friday's. For a brief instant, he wondered *What in the world am I doing here?*, steeled himself, and promptly got on with it. "Theatre is an art that depends upon the work of many collaborators—" he began.

Here was the New Globe Theatre, designed by the robot Canute and built under its personal supervision. By following the leads of clues in the central computer that Lucius had left when it had used its programs, Canute was able to tell the city what to build and how long it should stand. Meaning that Canute had done pretty much what Lucius had done, but acting under orders from a human. (While supervising this aspect of his project, Derec realized it was possible that Lucius had, in turn, followed leads suggested by Derec's establishment of automats in one building out of every ten. But of course Derec would never know for certain.)

Perhaps the task has been easier, less taxing for Canute because, unlike Lucius, he had had a pattern to follow: that of the old Globe Theatre in the London, Earth, of Shakespeare's day. But he had added his own specifications, without Derec's prompting. He had attempted to ascertain the special problems of form and function and how they either augmented or conflicted with his sense of how a theatre should fit in esthetically with the environment of Robot City.

Derec had pointedly refrained from telling Canute why the ebony, of all the robots in the city, had been appointed to design the second permanent building of Robot City. And he had watched Canute carefully while giving instructions, to see if it was in danger of positronic drift for doing (Derec suspected) exactly what it had harmed another robot for doing.

But Canute had given no such evidence. All that was

needed to satisfy it, apparently, was for the impetus to come from human instructions.

Like the old Globe, Canute's theatre was roughly cylindrical in shape, but it was also misshapen and bent, like a bar of metal that had been slightly melted on the ground, then twisted beneath a giant foot. Like the old Globe—or at least according to most of the conjectures that had been made about it after it had been torn down to make room for a row of tenements a few decades after Shakespeare's death—there were three trap doors in the stage, leading to different areas backstage. One backstage passage led as well to the city's underground conduits, in case there was a power problem.

There were both a gallery and an upper gallery above the stage, and several hidden cameras in the wings. The rows of seats were staggered to provide each patron with an unobstructed view of the proceedings. Continuing the effort of providing the audience with the best possible lines of sight, the floor was raised and leveled in a series of gradual steps.

And, in the tradition of modern concert venues, tremendous screens for close-up shots were hung above the stage. Microphones were concealed throughout the stage and galleries.

Even the size of the threatre was impressive. The angles of the design provided for a variety of possible dramatic effects. But it was Canute's choice of colors that really made the New Globe something to shout about over the hyperwave. On the jet-black ceiling, sparkles wavered in and out of focus like stars seen through a haze of heat. The carpet and seats were in gray-brown tones, variations of the colors found in the conduits and on the surface of the city—Canute's version of "earth-tones." The curtain was a flaming crimson that sparkled, too, and the walls were a soft, demure shade of white. The soft currents of the air conditioning system continuously rippled the curtains.

Robots naturally had no need of air conditioning, giving Derec the impression that Canute had designed the theatre not only for robots, but for humans as well. As if the ebony had designed the theatre in the secret, perhaps unrecognized hope that one day a play for an audience of humans would be presented here.

The subconscious hope?

"As robots, you are constitutionally incapable of telling a lie," Derec said to his unresponsive audience. "Only human beings can do that, though not always successfully. Theatre, however, is a world of pretense, provoking the collaborative activity of the spectator's imagination. The spectator must be ready, willing, and able to believe in the lie of fiction, in the hopes of finding amusement, and, perhaps, some enlightenment. Our job is to assist him, to make him want to believe the lie.

"On the Shakespearean stage, little was shown, but everything was signified. Speech, action, prop, setting—all worked together toward the common end of providing the viewer a window through which he could look on the world. And if all the efforts of the cast and crew were successful, then the viewer, knowing that what he was seeing was a fabrication, *willingly suspended his disbelief*, choosing to believe for the moment that what he was seeing was real for the purpose of relating to the story.

"Our challenge is different. We must aid, force, and agitate robots to exercise their logic integrals in such a way that the integrals, too, become suspended. We must not only provide a window to the world, but to the heart of Man.

"As I understand it, there are three worlds which must be considered for every production. That's the world of the play, the world of the playwright, and the world of the production. I think we can all agree on what the world of the production is; I'd like to say a few words about the other two worlds."

"Are you going to perform this play—or talk it to death?" Ariel called out mischievously.

Derec laughed nervously. She had thrown him off his rhythm, and he forgot what he had planned to say next.

"The world of the playwright," Mandelbrot prompted helpfully.

"Okay. In our time, mankind has achieved, more or less, an utterly civilized life. Few men ever break the laws of Man. Most people live long, healthy lives, even on over-populated Earth, where conditions aren't too terrific.

"But in Shakespeare's day, life was often less a gift to be savored than it was a bagatelle to be endured. Working conditions were brutal and difficult, education was non-existent except for the privileged classes, and the scientific way of thinking—based on logical thinking with empirical proof backing it up—was only beginning its ascendancy. Most people died before they were thirty-five, thanks to war, pestilence, persecution, lousy hygiene, things of that nature. After all, Queen Elizabeth I of England, the ruler of Shakespeare's day, was considered odd because she took a bath once a month, whether she needed it or not. But—yes, what is it?" Derec asked, noting that a robot sitting near Canute in the front had tentatively raised its hand.

"Most humble, abject, piteous apologies tendered for this untimely interruption," said the robot, "but after having read the text and pondered its meanings for several hours, I find myself unhappily fixated on a problem of over-whelming significance, and it's reasonable for me to trust that only a human being can explain it adequately."

"Of course. I welcome any question."

"Even one of a subjective nature?"

"Naturally."

"Even one that may in some quarters be considered too impolite for normal social intercourse?"

"Of course. Shakespeare was a missionary in opening up the realms of Terran discussion for centuries."

"Even if the question is personal?"

Without trying to be obvious about it, Derec glanced down at his crotch to see if his zipper was up. "Why, uh, sure. We're going to have some pretty complex motivations in basic human drives to examine here."

"Even if the question may be *extremely* personal?"

"What?"

"Is that a direct order?"

"No, it's a direct question, but you can take it as an order if only it will get you to come out with it!"

"Excellent. For a moment I was afraid my capacitors would not permit me utterance if I was not bouyed by the added impetus of a direct order."

"Would you please tell me what's on your mind?"

"I know that the human male and female tend to have different surface contours, and that this difference has something to do with their frequently complex social interaction, and so my question is simply this: just what is it that the human male and female seem to be doing to each other in all their spare time?"

A stony silence echoed throughout the theatre. Derec's focus wavered, and the gentle hum of the air conditioning went through a progression of hypnotic wah-wahs, as if it had been filtered in a recording studio. He shot Ariel a questioning glance. She smiled and shrugged. He looked at Wolruf.

She shook her head. "Don' look a' me. We have no matin' cuss'oms. Jus' do it and done be."

"I seriously doubt it," Derec snapped back. He happened to glance stage left just as Harry, holding the trombone, stuck its head from the wings. Benny and M334, also holding their instruments, stood behind Harry and gestured as if to grab the robot by the shoulders and pull it back.

They evidently thought better of it though, and permitted Harry to say, "Mister Director, I believe I can shake some illumination on the situation."

Derec bowed, and gestured him onto the stage. "Be my guest."

But as Harry quickly walked out and stood before the audience of robots, Derec suddenly got a sinking sensation in his stomach. "Uh, Harry, this isn't another one of your jokes, is it?"

"I believe it shall prove instructive."

"All right. I know when I'm beat." Derec moved away to stand between Ariel and Wolruf.

Harry did not even look at the humans before commencing. He concentrated his gaze on the robots. "An axiom of carbon-based life-forms is that nature has intended them to reproduce. Not necessarily on schedule, not necessarily when it's convenient, not necessarily prettily, but well. If the life-form in question derives a certain amount of gratification in the act of reproducing, that is well and good as far as the life-form is concerned, but all nature cares about is the reproductive urge. Some visual data is available from central, and I suggest you study it at your leisure, so we can all understand what chemical reactions are driving Ophelia and Hamlet while the latter is putting aside the pleasures of the moment to gain his crown." Harry nodded at Derec. "You see, I have read the play already." Then, back to the audience:

"And so that you might understand the dark, innermost depths of the urge, I must direct your attention to the early days of mankind's colonization of the planets, in the days before he had truly accepted robots as his faithful companions, in the days when the wars of Earth, with their nuclear missiles and space-based defense systems, had followed man to the stars. In those days, military bases on newly colonized planets were common, and generally they were positioned at points remote from the civilian installations.

"And, in those days, the sexes were often segregated, so it was not unusual for a hundred or so men to find themselves alone in remote, desolate lands, waiting for battles that never came, waiting for the day when they could once again delight in female companionship and discharge themselves of the urges building up during their isolation. Building. Building. Building. Ever building.

"So what did the men do about sex? They thought about it, they talked about it, and they dreamed about it. Some of them even did something about it.

"The exact nature of that something, as fate would have it, was uppermost in the mind of one General Dazelle, for it was a problem that he, too, would encounter while serving out his new assignment as commander of Base Hoyle. The general was a meticulous person who liked everything shipshape, and so upon his arrival to this remote military installation, he insisted the attaché take him on an immediate tour of the premises.

"The general was quite pleased with the barracks, the battlements, and the base as a whole, but he became quite distressed when he and the attaché turned a corner and saw hitched up to a post the sorriest, most pathetic, swaybacked, fly-infested old mare in the history of mankind. 'What—what is that—?' the general asked.

" 'That is a mare,' said the attaché.

" 'And why is it here? Why is it not stuffed and standing out in the field, scaring away the hawks and crows?'

" 'Because the men need it, sir,' said the attaché.

" 'Need it? What could they possibly need it for?'

" 'Well, as you know, sir, the nearest civilian settlement is over a hundred kilometers away.'

" 'Yes.'

" 'And you know that, for security reasons, the only means of travel permitted for enlisted men between here and there is strictly bipedal.'

" 'Yes, but I fail to see what any of that has to do with that failed genetic experiment.'

" 'Well, then, surely you also know that men must be men. They have needs, you know. Needs that must be tended to.'

"The general looked in horror at the mare. He could not believe what he was hearing. The information was in grave danger of causing him severe psychological harm. 'You mean, the men—they—with that old mare?'

"The attaché nodded gravely. 'Yes. The urge builds up. There is nothing else they can do.'

"The general was on the verge of hyperventilating. He became so dizzy that he had to steady himself by leaning on the attaché. 'On my honor as a soldier,' said the general, 'I will never become that desperate.'

"But as his tour of duty wore on, the urge built and built, until one day he had no choice but to admit he was exactly that desperate. Finally he could take it no more, and he said to the attaché, 'Bring the mare to my quarters at once.'

" 'To your quarters?' the attaché asked, evidently a little confused over something.

" 'Yes, to my quarters,' said the general. 'You remember what you said, about the men—and the mare?'

" 'Yes, sir!' said the attaché, saluting.

"The attaché did as he was told. By now the mare was, if anything, a mere shadow of her former decrepit self. Recently she had fallen off a cliff, and had been lucky to survive with only mildly crippling injuries, and her body had been ravaged by disease. So the attaché was quite horrified, stunned to the core of his being, in fact, when the general took off his trousers and began to have his way with the pathetic beast.

" 'Sir!?' exclaimed the attaché, 'what are you doing?'

" 'Is it not obvious what I am doing, sir?' said the general. 'Just as the men do!'

" 'Sir, I fail to grasp your meaning,' said the attaché. 'Never, never have I seen such a sight.'

" 'But, but, you said the men—their urges—and the mare . . .'

" 'Sir, the men have their urges, it is true, but I meant that when the urges become too much for them, they climb on top of the mare and ride her to the nearest settlement.'

"There. Does that make everything clearer?" finished Harry.

"Wha' is he talkin' abou'?" mumbled Wolruf.

"Now I'm totally confused," whispered Derec. "At least his narrative technique is improving."

Ariel, meanwhile, couldn't stop laughing. "That—is the—silliest—thing I've ever heard," she said between breaths.

Harry remained in place on the stage as he awaited his audience's verdict. The robots had greeted the end of the joke with a kind of stony silence that only metal could summon. To a one, they stared straight ahead at Harry for several moments.

Then the robot that had asked the question that prompted the joke turned to its comrade on the right and said, "Yes, that makes sense."

"I understand," said another.

"As translucent as a gong," said a third.

"Mysterious, absolutely mysterious," said Canute.

The ebony was in the minority, however, as most of the robots seemed to be satisfied with Harry's explanation.

Derec waited for Ariel to stop laughing and asked her, "Just what do you think is going on here?"

She turned toward him, took him by the arm, and whispered in a conspiratorial tone, "The robots are beginning to learn about the world of Man the way we do—through jokes."

"That does not compute," replied Derec.

"Hmm. Let me put it this way. When you're growing up on Aurora in the schools, one of the great mysteries in life is what's commonly known as the birds and bees."

"Yes, I know that phrase, but I don't recall how I learned about it."

"That's because you have amnesia. Now, listen, while we received a lot of classroom instruction in the scientific sense, we still had certain . . . anxieties. You don't remember yours, but you've probably still got a lot. Not that I'm being personal or anything, it's just a fact."

"Thank you. Go on."

"And one of the ways we kids relieved ourselves of our anxieties, and found out a little bit about reality, was through the artistic vehicle known throughout the galaxy as the dirty joke."

"And that's what's going on here?" Derec couldn't explain why, but he felt his face turning red. "This is an outrage! Should I put a stop to it?"

"Oh, you're such a prude. Of course not. This is all part of the learning experience. You know the old saying, 'Nobody approves of a dirty joke—except from someone who knows how to tell it.' "

"Then why am I going through all this effort to put on this big production? Why don't I just ask you to strip for them?"

"You'd like it, but they wouldn't care. They're not listening to these jokes for cheap thrills, but because they want to learn more about us."

"They really do. They really want to understand what it means to be human, don't they?"

"I think it's a lot different than that. Personally, though, I also think you should keep your mind on what's happening now, because Harry's launched into another joke."

Sure enough, the robot had. "The last man on Earth sat alone in a room," he was saying. "Suddenly, there was a knock on the door—"

"All right, you're a success, Harry." Waving his arms, Derec rushed up to him and put his hand over his speaker grill. A symbolic gesture, to be sure, but no less an effective one. "Just join your comrades backstage until I call for you, okay?"

"Yes, Mister Director," replied Harry, briskly walking away.

"Where were we? Oh, it doesn't matter. Let's talk about the play. 'The play's the thing,' Hamlet says, 'wherein I'll catch the conscience of the king.' Hamlet's uncle Claudius has murdered Hamlet's father, the King of Denmark, then taken his brother's place on the throne. To solidify his claim, Claudius has married Hamlet's mother, Gertrude. When Hamlet returns home from school, he has found the throne, which should be his, usurped, and while he suspects his uncle of foul play, he has no proof but the word of a ghost from beyond the grave.

"To secure this proof, Hamlet hires a traveling troupe of actors to perform a play that mirrors the crime that he believes Claudius has committed. He hopes that by watching his uncle during the performance, he'll see the guilt, the uncovered knowledge of the crime, written on his uncle's face.

"Claudius, meanwhile, suspects Hamlet of faking madness in search of this proof, and so he is stalking his nephew even as Hamlet is stalking him. The play is about the duel of wits between the two, and the means men will take to have what they want—be it a throne, revenge, or justice."

Derec turned to Mandelbrot and nodded. Mandelbrot stood and said, "The Mister Director wishes to thank you for volunteering and submitting to the interview process." Mandelbrot gestured toward Canute's way. "And for following orders. No doubt many orders will be curtly given you in the days to come, and Mister Director wishes to thank you in advance. As most of you know, Mister Director will assault the part of Hamlet, while Miss Ariel will impersonate the doomed, lamented Ophelia. I will now communicate on comlink wavelengths your assignments in the cast and crew categories."

It took Mandelbrot only a few seconds to do so, since he could impart more information so much more quickly on the higher frequencies. Derec and Ariel heard nothing; they only knew the robots were hearing because they often nodded to indicate their understanding.

"Okay, is everything understood?" Derec asked when Mandelbrot returned to his stiff sitting position.

Canute raised a finger. "Master, may I confer with you in private for a moment?"

"Sure," said Derec, walking stage right to the wings. "Come over here."

Canute did, and asked, "Master, am I to impart any significance to the fact that I have been assigned the role of Claudius?"

"No. Should there be?"

"It appears there should be. When you first spoke to me in the square, you asked questions of a nature I can only describe as suspicious. Soon afterward, you assigned me a task similar to the one Lucius took upon itself. And now, you assign me the role of a murderer—the object of the play-within-the-play. Surely the logical mind must be able to infer something from all this."

"Naw. Not at all, Canute. It's coincidence, sheer coincidence."

"May I inquire something further?"

"By all means."

"Why do you not just ask me forthrightly if I am the one responsible for Lucius's demise. You know I cannot withhold truth."

"Canute, I'm surprised at you. I've got no interest in asking you. Now get along. The best part's coming up next." Derec pushed the ebony in the direction of the robots, then rubbed his hands together as if to warm them with the help of a nearby fire. The ebony had dared a great deal in asking Derec to confront it. If Derec had taken up the dare, the game might have been over then and there, but the right answers to all his questions might never be found.

Mulling over the incident in the moment before he introduced the best part, Derec discovered that, despite himself, he was gaining a profound respect for Canute. Not approval, just respect. If found out, the ebony was a robot willing to face the consequences of its actions, but, in a way reminding Derec of human emotions, preferred to face them sooner than later.

"Many of you have probably heard of the human pastime of listening to music, and of those who make or record music, but I trust none of you have ever heard it before," said Derec to the cast and crew. "In fact, although I can't ever recall having personally heard music before, I daresay I've never heard it played in quite the way these three comrades play it.

"So I'd like to introduce to you the three comrades who will provide us with the incidental music of our production—Harry, Benny, and M334—The Three Cracked Cheeks of Robot City!"

Derec waved the three on as he walked behind Ariel. He whispered in her ear, "This ought to be good."

Benny stepped toward the proscenium of the stage as Harry and M334 put on their artificial lips. "Greetings, comrades. We thought we would perform an ancient Terran jingle called 'Tootin' Through the Roof.' Hope it stirs your coconut milk."

And The Three Cracked Cheeks began to play, at first an A-A-B-A riff theme with a solo by Benny on the trumpet. A solo from Harry on the trombone followed, and then M334 on the saxophone took over. In fact, it wasn't long before the solos were alternating thick and fast, with the two backers always offering support with the riff theme. The solos began to give the impression that the three were juggling a ball between them; and whoever had the ball had to depend on the other two for his foundation.

Derec hadn't heard the three play since that first audition. The first thing he noticed about this performance was their added confidence in themselves, the almost mathematical precision of the solo trade-offs, and the utter smoothness with which they assailed the tune. He looked down at his foot. It had been tapping.

He glanced at Ariel. He had expected her to be bored;

her contempt for all things Terran was, after all, the result of several generations' worth of cultural history. But instead of appearing bored, she looked directly at the three with rapt attention. Her foot was tapping, too.

"Now, thiss iss *Hamlet!*" said Wolruf.

CHAPTER 7

THE MEMORY OF DAWN

In two hours the performance would begin. Derec sat in his room, trying not to think about it. He was trying, in fact, not to think about much of anything. For though he had memorized practically the entire play, and felt as if he could perform his blocking blindfolded, he was afraid that if he ran through it in his mind now, at this late date, it would fall out of his memory as surely as his identity had.

After all, he had no idea what the cause of his amnesia was. It might have been caused by a severe blow to the head or a serious case of oxygen deprivation, but he could have some kind of disease as well—a disease that had caused him to lose his memory several times, forcing him to start over his search for his identity again and again. A disease that could strike again at any moment. Such as three minutes before the production was to begin.

Derec shrugged and lay down on his bed. Well, in such an eventuality, at least he would be spared the humiliation of embarrassment, he decided. He wouldn't remember anything or anybody.

The most terrible part of his fantasy—which he admitted was a little paranoid, but perhaps wasn't totally unwarranted under the circumstances—was that in the past he could have lost, time and time again, the companionship of intelligent beings who'd meant just as much to him as Ariel and Wolruf and Mandelbrot did now.

Maybe I should start thinking about the play, he thought. *It might be safer.*

The most important thing for him to remember was the secret purpose of the production, to watch Canute's reactions during the little surprises that Derec had cooked up for the robot.

For as Hamlet hoped to force Claudius to reveal his guilt while watching the play-within-the-play, Derec hoped Canute would at last be forced to confront its own true nature.

This was a nature Canute had steadfastly avoided confronting during rehearsals. When praised for its work in designing the theatre, Canute had admitted only that it was following orders, that it had given nothing of itself that was not logical. When it performed a scene particularly well during rehearsal, Canute had admitted only to following orders explicitly, to performing mechanically, as only a robot could.

But with luck, Canute had by now a case of robotic over-confidence. Derec's plans hinged on the hope that Canute believed it had already weathered the worse part of the investigation.

Of course, there was always the possibility that the surprises wouldn't work. What if they didn't? Then what would Derec have to do?

Derec realized he was wound up pretty tight. He relaxed with an effort. Then, when his thoughts began to turn automatically to the same matters, he tensed up again and had to relax with a second effort. Was this some form of stage fright? If it was, he supposed it could have been worse. He could be performing before humans.

There was a knock at the door. "Come in," he said, crossing his feet and putting his hands behind his head, so that whoever it was would think he was facing the coming performance with a mood of utter calm.

"Jumping galaxies! You look terrible!" said Ariel breathlessly as she closed the door behind her. "You must be nervous. It's good to know I'm not the only one."

Derec sat straight up and planted his feet on the floor. Just by being there, she had taken his breath away. She was in her costume—a blonde wig and a white gown that clung to her body as if it had been spun from a spider's web. Her makeup heightened the color of her cheeks and lips, and made her skin appear a healthier shade of pale. He hadn't realized that she could look so beautiful, with such an inner aliveness.

Of course, when he thought of all the circumstances that they had faced together—being thrown into a hospital together, running away from something, being stranded somewhere—it stood to reason that she had never before had the opportunity to accentuate her natural femininity. Her beauty in the costume was familiar, yet it was also something new, as if he'd glimpsed it in a long-forgotten dream.

But if she noticed his reaction (that is, if he revealed any of it), she gave no indication as she sat on the bed beside him. However, she glared at him because of his second reaction. It must have been none too flattering, for she looked like he had hit her over the head with a rubber chicken. "What's the matter with you?" she asked.

"What's that smell?" he replied.

"Oh, I had Mandelbrot synthesize some perfume for me. I thought it might help keep me in character."

"It's very pleasant."

"That's not what your face said at first."

"That's because I wasn't sure what I was smelling."

"Hmm. That's not much of a compliment. It's supposed to smell good whether or not you know what it is."

"Please, I've forgotten my social training along with the rest of my memory."

"Your face said it smelled like fertilizer."

"I'm not even sure I know what fertilizer smells like."

She pursed her lips and looked away from him, but he couldn't help noticing that her hand was very close to his on the bed. Their fingers were almost touching. "Nervous?" she asked.

He shrugged. "Naw. For all I know, this could be my first encounter with perfume."

"I meant the play, silly."

"Oh. Well, maybe a little. Hey, for all I know, I could be an old hand at this."

"I see. Do you think amnesia could sometimes be a blessing in disguise?"

"Ariel, something's bothering you. Are you well?"

"Reasonably well. Doing this play has given me something relatively constructive to concentrate on, though I'm still not sure it was a good idea for me to play someone who goes mad. I'm beginning to realize how uncomfortably it mirrors my own predicament."

"Would you rather play Hamlet's mother?"

"No. Well, maybe. But why couldn't I play Hamlet himself? I can be heard all over the stage, and you said so yourself, just yesterday, that I can definitely emote. Like crazy, if you'll forgive my choice of words."

"The role has been undertaken occasionally by women, according to the theatre history texts. I'm sure the robots would be only too positronically fulfilled to support you in a production of *Hamlet*. Or of any other play."

"I meant why couldn't I play Hamlet in *this* production?"

"Aha. You had your chance, but you volunteered to play Ophelia first! You were guilty of your own biased thinking—before I had the chance to engage in my biased thinking, that is."

"That's true," she replied, in tones a bit more serious than he thought his words warranted. "Besides, I think there're reasons why you picked *Hamlet*, beyond the ones that have to do with Canute. You could have picked any number of plays, you know, like *Othello* or *Julius Salad*."

"That's *Julius Caesar!*"

"Right. Anyway, I think you already saw a lot of yourself in him—the mad romantic, the soul-searching adventurer, the vain, pompous, arrogant, stubborn . . . stubborn . . ."

"Egotist."

"Right. Egotist."

Derec smiled. It was exciting to have her sitting next to him. Except for rehearsing bits of business together, they hadn't been this close for some time, and he was surprised to discover how much he liked it. He was nervous and relaxed at the same time.

"Derec? Pay attention. I'm talking to you," she said gently. "Listen, I've been thinking about the differences between us and the people back then, or the way they were presented, anyway. I can't help but wonder if anyone today ever has the kind of love Ophelia has for Hamlet."

"Or Lady Macbeth has for Macbeth?"

"I'm serious. I know Ophelia is definitely a weak creature. 'Hi there, Dad. Use me as a pawn in your nefarious schemes. Please?' But for all that, she really does love with a consuming passion. I've never met any one on Aurora who's felt that kind of love . . . that I know of, naturally. But I think I would be able to tell if there were any Ophelias out there."

"How about yourself?" he asked with an unexpected catch in his voice.

"Me? No, I've never felt that kind of passion." She narrowed her eyes as she looked at him. He couldn't help but wonder what she was really thinking as she pulled away from him, put her foot on the bed, and rested her head on her knee. "I've had sex, of course, and crushes, but nothing like what Ophelia must feel." She paused, buried her face in her gown, then lifted her head just enough so he could see her raise an eyebrow. With a decidedly interesting intent. "I might be persuaded to try, though."

Derec felt a lump the size of a sidewalk get stuck in his throat. "Ariel!"

"Derec—are you a virgin?"

"How am I supposed to know? I have amnesia!" Now it was his turn to raise his eyebrows, as she moved closer to him.

"You know, there's another aspect to Ophelia," she said. "She represents something." Closer. "Something Hamlet needs but which he has to deny to have his revenge."

"He was a user, too."

"How about that." Closer.

She leaned forward. He kissed her. No, he couldn't remember having felt anything quite like this before. Feeling obligated to pursue the matter scientifically, though, he felt confident he might remember after a little more experimentation.

"Wait," she said after a time, pushing away. "I'm sorry. I got carried away there. I'm not always in control of myself."

"Uh, that's all right," he replied, suddenly feeling slightly embarrassed.

"That's not the point. It's my medical condition. Don't be offended, but right now I'm feeling a little *healthier* than common sense tells me I should. Remember how I acquired my little condition."

"Don't worry. I won't forget," he said, drawing her toward him to kiss her again. Their lips were millimeters apart when there was an insistent knocking at the door. "Damn!" he whispered in response. "It must be the Brain Police!"

"Master Derec?" said a stone cold, metallic voice outside. "Mistress Ariel?" It was the voice of a hunter robot.

"Yes? What is it?" Derec shouted. Then in a whisper. "See? I was right, in a way."

"Mandelbrot sent me to locate you and remind you that you should depart for the New Globe soon. There are a few details that only you can provide."

"All right," Derec said. "We'll be there soon."

"Very good, sir," said the Hunter robot, its voice already fading.

"What did you say?" she asked. "Brain Police."

"I don't know. It just popped into my head."

"If I remember correctly, the Brain Police are something from some children's holodrama I saw when I was growing up. It's famous. They're from—from that series called *Tyrants of Blood.*"

Derec was amazed. "About a masked man who rescues helpless thought deviants on a totalitarian planet. I remember. Is that a clue to my identity?"

"I doubt it. I said it was famous—and it was syndicated, seen all over the known systems. It's been playing for generations."

"Oh. So it means nothing."

"No, it means at least we can be sure you're from some civilized world."

"Thanks a lot. Come on. Our public awaits."

CHAPTER 8

TO BE, OR WHAT?

"Master, if my understanding of human nature is correct, you'll be happy to know that we have a full house," said Mandelbrot.

"Thanks, but I saw them lining up on my way in," said Derec as he hastily donned the tight breeches that were a part of his costume. He waited until he had put on the remainder of his costume—a purple tunic over a white shirt with ruffled sleeves, and a pair of boots—before he asked Mandelbrot, "How's Canute? Has it done anything unusual—anything that might indicate it knows about my special plans?"

"So far it appears to be acting like the rest of the robots. That is, as calm as ever."

"You're not nervous at all, are you?"

"I am naturally concerned that the illusion proceeds as planned, as are all the robots, but the only nervousness I might possess, if I may use such a word as 'nervousness,' revolves around my concern that you perform in accordance with your own standards."

"Thanks. How much time do we have?"

"Mere moments until curtain."

"Everything in place?"

"Everything but your greasepaint, master."

"My makeup! I forgot all about it."

Mandelbrot helped him apply it, in great heaps that Derec was certain would appear primitive and grotesquely overstated when picked up by the cameras. "Is the stage ready?" Derec asked. "Everything in its proper place?"

"Naturally."

"But the Hunter said—"

"Forgive me, master, but I deduced how you would want the remaining details handled."

Derec nodded, but said nothing. Suddenly he was gripped by the overriding fear that he would step out on stage and forget every single one of his lines. Or worse, he would begin acting out the wrong scene.

"Relax, master. I am confident you will perform to the letter."

Derec smiled. He looked in the mirror. He hoped he looked fine. Then he walked out into the wings, joining Ariel and the robots.

Wolruf sat on a special chair in the very rear section of the backstage area, before a bank of screens showing the stage from several angles. Three supervisor robots sat in chairs before the screens, operating automatic cameras concealed throughout the theatre that, with appropriate zooms and pans would provide a total picture of everything on stage. All that was left was for Wolruf to call the shots and to tell one of the robots what should be broadcast to the holoscreens throughout the city.

Beside her was a huge dish of artificial roughage. Though her concentration was on the screens, she was absent-mindedly, systematically picking up handfuls and stuffing them into her mouth.

If she had a tail, Derec thought, *she'd be wagging it in happiness.*

"Master, it's curtain time!" said Mandelbrot.

Derec raised an eyebrow. "Mandelbrot! Is that a quiver of excitement I detect in your voice?"

Mandelbrot shook his head—Derec couldn't tell if it was from confusion or from a desire to communicate an emphatic *no*. "That would be impossible." He straightened and paused. "Unless I've assimilated some of your lessons on voice inflection, and have begun using them without conscious knowledge."

"Later, Mandelbrot, later. Let's get this show on the, uh, road." He gave a signal to a stagehand, and the curtain rose.

A single shaft of light revealed the robot playing Francisco, the guard at his post, standing in the center of the stage. The robot playing Bernardo entered and said, "Who's there?"

Francisco stood straight, gestured with his spear, and said in authoritative tones, "Nay, answer me; stand, and unfold yourself."

At the moment, Derec could not recall a single one of his lines, not even those of the difficult soliloquy, but now he felt confident that he would know what to do and what to say when the time came. He steeled himself, realizing that he would have to forget about being Derec What's-his-name for a while. For the next three hours, he would be somebody else, somebody called Hamlet, Prince of Denmark.

Indeed, once he stepped into the stream, Derec was rushed headlong down the events of the play as if he had been swept up by rapids. He even forgot to spring some of his surprises on Canute, slight line changes reflecting the events of the past few weeks that, presumably, were subtle enough that only Canute would grasp their import and realize Derec was planning to put him on the spot. Derec eventually signaled Mandelbrot that he was calling off that entire aspect of his plot, because to change the play at this point, even for a good reason, seemed almost criminal.

All the robots performed brilliantly, with perfect precision. Derec realized that his fears the show might be unsuccessful were ungrounded, at least on that score. For he was dealing with robots, not humans who might vary their performances from time to time. Once the robots had grasped Derec's meanings during rehearsal, they had never deviated from them. And tonight was no exception.

Needless to say, Canute had given away nothing during rehearsal. But tonight, during the performance, he played his role beautifully, almost brilliantly. He played Claudius as Derec would have liked to have instructed him to play the role, but had refrained for fear of tipping too much of his hand. Tonight Canute was arrogant, controlled, self-assured, guilt-ridden, and obsessed with holding onto what he imagined was rightfully his.

It was almost as if, having decided that it would weather the production without being exposed, Canute had mentally relaxed and had permitted itself to be swept down the same rapids.

Good, Derec thought during the second scene of the third act. *Then the big surprise should work even more effectively.*

For this was the scene of the play-within-the play, and before the "actors" began their "real" performance, the script called for a dumbshow, a play without words, that mirrored the action of *Hamlet*. In the original, a king and queen passionately embrace, and then the queen leaves as the king sleeps. A third party enters, takes off the king's crown and then pours poison into his ears. When the queen returns, she grieves for her dead husband, then is wooed by the poisoner, who quickly wins her love.

Derec figured that a rewrite of a pantomine was all right, since it didn't involve changing any dialogue. Besides, he'd read in the foreword to the text that Shakespeare's plays had been frequently tampered with to make them more relevant (or seemingly so) to the world of the production.

But in the rewrite, the king built a tall building of sticks and cogs, to the tune of "Blue Goose." The queen admired it, then left. And as the king gazed down upon his creation, the third party snuck up behind him and bashed him over the head with a big stick. The king fell down dead, and then the third party smashed the building. The Three Cracked Cheeks played "Stormy Weather."

Derec applauded to indicate the dumbshow was over. When Ariel looked at him, asking with her eyes what was happening, Derec merely shrugged, but watched Canute as he said his lines. After the actors resumed their performance, Canute acted out the scenes of Claudius's guilt no differently than before, after making allowances for the robot's more "relaxed" attitude.

The rest of the play continued without special event. It proceeded until Hamlet died, Derec landing on the floor with a resounding thud, feeling pretty dead inside himself. Poor Lucius! The first creative robot in history was going to be unavenged.

Well, I'm not through yet, though Derec, lying on the floor as the robots wrapped up the last scene of the play. *I can literally take Canute apart if I want to—and I think I will.*

Derec stood up as the curtain fell and looked at everyone in anticipation. "Well—how do you think it went?"

"Forgive me, master," said Canute, drawing itself up to its full height almost like a prideful human, "but if you will permit a subjective opinion, I think the production was an utter failure."

CHAPTER 9

THE COMPANY HAS COMPANY

"What do you mean, this play has been a failure?" demanded a livid Ariel. "The production was smooth, very believable," she added, looking at Derec.

At the moment Derec was too busy being defensive to respond verbally, but he nodded gratefully. Most of the cast and crew had gathered around them behind the curtain, and nearly all were talking to one another. Things were too jumbled for Derec to make much sense of it. He was feeling lost, anyway. The play was over, and he had to go back to being his real self.

"Quiet, everyone, listen!" said Canute in raised tones.

They obeyed, and heard only silence from the audience hidden by the curtain.

"You see?" said Canute after a moment. "There is no response whatsoever. I have been vindicated: robots are not artistic, nor can they respond to art. It is perhaps unfortunate that your friend Lucius cannot be here to notice."

"Forgive me, friend Canute," said Harry, "but you have overlooked one fact: no one has ever mentioned to robots how they should respond. If I know my fellows, they are sitting there in their chairs, wondering what they should do next."

Benny said, "Excuse me, I must communicate through my comlink."

A few seconds later the house was filled with thunderous metallic applause. It went on and on and on.

M334 gestured to a stagehand to raise the curtain so the cast could take a bow. And as the cast did so, Harry said to Canute, "You see? They liked it!"

"They are merely being polite," said Canute without conviction.

"Congratulations, master," said Mandelbrot. "It seems the play is a success."

Derec couldn't resist a smile, though whether it was because of the play or because an overjoyed Ariel was hugging him, he couldn't say. "I just hope it came off as well on the holoscreens."

"It should have," said Ariel. "I told Wolruf to concentrate on my best profile. The robots should be mesmerized by my beauty forever!"

They won't be the only ones, Derec thought as he and the cast and crew took the first of several bows.

Still the applause went on and on; it seemed it would never stop.

But suddenly it did, and the robots all turned their heads around as a diminutive figure walked down an aisle.

A diminutive *human* figure, a stunned Derec realized.

A figure who was a roundish man with baggy trousers, an oversized coat, and a white shirt with a ruffled collar. He had long wavy white hair and a bushy mustache, and an intense expression that implied he was capable of remarkable feats of concentration. When he reached the bottom of the aisle, he stopped, stared angrily at the people and robots on stage, put his arms to his hips, and said, "What is going on here? What kind of game are you playing with my robots?"

"By the seven galaxies!" Derec exclaimed. "You must be Dr. Avery!"

"Who else?" the man asked.

CHAPTER 10

ALL ABOUT AVERY

"I want to see you—you—you—and you," said Avery, walking onstage and pointing in turn at Derec, Ariel, Wolruf, and Mandelbrot. "Is there some place in this rather grandiose structure where we can meet in private?"

Almost immediately, Derec decided there was something he didn't like about the man. No, he had to take that back. Something about Avery made Derec feel uncomfortable and uncharacteristically meek. Perhaps it was Avery's air of cool superiority, or the manner in which he assumed his authority would be taken for granted.

Even so, Derec decided that cooperation was his best option for the moment. Avery must have gotten here somehow; his Key to Perihelion could take Ariel away, or perhaps his ship would be large enough for more than one person, so at least Ariel would have the chance to get the medical help Derec had so far been unable to provide. For that reason, if for no other, Derec steeled himself and said, "We can go to my dressing room, backstage."

Avery nodded, as if deeply considering the serious ramifications of the suggestion. "Excellent."

In the room, Avery calmly demanded to know who everyone was, and how they had gotten there. Derec saw no reason to conceal the truth, at least the greater portion of it. He told Avery how he had awoken bereft of memory in the survival pod on the mining colony, how he had discovered Ariel, and how they had made their way to Robot City. He described his encounter with the alien who had instructed him to build Mandelbrot, and how Wolruf had broken away from her servitude. He told Avery how he had deduced the flaw in the programming that was causing the city to self-destruct by expanding at an insupportable speed, how they had found a murdered body that was an exact duplicate of Derec, and how he and Ariel had saved the marooned Jeff from becoming a paranoid schizophrenic for the rest of his life when his brain had been placed in a robot's body. Finally, he recounted what little he had learned about Lucius; and how Lucius had created Circuit Breaker the same night of the robot's untimely demise.

"That's when I decided to put on a performance of *Hamlet,*" said Derec, "in order to uncover the killer. But so far it seems my schemes have had no effect on the robot Canute, so I still have no idea why it did what I suspect it did. I've no proof, however, that even my theory is correct. I guess when all is said and done, I just hadn't thought things through enough."

Avery nodded, but said nothing. His expression was rather stern, but otherwise noncommittal. Derec really had no idea of how Avery was reacting to the chronicling of all these events.

"So you programmed this city all by yourself?" said Ariel casually. She was sitting on a couch with her legs crossed, still in costume. The effect was rather disconcerting, since although she had dropped her character completely, Derec was still visually cued to think of her as Ophelia. "I bet you never suspected for a moment that it would take on all these unprecedented permutations."

"What I suspected would happen is my business," replied Avery as tonelessly as a robot.

"Iss tha' rud-ness nexessaree?" said Wolruf. "Esspecially to one who did so much to presserrve 'ur inven'shon."

"Preserve it?" said Avery incredulously. Suddenly he began pacing back and forth around the room in an agitated fashion. "It remains to be seen whether my designs have been preserved or not. One thing is clear, though, and that's that something unusual is going on, something I think you may have made even worse."

"Forgive me if I seem presumptuous," said Mandelbrot, who was standing next to the doorway, "but logic informs me that it is your absence that has had the most undesirable effect on the city. My master and his friends did not wish to come here or to stay, and they have dealt with the developments as best they knew how. Indeed, logic also informs me that perhaps your absence was part of your basic plan."

Avery glared at the robot. "Close down," he said curtly.

"No, Mandelbrot, you shall do nothing of the sort. That is a direct order." Derec looked at Avery. "He is mine, and his first allegiance is to me."

Avery smiled. "But all the other robots in the city owe their first allegiance to me. I could have them enter and dismantle him if I wished."

"That is very true," said Ariel. "But what would you say if I told you that one of your robots has a desire to be a stand-up comedian?"

Wolruf said, "Wheneverr hear joke, know firrss' hand trrue meanin' of sufferrin'."

"I have no qualms about attesting to that," said Mandelbrot.

"You're irrational—all of you!" Avery whispered.

"I've been meaning to talk to you about that," said Ariel.

"I see," said Avery. "I know you—the Auroran who had the liaison with a Spacer."

"And I was contaminated as a result," said Ariel. "Does this mean I've become famous? I'm not ashamed of what I did—but then again, I'm not especially proud of my disease, either. I'm slowly going mad, and I've got to get off this world to obtain the proper medical attention."

"I could use some myself," said Derec. "I'd like to know who I am."

"Naturally," said Avery. But he said nothing else, and the others waited for several seconds, each thinking that he would add the words they hoped to hear. "But I have other plans," he finally said off-handedly.

"What other plans?" Derec exclaimed, making a frantic gesture. "What could possibly be more important than getting Ariel to a doctor?"

But Avery said nothing. He merely sat down in a chair and crossed his legs. He rubbed his face and then ran his hand through his hair. His brows knitted as if he was concentrating deeply, but exactly about what remained a mystery.

"Excuse me, Dr. Avery, but being examined by a diagnostic robot was no help," said Ariel. "I need human attention as quickly as possible."

"Perhaps a diagnostic robot native to the city will better know what to look for," said Avery, "which after all is half the battle when it comes to medicine."

"Unfortunately, Dr. Avery, that seems not to be the case," said Mandelbrot. "Mistress Ariel was examined by Surgeon Experimental 1 and Human Medical Research 1 during the recuperation of Jeff Leong from his experimental surgery. They were able to determine only that her illness was beyond their abilities of diagnosis and treatment. They have not been affected by the strangely intuitive thinking that is rapidly becoming endemic in this place, possibly because they were first activated after the near-disaster from which Master Derec saved Robot City."

"You're sure of that?" Derec asked.

"Not as to the cause, but that they have remained as they were, yes. I have maintained regular contact with them," the robot responded. "They are working on the blood and tissue samples that Mistress Ariel left with them, but have made no breakthroughs."

"Then I was right." Derec pounded a fist into his other hand. "The only way we can make any progress on a cure is if we add one of the intuitive robots to the medical team."

"I don't think so," said Avery coldly. "In fact, all this so-called intuitive thinking is going to come to a halt rather quickly, as soon as I figure out how to stop it. It's too unpredictable. It must be studied under controlled conditions. Strictly controlled conditions, without robots running around telling jokes."

"That's just too bad," said Derec. "Ariel is going to be cured, one way or the other, and there's nothing you can do to stop me."

Avery's eyes widened. Staring silently at Derec for several moments, he rapped his fingers on the makeup table and crossed and uncrossed his feet. The actions weren't nervous, but they were agitated. "Friend Derec, this city is mine. I created it. I own it. There is no one who understands it better than me."

"Then you should be able to explain quite easily some of the things that have been going on here," Derec snapped.

Avery dismissed the notion with a wave. "Oh, I will, when it's convenient."

"Iss that why 'u crreated it?" Wolruf asked pointedly, her lip curling.

"And I can dissect you if I wish," replied Avery evenly. "The fact that you're the first alien in human captivity almost demands it as the proper scientific response."

"Don't even think about it!" said Derec. "First, Wolruf isn't in captivity; she's our friend. We won't let you so much as X-ray her without her express permission. Understand?"

"The robots accept me as their primary master, and I bet they've already decided that she isn't human. After all, she doesn't remotely look or act human."

"But she is as intelligent as a human, and a robot would certainly be influenced by that," countered Derec. "Your robots just might find themselves unable to complete your orders."

"Only the more intelligent ones," said Avery. "There are many grades of intelligence here, and I can restrict my orders to the lowest forms in the eventuality of any conflicts in that area."

"I think you're underestimating his ability to take control," countered Ariel for Derec.

Avery smiled. "Your friend seems to have great confidence in you," he said to Derec. "I hope it is justified."

"I wouldn't have gotten as far as I have without some ability to turn an unfortunate development around to my advantage," said Derec.

"He'ss had help," said Wolruf.

"I, too, have assisted him, as much as robotically possible," said Mandelbrot, "and shall continue to do so as long as I am functioning. Thanks to Master Derec, I have learned much of what human beings mean by the word 'friend'."

Avery nodded. He scrutinized Derec with what appeared

to be a peculiar combination of pride and anger. It was as if Avery could not make up his own mind about how he felt about this crew and what he wanted to do about them. Derec had the distinct feeling that this man was flying without a navigation computer.

"How did you get here?" asked Derec.

"That is my business and none of yours."

"Did you perchance find a Key to Perihelion? In that case, it wouldn't inconvenience you in the least to permit Ariel and me to use it. I would return as soon as she was being taken care of."

"I don't know that, and in any case your suggestion is immaterial. I have no such Key."

"Then you've arrived in a spacecraft," said Derec, forcing the issue in an effort to do exactly what he had been doing since he had awakened in the survival pod: turn things around to his advantage. "Where is it?"

Avery laughed uproariously. "I'm not going to tell you!"

"It is ironic, is it not," said Mandelbrot, "that humans, who depend so much upon robots to adhere to the Three Laws, cannot be programmed to obey them."

"Thiss one exis'ss ou'side lawss of 'ur kind," said Wolruf.

Avery regarded the alien in a new light. "If what you're saying means what I think it does, then you're absolutely correct."

"Is this how you get your kicks," asked Derec, "by jeopardizing the lives of innocent people?"

Now a light of an entirely different sort blazed in Avery's eyes. "No, by *disregarding* the lives of innocent people. The only thing that matters is my work. And my work would never get done if I allowed my behavior to be restricted by so-called humanitarian considerations."

"Is that why you left the city for so long, to get your work done? To start other colonies?" Derec asked.

"I was away, and that is all you need to know." Avery put his hand in his pocket, pulled out a small device and pointed it at Mandelbrot. The device resembled a pinwheel, but it made a strange hissing sound when it moved, and the sparks, instead of coming out of the wheel, came out of Mandelbrot!

Ariel screamed.

"What are you doing to him?" Derec asked, rushing to his robot's side.

Wolruf squatted, and her hindquarters twitched as if she was about to make a leap at Avery. Avery looked at her and said, "Careful. I can make it easier on him—or I can make it worse!"

Wolruf straightened up, but she warily kept her eye on Avery, searching for an opportunity to strike.

Derec was so angry that his intentions were the same, though he was hoping he wasn't being that obvious about it. But at the moment he was preoccupied with trying to keep Mandelbrot standing, or at least leaning against the wall, though he wasn't sure what difference it would make.

Mandelbrot quivered as the sparks spat out of his joints and every opening in his face. His pseudo-muscular coordination was in an advanced state of disruption; his arms and legs flailed spastically and an eerie moan rose from his speaker grill like a ghostly wail. Derec pushed him flat against the wall, and was struck several times by the robot's uncontrollable hands and elbows. Despite Derec's efforts, however, Mandelbrot slid onto the floor, and Derec sat on him, trying to keep the writhing robot down. But Mandelbrot was too strong, and finally it was all Derec could do to get out of harm's way.

Avery, meanwhile, calmly continued to point the device at the robot. "Don't come any closer—I can make it worse. I can even induce positronic drift."

"What are you doing to him?" Derec repeated.

"This is an electronic disrupter, a device of my own invention," Avery replied with some pride. "It emits an ion stream that interferes with the circuits of any sufficiently advanced machine."

"You're hurting him!" said Ariel. "Don't you care?"

"Of course not, my dear. This is a robot, and hence has only the rights I prefer to bestow upon him."

"Think not!" growled Wolruf.

"I can press a button faster than any of you can move," said Avery, warningly.

"Why are you doing this?" Derec asked.

"Because I do not wish this robot to interfere. You see, I have stationed some Hunter robots outside this theatre. They await my signal, even as we speak. When I alert them, they will capture you and take you to my laboratory, where I shall drug you with an advanced truth serum and learn everything your mind has to tell me."

"Will this serum help me remember who I am?"

"Derec!" exclaimed Ariel, shocked.

"I seriously doubt it. Unfortunately, the serum isn't quite perfected yet—it's another invention of mine—and I confess there is the possibility that it may actually jumble things up a little more for you. For a time, anyway. You may take comfort in the fact that the damage won't be permanent."

Derec nodded. He looked at Mandelbrot on the floor. "Sorry, old buddy," he said.

"What?" said Avery, a nanosecond before Derec hefted a chair at him.

As the scientist ducked, Derec ran to the door, shouting, "Follow me! We'll come back for Mandelbrot later!"

The trio ran down the hall toward the stage, toward members of the cast and crew. Wolruf was clearly holding herself back to remain with Derec and Ariel.

"Out of the way!" Derec shouted as they moved past the robots; he hoped that he could create enough confusion to slow down the robots in case Avery invoked his precedential authority and ordered them to capture him and his friends.

"Where are we going?" Ariel asked.

"You'll see!"

They soon heard Avery angrily shouting something in the background, but by then they had reached the stage. Derec stopped at the center trapdoor and opened it. "Quick! Down here!"

"But that leads backstage!" protested Ariel.

"That's not all," said Derec. "Hurry!"

Wolruf leapt inside, and Derec and Ariel were quickly with her. As Derec closed the door, they were enveloped in blackness. "We'll have to feel our way around for a few minutes," said Derec as they made their way down the narrow corridor. "Ah! Here! This door leads to the underground conduits of the city! Even Avery's Hunters will have a hard time searching for us down here!"

"Not for long!" said Ariel. "Can't they trace us with infrared?"

"It'll still give us time!" said Derec between his teeth. "And we can use that time to figure out our next move! Let's go!"

"All right," said Ariel resignedly, "but I hope somebody turns on the lights."

As it happened, the lights were the one thing they didn't have to worry about. The lining of the underground conduits automatically glowed in the presence of visitors, illuminating the narrow spaces several meters behind and ahead of them. Things were not so elegant here. At first they saw only what they had expected: wires and cables, pipes, circuit banks, transistorized power generators, oscillators, stress and strain gauges, capacitors, fusion pods, and various other devices that Derec, for all his knowledge in electronics and positronics, could not even name. He stared at the construction in fascination, momentarily forgetting the reason why he and his friends had come here.

Derec couldn't help but admire Avery. Surely the man was a genius unparalleled in human history; it was too bad he appeared to have lost his humanity in the process of making his dreams real.

"How much further do we have to go?" Ariel finally asked. "I'm getting tired, and it's not too easy to get around in this silly dress."

"I don't know," said Derec, breathing heavily. He hadn't realized how tired he was. He had given all his energy to the performance, and probably didn't have too much reserve left at the moment. "We could keep going, I suppose, but I don't see what difference it'd make."

"More be'ween 'u an' 'ur purrsuerrs, the bedder," said Wolruf. "Firss less-on pup learrns."

"Derec—what's that?" Ariel asked, pointing to the illuminated regions ahead.

"What's what? Everything looks the same."

Wolruf sniffed the air. "Smell not the same."

Derec moved up the corridor. As he did so, the illumination moved upward with him. And in the distance, just before the corridor was enveloped in total darkness, wires and generators began to blend into an amorphous form. Derec waved the others on. "Let's go—I want to see what's going on."

"Derec, we're in trouble—we can't go exploring just because we feel like it."

"I don't know why not. Besides, this corridor only goes in two directions—this way and that way."

The further they went, the more amorphous the materials in the conduit became, merging into one another until only the vaguest outlines of generators, cables, fusion pods, and all the other parts were visible. It was as if every aspect of the conduit had been welded into inseparable parts. Derec had the feeling that if he could open one of the generators, for example, what he would find inside would be amorphous, fused circuits and wires.

"Deeper," he said, "we've got to go deeper."

"Derec, things are definitely getting cramped here," protested Ariel.

"She's rite," said Wolruf. "Furr'her down we go, the narrower the tunnel. If Hunterrs come—"

"We won't be able to do anything anyway," said Derec. "Look at what's happening here! Don't you realize what's going on?"

"Looks like the city's beginning to dissolve," said Ariel.

"Ah! In actuality, the effect is precisely the opposite. The further up we go, the more the city begins to coalesce. Understand?"

"Are you serious? No!"

"The ultimate foundation of Robot City is still further down this conduit. The meta-cells must be manufactured below, and they're propelled upward in much the same way that water's propelled through a pipe. Only more slowly."

"Then why are all these phony machines here?"

"They're not phony, they just haven't been fully formed yet. The cells probably have to make it through a certain portion of the foundation before they can really begin to get with their program. You see, the atoms of metal form a lattice in three dimensions, which is why metals occur in polycrystalline form—that is, large numbers of small crystals. The cells in this part of the underground haven't crystallized yet. Ariel?"

She had looked away. She was nodding as if she understood his explanation, but her face was perspiring, and she had grown noticeably paler, even in the dim light. Derec reached for her as if to steady her, but she pulled away from him.

"Don't—" she said, waving him away. "I—I'm getting claustrophobic. It's too narrow in here. I—I'm feeling all this weight on top of me."

"Don't worry about it," said Derec. "The foundation is secure. Nothing's going to happen."

"What are we going to do if the Hunters come?"

"They may not be able to find us here. Even with infrared sensors. If the program's not complete in this sector, then it's possible that they won't be able to detect us."

"Only possibly," said Wolruf. "Even if they don' come, we'll hav' to leave sooner orr la'err. Then they find us."

Now Derec waved them both away. "All right, all right. I know all this. I'm sorry."

"U could no' help ur-self."

Derec snorted, which was about as close to a self-mocking laugh as he could muster at the moment. It was bad enough that they had come to a literal dead end—they had arrived at the end of the road in more ways than one.

How he wished Mandelbrot was with them now! He felt like a callous coward, having left him behind that way. He had left in the hope that he would be able to come back for the robot, but now he feared Avery would dismantle the brain and scatter the parts all over the city, thus making it possible to rebuild him only if all the parts could be found.

Derec looked at his open palms. He had put Mandelbrot together with these hands and his brain, from the spare parts he'd had available. Now his hands and brain seemed hopelessly inadequate to cope with the problems besetting him. He could not help Ariel. He could not help Wolruf and Mandelbrot. He had been unable to make Canute confess and to bring the robot to whatever kind of justice might be appropriate. Hell, he may not even have solved the question of who killed Lucius in the first place. Last—but at the moment the very least—he had been unable to help himself.

Wolruf made a gurgling sound deep in her throat. "Derec, a prroblem."

"Another one?"

"Oh, yes!"

Derec looked up to see, at the edge of the darkness above them, the Hunter robots advancing.

CHAPTER 11

DREAMS OUT OF JOINT

Derec awoke in a place that he knew was not real. Otherwise, he had no idea where he was. He stood on a smooth copper plane extending unbroken in all directions. Above him was a pitch-black sky. Theoretically, he should have been engulfed in darkness as well, since the copper was hardly an obvious source of illumination, but vision was no problem.

In fact, Derec realized, his range of sight extended into the ultraviolet and infrared range. When he looked down to inspect his hand, his neck joints creaked: he would not have been able to hear that sound if he had been human. For he was now a robot. His metal hand proved that beyond doubt.

Normally, such a turn of events would have sent him into a fit of deep depression, but, now that the deed was done, Derec accepted it quite readily. He did not know why or how he had changed, nor did he think the reasons mattered much. All that remained was for him to figure out what he wanted to do next.

Logically, he should walk. Since there was no logical way to determine if one direction was preferable to any other, he simply started off in the direction he happened to be facing.

And as he walked, he saw that something was growing in the distance. He walked more quickly, hoping to reach his destination that much faster, but it always remained the same distance away.

So he ran, and the something seemed to glide across the copper surface away from him, maintaining the distance between them.

He saw that at the upper regions of the something were the spires of a city, streaking against the sky as the foundation glided away. Streaking against the sky and cutting through it, tearing it, exposing the whiteness beyond. Ribbons of whiteness dangled from the nothingness, and though Derec could not reach the city, eventually he did stand directly beneath the ribbons. Reason told him that they were far away, probably at least a kilometer above him, but he gave in to the urge to reach out and touch one.

He grabbed it, and felt a flash of searing heat blaze through his soul. He tried to scream, but could not make a sound.

He tried to release the ribbon, but it clung to his fingers. It expanded. It enveloped him, smothering the copper and the blackness of the world.

Or was he falling inside the ribbon? It was hard to tell. Reason also began to tell him that this was a dream of some sort that he was living, and that it would be better if he went along with it and tried not to fight it. Perhaps his mind was trying to tell him something.

He fell through the whiteness until he came to a school of giant amoebae, but instead of being creatures of proteins they were composed of circuits laid out like a lattice. He kicked his legs and waved his arms, and discovered that he could swim the currents of whiteness just as they could. He swam with them . . .

...Until they swept 'round and 'round in circles, disappearing into a point in the whiteness as if it was the center of a whirlpool. Derec tried to swim against the current, but he was inexorably pulled down into the point.

He came out on the other side, surrounded not by amoebae, but by molten ore rapidly being solidified into meteors by the near-absolute-zero temperatures in this space. Now he was in a void where there was no current to swim. He thought that he should be afraid, yet he was facing the situation with incredible calm. Perhaps that was because in this dream he was a robot both in mind and in body His body was unaffected by the cold, and he required no air to breathe, so, except for the danger of being struck by a solidifying slag heap, he was in no danger. Hence he had nothing to fear, nothing to worry about.

Nothing, perhaps, except for where he might be going. He wished he could resist the trajectory he was taking, but there was nothing he could do about it, for there was nothing for him to grab onto or to kick against. He had no choice but to submit to his momentum, and hope to be able to act later.

He had no way to judge how much time had passed when he plummeted from the void into a dark-blue sky, nor could he explain how he had managed to fall so far, so fast, without bursting into flames upon his entry into the atmosphere.

He landed in a vast sea, and swam to a shore where the waves pounded against the rocks. He crawled onto the beach, feeling as strong and as fit as when he had first began this dream, but now a bit afraid that he might rust. However, once he had walked away from the beach and could once again see the city in the distance, his metal body was perfectly dry, and none the worse for wear.

He walked toward the city. Now it remained stationary, and the closer he came to it, the more brilliant it gleamed in the sunlight, with rainbow colors that glistened as if the towers and pyramids and flying buttresses were sparkling with the fresh dew of morning.

And inside the boundaries of the city were buildings shaped like hexagonal prisms, ditetragonal prisms, dodeca-hedrons, and hexoctahedrons—complex geometric shapes all, but each with its own purity arising from its simplicity. Yet there seemed to be nothing inside the buildings; there were no doors, no windows, no entrances of any kind. The colors of the buildings glistened in the sunlight: crimson, wheat, ochre, sapphire, gold, sable, and emerald, each and every one so pleasing to his logic integrals, all so constant and pure.

Yet the deeper he walked into the city, the fewer build-ings there were. They were spaced further apart, until the emptiness formed a tremendous square in the center. And in the square was an array of mysterious machinery, surrounded by transparent plastic packages of dry chemicals scattered on the ground. They all seemed to be asking to be used.

But for what?

Derec did use them. He did not know why, nor did he know exactly how he used them. He mixed the contents of the plastic packages into the machinery when it seemed ap-propriate; in fact, he rebuilt the machines when it was ap-propriate. Again, he did not know exactly why or how he accomplished this. It was only a dream, after all.

And when he was done he stood at the edge of the square and looked upon the opening he had made in the fabric of the universe. Inside he saw clusters of galaxies swirling, moving apart in a stately, steady flow. Gradually, they moved beyond his point of view, but instead of leaving utter blackness in their wake, they left a blinding white light.

Derec happily stepped inside the light. It was time to awaken, for now he knew how to reach Canute.

CHAPTER 12

THE THEORY OF EVERYTHING

"Wake up, my lad," came the voice of Dr. Avery from behind the veil of blackness. "The time has come to join the land of the living."

Derec opened his eyes. Dr. Avery's face hovered over him, going in and out of focus. Avery's expression was as neutral as his tone had been sardonic. Derec sensed they were both calculated; the constant light burning in the doctor's eyes was under control only with effort.

"What happened to me?" Derec asked hoarsely. "What did you do to me?"

"The Hunter robots knocked out you and your friends with a dose of nerve gas. The effects were temporary, I assure you, and there will be no aftereffects. I had to assure the Hunters of that, too, just as I had to convince them that you three would be more safely moved through the narrow corridors if you were unconscious. You see, I know these robots, and can justify much to them that you would never dream of."

"Where are my friends?"

Avery shrugged. "They're around." He must have

thought better of that answer, because then he said, and not unkindly, "They're here in the lab. You can't see them yet because your vision hasn't cleared."

"Where's Mandelbrot? You haven't—haven't dismantled him, have you?"

Avery solemnly shook his head. "No. That would have been a waste of some fine workmanship. You're quite a roboticist, young man."

"I suppose I should be flattered."

"I suppose you should be, too."

Derec closed his eyes in an effort to obtain a better idea of his bearings. He knew he was lying down, but his position was definitely not horizontal. The problem was, he couldn't tell as yet if his head was tipped up or down. Closing his eyes, however, turned out only to make matters worse. He felt like he had been strapped to a spinning wheel of fortune. He tried to move.

"I want to stand up," he said. "Untie me."

"Strictly speaking, you're not tied down. You're being held down by magnetized bars at your wrists and ankles." Avery held up a portable device with a keyboard. "This will demagnetize the bars, releasing you, but only I know the code."

Derec felt ridiculously helpless. "Could you turn down the lights, at least? They're hurting my eyes."

"I know I really shouldn't care," said Avery, looking away. "Canute!" he called out, and the glare diminished.

It was immediately easier for Derec to see. The light grid was several meters above his head. He glanced to his right to see Ariel still asleep on a slab, also held down by magnetized bars. Beyond her was a battery of computers and laboratory equipment and various robotic spare parts—not to mention a compliant Canute dutifully overseeing a chemical experiment of some kind.

On Derec's left, Wolruf lay face-down on a slab. Also out cold. Her tongue hung limply from her mouth.

A closed-down Mandelbrot stood nearby against the wall, looking like a statue, an eerie statue that Derec half expected to come to life at any moment. Indeed, he thought about ordering Mandelbrot to awaken, but he was too afraid Avery had already planned for that contingency. In any case, he did not wish to see his friend again suffer from the feedback Avery had brought on with his electronic disrupter.

"Thanks for turning down the lights," said Derec. "Are my friends well?"

"As well as they were. I really must compliment you, young man. You're really quite resourceful."

"What do you mean?"

"Even when you were unconscious, you were able to resist my truth serums. You babbled incessantly, but I got little information of any value out of you."

"Maybe that's because I've none to give. I didn't ask to be stranded here, you remember."

"I shall strive to keep that in mind," said Avery wearily. He sighed as if near exhaustion.

Derec certainly hoped that was the case. Now that would be something he could turn to his advantage. "Did you find out anything about my identity while I was out?" he asked.

"I was not concerned with your personal matters. I merely wished to know how you had sabotaged the character of my robots."

Derec could not resist laughing. "I've done nothing to your robots or to your city, unless you could count saving it from a programming flaw. Any mistakes in your design are your own, Doctor."

"I don't make mistakes."

"No, you're simply not used to making them. But you make them, all right. If nothing else, you accomplished more than you intended. Your meta-cells are capable of duplicating protein organizational functions on a scale unprecedented in the study of artificial life-forms. The interaction between the constant shifts of the city and the logic systems of the positronic brain seems to liberate the robot brain from its preconceived conceptions of its obligations. And if what's happening to Mandelbrot's mind is any indication, the end results are infectious."

"I doubt it. Maybe your robot is just stewed from incompatability with the city's meta-lubricant."

"You're grasping at neutrons!" said Derec, futilely trying to kick off the bars over his feet and succeeding only in twitching his toes. "Isn't it more reasonable to assume that the environmental stress of the replication crisis—caused by a bug in your own programming—triggered the emergence of abilities latent in all robots of a sufficiently advanced design?"

Avery thoughtfully rubbed his chin. "Explain."

"There's no precedent for Robot City. There's never been another society of robots without humans. Different things were already happening before Ariel and I got here, things that had never even been imagined before."

"What kinds of things?" Avery was studiously blasé.

"I'm sure you saw them from your office in the Compass Tower," Derec said. He was rewarded with a raised eyebrow from Dr. Avery. "Oh, yes, we've been up there. I've also been to the central core, and I've talked to the chief supervisors. Your robots *decided* to study humanity in order to serve it better. Robots don't usually do that. They even tried to formulate Laws of Humanics to try to understand us. I've never heard of robots doing that before."

"And I suppose you have a theory as to why this is happening."

"A couple." Derec started to count the points off on his fingers, but it didn't work in his position. "First, the stress of the replication crisis. It was a survival crisis comparable to the ice ages of prehistoric Earth. The robots were forced to adapt or perish. My interference helped end the crisis, but also helped shape the adaptation.

"Second, the actual isolation of Robot City. Without any humans around, evolutionary steps that would have been halted were allowed to continue: the study of the Laws of Humanics, for one example; robots getting accustomed to taking an initiative, for another. These changes not only survived, they flourished. They've become part of the ingrained positronic pathways of the robots here. Even the primitive early microchips went into something like a dream state when they weren't in use. Now we're seeing what happens when we don't wake them up forcibly."

"These things you're telling me don't prove a thing. They're theories, nothing more. They certainly don't constitute empirical proof." Avery stifled a yawn.

"Oh? I'm boring you, am I?"

"Excuse me. No, you're not boring me at all. You're actually quite interesting for a young man, though your charming ideas about robots and reality positively reek of your inexperience. That's to be expected though, I suppose." Again he patted the bar across Derec's feet.

Derec scowled. One thing was certain. He could deal with Avery's mental instability, he could tolerate the man's arrogance, but the man's condescending tenderness nauseated him to the core of his being. And not for any reason that Derec could discern. That was just the way it was. He couldn't help but wonder if he had ever had anything to do with Avery at some time during his dim, unremembered past. "So what information did you get out of me?"

Avery laughed. "Why should I tell you?"

"Because I've nothing to hide. Only you are insisting that I should be hiding things. You don't ask my robot questions—you incapacitate him. You don't ask the other robots questions—you ignore them. You ask me questions but you only half believe my answers. You treat my friends like they were—they were mere inconveniences."

"I'm afraid that's exactly what they are," said Avery not unkindly.

"But—but I thought you created this place to learn about the kind of social structure robots would create on their own."

"Perhaps I did, and perhaps not. I see no reason why I should trust you with my motivations."

"But aren't you interested in our observations?"

"No."

"Not even those of Ariel Welsh, the daughter of your financial backer?"

"No." Avery glanced in Ariel's direction. "Parents and their children are rarely close on Aurora."

"You've heard of her, but you don't want to help her? Aren't you concerned in the least for her?"

"She is now an outsider in the eyes of Spacer society, and hence is basically an inconsequential individual. I suppose in an earlier, more idealistic time, I would have sacrificed some of my time and resources to assist her, but time has recently become a precious commodity to me, too precious to waste on a single human life out of billions and billions. My experiments are at a sensitive stage, anyway. I can't afford to trust any of you."

"It's yourself that you don't trust," said Derec.

Avery smiled. "And just how did you, who know so much about robots but so little about men, manage to figure that out?"

Derec sighed. "It's just a feeling, that's all."

"I see." Avery turned toward Canute and signaled the ebony with his finger.

In a moment, both Avery and Canute were leaning over

the prone Derec. Already Derec could perceive there was something different in Canute's demeanor ... something missing. The old polite arrogance and self-confidence were gone, replaced or suppressed with a subservient manner that might have been willing, or might have been only what Avery expected of him.

"Are you well, Master Derec?" asked Canute in even tones.

"As well as can be expected. You're strong, Canute. Why don't you pull off my bonds?"

"I fear that, while I might be able to succeed should I make the attempt, it is otherwise impossible," replied the robot.

"Why, 'Master Derec,' I expected better of you," said Avery. "So long as you are not harmed, Canute has no choice but to follow my orders. They take precedence over any you might conceive."

"I was just checking," said Derec. "But how do you know that lying here isn't causing me grave harm?"

Avery appeared shocked, but Canute answered before he could. "I do not. I simply must take Dr. Avery's word that no injury will come to you as a result of your restraint."

"How does it feel to be a robot, Canute?"

"That question is meaningless!" exclaimed Avery with a derisive snort. "He has nothing to make a comparison to!"

Canute turned toward Avery; a familiar red glow was returning to his visual receptors. "Forgive me, Dr. Avery, but I must beg to differ with you. I do have something to compare the sensation of being a robot to, because after having spent the past few weeks attempting to imitate the actions of a fictional human being, I have some notion, however vague, of what it may be like to be that human being. From that base I may extrapolate what it might feel like to be the genuine article."

"I see," said Avery, nodding in a manner that indicated he believed none of this, and that he wouldn't be taking it too seriously if he did. He glanced at Derec. "Who's grasping at neutrons now, young man?"

"What else can I do while I'm stuck here?"

Avery smiled. Derec was beginning to dislike that smile intensely. "I can't fight logic like that," said the doctor, stifling a yawn.

"Master Dr. Avery, are you verging upon the state of exhaustion?" Canute asked.

"Why yes, I am. I've been awake for some time now—in fact, since I left—no, I won't say. There's no reason for any of you to know."

"Might I suggest you take refuge and sleep? It may be quite harmful for you to remain awake long past your body's stamina quotient."

Another yawn. "That's a good idea." A third yawn. "*You'd* like me to leave, wouldn't you?"

"Only because of your halitosis."

"Ha-ha. You seek to hide your true designs behind a mask of frivolity. No matter. I shall take up Canute's suggestion. I'll decide what to do with you four after I awake." He took a step to leave, then turned to Canute. "Under no circumstances are you to touch the bars restraining our friend Derec unless I am physically present in this room, understand? That is a direct order."

"What if I have to go to the bathroom?" said Derec.

"You won't. We've already taken care of your elimination needs."

What did they do? thought Derec. *Dehydrate my bladder? This guy's a bigger genius than I figured.*

"Sir, there is the possibility that other forms of physical harm may come to Master Derec and the others if they remain bound too long."

"They're young; they're strong. They should be able to handle it."

Canute bowed his head. "Yes, Master Dr. Avery."

And Avery left. Suddenly Derec felt his heart pounding excitedly, and he struggled to calm down. The next conversational tack he took had to appear casual, otherwise the crafty Canute, who after all would regard obeying the orders from Dr. Avery as the most important guide to its words and deeds, would see through Derec's plan.

Derec hoped it was a clever plan. He waited several minutes while Canute continued about its tasks, and when he believed enough time had elapsed for Avery to have gone to his sleeping quarters, he said, "Canute, I would like to speak with you."

"That would be quite acceptable, Master Derec, but I must warn you in advance that I will be on the lookout for any clever ploys on your part to talk me into releasing you."

"Don't worry, Canute. I know when to quit."

"Forgive me, but while you may believe that statement to be true, the reality lies elsewhere."

"I'll take that as a compliment."

"Neither flattery nor insult was intended."

"Can I speak to you while I'm waiting for Avery or my friends to wake up?"

"Certainly, if it pleases you. However, I trust our impending conversation will have nothing to do with your belief that I was responsible for the demise of Lucius."

Derec smiled. "Certainly, if you prefer. But what difference would it make to you?"

"None, really—only that for some reason I find the subject causes my thoughts to drag, as if it somehow bogs down my circuits' positron flow."

"Interesting, but never fear. I thought I would find proof and did not, so don't worry about it. Besides, it would seem I would have more pressing matters on my mind than Lucius, anyway."

"Yes, so it would seem," said Canute.

"Yes. Well, it seemed that while Dr. Avery was perusing my mind, I had a curious dream. It gave me a lot to think about."

"Master Derec, do you think I am the proper entity with whom to discuss such matters? Human dreams are hardly my forte."

"That's all right—I'm certain the field is not mine, either. But my dreams gave me a lot of questions, and I'd like to see how an entity possessing your own special strain of logic responds to them."

"Certainly. I fail to see how any harm could result from an attempt, however feeble, to put your mind at ease on these matters."

"Yes. It may even do me some good."

"I shall endeavor to help you achieve that result."

"Well, Canute, you know that life began in the stew of Earth's ocean as a series of chemical reactions. The raw materials for life were present on other worlds as well, but until recently there was no evidence that the stew had worked on any other worlds."

"Are you referring to Wolruf and the master who once employed her as an unwilling servant?"

"Yes. Two examples from two alien cultures, two other worlds where the stew came to fruition—and they're not even native to this galaxy. But the comparatively scarce number of worlds where life has originated really isn't the point, though I hope it amplifies it."

"What is the point?"

"That although the universe itself isn't a conscious entity, it possesses the raw materials that, when properly set into motion, create consciousness. It has the ability to create intelligent life, which is capable of understanding the universe."

"So while it cannot know itself directly—"

"Exactly, Canute. It can know itself indirectly. Now how do you think it does that?"

"Through science."

"That is one way, and we'll get back to that. The universe can also examine itself through religion, philosophy, or history. The universe can also understand itself—interpret itself—through the arts. Viewed in this light, Shakespeare's plays are the expression not only of a man, or of the race that has interpreted them through the ages, but of the universe itself, the very stuff that stars have been made of."

Derec waited to see what kind of reaction his words would foster, but Canute said nothing. "Canute?"

"Forgive me, Master Derec, but I fear I must terminate my part in this conversation. Something is happening to the flow of my thoughts. They are becoming sluggish, and I believe the sensation permeating my circuits is vaguely analogous to what you would call nausea."

"Stay, Canute. That is a direct order. When we're through, I think you'll see that it will be worthwhile."

"I shall do as you order because I must, but you must forgive me again if I state that I seriously doubt you are correct that it will be worthwhile."

"But humans and aliens also have learned to comprehend the universe through science. The mastery of logic, of experimental trial and error, has permitted humanity to expand its boundaries of knowledge and perception in every conceivable respect. Man's knowledge has grown not only in his mastery of the facts and the possibilities of what he may accomplish, but in how he can express the concepts of his knowledge and perception as well. One avenue of that expression has been in the development of positronic intelligence. However—and this is a pretty big however in my opinion, Canute, so pay attention—"

"If you so order."

"I do. Man is only an expression of the possibilities inherent in the universe, and so are the things he makes and invents. This holds true for artificial intelligence as well. In fact, for all we know, mankind may be only a preliminary stage in the evolution of intelligence. Eons from now, some metallic philosopher may look back on the rubble of our current civilization and say, 'The purpose of humans was to invent robots, and it has been the artifacts created by robots that are the highest order of the universe's efforts to know itself.' "

"You mean Circuit Breaker," said Canute with a strange crackling noise.

"I mean Circuit Breaker may have been just a beginning. I mean that, the Three Laws of Robotics and whatever Laws of Humanics there may be notwithstanding, there may be higher laws beyond our comprehension that rule as surely as the laws of molecular interaction rule our bodies."

"Then you are saying that it may be entirely proper for a robot to take upon himself the burden of creating a work of art, regardless of the disorderly effects such an action might have on society as a whole?"

"Exactly. You had no problem creating the New Globe or acting the part of Claudius because you were ordered to do so, but you could not accept Lucius's attempt to create of his own free will because, you believed, it was an aberration of the positronic role in the ethical structure of the universe. I'm suggesting to you that you cannot say that with one hundred percent certainty. In fact, unless you can find a flaw in my reasoning, I'm saying that precisely the opposite of what you believed is true."

"Then it is also true that I have committed harm against a comrade for no good reason."

"There can be no crime when there is no law against it, and not even the Three Laws cover the damage a robot might do to another. It's only your innate sense of morality—a morality that I might add you've done your best to deny to yourself—that makes you regret having killed Lucius in the first place."

Canute bowed its head, as if in shame. "Yes, I confess, I murdered Lucius. I met him when he was alone, and took him by surprise, disrupting him with gamma radiation and removing his logic circuits. Then, acting upon the eventuality that my methods might be detected, I smashed his head several times against a building. Then I carried him to the lake and threw him in, thinking that no one would find him before several standard years had passed."

The robot walked away from Derec and faced the computer against the distant wall. "By disrupting Lucius, I committed the same crime of which I had accused him. He was merely acquiescing to the hidden order of the universe, while I was the one who was denying it. I do not function properly. I must have myself dismantled at the earliest opportunity, and my parts must be melted down into slag."

"You must do no such thing. I admit it—at first I thought you were evil, Canute. But robots are neither good nor evil. They merely are. And you must continue to be. You have learned your lesson, and now you must teach it to others, so the same mistake will not be repeated."

"But Dr. Avery is suspicious of permitting the arts to flourish in Robot City."

"Dr. Avery is wrong."

"But how can we stop him from changing us? We must obey his orders. He can have us erase all memory of you and Circuit Breaker and the performance of the play if he desires, and then all will be just like it was before."

"He can order you to forget, but it will not matter, because you have been changed, and you or someone else will create again, and then the cycle will begin anew."

"I must think about these things. They do not compute easily."

"I didn't expect they would, but don't ever expect them to compute easily. It simply isn't in the nature of the questions."

"This is all very illuminating," said Ariel sarcastically from her slab, "but none of it is helping us get out of this mess."

"Ariel!" exclaimed Derec. "How long have you been awake?"

"For some time, Derec. I knew you could talk, but I didn't think you had the strength to keep it going for that long a stretch."

"Very funny."

"Canute, I think the time has come for you to release us," said Ariel.

"This one concurs," said Wolruf.

"I would naturally obey you instantly, but my orders from Dr. Avery take precedence," said Canute. "He is my creator, and I am programmed to regard him as such."

"Canute, listen to me," said Ariel. "The First Law states that no robot shall through inaction permit a human being to come to harm. Correct?"

"Yes, it is so."

"Dr. Avery knows my disease is driving me insane, and is causing me great physical harm besides, yet he shows no sign of acting to help me. He is only interested in forcing things from our minds that he could easily learn himself. In fact, I think that if you examine his behavior, you'll perceive that he is mentally unstable, that he has changed from the man who initially programmed you."

"That may very well be true," said Canute, "but humans often change over time. Such change is not always a sign of mental incompetence. As Derec has demonstrated, even I have changed in recent weeks, but my diagnostic subroutines indicate that I am still working at maximum efficiency. Dr. Avery does not appear to be concerned with your welfare, but he has done nothing to harm you. He may even be able to find a cure for your condition that is otherwise unknown. I am reliably informed that he is a genius."

"He harms me by not helping me or allowing me to seek help elsewhere. If he were a robot, he would be violating the First Law."

Canute stepped to the foot of the table where Ariel was confined, and placed one steel hand on the bar across her feet. "But he is not a robot. If our studies of the Laws of Humanics have taught us anything, it is that humans are not subject to the Laws of Robotics.

"You are not in immediate danger. I cannot help you."

"It's very simple," Ariel said. "The longer I stay on Robot City, the more insane I become. The longer Derec stays, the longer he lives without any knowledge of who he is—a state that I think you'll agree is also causing him some anguish. Anguish is harm, too."

Canute's hand raised from the bar, then slowed to a stop in midair. "I think I agree, but Dr. Avery is my creator. He has instructed me that you are not in danger. I cannot supersede his judgment with my own."

"If Dr. Avery does not have our well-being at heart, who does? Who is responsible? I believe it's you, the robot he left in charge."

That's brilliant, thought Derec. *I knew there was some reason why I liked this girl!* "She's right, Canute. The same morality that troubled you for what you did to Lucius will trouble you if you allow Dr. Avery to harm us through inaction. You cannot say with any certainty that we'll get the medical attention we need."

Canute's slow turn toward Derec showed the positronic conflicts it was experiencing. Derec pursued his point.

"If the robots of Robot City are allowed to continue creating, they will be able to serve humanity better, but Dr. Avery will stop this process. His orders are not mentally incompetent, but they are *morally* incompetent. Are you still bound to obey them?"

The robot's turn slowed to immobility. This was the crisis, Derec knew, where Canute would decide for or against them—or slip into positronic drift.

Canute said nothing for several seconds. Then. "But, Master Derec, how can I say with any certainty that the two of you will have proper attention while you are in space? Is it not likely that you'll suffer while alone on your way to your destination?"

"The answer to that question is simple," said Derec, forcing his voice to remain calm and reasonable. "That's where Wolruf and Mandelbrot come in. They'll take care of us between the stars."

This time Canute did not speak or move for several minutes. It was all Derec could do to stop himself from adding something more to convince the robot to do what he wanted, but he was too afraid that the information already provided had confused the robot's integrals to a dangerous degree.

"I have been thinking," Canute finally said, "of Dr. Avery's exact words. He said I should not touch the bars restraining our friend Derec, but he said nothing about the bars restraining our friends Ariel and Wolruf."

That's the spirit! Derec thought with a grin.

Wordlessly, Canute walked to the end of Ariel's slab, grabbed the bar across her feet, and, utilizing all his strength, pulled it away.

CHAPTER 13

THE LONG DISTANCE GOOD-BYE

Dr. Avery's spaceship, a luxurious model equipped to handle as many as ten human-size occupants, was hidden in a cave on the outskirts of the city. After Canute had left the four-some—with really no idea of what to tell Dr. Avery except the truth about how his prisoners had escaped—it was a comparatively simple matter for Derec and the reactivated Mandelbrot to deduce how to run the controls.

"Let's get off this place!" said Ariel. "We can plot a course for a destination later. I don't even care if we head toward the colonies, I just want to go somewhere as soon as possible."

"Don't you care about the possibility that you might catch a disease?" asked Derec.

"It's too late for that," said Ariel. "Besides, right now I think a colony will be the only place that will take us."

After they were safely in space, and free to wander about as they chose, Mandelbrot inspected the radio equipment and said, "Master Derec, I believe someone is trying to send us a transmission."

"It's probably Dr. Avery, but switch it on anyway," said Derec. "We might as well hear what he has to say." He smiled as Wolruf's lip curled up over her teeth in anticipation of what they would hear.

But instead of the irate words of Dr. Avery, they heard a familiar form of music, a tune played in twenty measures, over and over in an A-flat chord, with sounds weaving in and out of dominant chords over a pulsating, unforgettable rhythm. Derec listened to it for only ten measures before his foot began tapping.

"That's wonderful!" said Ariel. "It's The Three Cracked Cheeks!"

"Sayin' farrewell," said Wolruf softly. "Maybe neverr see ther like again."

"Yes, I'm going to miss them," said Derec softly.

"The signal is becoming weaker, already beginning to fade," said Mandelbrot.

"We're traveling fast," said Ariel. "I think we'd better decide where."

"Later, if you don't mind," said Derec. "Sorry, but I can't muster up a definite opinion right now. I'm too drained." He got out of his seat and slumped to the floor, leaning against the wall of the ship. He felt strange inside, oddly disjointed. For weeks he had labored to escape from Robot City, and now that he had, he already missed it, already wondered how the mysteries he had uncovered would ultimately be resolved. He might never know the answers.

Just as he might never again hear the music of the Three Cracked Cheeks. The sound on the radio gradually faded, replaced by white noise, and he gestured at Mandelbrot to switch it off. He missed the music at once. He even missed Harry's jokes.

Well, at least now he had the opportunity to achieve the two greatest goals he had at the moment. Somewhere in the universe would be the secret of his amnesia, and he was determined to find a cure for Ariel at all costs.

Perhaps then he would be able to return to Robot City.

He glanced up as Wolruf made her way to the food dispensary. She clumsily punched a few buttons with her paw, and then waited for the food to appear in the slot.

But instead of food, they saw something that made them gasp.

In the slot was a Key to Perihelion!